ANNE
HILLERMAN

D0038567

THE SACRED
BRIDGE

A LEAPHORN, CHEE & MANUELITO NOVEL

DON'T MISS THE
OTHER NOVELS IN THE
LEAPHORN, CHEE & MANUELITO
SERIES BY *NEW YORK TIMES*
BESTSELLING AUTHOR
ANNE HILLERMAN

HARPER
U.S. **$9.99**
CAN. **$12.99**

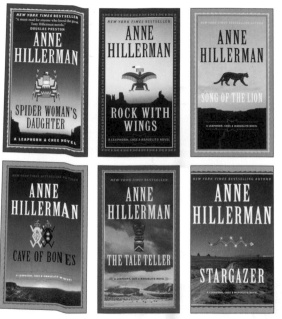

"Anne Hillerman's taken
familiar characters and
locations and struck out on a
literary legacy all her own."
—CRAIG JOHNSON,
author of
the Walt Longmire series

ISBN 978-0-06-290837-7

9 780062 908377

50999

EAN

Praise for
Anne Hillerman

THE SACRED BRIDGE

"Captivating. . . . Series fans will be well satisfied."
—*Publishers Weekly*

"Gripping."   —Bookreporter.com

"Anne Hillerman has carried on the franchise of Joe Leaphorn and Jim Chee mysteries started by her father, Tony Hillerman, with great aplomb and a deft writing style. The Southwest setting and the weaving in of Navajo culture are always a treat for readers. The characters are genuine, the story is compelling and complex, and the writing is gorgeous. . . . It reads well as a stand-alone story. Mystery lovers will love this one."

—Portland Book Review

"As always, the characters are a joy."
—*Santa Fe New Mexican*

"Anne Hillerman brilliantly continues the Hillerman legacy, expanding the mystery genre by making Bernadette Manuelito America's most popular Native American female law enforcement officer."   —David Morrell, *New York Times* bestselling author

STARGAZER

"Tony Hillerman fans will appreciate her keeping his fictional creations, Jim Chee and Joe Leaphorn, alive and thriving. The storytelling gene has been proudly passed on from father to daughter."

—Bookreporter.com

"Anne Hillerman is a star."

—J. A. Jance, bestselling author

THE TALE TELLER

"Hillerman's writing becomes stronger with every new installment in the series, deepening the development of each character. . . . The picturesque Southwest, as well as the history of the Navajo, come through on each page.

—*Library Journal* (starred review)

"*The Tale Teller* is more than just a police procedural set in the Southwest, it's a reading experience not to be missed. Anne Hillerman has reached a new level of storytelling in this one, and she deserves recognition as one of the finest mystery authors currently working in the genre."

—New York Journal of Books

SONG OF THE LION

"Fans of Leaphorn, Chee, and Manuelito, characters created by the author's father, Tony Hillerman, will savor this multilayered story of suspense, with its background of contemporary environmental vs. development issues."

—*Library Journal*

"Hillerman seamlessly blends tribal lore and custom into a well-directed plot, continuing in the spirit of her late father, by keeping his characters (like Chee) in the mix, but still establishing Manuelito as the main player in what has become a fine legacy series."　　*—Booklist*

"The latest from Hillerman continues worldbuilding in a tale that will reward long-term readers."　　*—Kirkus Reviews*

ROCK WITH WINGS

"Hillerman uses the southwestern setting as effectively as her late father did while skillfully combining Native American lore with present-day social issues."　　*—Publishers Weekly*

"With a background of tribal law and custom, Anne Hillerman ties up multiple subplots in concise prose, evoking the beauty of the desert and building suspense to a perilous climax. Tony would be proud."　　*—Booklist*

SPIDER WOMAN'S DAUGHTER

"From the utterly shocking opening scene to the final twist, Anne Hillerman offers a thrilling Southwestern tale featuring the unforgettable characters of Jim Chee and Joe Leaphorn, set in the vivid landscapes of Navajo country. *Spider Woman's Daughter* is a must-read for anyone who loved the great Tony Hillerman novels."

—Douglas Preston, #1 New York Times bestselling author

THE SACRED BRIDGE

Also by Anne Hillerman

ANNE HILLERMAN

THE SACRED BRIDGE

A LEAPHORN, CHEE & MANUELITO NOVEL

HARPER

An Imprint of HarperCollinsPublishers

THE SACRED BRIDGE. Copyright © 2022 by Anne Hillerman. All rights reserved. Printed in the United States of America. No part of this book may be used or reproduced in any manner whatsoever without written permission except in the case of brief quotations embodied in critical articles and reviews. For information, address HarperCollins Publishers, 195 Broadway, New York, NY 10007.

First Harper premium printing: January 2023
First Harper hardcover printing: April 2022

Print Edition ISBN: 978-0-06-290837-7
Digital Edition ISBN: 978-0-06-290838-4

Cover design by Jarrod Taylor
Cover photographs © Universal Images Group/Getty Images; © Alamy Stock Photo

Harper and HarperCollins are registered trademarks of Harper-Collins Publishers in the United States of America and other countries.

23 24 25 26 27   BVGM   10 9 8 7 6 5 4 3 2 1

To the brave men and women who devote their
lives to law enforcement on the Navajo Nation

1

The young Navajo man froze for a moment and dealt with his fear.

Even all these years after the accident, looking at the vast expanse of cold lake water still left him frightened. When the nightmarish idea arose that his boots might slip and that he could tumble down the pale sandstone and into the lake, he shoved the thought to the back of his brain. But his palms had started to sweat. He took a deep breath and ordered himself to get a grip, to calm down, to go in beauty.

His apprehension had begun years before, when Lake Powell was higher and he was smaller, just a boy. He had been walking along the shoreline, looking for insects. Then he tripped on a rock and lost his balance. He could still taste his panic as the icy, bottomless water enveloped him. He could still feel the iron grip of the terror that paralyzed him. Unable to keep his head above the deadly lake, he sank, breathless, too scared to struggle.

Finally his brother's strong arms pulled him back to life, to the surface where he could gasp for breath. After an eternity they reached the dry safety of the shore.

He was only eight, but the experience changed him from the inside out. His brother wanted to teach him to swim, but he had none of it. He knew Lake Powell was a lurking, evil monster, ready to suck him into its frigid depths. He respected its power, and now, after decades, he could sometimes see its beauty. But only from afar.

When the ancient ones he admired, the ones who had left their marks on the rocks here, saw water, they beheld rivers, the area's flowing lifeblood. Not this giant, human-made pool trapped by a dam.

The young man forced his gaze from the water's dangerous, seductive shimmer to the sky. He took a long breath and made himself move with caution across the unforgiving sandstone, heading back toward his campsite and then to the boat dock.

But a sound behind him stirred his curiosity and he turned, careful not to lose his balance on the steep slope.

Time compressed. First, a whooshing noise, then a heavy thunk against the back of his head. He fell forward with the sound. The searing pain lasted only a moment. After that, his damaged skull couldn't protect his brain. If he had been conscious, he would have noticed the warmth of the rock cliff, a gift from the October sun, against the skin of his torso. But he had transitioned to the space beyond human senses. He didn't fear his body's growing momentum as the energy of the fall and gravity's pull drew him toward the water. He didn't feel the abrasive stone bloodying the skin of his arms, cheeks, and forehead. When his physical self finally slid into the deep icy water of his nightmares, he didn't even flinch.

Death had come quickly. And now the place that had long terrified him began to make its amends. The lake gently rocked him as it washed away the blood.

2

Jim Chee looked out at the broad expanse of water known as Lake Powell.

The huge dam that created this immense desert lake had destroyed the sacred junction where two vital rivers merged. The San Juan River, the Male Water, forms one boundary of the Navajo Nation, whose people Chee served as a police officer. The water from the San Juan flowed into the Female Water of the Colorado River, whose spirit is called Life Without End, when they met in Glen Canyon. The old stories spoke of the two Navajo deities embodied in the rivers. When they joined, they created the Water Children of the Cloud and Rain People.

Some said that the dam's dishonoring of the confluence led to the long-standing drought that had reduced the volume of the lake itself to less than half.

Chee stretched his tired legs along the sand and readjusted his back against the cliffside. A few more moments of rest, and then he'd hike on toward

Rainbow Bridge. This combination of vacation and personal retreat had left him frustrated on several levels, but standing in the presence of that sacred site should provide a cure. Then the three-hour drive to Shiprock, reuniting with his smart and lovely wife, and finding time to further contemplate the future and shake off his disappointment at yet again failing his mentor, the retired Legendary Lieutenant, Joe Leaphorn.

Perhaps, Chee thought, the imprisoned water from the two sacred rivers had washed away the images of the Holy People that had left Leaphorn in awe decades before. Perhaps the water had transformed the sand paintings Leaphorn recalled so vividly into rainbows of tiny specks of colors and washed the sand away. Perhaps the sand rested on the bottom of the lake or had washed onto a beach where coots and grebes strolled and boaters pulled ashore.

Or perhaps the rising water had stopped before it reached the cave that sheltered those precious things. Perhaps. Perhaps.

This morning, as he sang his morning prayers in this soulful place, he realized that he knew of nowhere else to search for the cave that still burned in his mentor's memory. Using the Lieutenant's old map and his own acute sense of the geography of the Colorado Plateau, he had discovered a few caves that seemed appropriate, but none sheltered a trove of sand paintings.

He looked forward to Rainbow Bridge, a holy place near the lakeshore. He would be there in a few hours.

And then he would go home. He missed Bernie and their cozy little place along the San Juan River. He missed the men and women he worked with at the police station and beyond. He missed those assignments where his presence and something he said or did made life better, or at least more tolerable, for the person who had called for the police. He missed being of service.

But he didn't miss the reports. He didn't miss his role as backup in charge at the substation when Captain Largo was away. And, especially and with all his heart, he didn't miss having to be Bernie's boss when the captain left.

Chee took another sip of water and listened to the distant, muffled roar of a powerboat. Then he unzipped the backpack that sat in the sand and spread the map Leaphorn had given him on his lap. He studied it again. According to what he saw and the Lieutenant's story, the cave should have been inside the cliff that warmed his back. But he had looked there, closely, and only found solid rock. The expansive, rugged landscape between Lake Powell and Navajo Mountain could have confused the map maker. Or, Chee thought, perhaps he had misread the map and made a mistake.

He heard the low vibration of the boat motor again.

Later, he realized that if he had positioned himself with eyes toward the lake instead of away from it, and if he had pulled out his binoculars at the sound of the boat, he might have seen something important. He might have seen a murderer fleeing the scene of the crime.

3

Lake Powell, a desert lake born in controversy, is an infant finding its place in the ancient geological environment of the Colorado Plateau. Its creation in 1963 as America's second-largest human-made lake (only Lake Mead holds more water) captured the Colorado and San Juan Rivers, two of the Southwest's major waterways. Glen Canyon Dam, constructed to provide hydroelectric power and water storage, imprisoned the water between beautiful sandstone walls. The lake had taken seventeen years to reach its high-water mark. Chee knew water levels had been declining due to both use and drought in the southwestern United States. By the summer of 2020, Lake Powell was a hundred feet lower than full pool, and at less than 50 percent capacity. And the drought continued.

Trees, shrubs, and native grass often surround natural lakes throughout the Colorado Plateau, but the rock shores of Lake Powell combine with scorching summer heat and scouring winds to prevent the verdancy that presents itself in a more hospitable environment.

Having paused in his hike to the lake's most famous site, Rainbow Bridge, Chee considered the untouched lunch in his pack. He'd eat in a few minutes, but first, a rare nap under the clear blue October sky. Doug Walker, his wife's clan brother and an area tour guide, had shown Chee where the trail to the sacred site began. After reminding him that it would be a lot easier to reach the bridge by water, Doug had promised that a boat would pick Chee up at the closest dock.

Chee closed his eyes and replayed Doug's instructions. "The bridge is nine miles from the trailhead. You'll be coming into it here." Doug had pressed the spot with his index finger. "Our boat leaves the big marina every day around one p.m. with the last group of sightseers and arrives around three. If you miss it, either I or one of the staff will come and get you that evening."

"No need for that," Chee said. "I can catch up with the tour boat the next day." Another night beneath the diamond stars and a chance to enjoy the power of Rainbow Bridge in evening's quiet sounded appealing.

Doug nodded. "I'll tell Curtis or Sunfish to watch for a big, tired-looking Navajo guy. If you're there before we leave, you'll get a seat. We're not as busy now that kids are back in school. That's good, because Curtis and I are cooking up something new."

"What's that?"

"Ah, it's too early to talk about it." Doug

shrugged off Chee's curiosity with his own question. "Can you guess which story of Rainbow Bridge we share with tourists?"

"Well, I prefer the tale of how one of the Hero Twins was hunting and got trapped by a flash flood. His father, Jo'hanaa'éí, the Sun and Changing Woman's husband, sent a rainbow to save the young man from drowning. Afterward it turned to stone as a symbol of the strength of a father's love. I also like the one about the measuring worm that transformed itself into a solid rock bridge to help the twins escape from rising water. That story has value, too. It shows how little things can make a huge difference."

For the Diné, the graceful sandstone bridge represented more than interesting geology. Here, the supernatural and humanity had interacted, and that made Tsé'naa Na'ní'áhí a sacred place. Other tribes of the area also held the natural bridge in reverence as a blessed marvel and had their own stories of its origins and importance.

Doug had rubbed his chin. "Nope. The story we share concerns the controversy about the lake's creation. About how the ones who built the lake disrespected the bridge and how the People stood up for it. Navajos, Hopi, Zuni, Paiutes, even some Utes. The enviros joined in, too."

Chee recalled the struggle to preserve the bridge as a pilgrimage site instead of a tourist attraction to minimize the inadvertent and inevitable desecration that might be caused by uninformed visitors who would walk beneath the bridge—an action of disrespect—or talk too loudly or laugh too much. "Were you involved in trying to protect it?"

"Not me, bro. I wasn't born. That was in the 1970s." Doug laughed. "My baby brother, Curtis, he did a lot of research about the protests and the controversy. He started working with Dr. Peter Hendrix, the archaeologist from the University of Utah who was involved with all that. You heard of him?"

"No."

"Dr. Pete is famous in these parts," Doug said. "He did a lot of the archaeology that went down before Lake Powell started to fill. Curtis met him when he spoke at our school. My brother really got into that archaeology stuff. Every year on the anniversary of the dam's completion, Dr. Pete encouraged us to write letters to the newspapers about the old ones who lived here. One year Curtis wrote about why Rainbow Bridge matters and included a sketch he made. We all were so proud of him when we saw that in the newspaper.

"The National Park Service, the state of Arizona, even the conservation groups, tried to help protect Rainbow Bridge from tourists, but the fact is that Lake Powell is government property, open to all comers. Then Mother Nature stepped right in. Now that lack of rain, miserable snowpack, and evaporation have lowered the water level, everyone has to walk farther. Most of them just stay in the boats." Doug chuckled. "When we do our tours, we tell the traditional stories you mentioned and let the customers know that we've heard about people who died unexpectedly not long after they walked under the arch."

"I thought that was only us Navajos who didn't know the right prayers."

Doug grinned. "We don't share every detail. It keeps them from being disrespectful."

Refreshed from his rest, Chee hiked toward the bridge. He startled a cluster of bighorn sheep. Two of them glanced up from their browsing and scampered higher over the russet sandstone. The third watched a moment longer before joining the herd. The human herd was more elusive; he only encountered two other hikers, a pair of Hopi women.

Eventually he came to a faded sign that read "Rainbow Bridge National Monument," and a wooden fence that created a hikers' maze. He stopped and searched the arid landscape for the first sight of the towering stone bridge, beautiful Tsé'naa Na'ní'áhí.

And then he saw it.

He breathed in its majesty as he approached, following the trail to the point where he could stand in the narrow band of shade the bridge created. He admired the height of the graceful arch—roughly as tall as the Statue of Liberty—and its strong span across the river. Some said that it represented the union of male and female as well as the cooperation of the Hero Twins who made the world safe for humanity by destroying most of the monsters who threatened to elimi-nate us Five Fingered beings. The reality of its

presence calmed his disappointment at his failure
to find the cave. He paused in gratitude, sang his
prayer, and blessed the spot and the day with sacred cornmeal.

Based on the angle of the sun, he had plenty
of time before the boat arrived, bringing its tour
group. With the arch at his back, he walked along
the lakeshore, watching the deep-blue water lap
against the floating dock. What a gift, he thought,
to have this powerful place to himself.

Wanting a panoramic view of the lake, he studied the sandstone for a trail that could provide
such a vista. He found one that seemed promising
and began to climb. The hike grew steeper, and
when he paused to catch his breath, he noticed a
packrat nest at the foot of the cliff with something
shiny on top. Curious, he left the trail to examine
the anomaly. When he pulled it from the sticks,
weeds, and debris, he realized the object was a
miniature thermometer. It resembled something
a hiker might add to the puller on a jacket zipper. The attachment had broken, but the device
still worked—if, in fact, the day was eighty-five
degrees warm. He smiled, thinking of a packrat
checking his thermometer. As he flipped it over
in his palm, he saw a logo, a sketch of a houseboat with the words "Laguna Blue" on its side. He
slipped the device into his pants pocket to dispose
of later.

He climbed until he reached the mesa top and
stopped to savor the view. The lake stretched below him, vast and as blue as the October sky, with
a broad band of desert-brown rock separating the

two. He searched the water for the tourist boat and didn't see it—just late-season houseboats bobbing gently in the distance. He pulled out his phone to take a picture and, as he framed the shot, something bright green caught his eye. A tent. Someone had carefully positioned it to catch afternoon shade from a wind-carved overhang. Except for the thermometer, he hadn't seen signs of human presence. Not even a boot print. He wondered who had camped here and where they were now.

He told himself he was on vacation, and the tent was none of his business. But it was on his way to his next goal—soaking his toes in the cool water. So instead of heeding his own advice, he approached it. He saw where a fire had been, but none of the cooking utensils, drying laundry, or other signs that indicated an occupied campsite.

"Hello. Anyone home?" Chee waited, then called again. "Anybody in there?" He heard no response.

He strolled to the tent. It looked expensive and well loved, lightweight and designed for backpacking. Someone had zipped the entrance flap closed. It had been untouched long enough to attract a spiderweb between a supporting pole and the emerald fabric nearest the pole. The relatively flat surface at the top had accumulated a fine layer of sand, and more sand had piled into a small undisturbed dune at the tent's entrance. Odd, he thought; the day had been calm and windless. The tent had been here awhile.

"Hey, I'm a cop. Everything OK here?"

With nothing stirring inside the tent, and no

one approaching, Chee found the zipper, scared the spider away, and opened the flap. With some dread, he squatted to look inside. As he'd expected, no one was there, but what he saw took him by surprise. No decaying corpse, but half of a large broken pot decorated with the classic black-and-white geometric shapes of the early Pueblo people lay on the waterproof tent floor. Next to it was a fiber object he identified as an ancient yucca sandal. There were three large, dark stones, which looked as if the hands of the ancient ones had shaped them into tools for grinding grain. A small group of potsherds sat next to them, as though someone had arranged everything for a photograph.

He again took out his cell phone—a device that had proven useless except as a camera in this cell-tower-scarce landscape—and snapped some photos of the display. If this were a case of grave robbing—stealing from the dead for sale to collectors—the person responsible would face serious consequences.

Someone also had left a backpack, a water filter, a rolled-up sleeping bag, and a pad, all stashed across from the entrance. He hesitated. If whoever camped here returned to find a stranger rooting around in the tent, Chee risked an angry confrontation before he could explain that he was a policeman with legitimate concern for the owner's safety. But the person who set up this campsite could be hurt or lost and he wasn't a man to ignore the situation.

He grabbed the pack, noticing that it was surprisingly light, and took it outside the tent's tight space to look for any identification of its owner. He opened the main pocket and found a small digital camera, a half-empty water bottle, some energy bars, sunscreen, and a ziplock bag. Inside the bag were Band-Aids of various sizes, a tube of antibiotic ointment, gauze, tape, and other components of a first aid kit.

The smaller pockets were equally unhelpful in terms of identification. He found a bag of nuts, a pocketknife, and a rock.

Chee held the rock in the palm of his hand, wondering what about it had caught the interest of whoever had camped here. It looked like granite, and had several colors—streaks and mottles of white, black, and brown with green the most prominent. It was about the size of a flattened golf ball. When he spun it on its side, he realized it had the shape of a frog. Frogs meant rain, and rain meant everything to indigenous people of the desert.

He replaced the rock and, in the final compartment, discovered a small notebook. It reminded him of the one Leaphorn kept in the breast pocket of his uniform shirt. Chee opened it. The cursive handwriting, small and neat, was in the Navajo language, Diné Bizaad. The words were poetry, poetry about love, directed to a woman. He spent a moment thumbing through it for the name of the writer, then closed the book and zipped it back into the pack. He returned the backpack to the tent, shut the entrance flap, and left everything as he had found it. The scene troubled him. He'd mention the abandoned campsite to Park Service authorities when he returned.

Chee resumed his hike to the lake. He looked up when he heard an animal cry and searched the honey-colored sandstone for its source, seeing only a moving shadow, a golden eagle soaring silently. He followed the eagle's course as it settled on a stone ledge. The noise must have been a warning from its potential prey.

He pulled his binoculars from the pack and, through them, scanned the rocks for rodents. Instead, he found ancient art: concentric circles, handprints, shields, a snake near the place where two large boulders touched, a four-legged creature with antlers. He envisioned the hunter, waiting here for his prey and returning to mark the site to honor the animal. Or perhaps pecking the image in the stone to draw the deer. Whether the signs carved on the rocks were clan markings, records of successful kills, or just done for their beauty, they reflected humanity's long-held wish not to pass away unnoticed. Chee wondered what stories these old ones told to explain the sacred bridge, and if, like himself, they viewed it as a link to another reality.

As he scanned the terrain for the safest route to the water, he saw unusual red marks on the cliffside, and then found what could have been a trail to the lake. Putting down the binoculars, he set off for it, but again the steepness of the slope made the descent a challenge. He watched his steps as he crossed the sandstone, eventually finding switchbacks that seemed to head to the lake. After negotiating the first few, he stopped at a flat ledge to savor a stunning view of the water below.

Chee removed his heavy backpack, letting the coolness of the gentle breeze evaporate the sweat that had soaked through his T-shirt. The water rippled along the shore, and he could hear the waves slap against the caramel cliffs. Ducks bobbed in the cove, diving headfirst and quickly popping back to the surface. He wondered if they were visiting on their migration south or if they were full-time residents. No matter how hot the air and sandstone, only the top few inches of the lake warmed. The deep water just below the sun-heated top few inches remained numbingly cold, in the mid-to-low forties. That might be why the ducks resurfaced with lightning speed.

He scanned the terrain again, hoping for an easier path to soak his toes a few moments. As far as he could tell, only lizards and birds could get to the water without a struggle. As Doug had said of Rainbow Bridge, the best access to the lake here was by boat.

Thinking of boats reminded him of his own marine pickup. He gave the hunt for a better trail a final try. This time, he observed something yellow bobbing in the water. It looked like cloth trapped against a cream-colored rock face and a large boulder. Probably an item that washed overboard from one of the houseboats. It spoiled the pristine view. It bothered him.

Chee watched the fabric dance with the lake's motion, wondering why it had wedged there instead of washing onto the beach or sinking into the depths of the lake. A puzzle. He squinted toward the water, and noticed something dark and alive, with a dancing motion, near the patch of yellow. It reminded him of the anemones he and Bernie had seen on their honeymoon in Hawaii. As he watched the dance, he realized that he wasn't observing a marine creature. He felt his stomach tighten with anticipation.

He used the binoculars to look more closely. What he'd taken for tentacles was long dark hair moving with the tide and attached to a human head. A dead person floated facedown, the body rocked by the rhythm of the lake.

4

Bernadette Manuelito pulled her Toyota Tercel to the side of the road and turned off the engine. "OK. You drive."

Bernie had invited her sister, Darleen, to join them on a tour of amazing Antelope Canyon. Now the sisters were on the way home. Darleen hadn't been part of the original plan, but Mr. Natachi, the elderly gentleman Bernie's younger sister worked for in Chinle, had passed away. Bernie had thought some sisterly love might nudge Darleen to figure out what came next, and her sweet husband agreed.

The three of them had walked with the other visitors through the amazing grottoes in the upper canyon, sandstone carved into swirling shapes by wind and water. Bernie marveled at how the sunlight seeping through the narrow slot between the walls made the rock glow. Darleen took pictures of everything, including the three of them against that special background.

Then they had climbed down a long flight of stairs to see a different and equally spectacular magnificence in lower Antelope Canyon. Doug Walker, who with his brother, Curtis, ran a business called Antelope Canyon Tours, kept the small groups of tourists entertained with amusing dialogue. Bernie hadn't met her clan brothers before the tour, but she suspected that Doug told those same jokes on every trip, and she gave him credit for making them seem fresh.

They climbed out of the car.

Darleen, who had been fiddling with her phone, punched Bernie playfully on the shoulder. "I'm glad you didn't fall asleep behind the wheel. I'm happy to take over. I've been editing my pictures from the tour. I have to show you."

Bernie leaned toward her toes, stretched, then straightened up again. Fatigue hung on her like a blanket, and the sun's warmth through the windshield hadn't helped. But she was glad for the trip, happy at the chance to travel again after Dikos Nitsaa'igii-19, or the Big Cough, the virus that had ravaged the world, and especially the Navajo Nation. Doug mentioned that their business had taken a huge hit from the pandemic. Per capita cases on the Navajo Nation had surpassed those in New York State. Navajo health officials reported that roughly 33,000 people on Navajo land—out of a population of 175,000—tested positive for the coronavirus. More than 1,400 people had died from the virus, among them precious elders like Mr. Natachi who carried tradition and irreplaceable memories. And those numbers came before the new wave of illness from the Delta and other variants.

Darleen walked toward the driver's door. "Look at this one." She extended her phone to Bernie. "I love the way the shadows fall. And the color is really intense."

Bernie took the phone. The photo showed the strata of a narrow passage in Antelope Canyon to great advantage. The light accentuated the curves in the rock, the color flowing like liquid gold. Doug stood out in his bright shirt with the Antelope Canyon Tours logo.

"That is beautiful." She handed the phone back. "I loved that tour. That place is magic."

"I might make a print for Mama and Mr. . . ." Darleen stopped. "I keep doing that."

"It's OK. He was part of your life for a long time." Even as she said it, Bernie realized it wasn't perfectly true. Although her family had known Mr. Natachi ever since she and her sister were children, Darleen had come back into his life less than a year before. The gentleman had been hospitalized and needed some assistance when he came home, and Darleen had moved to Chinle to help him. The old one, like so many others, had died of the virus during that sad, lonely time. Darleen tested negative, but even so she stayed away from Mama during that time for fear of spreading the infection. Bernie had helped Mama set up some video calls. Now Darleen could live with Mama in Toadlena once more and figure out, yet again, what came next for her.

"Will you make a copy of that picture for me, too?"

"OK."

"Do you have shots of Lake Powell?"

"A gazillion, but none of them do it justice. It's spectacular."

"Right." Bernie recalled her first view of Lake Powell, glistening as it stretched farther than she could see. The rock walls that framed it run from northern Arizona into southern Utah. She'd read that it was one of the West's largest bodies of water—two thousand miles of shoreline. Other than her honeymoon in Hawaii, she'd never seen so much water.

Darleen paged through her photographs. "I've got something better, a really cute shot of you and Cheeseburger."

Cheeseburger. The nickname Darleen and Mama had given Bernie's charming husband. "Let me see."

"No way. It's a surprise. But here's a nice one of us with the Walkers."

After their visit to the stone wonders of Antelope Canyon, Doug Walker invited them to dinner. They enjoyed meeting Doug's wife and sons. Bernie remembered that Chee had asked a few discreet questions about Leaphorn's cave, but Doug knew nothing about it. Curtis might know something, Doug said, but his brother had left after work for a camping trip.

Darleen opened the driver's door and moved the seat back to make room for her longer legs.

Bernie walked to the passenger side. "It's

strange to be sitting here with you behind the steering wheel."

"Strange but true."

"You've driven my Tercel before."

"Barely." Darleen adjusted the rearview mirror. "You're so protective of this car."

"I am. That's why it's in such good shape for something this old. Although I wouldn't mind driving something different."

"Something different? That reminds me. Do you have any news about your job change, the criminal investigation stuff?" Darleen punched her shoulder again, harder this time. "My big sister as a detective. How cool!"

"No, not yet." Bernie hadn't heard because she had delayed putting in her application. The wait came partly from problems getting the right forms, and mostly because her indecision had returned. She liked her current job as a police officer, and the flexibility it gave her to spend time with Mama and her husband. Sure, she felt restless, ready for more of a challenge, but she was basically happy. When she finally submitted the paperwork, she'd told herself she didn't have to decide if she really wanted a change until she got called for an interview—or even if and when a job offer came her way.

Darleen started the car and headed east on the paved two-lane highway Arizona State Route 98.

"I'm gonna stop for lunch when we get to Kayenta. I'm starved." She lowered her window. "Are you ever going to get the air conditioner fixed?"

"Probably not."

Darleen laughed. "That's what I thought."

"It's good to be with you, Sister. I'm glad you're home again."

"At least for a while."

"I'm glad you'll be living with Mama." Bernie had spent more time with their mother as caregiver during the pandemic and noticed Mama's memory slipping. Equally disturbingly, she'd seen changes in her physical health. "We're lucky Mrs. Darkwater is around to help, too."

"I used to think she was, you know, just an old busybody of a neighbor, but now, well, I appreciate how much she loves our Mama."

Bernie recalled that sometimes when Mrs. Darkwater phoned her with an upsetting report about Mama, it turned out to be a false alarm. But usually her concern was justified. "I'd like to get Mama in to see a doctor."

"Good luck with that." Darleen laughed. "Mr. Natachi had an aide from the VA who came about once a week. The guy took his blood pressure and then showed me how to do that. He had a little monitor that clipped right on to his finger to show how much oxygen was in his blood. Sometimes when that old soul was confused, it turned out that his oxygen level was low. The aide taught me how to work with Mr. Natachi's oxygen machine. Maybe that would help Mama."

"Sounds like you learned a lot."

"I did. I never expected a job like that to be so interesting." Darleen took a hand off the steering wheel to push a strand of hair back from her forehead.

Bernie's fatigue returned as she gazed out at the starkly beautiful country they drove through, land with space enough for people to think and breathe. Mama and Darleen had plenty of room to be together in Mama's house. But given past experience, she wondered how long her sister would stay. She closed her eyes and felt sleep approaching.

Then the car swerved, and she popped awake. Darleen had taken her right hand off the steering wheel to reach behind her, feeling for something in the back seat.

"Hey, you scared me."

"Sorry. I can't find my water bottle. Do you see it?"

Bernie turned, grabbed the purple container, and handed it to her sister.

"You know, while you were sleeping, I've been thinking about doing something in the medical field. Taking some classes, getting certified as a nurse's aide or a home health worker. Something like that. What I'd learn would help Mama, too."

"That sounds good, but what about art?" For the past few years Darleen had pursued her drawing with clear focus, even enrolling at an arts college in Santa Fe one summer. "I thought drawing was your passion."

"I can do both. I'll always love art. I got a big kick out of teaching it at the senior center, you know, painting and weaving and making collages with those elderlies. But . . ."

Bernie waited for her sister to continue, but Darleen seemed to have lost her train of thought.

"But what?"

"OK. This is weird, but a lot of people don't value art, and I think it would be a hard way to make much money. Not that I want to be rich but, you know, I want to support myself and help Mama. If I got a certificate in something medical, I could make a difference in a good way with my work. If I ever wanted to live somewhere else, you know, like Gallup or Flag or even Phoenix, I could find a job."

"I didn't know you enjoyed that kind of work."

"Me neither, but I liked helping that old man. One of his helpers from the VA told me she'd trained at Navajo Tech. I could do that."

"That's an interesting idea."

"By interesting, do you mean dumb?"

Bernie chuckled. "Not at all. I mean *cool*. You surprised me."

"I surprised myself. You know, it felt good to do something for someone else. Even though I missed Mama, being away from her gave me time to think about a lot of stuff. You remember that dude I was hung up on?" Bernie heard the change in Darleen's voice. "That video guy? I really liked him, and I thought maybe we'd be, like, you know, like a couple or something. And then it turned out he wanted to focus on his work and didn't need a girlfriend."

Bernie listened as Darleen talked about how some of her friends were partnered up and had a child or two already, and how some were in college. Bernie remembered a few of the names she mentioned. Then her sister came to Slim, a quiet, intense young man Bernie clearly recalled. They had given him the teasing name Stoop Man.

"Slim got his AA degree, and he's working as a teacher's aide at Nizhoni Elementary. He wants to go back to school to become a school counselor. He's a great listener, so I know he'd be good at that." Darleen took a drink from her water bottle. "He's nice."

"So, have you seen the guy since you've been back?"

"Yes, and we text once in a while." She heard new joy in her sister's voice.

"He was at Chaco helping with a group of kids on the field trip when I was there a while ago." Bernie recalled the shy young man who seemed to enjoy working with children. "He knew how to manage those little ones and keep them happy. Do you like him?"

"A lot." Darleen nodded. "But I think he looks at me as just a friend. He hasn't tried to kiss me. How can I tell if he likes me, I mean, more than just a friend?"

"What do you think?"

Darleen shrugged.

"Give it time."

"It's just . . ." Darleen hesitated. "He and I get along great. But it's not like with Mr. Video, the guy I made a fool of myself over. He was always trying to kiss me and . . . well, you know. But Slim is almost too nice, too polite. I wish I could take the best of both of them and squeeze that together." To demonstrate, she took her hands off the steering wheel, using her knee to steer.

"I'd like to meet someone like the Cheeseburger, smart and nice and sorta good looking but, you know, younger and not a cop."

Bernie laughed. "I think he's sorta good looking, too."

She felt her phone vibrate. A text from Detective Tara Williams, her friend from the Socorro, New Mexico, sheriff's office.

> Manuelito. I've got time off next week. You free? Hiking? Let me know.

Bernie sent a thumbs-up emoji. She'd call Tara later when she knew the signal would last through a phone call.

Darleen stopped at the Burger King in Kayenta. A family had erected a flea market next to the restaurant parking lot. They noticed a poster behind one of the tables with a picture of a pretty little round-faced girl.

Bernie and Darleen looked at the items for sale and found some salt and pepper shakers they thought Mama would like. Nothing fancy, but nicer than the big, banged-up aluminum shaker Mama used for salt. Bernie picked them up and asked the young woman behind the counter for a price.

"They're a dollar. For both."

"OK." Bernie removed her wallet from the backpack. "Who is the girl on the poster?"

"That's my sister, Morgan."

"She's pretty."

"She's why we're having this sale, you know. She has seizures, and she has to take medicine to keep her healthy. Sometimes with the trembling, she hurts herself. Mom had to start homeschooling Morgan because of her health, so now she can't work."

"What makes your sister tremble?"

"It's a rare form of epilepsy. Here." The woman gave Darleen an information sheet, *Facts about Childhood Epilepsy.* "Because not many people have it, her medicine costs a lot."

"How much?"

"More than thirty thousand dollars a year. And she'll have to take it the rest of her life."

"Wow." Darleen's eyes widened. In a place where the average annual family income was about $22,000, the amount was formidable.

Bernie put a $5 bill for the salt and pepper shakers on the table. The woman started to make change.

"No, keep it for your little sister."

They went inside for a drink and something to eat. Bernie paid for Darleen's large fries and milkshake and got a Coke—extra large, because it was still a long drive to Shiprock—and a burger. She'd promised herself to cut back on Cokes and drink more water. But not right now.

They sat at a table by a window. Two more hours, Bernie thought, and they'd be at Mama's. She was tired. She hoped Mama's mood had improved since the last time they'd spoken.

Darleen dipped a fry in catsup and pushed the

bag toward Bernie. "They're really good." She took a bite and lowered her voice. "You see that guy over there, the one with the brown shirt?"

Bernie quickly glanced at the next table. "Yeah."

"He's really staring at us. I don't recognize him. Do you?"

Bernie shook her head. "I don't think I've seen him before."

The man in question rose and walked to their table. He stood in front of Bernie for a moment before he spoke, and her heart rate increased with dread and anticipation. "Excuse me. Do either of you know Lauren Lapahie?"

"No, sir," Darleen responded. Bernie shook her head.

"Sorry to bother you." He smiled. "You surely do look like someone I've met."

"My sister has one of those familiar faces," said Darleen.

"No, it's her earrings."

Bernie moved her left hand to her ear, remembering the turquoise and silver earrings Mama had given her a long time ago. She took the first sip of her big Coke. Seldom had one tasted so sweet and good. She sat the cup on the table.

The man kept talking. "Lauren had a pair just like them . . . and a lot of friends. I thought maybe she had given them to you, and I'd seen you with her or something, and that's why you looked familiar."

Bernie shook her head and stayed silent, waiting for the intruder to go back to his own seat. She looked down at the table. Her burger was getting cold, and the earrings were none of his business.

"Who's Lauren?" Darleen asked.

"My niece, who disappeared last month. Your sister here wants to eat that hamburger. I'm sorry I interrupted your lunch." The man walked away.

Darleen frowned. "You weren't very nice to him."

"I answered his question." Bernie began to unwrap her burger. "Helping people is what I do for a living. I'm tired and I'm off work until tomorrow morning."

"Saving all that natural sweetness to share with Mama, right?"

"I'll need it. Mama has been extra cranky with me lately. I have to call on my inner nice girl not to lose my temper."

"I'm glad to know you have one. Here." Darleen pushed the bag of french fries toward her sister again. "Try this. Maybe it will cheer you up."

"Has Mama been nice to you?"

"All lovey-dovey. I think that's because I haven't been around because of Mr. Natachi. Maybe you can help me figure out which of my Antelope Canyon pictures are the best. I don't want to deluge her with too many. Here, I'll show you . . ."

As Darleen pulled out her phone, her arm brushed against Bernie's giant Coke. The cup overturned, and soda poured like a waterfall onto Darleen's lap. A fleet of ice cubes floated across the tabletop, then sailed on toward Bernie and the floor. Bernie stood, grabbed a napkin, and pushed

the few remaining ice cubes from the tabletop into
her now-empty cup. Then she started to clean up
some of the mess.

Meanwhile, Darleen jumped up. The Coke had
soaked the front of her shorts, dripped down her
legs into her shoes, and puddled on the floor. She
grabbed the remaining napkins and began mop-
ping until they became soggy globs of stickiness.
"I'm sorry about this. What a mess."

"Don't worry about it. Go wash the sticky stuff
off your legs so it doesn't get in the car. I'll find
someone with a rag and a mop to work on this."

Darleen left.

The man who had asked about Bernie's earrings approached from the counter with a stack
of dry napkins and began to help absorb the biggest puddles. "I talked to them up there." He motioned toward the front of the restaurant with his
chin. "They say the cleanup guy will be here in a
minute."

"Thank you."

"You're a cop, aren't you?"

Bernie nodded. "Navajo Police."

"That's why you look familiar."

Bernie felt a tightness in her throat. She'd had
too many conversations that started like this.

"I'm George Lapahie." He stopped, remembering his manners, and introduced himself in Navajo with his clans.

Bernie reciprocated.

"Even though you're out of uniform, I knew I
recognized you. You pulled my dad over for driv-

ing funny a few weeks ago. It turned out he was having a stroke. I was in the car with him, but I had fallen asleep. Your siren woke me up, and I grabbed the wheel. You saved both our lives. *Ahéhee'*. I didn't have the presence of mind to thank you then. *Ahéhee'*."

She remembered the incident. "How is your father doing?"

"He's OK. Good, I'd say for a person almost ninety. They gave him the antistroke medicine real quick to reduce the damage to his brain. We don't let him drive on the highway anymore."

Her heart had opened to the man. "Tell me about the woman with my earrings."

He nodded. "How much time do you have?"

"Until my sister gets back from washing off the Coke."

George laughed. "OK, then, I'll give you the short version. Mind if I sit down?"

She motioned to an empty chair and took the dry seat across from him.

"The lady I mentioned, Lauren Lapahie, is a clan sister of Morgan, the little girl our family is raising money for out there. Morgan loves Lauren. I think if Lauren came home the little one would feel better."

Bernie sighed. Too many indigenous women went missing. Some came home alive but damaged. Sometimes their bodies turned up. Sometimes they vanished without a trace. Sometimes, but far too rarely, law enforcement found them.

"She wrote a note to her scumbag ex-husband,

saying she had something she had to do, and she wished him and all her relatives well. She left behind her wedding ring, her car, her credit card, most of her clothes and jewelry, her other belongings, you know? And that was it."

Bernie nodded. "I'm sorry you have to deal with this sadness on top of Morgan's illness. I know my mother worries about me even though we see each other several times a week. She's always concerned that something bad might happen."

"Relatives are like that. I know how your mother feels."

Bernie waited for him to say more, and he had more to say.

"We've had no sign of Lauren. No phone messages, texts, emails, nothing. After a couple of weeks, we pooled our money and hired a detective." George made a hissing sound. "He shoulda given us a refund. I've told you only the basics. I left out the confusion, anger, blame, questions and repercussions, and the worry. It's like throwing a rock in a lake and watching the ripples roll out, ya know? Sadness builds up on you. It's been hard, especially with my dad not doing so well. We all miss her like crazy."

"I hope she comes home soon."

George stood, reached into his pocket, and pulled out a cell phone. "I want to show you something." He fiddled with the phone a moment and then held it out to Bernie. "Here's the last photo I have of her. Just in case, you know."

Bernie looked at the attractive Navajo woman about her age, staring at the camera with a solemn expression. "What's that on her shoulder? A bruise?"

George used his thumb and index finger to expand the image.

"See? It's a blue feather." He moved the phone closer to Bernie to show the tattoo. "Lauren wanted a bigger one, but she couldn't afford it. She told me she'd start with this and work up to a whole eagle." He laughed. "That girl. What a bright light."

Bernie looked at the feather, unusual and nicely done. That photo would make it easier to identify the body, and as the thought flashed by she realized, again, that she knew a lot about the sad side of life.

"Want me to send it to your phone in case you see someone who looks like Lauren?"

"No, I have a good memory." She never gave her cell number to strangers.

"Well, here." He pulled a black leather wallet from his pocket and offered her an old-fashioned business card. "You never know."

A woman and little girl who had shared the booth with George came up behind him. The woman had car keys in her hand. George turned to her. "This is my friend Hannah, and the short one is Morgan, the reason we're here. The girl on the poster."

Bernie greeted the woman and then said to the child, "Morgan, that's a pretty name. How old are you?" The girl started to speak and then seemed overcome by an unseen distraction. Her closed eyelids were fluttering. "Are you OK?"

Hannah glanced at the little girl's face. "That's called an absence seizure. They usually pass quickly. But she needs her nap."

Morgan opened her eyes. Bernie read the surprise in her face.

"Hi there. I'm Bernie. Nice to meet you."

"Nice to meet you," Morgan mirrored.

"You be safe out there, Officer," George said. "I apologize for interrupting your lunch." He set another card on the table. "This is for your sister." Like the one he'd given Bernie, the card had a photo of Lauren Lapahie on one side and information about how to contact the family on the other.

When Darleen returned, she was holding two cups. Bernie told her the story of Lauren and showed her George's card.

Darleen studied the picture. "I bet Lauren had a secret boyfriend, and they ran off together. She didn't want to tell anyone because she already had an ex-husband. She thought her family would hate her."

"You make it sound romantic, but that's a cowardly thing to do, and hurtful to your relatives."

"Don't you believe in love?"

"Well, sure, but you need to be honest with people. Not just run away."

"Here's a different idea. What if Lauren has some terrible disease that everyone she came in contact with could have caught? She knew she would die, and she wanted to be alone, you know, not make other people take care of her and risk getting sick."

"I like that story better, but I don't buy it."

Darleen looked at the drink lids and eased one toward her sister. "Here's a fresh Coke. Don't spill it."

"Ahh. You didn't have to do that."

"Sure, I did."

Bernie grabbed the cup and her backpack, and they headed to the car.

Darleen had the keys in her hand. "Want me to keep driving?"

"No, thanks. I'll take it from here." Bernie grabbed the keys, slid in behind the steering wheel, and scooted the seat toward the windshield.

Darleen fished her phone from a back pocket before she fastened her seat belt. "We need to let Mama know when we'll be there."

"Use my phone and put it on speaker so I can hear, too, OK? You'll find it in the front pocket of my backpack."

Darleen reached into the back seat to grab the pack and bring it onto her lap. She unzipped it. "Your phone isn't here."

"It has to be. Keep looking."

Bernie watched the road as she heard her sister unzipping pockets and rummaging around.

"A book. A water bottle, a notepad, a pen, sunscreen, a plastic bag with seeds or something weird. Granola bars. Phone charger. Is it in your pocket?"

Bernie patted her jacket again. "No. Check on the floor back there."

She waited, her anxiety rising.

"I can't find it. It's not here, unless it slipped under your car seat. I can't reach that far."

Then they heard a phone ringing.

"Ah. Wait a minute." Darleen had her purse on her lap. She reached inside and pulled out Bernie's missing phone just as it stopped ringing. "It was Mama."

Bernie waited for her sister to explain.

"Remember when I spilled the Coke? Well, I picked up your phone before it could get sticky and put it in my purse, and then, with all the confusion, I forgot. Sorry. I'll listen to Mama's messages, if she left any." Darleen studied the screen for half a second. "This is the first one." She put the phone on speaker.

"*My daughter, when are you coming to help with my groceries? I'm waiting for you.*" Mama hung up.

Then Darleen played the newer message. "*My daughter, did you have an accident? Are you doing a dangerous job? I'm calling your work and that other phone. I am worried about you. Why can't you be like your sister? She's gone, too, but she's working for that nice man.*"

Bernie frowned. "Poor Mama. I told her you and I would be gone for a few days, back this afternoon."

"I told her, too. I guess she forgot. I've been noticing more of that. I mean, I know that can happen to anybody, like I forgot that I'd rescued your phone. But Mama seems to be getting worse. We should take her to the clinic again."

"You know what she'll say to that."

"I could tell her I wasn't feeling good and make an appointment and then she'd come with me and . . . you know. I'm sure the doctor would work with us." Darleen looked out the window. "If you get that new job, you'll be traveling more, won't you?"

"Probably."

"So more of this stuff will be up to me."

"Yes." She paused. "Sister, I won't abandon you. And my husband can help, too."

Mama still had some of the old thinking that said sons-in-laws should avoid mothers-in-law. For his part, she knew Chee had begun to reevaluate his career in law enforcement: that was part of the reason he had stayed at Lake Powell and planned the hike to Rainbow Bridge. Her husband had been at the job long enough, she realized, to feel the need to do something else. And who knew where that would take him?

US 160 stretched north and east toward Dennehotso, Red Mesa, and Teec Nos Pos, Arizona, and then to the New Mexico border. Bernie watched the arid landscape she loved pass by.

Darleen looked at the cell phone. "I'll call Mama as soon as we get some service. Did you ever try a video call with her?"

"She just has that landline, remember?"

"Oh shoot. That's right."

Bernie's phone rang, surprising them both.

"It's not Mama. Someone named Williams." Darleen handed her the phone. Bernie glanced at the screen, then took the call.

"Hello?"

"Hey, it's Tara." Bernie realized that the phone was still on speaker from when Darleen had played Mama's messages. Good, since the Tercel didn't have Bluetooth and she liked to keep both hands on the wheel. She put the phone on the center console.

"Listen, Bob and I are coming to Farmington to look at a horse tomorrow. You wanna . . ." The voice disappeared and then was back. ". . . or lunch?"

"The coverage here is spotty. I'll call you when I get home, and we'll make a plan."

"OK. Don't forget. I want to . . ." Her voice grew faint, and then, ". . . something else . . . ," and then they heard the chimes of signal death.

Bernie handed her phone to Darleen.

"Is Tara a friend?"

"Yes. She's a detective in Socorro. We worked a case together."

"Cool. Is that what encouraged you to apply to be a detective yourself?"

"Sort of. Part of the idea anyway. What do you think of it?"

Darleen stretched her legs away from the car seat. "What would you do?"

"It depends on the case. Basically, go to the crime scene and try to figure out what happened." Bernie explained in more detail.

"Could you work with someone like George back there and help him find Lauren?"

"Probably, if he called when they discovered she was missing, and especially if it looked like she'd been kidnapped or hurt or something. The law says an adult has a right to go missing. After all this time, it could be really hard to find her."

"If Lauren was related to a tribal councillor, or

a judge, or some big shot, I bet someone would have figured out what happened."

Bernie nodded. "The other thing to consider is that an adult can break off contact with her family, with whoever."

Darleen reached for her drink. "I don't believe in that. Even if you argue, get in a big old fight, they are still your relatives. I bet there were times when you and Mama and Cheeseburger wanted to disown me, wanted me to disappear. I'm glad you stuck with me. It's *k'é*."

Bernie laughed. "We wouldn't know what to do without you. Mama didn't raise her girls to act like we have no relatives."

They drove a few miles in silence. Darleen looked at her phone again and put it away. "I'm not sure what's next for me. You've heard that before, haven't you?"

"Oh, once or twice."

"A lot of it depends on Mama's health." Darleen turned toward the window, and then back to Bernie. "I've been thinking about Mama a lot since the man I was working for died. I realized that I missed being with her, even though she can drive me crazy. I missed fixing breakfast for her, making sure she got out of the shower without falling, giving her those morning pills. I think living with her again will be good."

Bernie felt herself relax. "So, it's really OK with you to move home to Toadlena?"

"Yes, I'm looking forward to it. You know, because of the virus, more classes are online. I'm sure I can learn a lot in the next year or so without ever going to a school campus." Darleen looked at her phone again. "When will the Cheeseburger be back?"

"Oh, in a couple of days, I guess. He's got a lot of time off from work."

"You don't know?"

"He's looking for a cave with some special sand paintings. It might take him a while to find it."

"A cave? That's weird."

Bernie remembered the evening when the idea arose, at a dinner with the Lieutenant and Louisa Bourbonette, his housemate. She could still hear the reverence in Leaphorn's voice—something unusual for a man who seldom spoke about the sacred—as he told them about the cave. "I realized that I had come across a sanctuary," he'd said, "where some wise person or persons had stored what we would need to start the world again. I know enough about our traditions to understand that these paintings came from different ceremonies and, well, all the rest."

"The rest," she knew, included this caveat: the *hataɫii* who created the images of the Holy People with colored sand for the patient at the time of the healing ceremony always made sure the images were destroyed when the praying and chanting concluded. Always, until this odd exception Leaphorn had accidently discovered.

"My husband mentioned to the Lieutenant and Louisa that he had some days off and that we planned a quick trip to Antelope Canyon. The next afternoon, the Lieutenant called and said he'd found a map showing where the cave might be."

"So the Cheeseburger took off on the quest for the mysterious cave. Is he ever coming back?"

Bernie laughed. "Yep. I'm sure of it. But besides the cave, he has a lot on his mind. He needs to think about his future."

"I get it. How long he's gone depends on how it goes. I want to talk to him about something, but it can wait."

"What?"

"It's a Who. That guy, Slim." Darleen sighed. "I mean, I wonder if he can tell me why that man acts so edgy around me."

"I think it means he likes you."

"But why would that make him nervous?"

Bernie laughed. "You're right. That's a question for the Cheeseburger."

5

Over the past few days, Chee had hiked for miles, slept beneath a million shimmering stars, seen hawks, coyotes, rabbits, deer, ravens, several kinds of lizards, and enough rattlesnakes to fill a cowboy hat. Best of all, he had relished the deep silence and the sounds of creation uninterrupted by police radios. The last time he'd felt this settled, he'd recalled, was the day he had asked Bernadette Manuelito to marry him. No, he thought. Not when he'd asked her, but when he'd heard her say yes.

But now death had again intruded on his peace of mind. He turned from the body, but the sight had burned itself into his consciousness.

Chee felt his heart pounding as he lowered the binoculars. He replaced them in the backpack, slipped it on, then began the slow, cautious descent to the place where, together, rocks and waves had trapped the victim.

Using gravity as an assistant, he reached a stone

ledge that overlooked the shore but offered no way down except to leap. He walked as close to the edge as he could, keeping his balance and praying that the eroded rock would hold his weight. He had a clearer view of the body that floated below him, wedged against a cliffside. He could tell the person was deceased by the total lack of resistance to the water's pulse. The body lay facedown. Both from the clothes and the bulk of the corpse, he assumed that the deceased was male. Removing him from the lake would require a crew and a boat.

Even if Chee had seen this person as he struggled in the water, he knew he could have done nothing to help because of the steep angle of the cliff face. If he had to guess, he'd assume that the person had been hiking on the sandstone, as he himself had, but then slipped, fell, and drowned. He couldn't tell for sure if the accident had left evidence on the rock, but he recalled the red streaks he'd seen earlier. Perhaps they were made by the victim's blood as his body slid to the water.

Chee sighed at the way an unexpected death— and his devotion to police work—had intruded on his vacation. Interesting, he thought, that the situation stirred up a conflict that he'd never quite settled. As a younger man, he had trained long and vigorously under the guidance of his uncle, an esteemed singer and healer, with the idea of becoming a *hatałii* himself. Then his beloved mentor died, and the difficulty of pursuing the additional training he needed to assume the duties of a *hatałii* become more apparent. He put the dream on hold partly because he loved his job as a cop. He thanked his lucky stars that the career had also introduced him to rookie officer Bernadette Manuelito, the smart, strong young woman who'd become his wife. He'd committed himself to marriage, helping Bernie's family, and providing some leadership to the Shiprock division of the Navajo Police.

Superstition didn't rule Chee's world, but he accepted that there were things he couldn't understand or explain using either logic or past experience. He recalled the artifacts he'd seen in the tent. Mostly material like this came from ancient, abandoned pueblos and from looted graves. It was said that *chindis*, the spirits of the dead, lingered strong and angry around the old sites. He pictured the dead man in the act of disturbing the graves to extract his booty. A person rooted in tradition might assume that the ancient ones had exacted their revenge on a grave robber.

Chee said a silent prayer for the deceased. Then, because he was a trained police officer, he took photos of the scene with the camera on his phone and recorded a narrative of what he saw. If this dead person was the man from the green tent—and that was Chee's best guess—he hoped someone who missed and loved him had already called the Park Service or the police with his name and description.

He didn't like leaving the body, but he had no choice. He started back to the Rainbow Bridge dock along the steep, rocky trail that sometimes was no trail at all, now more aware of the racket the approaching boat made and the way the sound echoed off the cliffs. As he listened, Chee took a break from his self-imposed role as detective, and his brain turned to Bernie. If she became a detective, she might be called to investigate a case like this. Bernie knew how to take care of herself and was as smart as their mentor Joe Leaphorn, the Legendary Lieutenant. But grounding in Navajo tradition warned him that association with the dead carried risks. And if and when they started a family, mothers-to-be and babies-in-the-making were especially vulnerable.

As he grew older, the gravity of the risks he and Bernie faced as police officers had grown clearer to him. He had seen colleagues die or receive grievous physical injuries in the line of duty and known officers with deep invisible wounds to their psyches. Like many seasoned officers, he had tried a desk job. With it came the political decisions that rising in police bureaucracy entailed. It didn't suit him.

He knew many fine officers who put in their time and retired with a pension and enough energy to do something different. He had considered it himself, but he didn't see the point in leaving police work until he knew what came next. Much of the crime he'd seen stemmed from loss of connection with Diné cultural foundations. Many of the Navajo offenders he arrested had forgotten how to stand in *hózhó*—the special peace, balance, beauty, and harmony; a way of walking the earth that is inherently good. And, he knew, they had also lost touch with *k'é*, seeing oneself as part of an extended network of immediate family, relatives, the entire clan, and the related clans. That web of connection gave a person stability and provided strong supportive links when times got tough. The gift of helpful clan brothers came with the obligation of reciprocation, the understanding that you would be there to stand with them when the time came. As he thought about *k'é*, he understood that the web stretched to include all living creatures.

These values had for centuries set his people apart as strong, resilient, flexible, and adaptive. The old stories, including the lexicon he'd learned from his uncle, offered the tools needed to rescue lost ones from the disaster they sometimes encountered in mainstream culture. Those tools included respect for elders, caring for little ones, and living with gratitude to Changing Woman and her husband, the Sun, for their many gifts.

He inhaled deeply, pushed distracting thoughts aside, and focused on the trail, picking up his pace. He had to get to the dock before the boat captain decided he wasn't coming and left with the load of sightseers. A rock slipped beneath his boot, and he stumbled, struggling to regain his balance. He paused to let his heartbeat settle. Hiking downhill might be easier on the lungs, but it challenged his knees and thighs and created tension between momentum and stability. The weeks at a desk as fill-in for Captain Largo had not improved his fitness level, but the hiking here had stirred some muscle memory. He set out again, at first more slowly and then faster, finding a confident rhythm and sensing the direction of the trail with increasing surety.

Although Leaphorn's cave eluded him, Chee had uncovered something precious: peace of mind. He still hadn't discovered the path he would take for his future, but after four days alone under the sun and stars, he felt comfortable with that indecision. He put the vision of the dead man aside and promised himself a sip of water when he reached the dock.

As the trail flattened, he noticed a woman in brown shorts and a striped sleeveless shirt on the path ahead of him. When he was close enough, he called out, "Lady, stop. I need your help."

She turned, saw him, and froze.

He repeated himself. "I'm a cop with the Navajo Police. There's a problem down at the lake."

He read her expression. "Don't panic. I want you to stay right where you are. All you have to do is make sure no one climbs up this trail."

"What . . ."

"What's your name, ma'am?" He walked toward her.

"Marilyn."

"I'm Chee, Sergeant Jim Chee." He showed her his ID. "I'm going to the dock right now to report this and get help. Will you please stay right there?"

"What happened?" She didn't wait for him to answer. "I have to get back to the boat or . . ."

"It won't leave without us. I promise."

Marilyn studied the clouds a moment. "OK. I'll do it."

"Thank you." He nodded to her as he walked by, then scrambled down the trail, seeing only one other hiker before the dock came into view. The Antelope Canyon Tours pontoon boat was there. A few people sat on the bench seats, under the canopy that shaded the deck. He approached, scanning for Doug Walker, but the captain's seat was empty. Chee stepped back onto the floating dock, wondering where Doug was and thinking of a way to announce that he'd found a body without causing passenger panic.

He spoke to a passenger as he slipped off his pack and set it in the boat. "Sir, I'm supposed to meet the tour guide. Do you know where he is?"

"He's a she. Miss Sunfish. She's over that way." The man's life jacket rose around his chin as he pointed to a deeply tanned woman in a yellow shirt with a floppy hat. She stood with her back to them, looking toward Rainbow Bridge.

Chee hurried to her. She turned and spoke before he could. "Hey, you must be Chee. Doug told me to keep an eye out for—"

She broke off when she saw his expression. "What's wrong, buddy? You look like you've seen a ghost."

"There's a body in the lake. I spotted someone floating facedown in the cove to the south of here." Chee indicated the place with a jut of his lips. "I think it's a male."

She stared at him in stunned silence.

"There's a dead man in the lake." He said it again, kept it simple.

Sunfish's green eyes widened. "You found someone who drowned . . ."

He nodded once. "You have a radio?"

"Dead guy?"

"A radio?"

"Yeah, sorry. It's in the boat." They both knew cell phones didn't work there. She opened her mouth as if to ask a question, but Chee had already started toward the boat. She ran to catch up.

"Sunfish, is there a name for the cove up that way?"

"Yes. You mean Crimson." She walked beside him and looked south toward the lovely, deadly place. "That place is off-limits, and we always tell the tours no hiking up that way. And not just us; no one should have been near there. The trail is treacherously steep. I'm glad you didn't slip."

"Yeah. Me too."

They reached the pontoon boat, and she climbed on, lithe as a bobcat, stepping over Chee's backpack.

"Put your pack down here while I find the radio." She opened a large cabinet in the bow, rummaged around, and pulled out a battered walkie-talkie. She examined it closely. "I've been fortunate and never had to use this. I'll get the base, then you give them details about what you found."

Chee stowed his pack under the watchful eyes of five passengers—three portly dark-skinned women and a gray-haired *bilagáana* couple—all seated in their company-provided life jackets. They watched Sunfish fiddle with the radio, curiosity reflected in their eyes.

Chee spoke softly. "Does that thing work?"

"I don't know."

"Come on." He motioned with a tilt of his chin for her to follow him onto the dock. They headed away from the passengers toward a spot where someone had left a smaller boat.

Sunfish saw him looking at it. "That guy came in at the same time we did. I saw him head toward Rainbow Bridge." She adjusted some knobs on the radio phone and then pounded its flat base against the palm of her hand. "You're a cop, aren't you? That's what Doug said."

"That's right." He had no jurisdiction in a national park, or off the reservation. But he didn't tell her that. "I didn't want the passengers down there to worry about what we were doing."

"I can't get this stupid thing to work. You wanna try?"

"Sure."

"Here." She handed him the radio, and he studied it, then pushed the buttons. No lights or sound indicated power. He opened the back and looked at the batteries, then reclosed it and handed it back to her with a shake of his head. "Either there's a problem with its innards, or the batteries are dead. Do you have fresh ones?"

"Wouldn't that be convenient?" Sunfish scowled at the useless piece of equipment. "Doug should have made sure this was operational. What if my boat broke down? I'd be floating out there with a bunch of angry people. Ticks me off when stuff like this happens."

"I thought Doug was coming with the tour today."

"Yeah, so did I. He called last night and said he needed a day off. He asked me to work, and I didn't mind. Especially when he said I'd be picking up a mysterious male passenger with a backpack." She smiled at Chee. "It's not like I'm married or anything. The job is about it for me."

No one had flirted with Chee in a while, and it made him uncomfortable. "Sunfish, I need you to get to the marina and tell the rangers about the dead man."

She glanced toward the path to the bridge. "You got it. I'll leave as soon as all my passengers are back. I'm missing three."

"Is one a woman named Marilyn?"

"I'm bad with names."

"Slender. Curly brown hair." He searched his memory for more memorable details. "Wearing a striped shirt and brown shorts?"

"That sounds right. After a while, they all look the same."

"I asked her to guard the trail that heads toward the lake where the body is. She promised to stay there until I came back."

Sunfish crossed her arms over her chest. "So, Marilyn knows about the dead guy?"

"No. I just said there was a problem."

"Good." When she smiled at him, he noticed her slightly misaligned front teeth. "We try to keep these tours upbeat, you know? But accidents happen."

Chee raised his eyebrows. "Accidents?"

"Yeah. The majority involve alcohol. This guy

you found is the fifth drowning this season." She glanced toward the passengers in the boat and then back at Chee. "Crimson Beach looks tempting, but if you jump in the water there, you need to be a strong swimmer. Solid footing is five hundred feet of wet cold below you. How did you find the . . . um, the body?"

"Just lucky, I guess. I hiked up that way. When I stopped to look at the lake, I noticed something odd in the water."

"You're sure it's not some trash or an old life vest or . . ." She shrugged off the rest of the question.

"I'm sure."

She shook her head. "That's a locals' spot. The place is a secret that some of us who work here know about, not on any maps. That beach is sweet, private, beautiful, and peaceful." She cocked her head to one side. "There could be a boat anchored there that you missed. The guy might have been motoring, seen the beach, and pulled in there."

Chee looked at the white powerboat that shared the floating dock, empty except for some life vests and an ice chest. He wondered if it belonged to the dead man and if he had somehow not noticed it when he hiked down from Rainbow Bridge. "Have you seen that boat before?"

Sunfish gave it another look. "I might have. It's a Laguna Blue rental."

Laughter drew his attention back to the Rainbow Bridge trail. Some men were approaching the dock. "Are those the missing hikers?"

Sunfish glanced toward the arch. "Yep. They're

my guys." As if to confirm the observation, one waved to her.

"I'll pick up my pack, and then I'll go get Marilyn."

"Let me take that big thing back to Dangling Rope for you. I can leave it at the marina. It will be safe there until you come for it."

He hesitated. "Thanks, but I need my stuff—binoculars, sunglasses, phone, water. You know how it is."

"I have a spare daypack in the boat. Use that. You need anything else?"

He shook his head. What he really wanted, he thought, was better luck. It seemed like a bad joke: overworked cop takes a few days off, goes to a lake, and finds a body.

"Come on." She turned away, and he followed, noticing the strength in her step and the athletic way she carried herself. An attractive woman comfortable in her own suntanned skin. Doug was lucky to have her as an employee.

She handed him the daypack. "There's another water bottle, an apple, and some trail mix in there along with a first aid kit. It will be a while before anyone—" She stopped, noticing the passengers on the bench watching her, and lowered her voice. "Before the next boat gets here. The Rangers will bring the Glen Canyon dive team and then the body will have to go to the Utah medical examiner's office in Salt Lake City for an autopsy."

The pack had adjustable straps, and he configured them to fit his larger frame after loading his crucial supplies inside. It was many pounds lighter than the one he parked in the tour boat—a fact his shoulders appreciated after a full day of hiking.

"I'll leave your things at our tour office. If you're around for a while, let's go for a beer. It's nice to have someone new to talk to. Doug knows how to find me." Sunfish extended her hand to Chee. "Nice to meet you, even under these circumstances. And good luck."

Her handshake was a gentle touch, the Navajo adaptation of the white person greeting. He appreciated that.

The hike back to Marilyn, still standing where he'd left her, seemed longer than he remembered. "Thanks for staying. The group will leave as soon as you get back to the boat."

She walked in his direction.

"Glad I could help. I hope whatever the problem is on the trail gets fixed soon."

"Me too."

Marilyn seemed happy to abandon her job, scampering down toward the dock with an agility that surprised him. A few minutes later the rumble of the boat's engine echoed off the sandstone cliffs and faded into the distance.

He knew it was about two hours to the marina at Dangling Rope, and then at least another half an hour at best before the investigator and retrieval crew would be on their way. And then came the time to remove the body. A long afternoon stretched ahead of him.

He took a deep breath of the clear desert air, tinged with a hint of evaporation from Lake Powell. The desert light and colors fed his spirit: the contrast between the azure sky, the deep, deep blue water shimmering in the sun, the startling white of three small clouds that drifted overhead, forming shadows on the lake, and the sandstone's warm brown, vibrant red-orange, and black desert varnish. The discoloration on the rock, known as a bathtub ring, gave evidence of the once-higher water level on the cliffs that surrounded the lake.

The Colorado Plateau had been in drought for years, and the lack of rain and snow melt to feed the Colorado and San Juan had combined with evaporation to lower Lake Powell considerably. He'd read that some people wanted to abandon the lake altogether and let the rivers flow on to Lake Mead near Las Vegas. Chee remembered the angry controversy over the flooding of Glen Canyon and the fury stirred by the resulting destruction of the archaeological sites inundated by the rising waters of Lake Powell. From the outrage had come more protection for places where the ancestors had lived. The legislation hadn't been passed in time to rescue the homes and campgrounds of the old ones here.

Chee had long been a collector of stories, and the story of John Wesley Powell, the one-armed veteran from the American Civil War who had explored the Colorado River in his heavy wooden boats with a crew of fellow hardy souls and nothing to lose, was one of his favorites. The lake was named for Powell, and the recreation area, Glen Canyon, took its name from the intrepid explorer's description of the place long, long before the rising waters began to change the once quiet green oasis.

Chee studied the water, noticing how it reflected the subtle motion of the clouds. He was at peace despite his unexpected discovery. And because he knew that the emotion could fade quickly, he savored the feeling.

6

It would be hours before the crew arrived to remove the dead man from the lake, so Jim Chee used the time to hike back to where he had seen the body and examine the scene more closely. He took his binoculars from the daypack to study the terrain for a route to the water that wouldn't put his own life at risk. Not finding one, he looked closely for a boat that might have brought the victim here. Nothing.

He lowered the binoculars. His policeman's brain registered the thought that someone with a boat might have considered this isolated cove a fine spot to dump a body, or leave a man to drown.

Then he searched for possible trajectories of a person falling from the cliffside. He walked to a logical spot and studied the caramel-colored sandstone through the binoculars, noticing some dark stains. From the distance, he couldn't determine if they were nature's doing or caused by human blood as he'd initially suspected. He increased the magnification and scanned more closely. As he memorized the location, Chee realized that he was holding his breath. Just when he had decided to lower the binoculars, he noticed a strange rock, a different shape and color than the other stones, on a small ledge above and to the right of the splatters. Odd.

He sat and thought until his body was ready to move. Then, he headed back to enjoy another look at the sacred bridge and wait for the law enforcement team at the dock. The hike from the boat dock to the observation spot was little more than a mile. Just off the paved trail, he found the single dinosaur footprint he had heard about, the track of a two-legged, three-toed carnivorous giant who had walked through this area when the sandstone was sand.

Chee noticed that the sacred bridge had formed from two different types of sandstone. He knew that the reddish-brown base, sand and mud laid down by the wind and inland seas more than two hundred million years ago, was the Kayenta Formation, made up of sandstone, shale, and limestone. The span—the arch of the bridge—was Navajo Sandstone, slightly younger. He thought about rainbows, a sign from the Holy People that the Five Fingered creatures would be safe, that troubled times were over.

Far away, he heard a boat engine, the sound muffled by the distance. It was too soon to expect the retrieval squad, but perhaps Sunfish had brought the radio to life, and a ranger who happened to be nearby had received the call. He headed toward the dock, took out his binoculars, and after a minute of searching, located a wooden-sided powerboat. It carried only the driver, a man who wore a hat that flapped in the breeze created by the boat's motion.

Chee watched the boat move toward him. He yelled to the man. "Toss me the rope, and I'll help you tie it up."

"Here you go. We call it a line in the boat world. Thank you. I'm not used to having an assistant. I didn't see your boat."

"I hiked in."

The captain killed the motor, and Chee tugged the craft to the dock.

"You hiked? That's quite a walk. I used to do it way back when my father worked here before the dam. This area looked a lot different then." The man laughed. "Pop still talks about how lovely Glen Canyon was, and I have to put up with his diatribes about Lake Foul, as he calls it."

"Wasn't that Edward Abbey's name for this place?"

"Yes. Abbey is dead now, but my pop is still mad." The man picked up his daypack and climbed onto the dock with the grace of someone long accustomed to the process.

"Was your father an archaeologist?"

"Was, and is. How did you guess?"

"I've read about the construction of the dam and the men who came to do the archaeology work."

The man nodded. "How about you? What brings you here?"

Chee thought about how to answer. "I had heard of Rainbow Bridge for years, and I wanted to see it."

"Are you Navajo?"

"Yes."

"So the site is sacred to your people."

"Absolutely, to Diné who follow the old ways, and to the Hopi, Paiutes, and other native people."

"I sense something special here, too, and not just the geology. My father was a huge advocate for preserving this place, limiting tourists. He hated those years when the water rose high enough to reach the base of the formation." The man glanced at the path toward Rainbow Bridge. "Pop documented the archaeological sites along this part of the lake, making a record of what would be destroyed when the lake filled."

"That's interesting. I wasn't expecting to meet anyone with such a deep connection to the place."

"Rainbow Bridge's survival was a small victory after you Navajos, the Hopi, Paiutes, and save-the-planet environmentalists took the National Park Service to court. My father worked hard on that issue, too."

"Who is your father?"

"Dr. Peter Hendrix."

Chee recalled the name. "You can thank him for me. Jim Chee from Shiprock."

"I'm Paul Hendrix."

They shook hands. Chee said, "Have you heard of Crimson Beach?"

"Yes. Why do you ask?"

"I found something in the lake near there. I'd like to take a closer look at it, but I couldn't reach the water. I need you to give me a ride there in your boat."

Paul stared at him. "What? Jim, why would I do that?"

"Call me Chee. I'm Sergeant Chee, actually. Navajo Police."

"Sergeant Chee, I'm assuming what you want to look at is law enforcement business."

"The tour guide who was here is on her way now to Dangling Rope to contact the National Park Service rangers. I told her I'd wait until they get here to make sure no one hikes up that way to disturb the scene." Or, he thought, become disturbed at the sight of the body.

Paul shook his head. "I never take my boat in there. The current is swift, and there are no good anchorages. Ted Morris, the chief ranger, can negotiate it, but it scares me. I can show you a way to hike to the water, if that's what you want."

"OK. You know the area?"

"I do."

Chee didn't look forward to more hiking in the heat, but so it went.

Chee adjusted his daypack as Paul strode past him, heading up the steep trail chatting as he hiked. "I love this part of the lake. It has a lot of power for me. Whenever I have the blues, or something weighing on my mind, I come out this way. It brings me peace. I look at the bridge, I think of the way life combines light and dark, good and evil." He stopped. "I didn't mean to get all philosophical on you. That trail to Crimson Beach ought to be off-limits—even if it wasn't dangerous—because of the archaeological sites there. Are you OK with that?"

"Graves?"

"No. Not that I know of." Paul glanced toward the cliffside. "There's some rock art up that way, on the way to the beach. It's amazing. Would you like to see it?"

"Sure. I noticed petroglyphs earlier as I hiked down to Rainbow Bridge. I'm fascinated by those wonderful figures and designs." Seeing some interesting old drawings would make the hike more palatable.

"This area is rich with that ancient art. That's one of the many reasons I live here. My father worked on some sites in this area and brought me up many times to show me. I got comfortable hiking on trails like this." He chuckled. "Pop assembled a whole crew of graduate students and some Navajos who were interested in the work. They were under the gun to do as much as they could before the gates closed, the water rose, and the destruction began."

"Did your father ever mention any large caves up this way?"

"Caves?" Paul laughed. "I don't remember. He talked about sunburn, dust, hard work, the views, the beauty of the place, a few scorpions. Why do you ask?"

Chee thought about how much to say. "There's one a friend told me about. I'd like to find it."

"You should ask my dad. He may be getting

slower physically, but his memory is sharp. I'll put you in touch with him."

"I'd like that."

They walked until Paul stopped for a sip of water.

Chee pulled out his bottle, too. "Do you run into other hikers or campers up here?"

"At the bridge, for sure. You probably saw some of that."

"What about on this trail?"

"No. Well, hardly ever. There are a lot of easier spots for a hike."

They walked on without conversation, watching their footing. Chee could relax this time and appreciate the colors in a cliff face, the call of a bird, the coolness of the breeze. When the lake came into view, Paul paused again.

"It's something, isn't it?"

"Beautiful. Expansive." Chee smiled. "The contrast of all this water against the arid desert is really something. I'm sure this is a totally different kind of beauty than your father encountered. I guess he's famous."

"Famous and infamous. He raised some hackles in the world of archaeology."

"Why?"

"Pop has always been an outspoken maverick."

"Are you an archaeologist, too?"

"Yes. Like my father, but not as famous, or as disgruntled."

They hiked on. They autumn sun warmed Chee through his shirt. He wondered what the weather was like back in Shiprock, and if Bernie had built an evening fire in their woodstove yet. He wished she was with him and they could solve this problem together, but on second thought, he was glad she wasn't there. She didn't need to encounter another dead person.

Paul broke the silence as more of the lake came into view. "Are we close to where you stood when you found whatever we're looking for?"

"Not quite. It's a bit farther. We'll see a rock ledge. I was sitting there, enjoying the view, and I noticed something odd in the water."

"I think I know where you mean. We'll be there in a few minutes."

In the background, Chee heard the faint whine of an engine. "Stop a minute. Let me check to see who that is." He used the binoculars, found the boat, and scanned for the National Park Service's arrowhead logo. He saw that as well as three people in the trademark green uniforms. "It's them."

Paul grinned. "OK. I'm going to show you the quicker, local's-only path down to Crimson Beach so we can meet the boat. I'd blindfold you, but you'd kill yourself negotiating this without being able to watch where you were going. You have to swear to keep this route a secret."

They backtracked until they passed the place where Chee remembered he had hiked down the slope to avoid a large rock. Now, they hiked on the uphill side and then headed down. Chee trusted his feet to keep going in Paul's wake. The slope grew steeper, and gravity increased the speed of descent. Then, in a few more minutes, the trail leveled, and the boulders posed less of a challenge. Paul headed toward the water, detouring around domes of solid rock that towered over the lake's clear depths. Chee couldn't spot the body from here, he realized, and he hadn't been able to spot it for most of the hike. If he had rested at the ledge, he would have never seen the dead man.

Paul stopped again and sat. Chee gladly found his own perch a few yards away. Hiking down challenged the knees.

"I've been thinking as we hiked. I've deduced that you found something bigger than the remains of animals killed illegally, or even signs of looting at some of the old sites. I'm impressed that you don't mind being involved with this, even though you're not from here. Most off-duty cops would have gone back to Dangling Rope and let the Park Service handle it. Because you're sticking with it, I figure you've discovered something important."

"I'm a cop by profession, remember? This is how I'm trained to respond."

"So, am I right about you finding a body?"

Chee nodded.

Paul picked up a little rock and tossed it toward the lake. "What happens next?"

Chee noticed the strength of his arm. "Based on what I've seen in similar situations, the Park Service crew will include an investigator and at least one other person to help with the retrieval. They'll take a look around, photograph the body in the water, and do whatever else they need to do to document the scene and determine the chain of events that led to the death. When that's finished, they'll remove the corpse."

Paul stood. "Let's get to the water to meet the boat so you can show them where it is."

The route was indirect and fairly safe. They reached the water without mishap and stood watching the boat approach.

Chee heard the chug of the motor as the craft grew closer. He was turning toward it when a rock, about the size of a flattened golf ball, caught his eye. The brownish splatter made it stand out. He bent down to look at it more closely, then took out his phone for a picture of it.

Paul waved to the Park Service boat as it drew near, coming as close to shore as possible. Paul tied the line they tossed him around a big rock, and the passengers, two men and a woman, jumped onto the sandstone.

Chee introduced himself as a Navajo Police sergeant.

The older man had a grizzled, sunbaked face. "Ted Morris, chief ranger. This is Danny Nguyen and Bess Oppenheim." Danny nodded. Bess tapped the rim of her hat like a salute.

Ted glanced at Paul. "I think we know each other."

"Paul Hendrix. I live in Page. I ran into the sergeant at the bridge dock."

"Hendrix? You related to old Dr. Pete, the archaeologist?"

"He's my father." Paul didn't seem surprised at the question. "Do you know him?"

"Just by reputation. I heard that he raised a lot of hell out here."

The Park Service officer turned to Chee. "You're the one who found the body, right?"

"Yes." Chee explained how he had spotted it from his position up on the cliff. "I noticed the contrast between the brightness of his yellow shirt and the lake. I studied the situation with my binoculars but I didn't see any sign of life. I couldn't figure out how to get down here until Paul showed me the way. I'm glad Sunfish let you guys know."

The chief ranger seemed satisfied. "OK. Show me where it is." Ted turned to his crew. "Everyone, careful where you step."

Chee led the way, and all five walked to the edge of the water, making their way around a huge, partly submerged boulder. From that perspective, the shirt stood out, a glowing swath of color in the deep, clear water. They had to look closely to realize that it was attached to a submerged, clearly dead body.

Paul looked. "It could be Doug. I can't tell for sure." He quickly looked away.

"Doug?" Ted asked.

"Doug Walker, the Navajo guide who runs the boat tours to Rainbow Bridge and the Antelope Canyon walks. Yellow shirts are their uniform."

Chee inhaled. Association with human death always made him uneasy. The possibility that the dead man could be the guy who'd hosted Bernie and him at dinner a few days before greatly stirred his anxiety.

Ted shifted his weight to his heels. "I hope you're wrong."

The divers, Danny and Bess, returned to the boat and began putting on wet suits. Ted walked over to them and said something Chee couldn't hear, and they nodded. Ted removed a camera from the boat and walked along the shore slowly, stopping to bend down every so often, taking pictures and continuing his methodical search until he got to the place where he could see the submerged body. He glanced at the lake, then turned from the water and looked at the cliffside. Then he began walking with the lake at his back, stopping intermittently for more photos, before he returned to Chee and Paul.

"Did you guys hike down toward the water from up there?"

"Yeah." Paul looked at the cliffside. "But not directly down that way. Too steep. We came from the side."

Ted turned to Chee. "Did you see anything unusual before you spotted the body?"

"Yes. There's a green tent with some camping gear and a few native artifacts in it higher up the hillside. I checked the backpack but didn't find an ID. And, from the overlook, I saw what could be blood on the cliff face, and a rock that might have had some blood on it."

"OK. Thanks. It's showtime."

They walked together to the boat. Paul untied it, and Ted climbed aboard, nodded to the divers, started the engine, and cruised close to the body. Chee and Paul watched from shore as the two recovery people slid into the cold lake without hesitation. The divers did their solemn work out of view for a while. Finally, Chee saw the body move as they freed it. They swam with the corpse to the boat, taking turns supporting its weight. Ted worked with them to lift the corpse into the boat. When the divers were aboard, he started the engine again and brought the boat back to where Paul had tied it.

Ted motioned them forward toward the dead man. Paul stood frozen in place, but Chee moved closer to take a look. He noticed the clothing, the shoes, a silver band with gold edging on the man's right ring finger. The blue-tinged face was Navajo. He stared a moment, then turned away.

"I don't recognize him. It's not Doug."

Ted said, "Paul, come take a look at this."

"OK." Paul sounded shaky. He walked up slowly, and leaned toward the body. He stepped quickly back. "It's Curtis."

"Curtis?"

"Yeah, Curtis Walker. Doug's brother. The guy who works at the Laguna Blue boat rental place. He worked with me, too."

Chee remembered the thermometer he'd found with the Laguna Blue logo and imagined it coming loose from the victim as he fell along the steep cliff face.

Ted shook his head. "Curtis. Are you sure?"

"Yes. Totally. This guy was my friend, my brother. I'm . . ." Paul turned from Ted and the body and walked away from them a few yards. They heard him heaving.

Chee and Ted waited. After a few moments, Paul returned. He looked pale. "Someone needs to tell Doug and Ramona."

Ted said, "I'll take care of that."

Paul nodded. "I have to get out of here. Can you give Chee a ride back to Dangling Rope?"

"Sure thing."

Chee said, "I'm sorry about your friend."

"Thank you. Poor Curtis was scared to death of water. He couldn't swim. What a terrible accident." Paul walked away.

The crew members slipped off their wet suits. Then Ted, Danny, and Bess lifted the corpse into the body bag. Chee watched them work for a moment, struck by how they moved together with smooth efficiency. "Is Ramona the dead man's wife?"

"No. She works with him at the marina. She's someone else's wife. Did you notice his head wound?"

"I saw it." Chee put his hand on the back of his own skull. "Right about here. That would create a lot of blood."

"It could be the result of a forceful impact. It makes me think Curtis must have fallen from higher up the cliffside. If he slipped in from close to the water, near where the body got wedged, it seems unlikely that he would have hit his head hard enough to do that kind of damage. Did you notice his face?"

"Yeah."

"That damage could have come from sliding along the rock."

Chee agreed. "Did you know him?"

"Not well but we had met. Paul's father brought Curtis along to some of our National Park Service town hall meetings when we were talking about, oh, various issues that concerned park safety. Old Dr. Pete really took a liking to Curtis." Ted looked down a moment. "I'm glad Paul can tell his dad about this. I'd hate to be the one to break that news."

Chee knew what he would do next, if the responsibility for the investigation were his. Ted seemed to read his mind.

"I need to hike up to the place where I think the body may have come from. If you don't mind a climb, a second set of eyes never hurts."

Chee looked toward the diving team. "I don't want to step on their toes."

Ted called to the boat. "Nguyen. Oppenheim. I want Sergeant Chee to go up the cliffside with me to check on something. Wanna come instead?"

"Are you kidding?" The woman spoke. "Go ahead. No worries."

They walked toward the cliff face. "That retrieval is tough work on a lot of levels," Ted said. "I knew they wouldn't mind missing this. Show me the picture of that rock that looked suspicious."

Chee pulled out his phone and enlarged the photo with his fingertips.

Ted studied it and handed it back. "It might be blood."

"That's what I thought. I can find it, if you want to see it."

"I do." Ted studied the cliffside. "Notice where

the color of the sandstone changes from yellow to brownish? Now look just to the right of that little bush. See that?"

"A stain of some sort?"

"Maybe."

Chee stared at the spot, wondering if his imagination was overly active. They walked toward the cliff at an angle from the place where the body had been. Then he saw what he was searching for. "Take a look at this." Chee moved his foot toward a reddish stain on the sandstone.

Ted squatted to study it.

"Blood." He scraped off a sample, bagged it, and looked up. "Makes me wish I'd paid more attention in physics class back in high school. Then maybe I could determine if the body hit here and had enough momentum to roll into the water."

"It seems likely to me." Chee glanced at the slope and then at the watery place where he'd discovered the body. He felt a rush of sorrow. How had a day that began so beautifully devolved into an interlude with death?

Ted looked at the blood on the rock again and shrugged. "We're not getting any younger standing here. Let's go."

They used their arms and wits to climb the rock face, finding some threads that looked as though they matched the yellow shirt Curtis wore. Ted photographed and then bagged them. Finally they reached the top, sweating from the exertion. From here, they could see places where Curtis had hit the stone and, as the slope angled more gently, finally slid into the lake. Chee studied the marks and thought about the situation. He saw nothing to indicate that the man had tried to stop his fatal face-first fall.

Ted took more photos of the hillside and then put the camera away. "Most drownings here happen by accident, and I've been approaching this the same way. Does that seem on track?"

Chee didn't hesitate. "I'm not ready to go there yet. We have a man seemingly alone in a place where it would be easy to fall, hurt your head, and end up in the lake. Why was he here? I want to know more about the decedent and the actual cause of death."

Ted glanced out toward the lake. "Curtis was comfortable outdoors. Experienced. Maybe a medical incident caused the fall. You know, a heart attack or a stroke or something? I admired Curtis, even though I didn't know him well, but he made some bad calls. I hope it was a heart attack. I hope he was dead before he hit the water."

"What do you mean, made some bad calls?"

"Oh, in his personal life. He wasn't very circumspect in his choice of girlfriends." Ted sighed. "I don't want to speak badly of a dead man. You mentioned a campsite, right?"

"I noticed it before I saw the body. No ID, but in the backpack I found a little notebook where someone had written some poems in Navajo. You mentioned girlfriends. These were about love."

"Was there a name?"

"No. Writer and girlfriend both anonymous."

"Show me the site."

Chee's sense of direction, fine-tuned by years

of tracking on the reservation, led him to where he knew the camp had been. The tent entrance was still zipped. Chee opened it. The broken pot, the yucca sandal, the grinding stones, and the rest of that collection were gone.

"Except for the artifacts, things look about the same as when I was here the first time."

Ted nodded. "Strange. Because you were the first person on the scene, I'd like to get a written statement from you. Be sure to include the missing items. Can you stop by my office tomorrow?"

"Sure."

"Except for the fact that the writing in the notebook is in Navajo, there's nothing specific to tie the campsite to Curtis. All circumstantial." Ted looked at the tent again. "I'll tell someone to come back tomorrow, and if this stuff is still here, we'll remove it. It looks to me like Curtis fell, lost consciousness, and slid into the lake. We'll see what the autopsy says."

Chee knew an accidental death was infinitely easier for law enforcement than a murder.

Chee puzzled over the items missing from the green tent as they hiked back to the lake, and as he, Curtis's body, and the Park Service crew headed to Dangling Rope. Ten miles away, it was the closest marina to Rainbow Bridge.

After a while, Chee moved to the front of the boat and sat next to Ted. "Something's bothering me about this situation."

"Go ahead."

"Why was the dead man there, and how did he get there? We didn't see an abandoned boat. If that tent wasn't his, was he with someone? Did he and the tent person have a confrontation? Is that why he's dead?" As he spoke, more questions arose, but Chee didn't want to overstep his role as unpaid consultant.

"He probably left his boat at the Rainbow Bridge dock and hiked in. You spent some time down there. Did you see an unclaimed boat?"

"No. But someone could have dropped him off."

"Maybe." Ted squeezed his lips together. "People like Curtis, people who know the lake, know other places to come ashore. There are a few around Crimson Beach. Maybe he left his boat there." He looked up at the sky. "We have enough light to check some of those spots on our way back to Dangling Rope."

Chee knew Ted and his crew had hours of work ahead of them. He gave the man extra credit for his conscientiousness. As for himself, the death of a man he had never met energized his curiosity. It didn't matter that he was on vacation, and on a self-imposed mission to consider whether he should continue in law enforcement. He needed to know what had happened.

Instead of focusing on his own future, now he was wondering why a man who had been around this lake for much of his life and couldn't swim would walk on a dangerous lake-facing cliffside. He wondered what had made Curtis tick, and why he'd gone to that dangerous, lonely, and beautiful place.

So many questions.

He looked out onto the lake. What a huge amount of water confined here, at the edge of the Navajo Nation! And how ironic, when a lack of accessible water made life challenging for many Navajo families. People he knew still had to haul water for cooking and bathing and for their livestock. The Navajo Nation, the West—the world, for that matter—continued to surprise him.

True to his word, Ted took them to several coves close to Crimson Beach. The four of them searched the shoreline for a boat that Curtis might have used but saw nothing. After that, the steady, slightly rocking motion, the lack of conversation, and the fact that there was nothing he needed to do made Chee groggy. He closed his eyes.

Danny Nguyen and Bess Oppenheim had been silent for most of the trip, but now that Chee seemed to be asleep, they began to talk softly.

"Bessie, were you surprised to see Hendrix out there?"

"Not really. He and Curtis were business partners. But I wonder what happened to Ramona?"

The male voice didn't respond.

"I'm glad she didn't see him the way we did."

Ted fueled up at Dangling Rope, and they continued to the Wahweap Marina, pulling in to dock long after sunset. The vehicle Ted had requested had arrived and took the body.

Out of respect for the dead, they stood together and watched the van leave. Ted sighed. "Now comes the part I never get used to. Giving the bad news to the next of kin."

"It's tough."

"And I have to do it twice. Doug and then Ramona. At least I don't have to ask for anyone's permission for the autopsy."

Chee cringed at the thought of this desecration, even though he knew that it was a requirement in the case of unattended deaths. "I'm still wondering about that campsite."

"I think it belonged to Curtis. Did you mention it to Paul?"

"Yes."

"That's what I assumed. I think Paul has those artifacts you saw."

"I hear Paul's dad is an expert on what this area was like before the lake rose."

Ted laughed. "To say the least. Dr. Pete loves talking about the geology and history of this place. It's his favorite topic. He can be an ornery cuss, but he spent a lifetime exploring out here. If you get on his good side, he's full of stories." Ted scratched his chin. "How long are you here for?"

"I don't know."

Ted laughed. "That's what I said ten years ago, and look at me now. See you in the morning for your statement."

Chee went to the Antelope Tour office to claim the pack he had entrusted to Sunfish. Instead, he found the door locked, and a note taped to the doorframe, addressed to him.

Jim Chee,
     You're reading this, so I figure the rangers got there, and everything worked out OK. Sorry about the radio. Your backpack

is in my truck. Call me, and I'll get it to you
and pick up that daypack you borrowed.

She left her number and a little drawing of a cat-
fish dancing under a smiling sun.

Chee called, and Sunfish answered on the second
ring.

"It's Chee."

"So you're back. Who came to get you?"

"Ted Morris and the retrieval crew."

"They're good folks. The owners at Laguna Blue
double-checked, and all their rental boats came in.
No one has officially reported anybody missing either. Well?"

"Well, what?"

"Did Ted identify the body?"

"Yes. He's calling the next of kin."

"Who was it?"

It came to Chee that she would know the dead
man. "Curtis Walker."

"Curtis? You're sure?"

"Yeah."

He heard Sunfish suck in a hard breath.

"How did it happen?"

"I don't know. Ted's investigating."

"And just when things were really looking up for
them and the business. I can't believe it." He heard
the sorrow in her voice.

Then the phone fell silent, and Chee realized
that his feet ached and his back hurt. "I appreciate
you getting Ted out there. I'd like to pick up my
pack."

"Oh, sure. Tell you what, I'll meet you at Doug's

house. I don't want him and Shawna to be alone when they get the news. Do you know where his place is?"

"Yes. Ted said he'd call him."

"This breaks my heart. How did it happen?" she asked again.

"I don't know."

She swore. "I'm sorry you landed in the middle of this, Chee. Aren't you here on vacation or something?"

"Something like that."

Chee remembered the dinner that Darleen, Bernie, and he had enjoyed with Doug, his wife, and their two boys the night before their Antelope Canyon tour. Doug had invited Curtis, but he hadn't shown up, much to the boys' disappointment. Doug had laughed it off—it was clearly not the first time their invitation had been ignored. They shared a special evening of good food, laughter, stories, gratitude, and *k'é*—a bond of kinship—in action.

Sunfish broke into Chee's daydream. "This is a good place to relax, unless you get involved in something like retrieving a body. Take care of yourself. I'll see you at Doug's house."

He walked to his truck, now thinking about Bernie and how she brightened his life, especially at the end of a day like this one. Before starting the engine, he took out his phone and called. While he waited for her to answer, or for her voice mail to ask him to leave a message, he looked at the photos he'd taken of the artifacts at Curtis's campsite and sent them on to Ted, with a request for his office address and a time to show up.

7

Bernadette Manuelito answered the phone as soon as she saw it was Chee.

"Hey, beautiful."

"Hey, yourself. I'm glad you have phone service. I've missed your voice." She smiled. "I'm at Mama's now. How was your hike?"

He told her at length about the landscape, about the birds, mammals, and reptiles he'd seen, and then about Rainbow Bridge itself. His enthusiasm and the visit's profound effect on him came through even over the phone. "I wish you had been here to share it," he said. "We have to come back together."

"I'd love that. Have you found the cave?"

"Not yet. I got distracted." He paused. She could practically hear him thinking. "Do you remember Doug mentioning his brother, Curtis, the guy who missed dinner?"

"Oh yes." She knew from his tone of voice that

this wasn't good news. Her chest tightened with anticipation. "What about him?"

Chee told her, focusing on the removal crew's skill, Ted's professionalism, and the mystery surrounding the death. She had to ask twice to get the details of Chee's own role. She knew he could have added more facts, but for now the story sufficed.

"Gosh, I'm sorry about Doug's brother," she said, "but you're right. If someone had to discover a body, it's best that it's a cop. This is not what you need while you're trying to sort things out for yourself and do a favor for the Lieutenant."

She heard his warm laugh. "It's not what I ever need any time, for that matter. But the National Park Service ranger in charge of the investigation knows what he's doing. He asked me to write out a witness statement, and I'll handle that tomorrow. What's on your schedule?"

"I'm helping Mama for a while, and then I'll head home, and relax until my shift starts."

"How was your drive home?"

He sounded tired, so she avoided the trivia. "Smooth. I even let Sister drive. We had a great talk. She grew up a lot in the time she spent with Mr. Natachi." She mentioned Darleen's idea to become a nurse's aide, or something like it.

"And there's more good news. She's helping this man we met in Kayenta find a missing relative. She borrowed a picture he had to begin to design some posters, and Sister is helping the family use social media."

"How goes it at the station?"

"Things are pretty quiet." She chuckled. "That always makes me nervous. We're getting a lot of complaints about that hemp farm. Bigman has been out there a few times talking to the neighbors. They don't like the dust from the traffic, and the fact that the farm seems to run twenty-four/seven."

Chee knew she meant Harold Bigman, her clan brother and fellow cop. "That sounds like a case of bad neighbors."

"Right. I'm surprised. I mean, Dino Begay Perez sold the council on the farm with the idea that he and his relatives would do everything they could to benefit the Navajo Nation." She remembered something else. "Largo has done some interviews and is considering who to hire to replace the rookie. He wants to do that pretty quick, in case I get to become a detective. Bigman and I are working overtime, and so are most of the other guys. I don't mind, especially because you aren't around to keep me company."

"I miss you, too, sweetheart. How's your mother?"

"She's holding her own." She didn't want him to worry. After all, he was theoretically on vacation. And, truthfully, there was nothing to be done.

Her husband didn't respond immediately. "'Holding her own.' What does that mean?"

"She's grumpy, and she's taking it out on me. I can't tell if she's having pain she doesn't want to talk about or if I'm seriously driving her crazy."

She heard his chuckle. "Give yourself credit, OK? She couldn't have two better daughters."

Mama came to the kitchen, opened the refrigerator, frowned, and then took out a pot of beans.

"OK," Bernie said. "Hey, I've got to run. Great talking to you. Call me again if you have service, or send a text. I love you."

"I love you more."

8

Jim Chee ended the phone call with Bernie and drove to Doug Walker's house to pick up his backpack and drop off what he'd borrowed. In the ideal scenario, he'd offer his quick but sincere regrets, get his belongings, and be off to set up his camp for the evening. He also had enough experience to know that the ideal and reality could be miles apart. He'd dealt with enough grief to have no expectations.

When he got to the house, he noticed that the van with the Antelope Canyon Tours logo that Doug drove was gone. An ancient blue Subaru occupied the driveway. He knocked on the door, and through the open curtains he saw one of Doug's sons, the six-year-old, walk toward the door, the smaller boy following him. Then he saw Sunfish.

Before he could speak, she did.

"Come on in."

"Is Doug here?"

"No. He called me right after we spoke. He and Shawna needed to go to Doug's mother's house to give her the bad news, and they asked me to stay with the kids."

Chee stepped into the living room. He could hear the boys laughing at something on television.

"I'll get your stuff, but would you like something to eat first? I fixed dinner for the boys, and there's plenty left."

"That would be great, if it's no trouble."

"Not a bit."

Sunfish walked with an easy grace in front of him to the kitchen, where she motioned him to a chair. She got a pitcher of iced tea and a pair of glasses and brought them to the table. "I can't stop thinking about Curtis. You know, he couldn't swim. He was always extra careful around the lake. I teased him about living in the wrong place, but he reminded me that the place he loved, Antelope Canyon, is nowhere near the lake."

"That's what Paul Hendrix said, too. He said Curtis hated water."

"What was Paul doing there?" She poured him some tea without asking, and without offering any sugar. He didn't mind, but he knew his Bernie would have protested.

"I met him at the Rainbow Bridge dock. He said he needed to get out of the house and think."

"Paul is an odd duck, but I guess anyone who grew up with Dr. Pete as a dad would be a little off. Did he tell you how his father practically adopted Curtis?"

"No. We didn't do much talking after we realized who the dead man was. He was able to identify Curtis, so it was good that he was there."

A big cast-iron pot, like the kind Chee's mother had used to heat the grease for the fry bread, sat on the stove. Thinking of those meals made him hungrier. "What are you cooking?"

"I call it campfire stew, although I guess now its stovetop stew. Ground beef, vegetable soup, whatever was left over that could be added to it. And I made some corn bread, too. Is that OK?"

Chee hadn't eaten since breakfast, he realized, and there was nowhere he had to be. "More than OK. Stew and corn bread sound great. Thank you." He watched the blue flame come to life under the big pot. She gave it a stir and then sat across from him.

"Poor Curtis. I can't wrap my head around this. He hiked by the lake all the time. He knew the Crimson Beach area well."

"What if he stumbled on the cliff face, lost his balance, and then fell?"

"Yeah, but . . ." She stopped, and he saw the start of tears before she glanced away. She brought him a bowl of stew and a slice of corn bread.

"This looks great. Nothing for you?"

She shook her head. "I'm too upset to eat. Go ahead."

The enticing aroma of the warm stew filled the kitchen, and it tasted as good as it smelled. Beef, carrots, potatoes, onions, green beans, celery, happily mixed together in a thick gravy-like base. Sunfish sipped her tea as he ate.

"I'm sorry you didn't have a chance to meet Curtis," she said. "You would have enjoyed him. He had a great sense of humor, and the boys loved him. He was so proud of them." She paused. "He could draw anything. He idolized Dr. Pete. Talked about him all the time."

Chee listened while he ate the stew. It was good, but not as good as Bernie's, and definitely not as delicious as the one Bernie's mother made. The corn bread was dry. But he knew the food came from a generous heart. He liked this woman with the strange name.

"Ted mentioned that he needed to tell someone named Ramona," he said.

"Curtis worked with her and her husband at Laguna Blue."

"Was Ramona his boss?"

"No. Her husband, Robert, theoretically runs the business, but they wouldn't survive without Curtis." She stopped. "I hope they do, but he did everything for them. They should have paid him twice as much."

"If Robert is the boss, why would Ted tell Ramona instead of him?"

Sunfish studied the ice cubes in her tea glass. "It's complicated. Let's just say that Curtis and Ramona were close." She stood and looked out the window into the evening darkness, closing the conversation.

Chee finished the stew and used the corn bread to mop up the last of the gravy. He put his empty bowl and the glass on the counter next to the sink. Sunfish pulled down the window shade. "I don't know when Doug will be back, but you're welcome to stay. I'm going to tell the boys it's time for bed."

"Do they know about their uncle?"

She shook her head. "Doug and Shawna will tell them tomorrow. He wanted to save his energy for his mother. Curtis was her baby. It breaks my heart to think of him dead."

"I'm sorry for your loss. I can tell he was important to you."

Sunfish nodded to acknowledge his sympathy, and he took that as his cue to leave. "I need to set up my camp. I better grab my pack and head on."

"It's there by the front door."

"Thanks again for dinner."

"Nice talking to you, even about such a sad thing. Your wife is a cop, too—do I have that right?"

"Yes."

"That must be intense."

"It can be. She's considering become a detective. And I'm in a transition stage myself." As he said it, he wondered why he was revealing so much. Something about this woman elicited his trust.

Sunfish smiled. "I believe in change, replanting yourself every once in a while. You never know what will happen." Her expression changed. "I guess what you found today reinforced that."

"Yeah."

"Do you get used to it?"

He shook his head and told her good night.

He loaded the pack into the back of the truck

and set out. He had only driven a block when he saw the white Antelope Canyon Tours van. He flashed his lights, and Doug pulled over. He noticed the exhaustion on Shawna's face and the sad tension in Doug's expression. Chee climbed out of his truck and expressed his regrets at Curtis's death.

"I'm sorry you were the one who found him. That stinks."

"Better me than some boater who wouldn't have known how to handle the situation."

"You're right. Are the boys still up?"

"Sunfish was getting ready to put them to bed."

Doug looked at the clock in the van and shook his head. "She's a lifesaver. I wish she and Curtis had, you know, hit it off. The only good thing I can think of about Curtis's death is that we won't have to put up with Ramona anymore."

"What do you mean?"

"She was cheating on her husband with my brother. No, that's not right. She *wanted* to cheat on him, but Curtis was too smart for that." Doug stopped. "At least, I think he was. It doesn't matter anymore. I shouldn't have brought it up. Thanks for your condolences."

"I'll be here a few more days. Call me if there's anything I can do to help."

The words rang hollow even as he said them, but Doug responded.

"You can let me know what really happened," he said. "Curtis drowning? The whole thing seems unreal."

Chee drove to the campground and found a

spot that offered some solitude. In peak season, the place would have been jammed, but tonight he found plenty of places to park.

He had not expected to have trouble sleeping; certainly, it had been a long day. His excitement about seeing Rainbow Bridge had made him restlessly excited the previous night. But now, as he lay alone in the dark, the blue-tinged face of Curtis Walker came to him. He pushed the image out of his mind with thoughts of the cave the Lieutenant had asked him to find and the encouraging idea that Paul's father might have heard about it. When he finally fell asleep, he dreamed of black caves, green tents, and a driverless boat on clear water with disturbing shapes beneath it.

He awoke cold and with a pain in his hip. His pad and sleeping bag had not been enough to buffer his bones from the hard ground. He thought of Bernie, missing her already as he let the sound of the lake lull him back to sleep.

9

Finding Peter Hendrix's phone number was easy. Chee called him after he'd fixed himself some coffee and breakfast over the camp stove.

"Who are you, again?" Peter Hendrix asked.

Chee gave his name and identified himself as a Navajo cop taking some time off, a first-time visitor to the area. "I met your son, Paul, yesterday at Rainbow Bridge, and he told me you know more about the area than practically anyone."

"Well, that's probably true of most of us old guys who have been here since forever. What's on your mind, Sergeant?"

"Well, sir, it's nothing to do with police work. I have some connections to the Navajo Medicine Man Association, and we have heard reports of something sacred in a cave in this area. I'd like to see if that cave still exists."

"Lots of caves out here. What's supposed to be in there?" The archaeologist's voice wore the patina of age.

Chee hesitated. "I'd rather not discuss that. It has to do with our Diné heritage."

"That's what I thought you'd say. Come on over. We should talk face-to-face." He gave Chee his address. "If you're lucky, there'll be coffee."

"What time would you like me?"

"Whenever. Before dark."

"I'll be there this morning."

Chee drove into the little town of Page. Bernie, Darleen, and he had stayed at the campground Doug Walker ran near Antelope Canyon Tours, so the town was new to him. He passed some hotels, gift shops, and restaurants, and stopped when he saw the public library. He could have researched what he needed using his phone and the internet, but a better idea came to him.

The librarian at the reference desk looked up from his book when Chee approached.

"May I help you?"

"I hope so. I have a meeting with the archaeologist Peter Hendrix this morning." The man's face brightened at the mention of the name. "And before I saw him, I figured it would be good to know a little more about the guy."

"I can tell you that old Dr. Pete's still sharp. He's full of information about the archaeology of the Colorado Plateau. He's a big reader. And he's a talker. Would you like to look at some of his research on the sites he helped excavate? Or are you more interested in the lawsuits?"

"I'm on a tight schedule. Maybe a comprehensive biography?"

"I have an idea." The librarian clicked a few keys

on his computer, stared at the screen, clicked some more. Chee heard a noise. Then the man reached under the desk and extracted some printed sheets.

"This is an article the local newspaper wrote about Dr. Pete a few years ago on his birthday. The reporter summarizes some of Dr. Pete's achievements. I printed his bibliography, too, for when you have more time. Dr. Pete's a community icon. He's lived here since the town was born, and he's a man of strong opinions." The librarian lowered his voice. "Are you a writer?"

"No. Why do you ask?"

"Folks have been after Dr. Pete to find someone to tell his story, you know, turn him into another Ed Abbey, but he's refused. From what I've heard, Page wouldn't be here if Peter Hendrix had had his way back then."

"What do you mean?"

"The more he worked on the archaeology of Glen Canyon, surveying the sites that the lake inundated, the more he decided that the dam that made Lake Powell was a devilishly bad idea."

Chee could tell the librarian was considering what to say next, or if he'd said too much already. "Dr. Pete likes Page well enough, but not the lake. He was one of the leaders in the movement to get rid of what they used to call salvage archaeology— the kind of quick-look science that happened here before the water obliterated the old sites. Whenever he talks about it, he always expresses his regret that he didn't have more time to study what was out there before it disappeared."

The man extended the pages he'd printed.

"This should be helpful." Chee folded the pages in half. "Thank you for your insight. I'm looking forward to meeting the man."

Chee took the article to an open seat, sat quietly, and read. Even if Peter Hendrix couldn't tell him anything about the cave of sand paintings, he looked forward to chatting with the man. On his way to the Hendrix home, he stopped at a bakery and selected a dozen cookies. When asking a favor, he knew, it never hurt to bring a gift.

Peter Hendrix, PhD, lived in a modest two-story house that looked like it had been built in the city's early days. The front yard was gravel, with a twisted mesquite tree in the middle, its leaves yellow with the changing season. Someone had parked a battered jeep in the concrete driveway, and a vintage outboard motorboat sat on a trailer to the side.

Chee rang the doorbell. After a few moments, he heard noise behind the front windows and then a man in a plaid shirt opened the door.

"Jim Chee?"

"That's right, sir."

"Dr. Peter Hendrix. Call me Pete. Come inside."

Chee followed Hendrix to a large room in the back of the house, noticing tables in the living room crammed with pots and rocks and old magazines in older baskets. He saw Navajo rugs on the floor, old weavings well used. The bookcase overflowed with books and bound manuscripts stacked on top of more of the same. Sunlight fil-

tering through the drawn shades gave the room
a pleasant golden tinge that went with its faintly
dusty scent. Chee spotted a huge stone metate
in one corner with a mano lying next to it. He
stopped to study them.

"They look authentic, don't they?"

"Yes."

"My grad students made them. They tried
grinding corn. Hard work. Other classes made
atlatls, rabbit sticks, slings for hunting. You ever
seen those?"

"I used to throw a rabbit stick fairly well. Atlatls? That was something the original inhabitants
around here used for hunting, right?"

"That's it. People haven't made them or taught
their kids how to use them for, oh, more than
a thousand years. The guys in my classes made
them, and a few got pretty good at hitting a tar-
get, but most of them would have died of star-
vation." Dr. Pete laughed. "A lot of those guys
couldn't have made it through college without a
care package from Mom."

"What about slings? Did they use those for
hunting out here?"

Dr. Pete nodded. "They are hard to find because
the leather or fiber disintegrates. Many different
cultures, including some tribes here in the Southwest, also used them, as weapons against opposing
groups." Pete glanced at the assortment of objects
on the table. "My son, Paul, made some. He's got a
good eye and a strong arm."

Chee followed the older man into the next

room, a den with a fine view of the desert landscape. "Perch over there so I can hear you better."
He pointed to a padded armchair to his right. "I'm
in Black Beauty." Pete patted the back of the dark
leather recliner, and then eased himself into position
and placed an oxygen cannula into his nose. Chee
sat and put the bakery bag on his lap. He watched
the birds that flocked to the feeders outside the
big windows, waiting for Dr. Pete to settle in and
catch his breath.

"What's in that bag you've got?"

"Cookies. I thought you might enjoy them."

"I like the way you think. There's coffee in the
kitchen. Bring me a cup and get one for yourself.
It'll go with those."

Chee set the cookies on the table next to the old
man's chair. He noticed Dr. Pete's swollen knuck-
les, a development he'd seen in other people with
arthritis. "Do you take anything in your coffee?"

"A shot of bourbon sounds about right, but it's
too darn early. I drink mine black. I don't have any
milk, but there's some of that fake stuff if you want
it, next to the sugar."

What he found in the kitchen—combined
with the collection on the living room tables—
confirmed his belief that, with a few exceptions,
archaeologists were the human version of pack-
rats. On the countertop, there was an impressive
lineup of vinegars and cooking oils, more than a
dozen tins and jars of spices, and large unlabeled
pill bottles with something inside. A light layer of
dusty grease gave the collection a dull patina.

He paused at the refrigerator to look at magnets

and notes. He saw an old photo in a red plastic frame of two smiling boys, one who seemed to be Navajo and one with Pete's blue eyes.

The sugar and creamer, along with two clean cups, sat next to an unplugged aluminum percolator, the old-fashioned kind with a glass knob on top. Chee filled both cups with the lukewarm coffee. He sat Pete's next to the cookies and settled in across from him.

"Just put your mug there, on top of those magazines. I'll get around to them one of these days." Chee noticed that the *Scientific American* at the top of the pile was dated two years back.

Pete took a cookie. "Thanks for these. My favorites. Almost as good as watermelon." He broke off a piece, chewed, and swallowed. "So, you want to know about a cave. Well, there are hundreds of caves out here, and I've explored a few dozen of them. What can you tell me about the cave you're interested in to narrow the search?"

Chee had expected the question. "One of my mentors worked on a case somewhere out here years ago and came across a large cave that he realized had spiritual importance to us Navajos. The cave was close enough to the lake that he got out of a tight situation using a boat. That man isn't much of a hiker these days, and since I had some time off coming, I told him I'd see what I could find." He paused, considering how much information to add. "This could be an important site for Navajo spiritual heritage."

Dr. Pete adjusted his glasses. "I'm an old desert rat, so I believe everything here has spiritual value." He motioned toward the view. "Everything except the man-made stuff designed to help somebody get rich. Did your man give you a hint about where to look for the cave?"

"He loaned me an old map—I have it in my truck. I can show you approximately where he believes he found it. He told me that the map might be wrong, and the cave could be below water now. That's the issue."

"Where are you from?"

"Shiprock. It's—"

Dr. Pete interrupted. "I know where it is. You probably understand the desert. You realize that water is always the issue out here. Did your guy find this cave before the lake filled?"

"I'm not sure. He hiked in from the Navajo Nation, but as I mentioned, he took a boat out."

"There's a man who lives at Navajo Mountain, a *hatałi* who has deep roots in the community. He might be of some help to you, too. I can't recall his name, but you can ferret it out."

Chee took note of this.

"You said you had time off from work to track this place down. What do you do?"

"I'm in law enforcement. I work with the Navajo Nation."

Dr. Pete made a hissing sound. "You told me that on the phone. I'm old, but I'm not senile. I mean, what kind of cases?"

"Whatever comes up. Lately, I've been in administration."

Dr. Pete nodded. "That's why you need time off. I get it. And your mentor is a cop, too."

Good deduction, Chee thought. "He retired a while ago. He does some private investigation cases. Are you retired?"

"Mostly. I help at the park if something turns up. I volunteer with their archaeology staff."

"I've heard that you were one of the main archaeologists working here before the lake."

"That's right. We did our best to document what we could. An unnecessary project directed by morons. An inexcusable waste of tax money, and a greedy and stupid destruction of something irreplaceable." Pete mentioned 1956, the year the dam construction began with a push of a button by President Dwight D. Eisenhower. "The last bucket of concrete was poured on September 13, 1963, and that's the year our work stopped. Between 1957 and 1963, we documented some two thousand sites."

"From what I've read, the effort that you and the other crew members put in really drew attention to the fact that America needed to take its heritage more seriously. It brought about a big change in archaeology, right?"

"I could talk all day about the foul thing that brought me to the Southwest, and I probably have. We weren't able to block the dam and the devastation the water caused to the old sites, but our work did help create better laws to protect antiquities. I'm proud of that." He chuckled. "But you're not here for a lecture. Let's get back to that cave."

Chee heard the rumble of a vehicle in the driveway, and a few minutes later, the door opened. He couldn't see who entered, but he could tell by the older man's expression that the visitor was welcome.

Paul strolled into the room. "Hey, Pop. Hey, Chee."

"You two know each other?" He heard the surprise in Dr. Pete's voice.

"We met yesterday."

"That's a surprise. Were you helping him find his cave?"

Paul sat on the couch across from his father, but he focused on Chee. "I haven't had a chance to tell my father what happened . . . you know, at the lake."

"I can come back later." Chee started to stand.

"No. I'm glad you're here. Stay." He turned to his father. "I came by last night to tell you something important, but you were so tired, I didn't want to mention it. I've got some bad news."

"The medicine makes me sleepy. Important? What is it? Did they reject your grant application?"

"No, it's not that." Paul leaned in toward his father. "Yesterday, Chee and I ran into each other at Rainbow Bridge dock. We hiked over to Crimson Beach, and there was a body in the lake there, trapped offshore beneath the water . . . against the cliffs." He took a breath. "It was Curtis."

"Curtis? Curtis Walker?"

Paul nodded.

"You're sure?"

"Ted Morris came with some other rangers to retrieve the body. I identified him."

After that, it seemed to Chee that time stopped.

Pete stared straight ahead. The only sounds in the room were the muffled tick of the clock on the wood-paneled wall behind the old man, the hum of his oxygen machine, and, after a while, the whirr of the refrigerator when the fan clicked on. The silence made sense to Chee, a way to honor the one who had passed.

He wanted to give Pete time to absorb the news. "If I go out to the truck for the map that shows where the cave might be, would you take a look?"

"Glad to."

Chee rose, thankful for an opportunity to go outside for a moment. He took his time. When he returned, Paul had left the room. Pete had moved to a table and cleared a space of the clutter. Chee spread the map in front of them.

Pete pulled glasses from his pocket. "This is a real old one. It doesn't show the lake."

"I know the lake had started to fill, because that's how my . . ." He was about to say "friend," but even after all these years, that wasn't exactly correct. "Like I said, the officer who found the cave left it by boat."

Pete ran his fingers along the edges of the map. "We hiked all over this country, me and the boys, Paul and Curtis. Back before I needed this oxygen machine. Paul complained about the heat, the snakes, about everything. He never seemed happy, never could just take in the experience, you know, and, like Ram Dass used to say, Be Here Now. But Curtis . . . he got it. He never whined much, enjoyed the process and the adventures. The more time we spent together, the more we came to love each other. That kid was like a son to me. I can't believe . . ."

He looked at Chee, then glanced away. "One day Paul and Curtis and I were out there, and Curtis asked why I was so interested in the old sites, you know? I told him that what the other archaeologists and I found helped fill in history because, as far as anyone could tell, the families who lived out there didn't write things down except in pictures. I told them the rock art was like a bulletin board. Paul thought that was interesting and started paying more attention to the artifacts, the ruins, the whole story of this place before us white people showed up. And Curtis loved the petroglyphs. Each of my boys got something different from the experience.

"Curtis liked my stories, but school never managed to grab his interest. Paul loved school, and once we found a doctor who gave him the right medicine for his low times, he did well. Next thing I knew, he had his college degrees."

Pete sighed and studied the view for a while before he spoke again. "Do you think Curtis suffered?"

"No." The question was unanswerable, so Chee assumed the best.

"I'm glad Curtis never married. One less heart to hurt over this accident. That was something he and Paul still had in common. They weren't lucky in love."

Chee listened. He knew luck had played a part in his relationship with his beautiful Bernie, but he always remembered how hard he had worked to win her affection.

"I wanted them to think of each other as brothers. Curtis told me Doug's boys, his little nephews, were like his sons. I thought of Curtis the same way, as a son, my second son."

Chee heard grief in the old man's voice.

Pete turned toward the map and, after a few moments, looked up at Chee. "You know, I can't focus on this right now. That news about Curtis knocked me flat."

"I understand." Chee began folding the map.

"Wait." He reached out to stop Chee's hands. "If you're comfortable leaving that here, I'll look at it later."

Chee hesitated. The idea of entrusting a treasure that Leaphorn had loaned him to a stranger made him uneasy, but there was something about the way Pete spoke of the past that prompted him to say yes. "Keep it for a while, if you'd like."

"Write down your phone number, and I'll call you to come fetch it. There's a pen in the kitchen and a pad of paper on the counter there."

When he got back to the den, he noticed that Pete had returned to Black Beauty. The old man had the oxygen tube in his nose. He opened his eyes at the sound of his name, and Chee saw the pain in them. He had aged over the past few minutes.

"Were you there when Ted and his crew removed the body, pulled Curtis out of the lake?"

"I was."

"I know the area. It's beautiful, isn't it? A pretty place to die. Curtis didn't swim. He joked that he'd take some lessons as soon as the lake warmed up.

He favored Crimson Beach because of the petroglyphs in the rocks above it, and he loved to camp
there. I was the one who showed him those images. If I hadn't, maybe he'd still be here."

"It was fate. No one's to blame." But as he said
it, Chee questioned the words. If Curtis's death
was not an accident, someone was responsible.

Pete took the paper with Chee's phone number
and slipped it into his shirt pocket. "Could you ask
Paul to come down? Time for my pills."

"Sure. Where is he?"

Pete looked toward the ceiling. "Upstairs in his
office."

Chee climbed the stairs and saw light coming from a large room at the end of the hall. He
knocked on the doorframe. Paul looked up from
his laptop, startled.

"Your father asked me to tell you he could use
his medicine."

"I'll get it to him in a few minutes. Come on in."

Chee stepped onto the carpet, noticing the
bookcases filled with ancient-looking pots and
sherds as well as books. The space was well kept.

"I need to move in with Pop full-time to keep
a better eye on him, but he wants to wait until his
lung issues get worse. So I use this as my work
space until I can ease him into letting me help him
more."

"Sounds like a good compromise."

"We're both cool with it." Paul rolled the chair
away from his desk. "I need to talk to you about
something concerning Curtis. I didn't want to do
it with Pop down there. He's pretty upset."

In terms of the upset people he'd dealt with, Chee considered the elder Hendrix fairly composed, but he didn't offer an opinion. "What's on your mind?"

"Yesterday, when we were hiking toward Crimson Beach, you mentioned that you'd seen a tent. Remember?"

"Sure."

"Well, when I left you, I went up there. I knew Curtis had a green tent, and it made sense—I mean as much as any of this makes sense—that he would have camped along the ridge. He loved that place. It didn't seem right to leave his belongings there. I decided to just take the artifacts and the water filter he borrowed with me. I thought you ought to know."

Chee frowned. "That was a bad move. You could be charged with disturbing the scene of a criminal investigation."

"The artifacts are in a box in the garage." Paul wrinkled his brow. "I'm not sure where they came from, but they probably shouldn't have been in that tent. They're right outside, if you need a picture of them. The water filter is out there, too."

Chee picked up something unsettled in Paul's tone. He waited.

"Curtis tried to borrow a filter from me for his trip. You know, the kind you use for camping? I didn't have one. He told me not to worry, he'd get one from the place he worked. The Park Service headquarters is near there. Would you mind taking it back when you go to give your witness statement?"

"Where do I return it?"

"Laguna Blue. Give it to Robert or Ramona at their rental office. I'd do it myself, but I've got to get this report out now that Curtis is gone." Paul hesitated again. "Ted Morris said he'd tell them about Curtis, did I hear that right?"

"Ted mentioned Ramona when he was talking about who he needed to contact."

"Ramona. I'm sure he took care of that."

"Your dad said that Curtis was working for you, too. Is that right?"

"He had been. Not for me but with me. We were working together on a project for my father. Curtis helped us to get another grant for more research on some of the sites Pop discovered way back before Lake Powell. He knew his way around the numbers, but it didn't work out for him to be an employee."

"What happened?"

Paul sighed. "He and Pop started talking about offering tours that focused on the early days of Glen Canyon, maybe taking visitors to some of these places."

"That sounds interesting."

"Pop and Curtis thought so. They believed the tours would help educate visitors. I think the idea is full of problems because there's so little protection for the sites. Anyway, Curtis couldn't work on that, work for me, work for his brother, and handle his job at Blue Laguna. Something had to give."

Chee nodded. "I enjoyed talking to your father."

"He's quite the guy, isn't he? I knew he'd take

the news about the accident hard. Pop saw Curtis as reliable, rock steady, you know the type? He overlooked his faults and focused on mine."

The water filter sat where Paul had left it. Chee put it in his truck and drove to the marina. The Laguna Blue Watercraft Sales and Rental Office was easy to find. From the well-tended look of the place, Chee assumed that the operation was prosperous, although he found only one customer in the office, a young man who had just offered the fellow in the Laguna Blue T-shirt his credit card.

Chee looked around as he waited, studying the pictures of speedboats and jet skis with brilliant blue sky above against the arid sandstone landscape of Lake Powell. Beautiful, with a unique enchantment all its own.

The customer left, and the man behind the counter approached Chee. The name Robert was printed on his shirt.

"Help you, sir?" He looked at the water filter in Chee's hand.

Chee turned the filter so Robert could see the Blue Laguna logo. "I'm returning this for Curtis Walker. I heard that he worked here."

The man's face fell. "Curtis."

The phone started ringing. "I've got to get that," the man said. "Go down that back hall and give the filter to Ramona."

Chee hesitated, disliking both the man's tone of voice and being treated like an errand boy. He'd finish the job and be gone. He walked down the hall to a large room with two desks and open shelving. Life jackets were stacked on the floor.

The woman at the first desk glanced up at the sound of his footsteps.

"Ramona?"

She was pretty, he thought, alive with the natural good looks of a woman who felt confident in her own skin.

"That's me. What can I do for you?"

"The man out front asked me to bring this in here." He walked toward her, lifting the water filter. To his surprise, her eyes filled with tears. He stopped, caught off-balance.

She recovered her composure in a few moments. "I'm so sorry. A friend who just died borrowed that."

Chee nodded. "I know about Curtis."

"You do?"

"You have my sympathy."

"Thanks. I can't get over the shock of that terrible accident. He sat right there." She waved a hand toward the empty desk. "Sweetest guy in the world. Are you one of his friends?"

"No." Chee saw her puzzlement. He introduced himself. "I was chatting with Dr. Pete and Paul Hendrix asked me to deliver this."

She shook her head. "Poor Pete. Curtis loved that guy. Does he know?"

"Paul told him this morning."

Ramona noticed that Chee was still holding the filter. "You can put that here. I'll take care of it." When she had motioned toward the floor near her desk, he noticed the diamond wedding band on her left ring finger and a broad silver band on the right.

"So, do you guys rent boats?"

"That's us. We're busy today. We're always busy on Fridays. Some people get a three-day weekend and drive here after work on Thursday. Saturdays are even crazier."

"Did Curtis take one of your boats to Crimson Beach?"

She shook her head. "Ted Morris told me that Paul made the ID on the body, and that a Navajo guy, a policeman on vacation, found Curtis and stayed until . . ." Her voice trailed off, and Chee saw her eyes widen. "So, were you there when the body was recovered?"

"Yes." The pain in her face prompted him to say more. "By the time I saw him, there was nothing anyone could have done."

He sensed that she wanted a longer story, but he had nothing more to say except that he was sorry the man she knew was dead. He gave her a moment, then continued. "Can I walk to Ted's office from here?"

"It's only a block away, and around the back of the building. Hold on." She tapped some keys on her phone and then gave him the address.

He offered her his condolences again, and trotted to the Park Service headquarters.

Instead of the receptionist at the front desk Chee had expected, Ted occupied the office alone. He looked up and smiled. "I was going to call and remind you to come in. I should have known that you'd remember." He motioned Chee to a chair. Chee studied the office, noting that it was small but well equipped.

"Anything new?"

"Only conjecture at this point." Ted folded his hands on the desk. "Have you dealt with many drownings?"

"No. That's the good thing about serving a district that doesn't have much water."

"Well, when a person drowns, the coroner finds water in the lungs. If the fall, or a heart attack, or whatever, killed him, and he was dead when he hit the lake, there will be no water in Curtis's lungs."

"So the autopsy could show that what looks like an accidental drowning might be murder."

Ted nodded. "Or a medical incident that led to the fall. But murder could be it. That's why I'd really like your help."

"Do you have sole jurisdiction because the body was found in the park?"

"No. The FBI will be involved. And given that the victim is Navajo, the Navajo Nation might want someone to assist with the inquiry—especially with the death's proximity to the Nation's border. I'm hoping that because you're already involved you could continue to help."

"This part of the Nation is a long, long way from Window Rock. I have to admit that there's something odd about this case, but my guess is that Navajo law enforcement will leave it to you." Chee shook his head. "We've got enough odd cases of our own on tribal land to solve."

Ted tapped his fingertips on the desktop. "I don't want to overstep, but I could make a call to headquarters in Window Rock, or your boss in Shiprock, and give you an attaboy for your help with the body. I can make an official request for your assistance as a consultant because of the artifacts you mentioned. If you find something that might give me a leg up to figure out why Curtis is dead, you'll pass it along. If you don't, you still get paid a pittance, and you can stay a few more days."

Chee thought about it. He'd like to help Ted get to the bottom of the death, and he knew he worked well as an investigator. But he already missed Bernie fiercely. "I'll think about it. You deal with many murders?"

"Not at all. The lake, the sun, the views, make people mellow. Only a handful in the years since the lake opened. That's why I'd really appreciate your assistance, Sergeant. No more than a few days. I promise."

A few days more might give him an opportunity to find the cave. "OK. I'll see what I can learn. From what I've heard, Curtis was a likable guy. Everything I hear about him is positive."

"I guess you haven't talked to Ramona's husband, Robert." The ranger whistled tunelessly. "He and Curtis had words a while back. It got so heated that she called us, and I had to give them both a talking-to."

"What were they arguing about?"

"Neither of them would say, and Ramona claimed she didn't know either. Doug, Curtis's brother, has been thinking about adding some hiking tours, and Robert might consider that competition, might have thought that Curtis was disloyal or something. When I called last night to give him the news, Robert didn't sound upset."

"That doesn't always mean something's wrong." Chee had experienced shock and silence after he gave the news of unexpected death to a loved one. "I returned a water filter Curtis had borrowed to his office and met Ramona. She cried when I gave it to her. I've heard that they were more than just coworkers."

Ted rubbed his chin and shrugged. "I plan to talk to Robert. Come on, let's get your eyewitness report out of the way."

Chee completed the statement about his discovery of the body, answering Ted Morris's questions and thinking how odd it felt to be the one responding to the inquiries instead of the officer in charge. As the interview progressed, Chee's respect for the man's competence and professionalism grew. A good thing, considering they could be working together over the next few days.

"Curtis and his brother have some connections to the Navajo community up at Navajo Mountain and at LeChee," Ted said. "I might ask you to go up there and talk to a few folks. If they see that a Navajo cop is dealing with the death, they might be more willing to chat about what they know."

"Whatever you want."

They said their goodbyes, and Chee walked back to his truck. He lowered the window to let in the afternoon air. If he went to Navajo Mountain, an isolated community in a beautiful place, he would have loved to have Bernie at his side. Hearing her voice and seeing her in a video call would be the next best thing. Before he started the vehicle, he dialed her number.

10

Bernadette Manuelito cringed as she clicked on the video call. She didn't look her best. But Chee never complained.

"There you are." He smiled at her. "I've been thinking of you. Figured I should call before it got too late."

"I'm glad you did. I'm getting ready to say good-bye to Mama and get to work. How's your day?"

"Great. I made some progress on the cave. I found a retired archaeologist who knows the area and agreed to look at the Lieutenant's map. He wasn't put off when I told him I couldn't say why I wanted to find the place."

"The Lieutenant will be happy that you're still searching for it. Do you know when you'll be home?"

Chee hesitated. "No, sweetheart. The ranger asked me to serve as the cultural consultant on the case, and I told him I would if it's OK with the powers that be out there. I miss you, but he needs the help, and the assignment might give me a few more days to look for the cave."

"And to think about what's next for you. I get it. Take as long as you want. This is a good opportunity for you to catch your breath."

"To return to *hózhó*." She heard the exhaustion in his voice.

When he asked, she told him Mama was fine, although that stretched the truth a bit. "Darleen went up to Navajo Tech to talk to them about their nursing assistant program and see what she thinks about the campus. You know her. That social stuff and the environment is as important as the coursework."

Chee chuckled, the happy sound that made her miss him all the more.

"Sister also needs online classes so she can stay with Mama most of the week. Mrs. Darkwater will probably help, too, and I can fill in if Sister has to be gone overnight or something."

Then Bernie remembered what Darleen had said. "She wants to talk to you about why men act the way they do."

"What does that mean?"

"She's reconnected with an old friend, a guy who she might like as more than a buddy."

Chee smiled again. "Tell her to call me. I'm full of free advice, but she gets what she pays for. Have you heard anything about your interview?"

She knew he meant for the detective position. "Nothing yet."

They chatted a few more moments. Bernie smiled as she put the phone down.

"Was that the Cheeseburger?"

"Yes, Mama. He says hello."

Mama nodded and went back to her television show. Bernie sat on the couch next to her, not because she wanted to watch TV but because she liked to relax in Mama's company before she left for work. They had made some applesauce together and then cooked and eaten meat loaf. They froze some for Mama and Darleen to enjoy later in the week.

"I have to work today, so I'll be leaving pretty soon. Is there anything you'd like me to do for you before I go?"

Usually Mama patted her hand and stayed quiet, but today she muted the TV.

"I need to talk to you about something important."

Bernie sat quietly, listening.

"There's a man who likes your sister. You know him. We used to call him Stoop Man. He asked me about her a while ago, and I said she was working in Chinle. That man is not right for her. You talk to your sister and tell her that."

Bernie's heart sank at hearing Mama's opinion of Slim, but she wasn't surprised. Mama had initially felt that way about Jim Chee, but his charm, brains, and good manners had won her mother's approval. She judged boyfriends harshly.

"Mama, I barely know the man. I only met him once or twice, and he seemed like a decent guy. Why don't you like him?"

"She says they are just friends, but I know he wants to be more than that. You tell her that man won't be good to her. You tell her."

Bernie tried rephrasing the question. "When I met him, I didn't notice any red flags. Why do you think he's wrong for Sister?"

"He's not the one. You can see that. Tell her that man is not right for her."

Bernie waited for Mama to offer a better rationale, but instead her mother turned the television sound back on. Bernie remembered the initial dislike Mama had taken to Jim Chee; she sensed that their mother wouldn't make life easy for her little sister.

"Mama, you know how Sister is. Sometimes if she's told *not* to do something, she does it just to see what will happen. The more you try to influence her about that man, the more she'll hang with him."

Mama's voice had a sharp edge now. "You think you know everything, my daughter, but you do not. You are one who does not listen to me and who wants to argue. Something is wrong with that man. Tell your sister."

Past experience taught Bernie that disagreeing with Mama left her frustrated and unhappy, while Mama's opinion remained solidly unchanged. She knew that exposing Mama to the facts without making an issue of it and letting the disagreement sit sometimes softened her mother's viewpoint. As they watched TV in stormy silence, she texted Darleen to let her know she was heading off to work. Her sister sent back a quick thumbs-up.

When a commercial came on, she rose. "I've got to go, Mama. I'll see you soon."

"Be careful out there, my daughter. I worry

about you. And don't forget what we talked about. Tell your sister as soon as you can."

She drove her old Tercel onto the main road, relieved that she hadn't gotten into a full-fledged argument. She felt an odd vibration and realized it came from the partially open window behind the passenger seat. The crank had broken, leaving the glass down a few inches. She hadn't been able to fix it herself, and she kept forgetting to ask Chee to take a look. Despite its wear and tear, her car still ran well, and for that she was grateful. Best of all, with the odometer approaching two hundred thousand miles, she'd paid off the loan.

Bernie turned onto the highway and a few moments later noticed a hitchhiker, a man in a blue T-shirt. From a distance, he looked like her sister's friend, the same tall, thin build, the same dark hair. She pulled over to the side of the road. But the person who staggered up to her car carrying a blue nylon sports bag wasn't Slim. This man was desperately pale, older, and Asian, not Navajo. He smelled so strongly of marijuana that even at arm's length the odor penetrated the air. She locked the car's front doors, then lowered the passenger window a few inches and leaned across the seat to speak to him. She saw him trembling as he moved closer, leaning against the car to support himself.

"Sir, are you ill? I'm a police officer, and I can—"

"Police! Help me quick." He gave her a nervous half smile, and she heard the panic in his voice. He tried to open the locked door.

"What kind of help do you need? What's going—" She stopped when she saw a black sedan speeding toward them. The driver slowed to stare at the hitchhiker as the car passed. Bernie thought the man had collapsed, then realized he was cowering, trying to hide behind her Tercel. She watched the black car pull onto the shoulder, the tires kicking up a cloud of sand.

It made a wide U-turn and headed toward them.

As the hitchhiker began a frantic run across the highway, the black car, close behind her on the shoulder now, swerved back onto the asphalt and sped up. The moving car struck the man as he fled, sending his body flying. She heard him hit the pavement with enough force to crack his skull. As she drew her gun, the sedan screeched to a halt, and then backed up over the man who lay sprawled on the edge of the asphalt. The sound as the weight of the vehicle crushed bones and organs would long burn in her memory. Then the car sped away.

The incident unfolded within the tiny sliver of time it took for an oncoming UPS van to slam on its brakes, fishtail, and barely avoid the body. The brown van pulled off the highway, and in another moment its emergency lights began flashing.

Bernie's heart was racing. She took a few deep breaths to steady herself, and called the station on her cell phone to report the incident. Then she rushed across the highway to the scene. From the bone and brain matter on the asphalt, she knew the double impacts had killed the trembling man. Death would have come quickly.

She heard the truck's door slam, and the UPS driver began to run toward her.

"Stop there," she yelled at him. "I'm a cop. Bernie Manuelito. Are you OK?"

"Yeah. He's dead, right?"

"Yes. I've called for backup. I need your help until they get here."

"I saw that car swerve to run him down and then back over him to make sure he was good and dead. I can't believe someone would do that."

"What's your name?"

"Roscoe Chipman."

"OK, Roscoe Chipman. Back up your truck and park it over there." She pointed to a spot near the place where the body sprawled on the shoulder. "Leave on the flashers. Be careful."

"OK." Chipman spoke louder as a car approached. "I was in the army in Iraq. I can do whatever you need."

"Do you have flares and cones in the truck?"

"Yeah. Definitely."

"OK." Bernie thought he looked solid enough to help. "After you park, get them all out and set them up to block the traffic lanes. Put on your safety vest, too, if you've got one. What about something that could cover the body?"

"A tarp?"

"Good. I'm moving my car to help with traffic."

She waited as the oncoming car slowed. The driver and passenger stared at the body on the shoulder, then sped up. Bernie raced back across the highway to her car and drove to the scene of the collision. She parked on the shoulder facing traffic, headlights and emergency flashers on. It was the best she could manage at the moment. She expected more official help soon. In the meantime, she had a job ahead of her.

She appreciated the way Chipman had now parked his truck to shield the body from passing traffic. She removed the flares from the back of her Toyota and put them out. She didn't need another collision. She noticed that Chipman had removed more flares and cones, placing them just as she would have. She was lucky he had stopped to help.

Most vehicles stopped out of caution and curiosity, but a few ran through the improvised roadblock, each doing its part to eradicate the important skid marks that showed the sedan's fatal route. She readied the camera on her phone.

"I need to get some shots of those skid marks before they disappear. Can you try to keep the traffic stopped?"

"Yeah, sure."

She rushed toward the fresh black tire marks on the highway, careful to avoid the traces of the victim on the asphalt. She grabbed a series of shots and looked at the pictures. Deciding they'd do in a pinch, she ran back to where the body lay and used her camera to document the disruption on the shoulder where the dead man had skidded. She photographed the mess of human biology that had been alive moments ago.

The cloying warmth of the afternoon amplified the stench of fumes from the vehicles and the heat that the pavement had absorbed. Bernie forced herself to focus on the work, not her queasy reaction to the hot stench, and this terrible, mutilating death.

After she'd taken enough pictures, Chipman helped drape the plastic sheet over the dead man. North-going traffic on 491 stopped, and those heading south gawked as they rolled slowly past the scene. The cacophony of engine noise and honking mixed with an occasional protest from a raven and the steady whistle of the dry October wind. Another driver, a volunteer EMT from Cortez, pulled off the highway, asked the pertinent questions, and helped with traffic.

As she waited at the death scene, Bernie replayed the incident in her mind, trying to recall every detail. The vehicle was a black Mercedes, a small, sporty-looking new sedan. She couldn't recall any body damage. She remembered a California plate, with 010 among the numbers. Had she picked up anything remarkable about the person at the wheel? The dark tinted windows and the speed of the incident had limited her view of the driver; she could only recall a large person who wore no hat or glasses. She'd seen no one else in the car.

She could describe the victim. That would come in handy. Unless he had ID, the extensive damage meant that the police would need to use dental records and fingerprints to give the body a name.

A black-and-white New Mexico State Police unit with its lights flashing and siren on arrived more quickly than she'd expected. She watched the vehicle drive over the median and park to block traffic. A tall, gray-haired officer stepped out, surveyed the scene, and then waved to her. She recognized Ned Holland, a nice guy she'd worked with before.

He crossed the highway lanes to talk to her. "Hey, Manuelito. We have to stop meeting like this."

"Hey, Holland. No kidding."

"What's the deal here?"

She told him.

"So, you watched this happen? Lucky you."

"A front-row seat. I was on my way home to change for my shift. The UPS driver over there saw the impact, too." She turned her head to look at him, and Holland did, too. "Roscoe Chipman. He told me the car swerved to hit the man and then ran over the guy again on purpose, in front of witnesses. That's exactly what I saw."

"I'll need you to give me a statement when the time comes. The investigation crew will be here shortly." Bernie knew law enforcement agencies in New Mexico treated all pedestrian traffic fatalities as crime scenes. This one had a cop as a witness to an obviously intentional hit-and-run.

"What can you tell me about the car?"

"It was a black Mercedes two-door sedan with a metallic sheen. Smallish, sporty looking, with a long hood. Either new or well tended." She mentioned the California license plate and the partial number. "Dark tint on the windows and the classic circle design on the front grill."

Based on her description, Holland called state police for a BOLO for the vehicle. They knew they could expect the full cooperation of San Juan County and McKinley County law enforcement, as well as the Navajo Nation and the Arizona Highway Patrol. He added possible damage to the car's hood from the body's impact.

"Did you see the driver?"

"I didn't get a clear look."

"But?"

"I'd guess a male, probably between thirty and forty. A big person. No hat or glasses. He was the only one I saw in the car."

Holland smiled. "For someone who didn't get a good look, that's a better description than I'd have from most witnesses. Any idea who the dead guy is?"

"No, I've never seen him before. He didn't look like a Navajo. He reeked of marijuana, and he was staggering. Pale skin, black hair, dark eyes, very thin. Maybe Asian. He was wearing a blue T-shirt with some kind of logo and jeans. From what I saw back there, not much is left of his face." She swallowed the wave of nausea that came with the memory. "Don't forget to talk to Chipman. He saw it, too."

To the enormous irritation of the drivers stuck at the roadblock, NM 491 northbound was closed for the investigation, with traffic diverted to the other side of the highway, which became a slow two-lane. As she helped with traffic, Bernie imagined herself as a detective, investigating this crime, figuring out who the victim was and why the driver of the expensive car had killed him.

When more officers arrived, she thanked Chipman and the Cortez EMT and retold her account of the incident to the crime scene investigators, again describing the victim, the car that killed him, and what she could remember of the driver. The investigators took photos and measurements and checked the body for identification, finding none. She watched the attendants remove the corpse and place it in the transport vehicle.

Having done what she could, she went back to her car and headed for home, her heart heavy. She wished Chee were there to help her decompress. Before she entered the house they shared, she burned some sage as a blessing, and smudged herself and her car. She said a prayer for the man who died, for her husband and his safety, for all their relatives, and for herself. Then she went inside.

Forcing her brain to think of something pleasant, she focused on their time together at Tsé Bighanilini, Antelope Canyon. She had loved the beautiful bands of sandstone created by water's erosion, and the way they seemed to swirl as solidified waves. The amazing play of light and shade and the beams of sunlight filtering into the cool depths of the slot canyon captured her imagination. The light rock made her think of caramel syrup, and the creases in the red-hued sandstone reminded her of the ribbon candy she and Darleen received at Christmas at the chapter house Késhmish party. Best of all, she had relished sharing the canyon experience with the man she deeply loved.

Darleen should be with Mama now, unless, as Mama suspected, she was distracted by a potential new boyfriend. Chee was at Lake Powell, looking into why a clan brother of hers had died. And she was home, about to begin a new shift and consider her own future.

She dialed Chee, hoping he was somewhere with phone service. As she waited for him to answer, she realized that she was exhausted but also exhilarated. She wondered what assignments Captain Largo had in store for her that afternoon.

Disappointed that Chee didn't answer, she left a message, took a shower, put on her uniform, and called the station to let the captain know she was on her way in.

"You sound kind of hoarse," he said. "You feeling OK?"

"I'm fine, sir. It's that talking over the traffic noise and breathing in the exhaust fumes gave me a sore throat."

"Take your time coming in, Manuelito. You get work credit for what you did at the crime scene. See me when you get here."

She walked to her car, looking at the great rocky bulk of Tsé Bit'a'í rising in the distance. How ironic, she thought, that the unknown man died in the shadow of holy Ship Rock. Perhaps blessings from this sacred site would ease his journey to wherever the souls of Asian men killed on purpose traveled.

She remembered the uncooperative rear window. Maybe if she gave the glass a tug, she could get it to roll up. When she opened the car's back door, she noticed a blue bag on the floor. A split second later it made sense—it was the dead man's bag, and the source of the lingering marijuana odor.

She called Captain Largo again to let him know what she had found.

"I just saw it. I haven't touched it."

"Don't touch it. Call me when you park. We'll get a picture of the bag in place before we move it."

She left the window alone, lowered the others, and drove to the Shiprock police substation. After someone had taken an official photo of the suspicious bag, she slipped on some gloves and took the bag inside.

Sandra looked up when she entered. "You look tired, Bernie."

"I've had a long day already."

"Yeah, I heard about the hit-and-run. The captain said to tell you to go right to the evidence room. He's waiting."

"Thanks."

Captain Largo got right to business as usual. "I called NMSP. They want us to check the bag and see if there's any ID for the victim inside. He didn't have anything on him, and they haven't figured out who he is. Have you already looked?"

"No, sir."

"Really?" He raised an eyebrow. "I would have."

"I think there's marijuana in there, and I wanted to make sure everything was done by the book."

"Go ahead. Let's see what Santa brought."

She unzipped the duffel. On the top they saw three neatly folded blue T-shirts, the same shade of blue as the victim wore. She took them out, one by one; each had some sort of Asian characters on the front. Next was a pair of neatly folded, well-worn jeans. She searched the pants pockets for a wallet or identification card and came up empty. Beneath these she found a plain gray sweatshirt, again with empty pockets. Under that were two books. The words "Mandarin/English Medical Dictionary" were printed on the cover of the first book, along with what she assumed was the same title in Mandarin characters. The second, larger book looked like a Bible with similar logogram writing on the cover, again, probably in Mandarin. She fanned the pages, and a piece of paper fluttered out.

"What's that?"

Bernie picked it up and turned it over. It was a photograph, a colored picture of an attractive, slender, dark-haired woman and a small girl. Behind them was a banner with Mandarin characters. Both smiled at the camera. She set the picture aside.

To no great surprise, below the books she found a nest of ziplock baggies. Each looked like it held about an ounce of marijuana buds. She glanced at the captain.

"Go ahead and take the bags out."

The bags were arranged in two layers. She put twenty of them on the table, one by one.

She found two pill bottles, devoid of labels.

"Shall I?"

"Go ahead."

She opened the first container, looked inside, and then gently shook a bit of the contents into her gloved palm. They were brownish-gray seeds, some with a pattern that reminded her of tiny turtle shells. Based on what was in the baggies, she assumed they were marijuana seeds. She put them back and opened the second vial. Inside she found a USB drive for a computer.

After that, she checked the two interior zipped pockets and found nothing more, nothing to help identify the dead man.

They looked at the assortment on the table.

Largo shook his head. "I know the tribal council approved that hemp operation out there, but this sure doesn't look like hemp to me."

She nodded in agreement. Because of her long-standing interest in plants, Bernie knew more about hemp and its cannabis cousins than the average cop. Navajo entrepreneur Dino Begay Perez had applied for the permit. After much discussion, he'd won approval from the tribal council because of his long-standing involvement in tribal agriculture, his good reputation, and his promise to bring jobs to the Navajo Nation before opening positions to outside labor. Begay Perez favored silver-toed cowboy boots and had a gift for making money.

"What do they call that place?" she asked.

"KHF." Before she could ask what that stood for, he added, "K'é Hemp Farm."

K'é. Kinship. A good name for a business, she thought. A unifying factor among the Navajo, and a word that expanded outside the clan system to symbolize a familial relationship with all living things.

"Or depending on who you talk to, Kelly's Happy Farm."

"What?"

"Kelly is Begay Perez's silent business partner, the non-native guy with money and connections."

"I didn't realize they were up and running already."

"Well, Begay Perez had trouble getting the permits for all the water they needed to operate full-scale, but his relatives helped with that. Now families who live out that way have begun to complain about the traffic and noise. And they say they notice men who aren't from here hitchhiking, and those who have given them rides say they work at the farm."

Bernie picked up a bag of buds. "Hemp won't get you high, unless you use it to make a rope. But whatever is in here might do the job."

"That's what the council was concerned about when they approved the operation, remember?" Black-market pot growers favor rural areas with few people and lots of empty, isolated space. The open landscape of the Navajo Nation offers those possibilities—although scarce water would always be an issue.

Largo looked at the flash drive. "I'll open this

later and let you know what's on here. Pack up the baggies to send to the lab. The seeds, too. No use speculating." He stood to leave. "You look a little worse for wear, Officer."

"That hit-and-run bothers me. No one should die like that. I want to do something to get justice for that poor man."

"Call KHF and see if they are missing an employee. Maybe we'll get lucky." The captain paused. "I want to talk to you about something else connected with this case. It's been on my mind for a few days, and murder by luxury car brings it to a head. But I've worked two shifts, and I'm beat. We'll talk tomorrow."

He had Bernie's full attention. "Sir, I could—"

"No, Officer, you need to get out on patrol." He asked her to check on an abandoned vehicle, talk to Mrs. Denetclaw about some vandalism, and then respond to a complaint about stolen sheep at the far end of the district.

"Go. We'll talk tomorrow."

11

Jim Chee had settled in for the night, this time not under the stars but beneath a small sprinkler head in the ceiling that would soak him and the bed in the unlikely event his motel room caught on fire. Ted Morris had an agreement with Sleep Inn for rooms for visiting law enforcement and had offered the lodging in exchange for Chee's advice.

Chee enjoyed camping, but after several days in the vast outdoors, he saw no reason to complain about a warm shower and a softer bed.

He plumped up the pillows and turned on the TV, but not even the syndicated sports show held any interest. He missed Bernie. She'd told him she was working the late shift, and he hadn't expected her to call. He answered before the second ring.

"I was just thinking about you," he said.

"Hey, yourself. How's it going?"

"Well, tonight I have a chance to watch college football on television, and I get a breakfast buffet tomorrow."

"That sounds like a fancy campground."

He laughed. "The captain approved my working with law enforcement here and being away a few more days. I ought to have a better idea of when I'll be home after our meeting tomorrow. I planned to call or text you then. I know you're busy."

"So, it seems like the death out there may not have been an accident." Bernie sounded exceptionally perky for a woman working a long night shift.

"Well, I have questions."

"From what you've told me, that's a very remote spot to kill someone. Did another person go camping with him?"

Chee put the television on mute. "It looked to me like he camped alone."

"Why don't you think it was an accidental drowning?"

"Everyone I've talked to stressed how cautious he was around water. And that he knew the place; he'd been there many times before. I didn't find any alcohol bottles to indicate he'd been drinking, so why wouldn't he have been as careful as always? And evidently a married woman at the boat rental company where he worked was having an affair with him, or at least wanted to. Her husband worked with them both and might have been jealous. I saw the dead man's injuries. He fell forward, not backward. Honey, it struck me as odd."

Chee took a deep breath and changed the subject. "So, how are you? Anything exciting in downtown Shiprock?" It was their joke. Shiprock had its charms, but no downtown. Or uptown, for that matter.

Bernie didn't answer immediately, and when she spoke, he heard the tension in her voice.

"We had a fatality, an intentional hit-and-run. I saw it happen when I was coming home from Mama's house. I was first on the scene."

"Ouch. Intentional, huh? Gang stuff?"

"I don't know. I watched the car make a U-turn so it could hit him, and then it backed up and ran over the man again."

"Did you know the victim?"

"No. He wasn't a Navajo. An Asian. He was hitchhiking. No ID."

"Where?"

Because he knew the road, she told him the approximate mile marker at the site of the accident. She mentioned the bag and its contents, and her surprise at finding it on the back-seat floor.

"What about a connection between the dead man and the drug scene?"

"It's possible. Because of the baggies, I wonder if he worked at the hemp farm and if they grow more than hemp. The murder was vicious."

He didn't like the distress in her voice. "I'm sorry you witnessed it."

"The person who killed that man ran him over on purpose. Twice. That's evil, Chee. It shook me to stand so close to it."

He tried to think of something clever, something to lighten the darkness, but came up short. The silence lasted until he offered his usual advice.

"Sweetheart, take care of yourself out there."

"You know I'm always careful."

Chee remembered the way Bernie had outsmarted a woman who tried to kill her on a stargazing trip. "Keep it up. Stay vigilant. Watch your back."

"I will. You do the same."

"I have to, because I can't wait to get home to you."

He heard her long exhale. "Remember that I love you. Now and forever."

"You too. Now and forever."

After that, he watched the end of the game, even though he couldn't focus on football. He switched to a late-night comedian without cracking a smile, then read the visitors' guide to Lake Powell from shiny cover to shiny cover. He struggled to find sleep. In his dream, he pictured Bernie at the traffic death, the murder car coming toward her, driven by the *chindi* of the dead man. In the logic of dreams, he was there, yelling at her to swerve out of its path. Then he saw her slipping away from him, sliding down a steep sandstone dome and tumbling, tumbling out of his reach toward the deep, cold blue lake. He awoke and waited for the sky to change from black to the darkest of gray.

He slipped on his sweatpants and went outside to greet the dawn with prayer and his special pouch of sacred corn pollen. Running had never appealed to him, but today it came naturally as the antidote to restless fear. As he moved, he offered a special prayer for Bernie, the love of his life, for Doug and his family, for Dr. Pete and his son, for Ramona and Sunfish, and for everyone Curtis had loved and who had loved him.

Back at the motel, he showered and dressed in his last clean pair of jeans and an unworn T-shirt. He packed up his belongings and left them in the room. He didn't know if he'd be spending the night at the motel again after the meeting with Ted Morris, probably a representative from the FBI, and whoever else needed to be involved.

He ate at the buffet, grateful for the cereal but disappointed that the coffee wasn't stronger. Oh well, he told himself. Law enforcement ran on coffee. He was sure the meeting with Ted would be caffeinated.

Chee showed up at the Park Service headquarters slightly early, as was his habit. Ted greeted him, finishing a cigarette outside the building.

"Glad you could join the team."

"Who will we be working with?" Chee liked to go into every situation prepared, if possible.

"If we're lucky, a good hand from the FBI will run the investigation. Besides that, probably someone from the Page PD and the sheriff—that's Bo Carter, a good guy."

"I'm not sure how much help I'll be. You all know the community. But I'm glad to do whatever I can."

Ted smiled. "We need you based on information that turned up yesterday about Curtis Walker's Navajo connections. His brother mentioned that there might be some bad blood out there, some problem back on Navajo Mountain."

"Sure." Chee felt his phone vibrate. "I've got a call coming in. I'll catch you in a minute."

He pulled the phone from his pocket, assuming he'd see Captain Largo's name on the screen.

But it wasn't Largo. Nor, as he had secretly hoped, was the call from Bernie. The ID read "P. Hendrix." By the time he answered, Paul, or Pete, had hung up.

In the office, Ted introduced him to Bo Carter, a fit-looking fortysomething who wore his battered black Stetson in the office, and to a strong middle-aged woman, Dorothy Malone.

"Malone is our chief detective," Sheriff Carter said. "She'll be running the investigation along with Agent Larry Lacabe. Lacabe couldn't join us, but Malone will fill him in."

She nodded to Chee. "You're the guy who found the body?"

"That's right."

"You speak Navajo?"

"Yes."

She glanced at Ted. "Hey, Ted. How's it going?"

"Fine, Detective. We'll get this done. Do you guys have some coffee for us before we get started?"

Chee had been thinking the same thing.

"Sorry, buddy. We're all out. You'll have to go to Starbucks when we're done here."

Chee stifled a sigh.

The sheriff asked Ted to give Detective Malone the background. He mentioned the bloody rock, the wound on Curtis's head, the streaks he and

Chee had seen on the sandstone, which had turned out to be blood, and Curtis's reputation as a fine outdoorsman and a person vigilant around water. And he reminded her that any unattended death could be either suicide, homicide, or from other causes, such as a heart attack or an accident.

Malone raised her eyebrows. "Accidents never make sense. But convince me that I should consider it a possible murder."

"If the skull wound Chee and I saw was caused by a projectile, say someone throwing a rock at the back of Curtis's skull, that would have caused him to fall facedown. He's unconscious and can't save himself from sliding into the lake. Chee and I have seen our share of violent deaths, and this one smells funny to both of us. Give us a day or two to do some background checking on the victim and his circle of contacts and acquaintances. By then the autopsy report should be back, and we can wrap things up."

She frowned. "I'm not ruling out an accident. Footing is tricky up there on that slick rock. I can see him falling, hitting his head, and, well, poor guy gets a lesson in why he shoulda taken a buddy camping with him."

Sheriff Carter nodded. "This could have been a freak accident. But it's worth looking into Walker's associates." He glanced at Malone.

"OK, then," she said. "We're not saying this is a murder investigation yet. We're just saying this death doesn't seem quite right." She turned to Chee. "Based on Ted's conversation with the deceased's brother, we believe there could have been some animosity between Curtis and a man who lives in the Navajo Mountain area, Brian Chin-chili. I'd like you to contact him and a few others Doug has mentioned. I'll give you those names."

"I can do that, but what about one of the Navajo officers from LeChee? That community is closer to their jurisdiction. I'm a Navajo, but I'll still be an outsider."

The sheriff answered. "I've talked to head-quarters there. Those folks are overwhelmed. Captain Largo has authorized your assistance with the investigation, so you are our man at Navajo Mountain. When I talked to the Navajo Mountain officer about the Chinchili guy Doug Walker suspects, he said he hadn't heard of him causing any trouble except for a fight out there with the dead man. This might have legs. I think you can get your interviews out of the way pretty quick."

Carter looked at Ted. "I will follow up with the coroner and track down some other leads here." He summarized the case, mostly repeating information Chee already knew.

Malone turned to Chee. "Here are the contacts I got from Doug. Talk to these folks, see what they know. You might save yourself a long drive."

The list consisted of about a dozen names. "Apart from Chinchili, do you have reason to suspect any of them?"

She shrugged. "Doug said Curtis made some bad decisions up there. He didn't want to get into details with me, but, knowing Doug, he wouldn't have mentioned it if he didn't think it mattered. He said the folks on the list might have insight into some of Curtis's secrets."

Chee examined the typed list of twelve names, only a few of them followed by phone numbers.

The sheriff leaned back in his chair. "Dottie and I agree that those Navajo Mountain contacts are a long shot, but we need to check them off the list."

"Do you have phone numbers for the ones who aren't listed here?"

"No. You can ask Doug, but I'm assuming you'll have to drive out there. And the road up that way is, ah . . ."

Malone finished the sentence. "So terrible it's not really a road. Talk this guy into letting you take Omar."

"Omar?"

The sheriff took the floor. "I was just going to say that the road is passable with the department's four-wheel-drive truck, if you take it slow. We call him Omar. No reason to screw up your own vehicle. I hope you're a better driver than our detective here."

"Or our sheriff." Chee heard the joking in their voices. "Doug said some of these people are more comfortable speaking Navajo. And all of them will be more interested in talking to a cop who looks more like them than I do."

Ted nodded. "If nothing else, you'll enjoy the drive. It's beautiful country. Especially if you like being alone."

"You all got anything else?" the sheriff said.

Chee said, "It looks like I should keep my room at the motel another night."

"That's right. Sergeant Chee, hang around a second and I'll deputize you. Make this job official. And on your way out, talk to Claretta at the front desk and she'll give you the key to Omar."

In addition to the key, Claretta, a woman about Darleen's age, gave him a department gasoline card and insider advice on the route. She told him where Omar was parked.

"How will I recognize the vehicle?"

She laughed. "It's the only thing out there that should be called Omar."

The truck was an aged gray Chevy with heavy-duty tires, high clearance, a few battle scars, and a faded version of the official Coconino County Sheriff's Office logo on the side. He would have preferred to drive his own vehicle, but he saw the logic in using Omar, beginning with the radio that connected him to the sheriff's dispatcher.

Driving another man's truck felt odd, like wearing another person's shoes. He called Doug Walker and left a call-me-ASAP message. Then his phone buzzed. Not Walker. The ID read "P. Hendrix," again. Chee remembered the earlier call he'd ignored.

"Hello?"

"Hey, Chee. It's Dr. Pete. Where are you?"

"Just leaving the sheriff's office."

"Good, you're in the neighborhood. I've been

studying the map you left here, and I've got some suggestions for you. Come on by to pick it up, and we'll talk."

Chee thought about it. "OK, but I don't have much time. I'm waiting for a phone call, and then I've got an assignment that probably involves a drive out to Navajo Mountain."

"You can wait here for the call. It will be good to see you. The front door is unlocked, so knock and walk on in. After yesterday's news, I can use the company."

Before heading to Pete's place, Chee drove Omar back to the motel. He went to his own truck and retrieved his traveling coffee mug, phone charger, and sunglasses. Then he walked inside and told the young woman at the desk that he would be staying another night.

He parked in Pete's driveway, knocked, opened the door, and announced himself.

"Come on in."

The house seemed the same as his last visit except for an unusual aroma, herbal or floral perhaps. It didn't smell like the coffee he was longing for and reminded him, again, that he hadn't had enough caffeine that morning.

The map lay where he'd left it, and Pete sat in Black Beauty, watching a morning news show. He turned off the TV at the sound of Chee's approach. "I could use a cup of tea before we talk. Get yourself one, too."

"Tea this morning? I took you for a coffee guy."

"Paul brewed it for me. It's supposed to help

with the congestion in my lungs. With all the dust in the air, it won't hurt you either, Sergeant. Bring out those doughnuts, too."

Chee poured a cup from the teapot for the old gentleman and, out of politeness, one for himself. He noticed something different on the kitchen table, a framed photo of Pete as a much younger archaeologist with two boys. All three were smiling. The boys, the same kids he'd seen in the other photo, looked to be about twelve in this picture. One of them resembled a younger Paul. He wondered if the other was the dead man. An open box with eight doughnuts sat next to the unused coffeepot. He balanced it on top of his cup and carried them to the table next to Black Beauty.

"No, put them there by the map." Pete unhooked his oxygen and eased himself up, bone by bone, as old people do. He stood a moment to confirm his balance, then moved to the map table. Chee followed.

Pete sipped his tea, made a face, and put the cup down. "First of all, just to be clear, I never saw anything in a cave that could be considered sacred. But based on what you told me and this, I think I've narrowed down the search." He pointed to a spot with his index finger. "You see here?"

Chee looked at the spot closest to the fingertip.

"I like this area for two reasons. First, it has the right sort of stone, you know, the appropriate geology for caves. Back when the lake began to fill, there could have been a beach here like the one you mentioned."

"Great. Thanks."

"Wait a minute. There's a problem."

The old man studied the doughnuts, then went back to the map. "The lake rose to its highest level in the summer of 1999, when it reached ninety-seven percent capacity. If the cave you're interested in was at the same elevation as the sites we investigated, whatever might have been there got flooded. The water went down for about ten years and then spiked again in 2010. The lake is at less than fifty percent full now, so you could probably get there. But it might not be worth your trouble."

He took a few steps and indicated another area on the map. "Now here, these caves are higher on the cliffside. We did some work there before the water came in. We didn't get to all of them, but they showed Ana—" He stopped. "I was gonna say Anasazi, but that's not politically correct. They showed that early Pueblo people lived here for a few decades and then moved on. After that, people who may have been your Navajo ancestors arrived. Apache, Ute, the other tribes that also are still around here showed up then, too. My crew and I took a bunch of photos of structures and rock art and artifacts we couldn't save from the water."

Chee digested the information. "What happened to the pictures?"

"Most of them went to the University of Utah or Northern Arizona University. Both schools were involved in what we called salvage archaeology work because the lake flows over the border between our two states."

The news made Chee smile. Even if the sand

paintings were no more, perhaps one of the other crews had seen the sand paintings. Perhaps photographs of them remained at one of those universities. He would mention that to the Lieutenant and Louisa, who worked at NAU, next time they spoke. Because Leaphorn was self-employed—or retired, depending on his mood—he could take a few days and look for those pictures.

Chee studied the Lieutenant's map more closely. "This doesn't show many roads, and it doesn't show the Navajo Nation border."

"I'm assuming the man who gave you this map walked in, right?"

"Right." Chee remembered Leaphorn's stories of the harrowing hike.

Pete tapped the map again. "If you are serious about needing to explore out that way, there could be easier access now, thanks to the lake. I want to talk to you about that, but I need to sit down."

Pete moved from the table to the recliner and eased his way into the chair. He reached for his oxygen. "Bring my tea over here, and I'll tell you my idea."

"Do you want a doughnut?"

"The chocolate one. And get us some napkins."

Chee smiled. Why was it that so many elders he knew gave orders instead of making polite requests? And that he complied without annoyance? He gave Pete his cup and a napkin with the doughnut on top. He put the extra napkins where the old man could easily reach them. He took the chair across from Pete, the one he'd used the day before.

"Your map doesn't show it, but there's a little beach to the south of this area. When I was there years ago, it was large enough for a boat to pull up. Because the lake is lower now, the beach will be larger. From the shore, the hike up to the cave will be a few miles. But without a boat, it's a long trek through tough country. A man could get lost without even knowing it. If Curtis was here, he could show us. That man knew this country better than anyone. Paul used to be good at it, but he's gotten lazy. And I'm too darn old."

"I noticed that photo in the kitchen. Is that the three of you?"

"Yes. The boys liked to go out with me when I was doing some research." He nibbled at the doughnut. "Paul and Curtis were like brothers that summer and for a long time afterward. I know seeing him dead was hard on Paul."

The old man paused and shook his head.

Chee could tell that Curtis's death had deeply affected Dr. Pete. "You know," he said, "despite all my years as a cop, death still shakes me. Even when it's someone I don't know, like your friend."

He rolled up the map, careful not to tear the vintage paper, secured it with a rubber band, declined Pete's offer of a doughnut for the road, and said goodbye. After climbing into Omar, he called Doug again from Pete's driveway.

"Antelope Canyon Tours . . . Can you hold a minute?"

He recognized Doug's voice. "No. It's Chee. I really need to talk to you."

He heard some muffled conversation, and then Doug was back.

"Do you have news about Curtis?"

"Not yet. It's about the names you gave Ted Morris. I may have to drive out to Naatsis'áán to find some of the people on your list."

"Where?"

"Navajo Mountain. Why do you think these folks might be tied to Curtis's death?"

"It's a long story. When our mother was with us, we lived there. We left after she died, partly because my brother burned some bridges, you know? Annoyed some people, pissed them off."

"All those on the list?"

Chee heard the hesitation. "Especially Brian Chinchili."

"What about phone numbers?"

"The ones I wrote down are the only ones I have. Curtis started going back there again, but I haven't stayed in touch very well. Before you talk to Chinchili, see if you can chat with Desmond Grayhair. He and Curtis were close." Doug paused. "Desmond speaks English, but you'd do better in Navajo."

Chee heard a woman's voice in the background and then a small chorus of laughter.

"Buddy, I've gotta get back to work. Keep me in the loop. Good luck with the calls."

Chee stopped at the bakery. He felt better as soon as he opened the door and the irresistible aroma of fresh coffee greeted him. An elderly woman behind the counter gave him a big grin. "I thought you'd be back. Those cookies are addictive, right?"

He had only planned to get a large cup of the hot coffee he craved, but he decided another box of cookies made sense. He took the cookies to the table, sipped the delicious caffeine-laden beverage, and thought about how to pose his questions about Curtis. Having a conversation with Desmond Grayhair, a stranger, that began with the news that someone he knew had died was fraught with problems. Doing it on the phone added abundant complications. Chee hoped Hosteen Grayhair would answer the call. He knew from experience the pointlessness of leaving a message.

A male voice came on the line at the third ring.

Chee spoke in Navajo, introducing himself as a police officer based in Tsé Bit'a'í, Shiprock. "I'm calling for Hosteen Grayhair. He's not in trouble."

"OK then. That's me." The voice confirmed Chee's guess that the man was elderly.

Chee then introduced himself in the polite Navajo way, beginning with his mother's clan, then his father's, then both his grandfathers'. Desmond did the same. They had no clans in common.

"Why are you talking to me, Sergeant Jim Chee?"

"I need some background information on the brother of Doug Walker. That man died unexpectedly. Doug gave me your name."

Chee heard the old man breathing heavily. "I am sorry to hear that person is dead. Why are you involved, Chee from Shiprock?"

"I was the person who discovered the body." He thought of what else he could say about the case, some way to build rapport, and decided to start at the beginning. "Here is how that happened. I came to this part of Navajo land to pray at Rainbow Bridge. I walked for several days on the long trail, and I thought about the Holy People and the meaning of the bridge. I said my prayer there. After that I hiked a trail the tourists use to the dock and then a difficult trail for a look at the lake. That's when I saw the body trapped beneath the water. It was too late to save him."

"He drowned?"

"The case is under investigation. That's the reason I would like to talk to you."

The phone was silent. Then Desmond said, "I don't have much to tell you. That man hasn't lived here for quite a while, maybe ten years."

"Do you know if he had any conflicts with his old neighbors or his relatives?"

"Maybe he did. Maybe he didn't. If he did, he doesn't now, not anymore."

Chee took a new tack. "I've never been to Navajo Mountain. What's it like, sir?"

Desmond chuckled. "Beautiful, isolated. Hard to get in here or out again. Sometimes we complain to Window Rock that they're ignoring us. But mostly, down deep, we like the peace and quiet. A lot of the people who live up here have been here quite a while, but there's a few newcomers. Spouses, teachers at the school, workers at the clinic."

"It sounds like you've been there awhile yourself."

"Only eighty years so far, but that's all my life. I

took my first breath here, and I wouldn't live anywhere else."

"Well, I hope that maybe you can help me. Doug Walker said I should call you first, but he gave me a few other names of people to talk to about his brother. But he didn't have phone numbers for them. Perhaps you do."

"Who are they?"

Chee read the names one by one, and Desmond obliged with a few numbers, including that of Brian Chinchili. The old gentleman had a good memory. The rest, he said, had no phones.

"Sergeant, let me give you some advice. Almost all of those people knew Doug's and his brother's parents and their aunties. I don't think they can help much in terms of what the one who died was up to lately. And I assume that's the information you're after."

"Yes. So, what about you? They say he had been coming to see you, Shicheii, is that correct?" Chee used the term for grandfather out of respect.

"It is. The man who died and I would sit together over coffee."

Chee sensed that there was more to the story and the relationship. He waited, but Desmond added no details.

"What about Chinchili?"

"We call him Chill. He's young. He and the dead man got crossways for a while, but things straightened out between them."

"In addition to the names I read to you, is there someone else I should talk to?"

"Have you talked to Wanda?"

"No, sir. Wanda who?"

The phone went quiet for a few moments, then Desmond spoke again. "Ask Doug about that."

"I have one more question for you, sir, about something very different. A colleague of mine found a large cave near the lake many years ago. There was some commotion associated with it. You might remember that a Red Power activist and his crew kidnapped a bunch of Boy Scouts and hid them there. The man who mentioned this to me asked me if I could find that cave because there could be something important still inside. They say you know about these things."

Desmond fell silent again. Chee could almost see the old gentleman pondering the question. "I know about that cave, Jim Chee. They say it was a sacred place."

"My colleague believes that, too. He mentioned something he saw to me because at one time I trained to be a *hataɫii*. I learned some of the Blessing Way. Then my uncle, my teacher, died, and . . ." He searched for the next words and realized he didn't have them. Except briefly with Bernie, he had never talked about why he gave up that dream.

Desmond broke the silence. "I will consider what you've asked. I have one of those old telephones that doesn't tell me your number. Give it to me slowly so I get it right."

Chee did as requested.

"Tell Doug Walker I am very sorry about what happened. Tell him I would like to see him again someday."

Chee disconnected, put his phone on the table, and looked at his coffee cup. He knew a little more than he had known before the conversation. But his hope for an easy lead to a killer with an old grudge had evaporated. He stood to shake off his pessimism.

The bakery offered free coffee refills, and while he was up, he selected an apple fritter. Normally, Chee wasn't big on sweets, but he took a couple bites, savoring the sugary goodness, before going back to his telephone. Two of the contacts, unfortunately including the number for Chill, solicited a number-is-not-valid message. The next phone number told him the person had not set up voice mail. At the following number, despite his better judgment, Chee left a brief message. He also sent a text to each. Probably futile, he thought, but worth the effort.

He sipped his coffee, warm and perfectly matched to the pastry. He looked out the window, thinking about Bernie for a few calm and pleasant moments, wishing she were there. He considered what he had learned so far about Curtis and his death. Two respected elders—Desmond and Dr. Pete—thought highly of the man. Curtis had had a disagreement with someone named Chill, and the two had evidently resolved their differences. His young nephews loved him, as did a coworker at Laguna Blue. And her husband could be jealous.

Doug had evaded the question when Chee asked if anyone from Curtis's past might have a motive to harm him, but Doug clearly knew more than he'd been comfortable saying over the phone from his office. In a face-to-face conversation, he might be more forthcoming. Time to pay the man a visit.

If Curtis's death was the result of an old grudge from Navajo Mountain, why wait so many years after the brothers had moved away to do him harm?

In his experience, violent Navajo-against-Navajo crime usually sprang from jealousy over a lover or other resentments with drugs or alcohol as the catalyst. From what he had heard, the Navajo Mountain community was close-knit and traditional. That made the idea that anyone from there would settle a disagreement with murder unlikely. It was not the Navajo way.

Chee had been a cop long enough to understand that almost everyone, even a seemingly straight arrow like Curtis, had something somewhere in their background to give people pause. He thought about sibling communication, and that led him to Bernie and her sister. His smart wife understood things about Darleen that Bernie wouldn't feel comfortable discussing on the phone with a stranger. Doug probably held at least some of his brother's secrets.

He finished his coffee, abandoned the fritter, and dialed the final number Desmond had given him. A woman answered. She sounded young. Chee asked to speak to the person on his contact list.

"Why?"

He identified himself as a cop and gave her a

brief explanation, leaving out the fact that the man about whom he sought information was deceased.

"My *shimá* had a stroke, and she's in the hospital. She can't talk. She can't even open her eyes."

"I'm so sorry to hear that." Sorry, and profoundly disappointed that this last lead had turned to dust. "Perhaps you can help me. Did you know a man named Curtis Walker?"

"Yep. Him and Doug used to live here until they got too fancy for us."

"Is your name Wanda?"

"Nope." She hung up.

Chee called Antelope Canyon Tours. He recognized Sunfish's voice when she picked up the phone.

"Hi. It's Chee. I need to speak to Doug. Is he available?"

"Hi there. Yeah, your timing is great. We aren't so busy now." She forwarded the call.

Chee got to the point. "I talked to Desmond, and I have some questions about Curtis that need answers before I go to Navajo Mountain. Desmond said he hadn't seen your brother for a while, but then Curtis started going back there. Do you know why?"

Doug hesitated. "Curtis was visiting with a girl. He didn't talk about her."

"You mean Wanda? Desmond told me to ask you about that."

"I don't know much, man. Curtis never even introduced us. Kept her a big secret. I didn't think it mattered. His love life was his business." Chee heard the man sigh. "I just heard something you might be interested in. Ramona, the woman Curtis worked with at Laguna Blue, collected some stuff from his desk she thought I might want. Maybe he had something there that could help you figure out what happened at the lake."

"Is she dropping it off?"

"She wants me to pick it up, but I can't leave here until tonight. If you could get that stuff, we can look at it together. Laguna Blue is on your way here."

"OK. I'm leaving now."

"I'll let Ramona know."

Chee found Ramona alone at the front desk. She gave him a weak smile. "Doug told me you were coming. I guess he didn't want to see me. I don't understand why he's never liked me."

"I was—"

"Yeah, I know. In the area. He told me. I could hear how happy it made him to give this job to you."

"Why?"

She pursed her lips. "Oh, Doug has a lot of rules, and I broke most of them. If you wait a second, I'll bring Curtis's things."

Ramona walked to the back office and returned with a cardboard box taped closed where the top flaps met. Chee could tell it was light by the way she handled it. She gently set it on the floor.

"What's in there?"

"Some family photos. A novel he read when business was slow. A comb for his lovely long hair. A nail clipper. His coffee mug. Some artwork

Doug's boys did for him. A sweatshirt he loved and left here. You know. Stuff. Was it a heart attack or something that made him fall?"

Chee shook his head. "The sheriff is looking into it, along with Ted Morris."

"I'm glad you could stay and help figure this out, too. If you can talk to his old Navajo friends they might respond better."

"Are you Navajo?" Chee had noticed her hair, as black and shiny as a raven's wing. He took in the regularity of her features and the clarity of her olive skin. She wore a silver bracelet with stones that matched the turquoise in her earrings.

"My dad was Navajo, but I don't know what clan. He left home early and lost contact with his family, so I wasn't raised to value that part of myself. Curtis, that dear man, made me feel proud to have some Diné blood. My mom's parents came from Italy."

"Do you and your husband own Laguna Blue together?"

"Unfortunately. He thinks he's too important to get involved in the details, so he focuses on how to expand, how to make more money, national trends in running marina rental operations like ours. He calls that the big picture. Curtis and I did the real work and kept track of everything: insurance on the rental boats, the price of fuel, the park regulations, customers who don't show up for their reservations or return the boats late. I couldn't do it without Curtis, but I guess now I have to."

When Ramona raised her head, Chee saw the silvery tracks of tears on her cheeks.

"He must have been quite a man."

She used the back of her hand to wipe the tears away, and he noticed her silver ring again. It reminded him of something he couldn't immediately remember.

"Did Curtis talk about his days at Navajo Mountain, or the people he knew before he moved here?"

"Oh, once in a while. He loved it there. Why do you ask?"

"There's some thought that there might be bad actors out that way."

She laughed. "They're everywhere. You know that as a cop, don't you?"

He nodded. "How did Curtis come to work here?"

"One of our boat rental customers said her family had done a tour with the nicest man, a big Navajo guy who loved this area and worked with Antelope Canyon Tours. I asked about him, and then I did a tour on a day he worked, just to see him in action. He was as wonderful as she said, so my husband, Robert, offered Curtis a job. He does the hiring. Robert figured Curtis had the brains to help us make more money. He was right.

"Curtis was a complicated, practical man. Those were two things I appreciated about him. Two of many, many."

"He was special to you, wasn't he?"

She said nothing, but unshed tears made her eyes shine.

Chee picked up the box. He had taken a few

steps toward the door when it opened. Ramona's husband entered, stopped, and stared.

"Hey, I remember you. Chee, right? Any news about Curtis's accident?"

"Not yet."

"Are you involved in figuring out what happened?"

"The investigation? I'm helping for a few days."

Robert shook his head. "Remind those guys that Curtis couldn't swim, OK? It shouldn't be much of a mystery."

"Sounds like you knew him pretty well." And, Chee thought, don't have much regret about the death.

"I guess so. He worked here . . ." Robert yelled across the room, "How long, Ramona?"

"Three years."

Chee heard the chill in her voice.

"So yeah." Robert nodded. "Why are you guys spending time on this accident? You pulled his waterlogged carcass out of the lake, didn't you? No gunshot wound in the back. No slit throat as far as I've heard."

"An investigation is routine in any unattended death. As far as we can tell, there weren't any witnesses. Why are you so sure it was an accident?"

"The guy liked taking risks. Right, honey?"

Ramona uttered an obscenity and disappeared into the back office.

Robert laughed. "She's touchy today."

"Death does that to most people."

"Ramona's always been emotional." He shrugged. "That's why she's in the back office. She lets her feelings get in the way of business. You're a cop. You can appreciate that, right?"

Chee ignored the jab. "I understand you and Curtis got into an altercation recently. Ted Morris said he had to step in."

"Don't believe everything you hear. It's a long story. Ted can tell you about that, if you think it matters." Robert smiled. "I gotta get to work."

Chee walked to Omar and put the box on the seat next to him. Robert's tough-guy reaction to the loss of his only employee, and his shortage of sympathy for Ramona's mourning, struck him as more than coldhearted. The man was acting like a jerk.

As he started the engine, Chee looked at his own large hands on the steering wheel. The sunlight caught his wedding ring. He realized that Ramona's ring looked familiar because he had seen one like it on Curtis's dead right hand. He considered Robert's lack of visible grief and the obvious possibility that Ramona and Curtis had been lovers. He added Robert to the mental list of suspects he began to compile in his head, right next to Chill from Navajo Mountain.

Two vehicles with Utah license plates had parked in the Antelope Canyon Tours office lot. Inside, Sunfish was explaining to a middle-aged woman in baggy shorts that the tours didn't start at the office. Instead, a driver took the customers to the canyon in a van and brought them back when the tour ended. When she'd finished the explanation, she said, "He's expecting you."

Chee took the box around the counter to a small

room filled with cases of water bottles. Doug sat on a folding chair with the phone to his ear, involved in a conversation that, from what Chee could gather, concerned a dispute over a group reservation. Chee pulled out the list of names Doug had provided and waited for the call to end.

"My brother always told me not to let the little stuff bother me—and that complaint would have qualified. I never told him how good he was at what he did." Doug looked at the phone in his hand and put it in his lap. "I miss him. My little brother. My friend. My right-hand guy in the business, good with details and with people. With the financial part, not so much, and that's all we ever argued about. He was smart, funny, a hard worker. He loved being outdoors. And he loved my boys. I don't know . . ."

Chee heard the man's voice crack and gave him time.

"My brother. No one can replace him in their lives or in mine. His death up there, his body in the water, none of it makes sense."

"Did he have enemies?"

Doug shrugged. "Not that he mentioned to me."

"No ex-wives, angry girlfriends, business colleagues who didn't like him, jealous husbands, people who thought he hadn't treated them fairly, people he owed money to or who owed him?"

Doug shook his head.

"What about Robert Azul?"

"He's an ass. He wants to limit our tour options."

"What about Brian Chinchili?"

"The only reason I know about him is that Curtis called me for a ride to work. He said Chill had slashed his tires. My brother thought the guy dripped with hate. He sounded scared of him."

Doug exhaled.

"But after that incident, he never mentioned Chill again. I put the guy on the potential bad-boy list because he was the only one I could think of who seemed to have ever had a beef with my brother, the only person who ever scared Curtis. At least that I know of."

"Did your brother say why Chill did that?"

"Never. Desmond might know more about it."

"So, let's talk about Wanda. Why did you leave her off the list?"

"I was thinking of people who might have, you know, held a grudge or something. When my brother started making more trips to Navajo Mountain I teased him about having a sweetie pie there, a long-distance relationship. He finally let it slip that he was seeing someone he called 'his Wanda.' I never asked for details like how they met, where she worked, who her family was, things like that. And he never offered any and never brought her here, so Shawna and the boys and I could meet her. All I can say is that knowing her made him happy."

Chee remembered how Bernie always probed her sister for information on any new potential boyfriend. Brothers were certainly different. "You don't know anything about her?"

"I had other things on my mind besides his love

life. We were busy putting together our plan to grow the tour business, and with both of us already working full-time, we tried to stay focused. I groused at him for driving to Navajo Mountain so much, but he reminded me of the time I spent with the wife and kids, so I shut up about it."

"What was the expansion?"

"Archaeology tours. Because of Dr. Pete, my brother learned about places with great ruins and rock art. He knew those sites like the back of his hand and loved hiking out there. He organized a collection of photos, and we were going to hire someone to make a video for the new tour promotion. We kept the idea quiet until we had a chance to run the figures. Curtis used to say you couldn't always count on people, but you could count on numbers." Doug frowned. "We hoped to start those tours in the spring."

"What do you think he was doing out there at the lake by himself?"

"I wouldn't be surprised if he was researching the rock art tour."

They sat for a while.

"Sorry I forgot to mention Wanda." Doug pulled out his cell phone, made a swipe, wrote something down, and handed Chee the slip of paper. "Here's a cell number my brother gave me for her. I remember that he told me she works for the Navajo Nation, or the chapter up there, or something like that."

"Thanks."

"Anything else I can do to help you get to the bottom of this?"

Chee stood. "Let's see what's in the box."

"I need to say something else before we do that. Desmond, the elderly gentleman I told you to talk to first, was a close friend of our Little Mother, our mom's sister. He helped raise us, especially my brother. I haven't seen him for a while. I should have called him to let him know about my brother. I'm sorry I didn't. I just couldn't face the idea of spreading the bad news."

"It's OK. I told Desmond that your brother died. He seemed to take the news in stride. It was as if he'd known he was dead before I even said it. Hosteen Grayhair wants you to come see him."

"Did you know that Desmond Grayhair's uncle was a famous *hataɫii* out there? He's a medicine man himself, very well respected."

"No, I didn't." Chee had observed that an appreciation for the power of the spirit, the supernatural, seemed to run in families. That explained the old gentleman's reticence to share what he knew about the cave over the phone with a person he'd never heard of or seen before.

Doug picked up the box and used scissors to free the tape. Inside, neatly folded on top, Chee saw a large black sweatshirt. Doug shook it out and pressed it to his nose. Chee noticed the tears and diverted his gaze to the box, studying a couple coffee cups, an old-fashioned Day-Timer datebook, a paperback novel, some rocks. Nothing that resembled a threatening letter to explain Curtis's death.

Chee focused on the rocks, noticing that they had the same rounded shape and were roughly the same color as the bloody, out-of-context stone he'd found on the cliffside.

A rap on the doorframe interrupted them, and Sunfish stepped in. "Sorry to bother you, but a customer is having a fit about her bill. I tried to calm her down, but she says she has to talk to the owner, not just a worker bee."

"Give me a minute. Tell her I'll be right there." Doug pressed the soft, warm shirt to his heart, and then handed Chee the garment.

"Do you mind if I deal with this later? We gave him that shirt from the boys for his birthday. They picked it out. He put it on the minute he saw it and wore it all the time. I wish I'd told Curtis how much he meant to my kids. Sorry, I . . ." Doug turned away.

"It's OK. Grief is strong medicine. Life loves on." Chee paused. "I saw some interesting rocks in the box. Do you know anything about them?"

"Rocks? No. Take them if you want them."

Doug wiped his eyes with his shirtsleeve, took a few breaths, and left the room. Chee put the stones in his pants pocket.

Sunfish returned. "Poor Doug. And you look tired, Jim Chee. You sure picked a strange way to spend your vacation."

"I'm getting ready for a long day." He grinned. "I guess I told you I came here for a break from police work, to enjoy being in a beautiful spot, collect my thoughts, and figure out what I wanna do when I grow up."

"You said something like that. Then you found a body, and things changed."

"I'm glad to help clear this up. It's just not what I expected to be doing."

She nodded. "That's what happens when you're good at something and you have a big heart. Come out on the lake with me for a while before you get to work. Curtis will still be dead, and there's nothing like this beauty to raise a person's spirits."

"I've got to do some interviews at Navajo Mountain."

"I know Curtis didn't accidently fall into the lake and drown. That man was super cautious. And he was healthy. Someone killed him."

"I can't talk about the investigation."

"I can. No one gets murdered here. We're all worried. That's why I'm being nosy. That's why you have to figure out what happened. I liked the man, but he wasn't perfect. He probably made a few bad decisions in business and in his personal life. And, well . . ." She shrugged off the rest.

Sunfish's candor reminded Chee of Bernie. "Do you recall him mentioning someone named Wanda?"

"Never. Here's some free advice. See what you can learn at Navajo Mountain, but if you want to find out why Curtis is dead, you need to focus closer to home."

12

Bernadette Manuelito awoke refreshed and ready for the day's challenges. She sang her prayers, did her morning run, and, after breakfast, headed on to work.

Sandra greeted her with a smile. "You look happier than the last time I saw you."

"I am. I had a nice talk with Chee last night. He'll be back in a couple of days. And Darleen can stay with Mama, and Mama seems to be feeling better. How are you?"

"OK, I guess. I don't like this time of year, the fall, *aak'ei*, always makes me sad. Leaves falling, gardens dying. And right before I left work yesterday, we got a weird call. It bothers me still."

"Did someone threaten you?"

Sandra opened her mouth, then quickly closed it. "No, nothing like that. The captain said he wants to tell you about it. But have some coffee first."

Bernie took her questions and her mug with her

as she rapped on the captain's office door. Largo motioned her in. "Close the door and have a seat. I want you to listen to something."

He put the phone on speaker. She heard a male voice with a heavy accent, not an inflection she was used to from Spanish or Navajo speakers. His words told her he wasn't comfortable using English. *"My brother missing. He been gone for two days. I know something bad happen to him. He arguing with the Boss Man. We work at the hemp farm. He stands five feet six inch and he named—"*

The voice on the phone said a couple of Chinese words. Then, the message was cut off suddenly, as though the caller had hung up.

"That's it. You wanna hear it again?"

"Yes, sir."

Bernie listened. "Did he say the brother's name was Arthur No?"

Largo raised an eyebrow. "I heard something that sounded like Proctor and the last could be Joe . . . The accent makes it hard." He told her Sandra had asked for the caller's emergency, name, and location when she picked up the call, but the man had ignored that and left only the message they had just heard.

"I had Officer Bigman contact the number that generated the call. The phone belongs to a Lester Nez. Bigman said the man who answered didn't sound like the caller. No accent. Nez didn't know what Bigman was talking about—he said he must have the wrong number. But the number was accurate."

"Maybe Nez loaned the caller his phone. Or

lost it or it got stolen. Does he have children who might have given it to someone else?"

Bigman had asked those important questions, and the answers were all no. "Nez swore his phone never left his pocket and that he didn't know anyone named No or Joe or whatever. Then he said he had to go and hung up. Like I told you, Bigman believes he was telling the truth."

Bernie pursed her lips together, a habit that seemed to help her think more clearly.

"So, a call comes in from a guy who could be Chinese, worried about his brother, who probably is also Chinese. This happens after I watch a Chinese guy who could be involved in drugs get creamed on purpose on 491. I don't like the coincidence."

Largo nodded. "That's what I'm thinking, too. And we've heard that the farm is bringing in Chinese workers."

"There's more to that phone story than Lester wanted to tell us. I trust Bigman's instinct on him telling the truth, but that doesn't mean the guy told the whole truth." Bernie frowned. "Is there anything yet from OMI on the fatality?"

"Not yet. But there is some good news. Based on your partial plate and description of the car, the New Mexico Motor Vehicle Division says KHF owns the vehicle involved in the accident. The company registered it a few months ago. State police haven't located it; the car seems to have disappeared. And, before you ask, no confirmation on what was in those baggies or the pill bottle either."

The lab had dealt with tons of cannabis over the years marijuana had been illegal, Bernie thought. Maybe they were backed up with too many requests ahead of this case. Perhaps whatever the dead man had was a special variety, maybe an experimental cultivar. Interesting.

"And the computer drive?"

"Odd. That was a bunch of data about epilepsy. You want to see it?"

She nodded.

"OK. I'll send you a copy." He typed something into his computer keyboard.

Bernie waited for the captain to bring up the next topic, her daily assignment. But before he could say anything, his phone rang. He let it go to voice mail and when the noise stopped, she raised the issue.

"I'd like to follow up on the dead man. I know the murder isn't in our jurisdiction, but the neighbors' complaints against that operation certainly are, and the call from Mr. No ties a person's disappearance to the farm. I'd like to chat with this Lester dude and check on the mystery call with someone in personnel at the farm."

"Sandra found the KHF business number for Bigman. But no one answered." Largo handed her a slip of paper. "Here are the farm's main contact number and Lester's cell. I've got to catch a conference call. Let me know if you have any luck with the Happy Farm phone, and we'll take it from there."

Bernie went to her desk, smiling at the Happy Farm designation for a business supposedly growing hemp to be used for medicine to help people sleep better and have fewer aches and pains. *K'é*, the Navajo word for extended family relationships, was a very good name for a business that ought to be behaving itself.

She brought the computer to life and glanced at the information Largo had forwarded from the dead man's computer drive. An abstract of a scientific paper from a medical school neurology department filled the screen with small print and footnotes. She glanced at it briefly, then set it aside. There were two other files on the disc, scientific notes about different varieties of cannabis. She jotted down the names of the various hybridized strains of *Cannabis indica* and *Cannabis sativa*. The more she read, the more she doubted that the lab would discover a match for the weed in the baggies or the seeds she'd found in the duffel. The number of officially named cannabis strains was in the thousands, with more being developed all the time.

She had been churning up a theory about the man's death-by-Mercedes, and the technical information on the flash drive didn't fit. She supposed he was stealing product, probably top-of-the-line marijuana, along with a cache of seeds to grow more of it. Maybe he planned to start his own business, and his boss had found out and decided to destroy the possible competition. Murder was harsh, but the drug trade was a deadly business.

She listened again to the recording of the man asking about his missing brother. This time the second part of the name he mentioned sounded like Joke. And for the first, did he say Proctor? Doctor?

She called the number Largo had given her for the hemp operations. The phone rang ten times without an answer. She hung up.

Frustration inspired her to stand and stretch, hoping that physical action would stir fresh ideas. She proceeded to the break room, poured herself half a cup of coffee, and thought about Chee, which lifted her spirits and made her remember a name from a long-ago world history course.

Back at the desk, she did a minute of research and found that Zhou—pronounced "Joe"—was a relatively common Chinese name. What if Proctor was "Doctor"? What if the dead man had been a PhD working with KHF to develop more potent strains of marijuana? What if there was some bad blood between him and management? Or what if her imagination was running away with her?

And how could she verify any of this?

She called KHF again and let the phone ring even longer, hoping that voice mail would click on. It didn't. She asked Sandra to check whether the number the captain had given her was correct, since Sandra had provided it in the first place.

Sandra double-checked. "That's the only number I found but I'll search again and let you know if something else turns up."

The KHF operation was about a ninety-minute trip from the station, on the remote edge of Navajo law enforcement's Shiprock district. Bernie wanted to drive out there and investigate. Who was the dead man? Why was a vehicle the company owned involved in a fatal collision? But first she needed another look at the duffel bag and its contents. She especially wanted to see the books and the photograph again.

She filled out the required paperwork, waited for the little suitcase to appear, then slipped on protective gloves and opened the bag. Everything she remembered was there—minus the seeds, thumb drive, and baggies. She unloaded the clothes and the books once more, placing each item on the table, silently asking them to tell her something of the man. She shook out each T-shirt again, noticing the smell of sweat and cannabis, finding nothing folded inside. Every shirt had identical Mandarin characters on the front. She took a photo of the logo or whatever it turned out to be, folded the shirts again, and stacked them in a neat pile.

Then she reexamined the jeans. Like the T-shirts, they needed to be washed. She patted the fabric, feeling for syringes or anything that could injure her hands. Then, she slid her slim gloved fingers inside the pants pockets to find what was there. She felt slightly uneasy, like an intruder in a stranger's personal space. She came to the tiny watch pocket and touched something firm and flat inside. Pinching it between her thumb and index finger, she pulled it out for examination. It was a small coin with a square hole in the center. She took a photo of it and left it out.

She thumbed through the Mandarin/English dictionary, noticing some underlined words:

anecdotal, intractable, synapse, developmental. Then she opened the second, larger book. Like the dictionary, it looked both well used and well cared for. From the cross engraved on the cover and its thickness, she assumed it was a Mandarin Bible. She turned to the page marked by a red ribbon, noticing that the book fell open easily to that spot, as though that section had been read many times. Someone had flagged other pages with small pieces of colored paper.

Finally, Bernie picked up the photograph. The woman and the girl looked happy and elegant, with a regal bearing that came from not only what they wore but the way they sat, their physical presence. Behind them was a banner with what she assumed were Mandarin characters. Who were they? What did it say?

She snapped a photo with her phone and put the picture back in its evidence bag. She waited a moment, wondering if a fresh question would tickle her brain. Then she slipped the coin into its own small evidence bag, reloaded everything as she had found it, and returned the duffel to the attendant.

Now she needed to persuade Largo to authorize her visit to KHF. Before that, as was her habit, she jotted down ideas to solidify the order and content of her request for the special assignment.

Ten minutes later she walked to the captain's office, and he motioned her in.

"Manuelito, any luck tracking that call?"

"No, sir, but I have an idea."

"Hold that thought a minute. Have you heard the name Dino Begay Perez?"

"Yes."

"Tell me what you know about him."

She glanced at the ceiling for a second. "He served on the tribe's Agriculture Review Committee and used to be the chairman. He's been active in the Shiprock chapter's governance. And he likes to wear silver toe covers on his cowboy boots."

"That's right. He's a big part of local government and tribal business. Anything else?"

"Yes, sir. Last year, he got conditional tribal approval to grow hemp, provided he could find the water for the operation. He promised to hire Navajo workers as part of the deal and said he planned to produce both fiber and CBD products."

"Well, we have a mess on our hands. Begay Perez convinced some of his relatives to assign water rights to him in exchange for a share of the profits from the hemp operation. Several of his clan brothers are complaining that he's not living up to his end of the bargain. They say that in addition to using more water than is allowed, the operation generates too much traffic, and leaves trash everywhere. They don't like the armed security guards roaming around and the big fences screened with black plastic. They say he wouldn't do that if he didn't have something to hide. They also complain that the workers are paid in weed, and that Begay Perez is hiring kids who are too young to work legally."

"Wow."

He looked at her as though he expected another comment.

"That *is* a huge mess. It ties in with what I want to talk to you about."

"Go ahead."

"A few days ago, I took a call from a lady who lives near KHF, and she wanted us to do something about the noise and the speeding." Bernie stood a little straighter. "She said that when she tried to talk to Begay Perez, she got transferred to someone else, a non-Navajo who told her to stop whining. He said what she saw was the price of progress. She was angry. A few days later, she called again to complain, and the person she talked to told her to shut up. Then someone poisoned her dogs. She didn't think it was a coincidence, and she says similar things have happened to other families who live near the farm."

Largo frowned. "I remember that incident. You were off so Bigman went out to investigate, but there was no way to pin it on KHF."

"That woman sounded devastated and terrified. It's not right. That's not the Navajo way." Just saying the words ignited Bernie's anger. "I want to drive out there and talk to Mr. Begay Perez. He or someone who works for him knows who killed the dogs. They probably know who was driving that car and who the dead guy was, too. I want to find the victim's brother, the man who made the call, and make sure he's OK, let him know what happened."

The captain remained silent, not the response she'd hoped for. She continued to press her case.

"Some deep evil is responsible for that man's death. It doesn't sit right with me. And the fact that a Navajo owns that place makes it even worse. I don't understand why Begay Perez is so standoffish about this. He used the word *k'é* in the name of that farm, but he certainly is not acting like a good relative."

Largo rose and closed the door.

"I've had some calls, too. Dino Begay Perez's relatives haven't been able to reach him directly to resolve any of their complaints. He's not responding, not even when they call his home number or stop by his house. They say it isn't like him, and they're worried. Bigman talked to some of them while you were at Antelope Canyon. Begay Perez's sister asked for a welfare check. Bigman went to his house, and no one was there."

"I'd like to get answers to some of these questions. Sir, I wouldn't be surprised if KHF is working on more than hemp and CBD. We know there's still a strong black market for pot. Not only in states where it's illegal but also in places where the price is higher because of the taxes the dispensaries have to pay."

"Don't lecture me, Manuelito." He leaned toward her. "Are you ready for a challenge?"

"Yes, sir. That's why I brought it up. I'm always up for a challenge—unless it involves Mama, Darleen, or my marriage. Or Lieutenant Leaphorn."

"Leaphorn. Have you seen him lately?"

"No, sir." She knew Largo's and Leaphorn's friendship spanned decades. "He's been traveling. After he and Louisa made that trip to Washington, he decided flying wasn't so bad." She smiled as she remembered the conversation. "You may not believe this, but they went to Hawaii."

"You're kidding!"

"It's the truth. Louisa's birthday was coming up, and he surprised her."

The captain's jaw dropped. "This is the same I'd-rather-drive Leaphorn I know?"

"The Legendary Lieutenant."

"Next thing I know, you'll be telling me my old friend is getting married."

Bernie smiled. "You'll have to talk to him about that."

"Back to business. The DEA's looking for links between Begay Perez and major drug operations. They had an agent investigating KHF after a load of ganja—not CBD product—was confiscated near Gallup. The man was going to be an informant, but evidently KHF sniffed him out and ran him off before he could learn anything. The FBI is involved, and an alphabet soup of other agencies. At this point, we're all monkeys in the circus. We need to know what's going on in that compound. Because you're Navajo and an attractive woman, you might have better luck." He emphasized *might*. "I bet you've already thought of how you'd approach it."

"I have. My first idea is to push, be obnoxious if I have to, until I can talk to Begay Perez. As the business owner, he might have been driving that

Mercedes. It makes sense. But if Begay Perez is out of the picture, I'll find out what happened, where he is, and who is running the operation now."

Largo cleared his throat. "Go back to your idea about Begay Perez as the driver. Can you ID him?"

"No, sir. It all happened too fast. But I'm sure the driver was a big man. And I'll never forget those eyes." She felt her stomach tighten at the memory of the raging anger she saw in them.

"Here's how it seems to me. If you go in as a cop, you'll run into the same wall of silence that Bigman bashed his head against."

"You mean on the phone?"

"Yes and more. Bigman drove out there to follow up on the poisoned dogs. The security guard stopped him at the gate, then a low-level management type came out to talk to him. The man denied any knowledge of the incident, and of course the woman had no proof. It was a useless waste of time. So if you do this, you'll have to be undercover. That's risky. I'd like you to think it over."

Undercover? She hadn't anticipated that response.

"Captain, you remember Arnold, the guy I arrested last week?"

Largo chuckled. "You bet. He's like a relative, he's here so often."

"He told me he's been working at KHF, and that they paid him in weed. He said he can go back there as soon as he's out of jail because it's harvest season, and they never check backgrounds. So what if I went in as a wannabe worker, got hired, snooped around for a day or two like the DEA person wanted to do? I could learn firsthand what's going on with the hemp, find the dead man's brother, and ask about the hit-and-run."

"Or you could waste a couple of hours, maybe a day. Or you could get killed. I don't want you there more than one workday. Too many unknowns."

"Sir, this case matters to me. Matters a lot. A day? That's not much time. I saw a defenseless man killed on purpose. And—"

He cut her off. "Think about it, Manuelito. A day. That's *not* a suggestion."

She took a deep breath. "Captain, I need to do this. The murder haunts me. And the sooner the better."

He gave her a long look. "I'll check with the other agencies involved in this, and we'll talk again. That death on the highway, as much as it bothers you, belongs to the state police for now, and maybe the FBI. See what, if anything, the DEA agent knows."

"Sir, when we started this conversation, you asked if I was up for a challenge. I am. Totally. I have a bad feeling about what's happening out there. The scumbags behind it need to be in prison." She recalled the sound the shiny new Mercedes made as it backed over the body. "The sooner the better."

She thought about the dead man, the phone call, and Begay Perez as she worked her shift. She dealt with a complaint about boys with BB guns harassing someone's horses, and a sad call about an elderly man who had wandered away from home. That assignment took most of the day, but it had a happy ending. When she returned to the office to write her reports, she found the name and number of the DEA contact, Agent Russ White. She called, left a brief explanation on his voice mail, and poured half a cup of stout coffee into her mug. She walked back to the desk just in time for Sandra to buzz her.

"A guy named Russell Bright White on the phone for you."

"Great."

She picked up the call and explained her pending assignment.

"I'm glad you called." White's voice had an easy, lilting tone. "I'm happy to tell you what I can about the KHF inside operation. It isn't much. My goal was computer access. We wanted to learn who the top dogs were at the farm, and who was responsible for arranging the orders on both ends. We knew that had to be in their computer system. Unfortunately, I got kicked out before I could learn much."

"I'm assuming you knew that Dino Begay Perez runs the operation. He won the go-ahead from the Navajo Nation."

"Yeah, and I knew he needed some deep pockets to finance the business. Early in my research, before I made the trip to New Mexico, I had some contact with him. Then, nothing. Radio silence."

"Couldn't you access their computers remotely?"

"We could, and we did for a while. Then they upped their security. The agency wanted me to get an idea of the operation from the inside. We tried to time things so I could investigate a reported outgoing shipment of high-grade 420."

Bernie knew 420 was slang for *naakai binát'oh*, also known as marijuana, ganja, weed, grass, reefer, Mary Jane, and probably a hundred other nicknames.

"My task was to find the weed's ultimate destination as well as KHF's link to the larger drug world. I went in with one assumption, and reality challenged it."

"What assumption?"

"I underestimated how smart and devious those guys are. You be careful out there, Officer. They're nasty, and they mean business."

Generalities didn't work with Bernie. She needed specifics. "Can you walk me through how things went down for you?"

"I'm not proud of it." White laid out the progression of his failure in meticulous detail for several minutes, beginning with bad information about the farm and an ill-conceived cover story of computer problems.

"We sent them a virus through an email spoofed from a known KHF client. KHF detected the virus, as we anticipated, and contacted me through that fake address. I sent a note apologizing and saying we were dispatching our top tech guy—that was me—to get rid of it, and that we were giving them a free laptop to compensate for the inconvenience. I promised that the trouble could be fixed in less than two hours."

The plan sounded OK to Bernie. "What happened?"

"I think they made me at the gate. Have you been out there?"

"Not yet."

"They have a security guard stationed along the entrance road, right at the start of the farm property—an armed man waiting in a truck, blocking access. He walked up to my car, informed me I was on private property and asked who I was and why I was trespassing. I gave him the Navajo name that the agency had assigned me and explained that I had official business at KHF because of a computer problem." White stopped. "I need to back up here. One reason the agency liked me for the assignment is because I'm Lakota. I don't look like what someone might think of as a DEA agent."

"I get it." Most Lakotas she'd met didn't look much like Navajos either, though. "Tell me about the guard."

"He seemed to buy the computer-problem story, maybe because I tossed in some of those five-dollar words. He used his phone to call the office and told the intake person I was on my way. He probably took my picture then, too, maybe with his cell camera. They must have matched that guy's photo to one of me on the web. That was it."

"I thought DEA investigators didn't post personal photos."

"We don't. I'm careful about that, but I think

they found an old picture from when I coached my daughter's soccer team. That photo is gone now, but it's too late." He paused. "Do whatever you can to change your appearance. The facial recognition system out there is state-of-the-art."

"Were you turned away at the road?"

"No. It took the system a while to find me. I drove into the compound, snapped a few photos, parked, and went to the intake office with the laptop gift. The guy there took the computer with a thank-you and told me they had their own tech guy who could handle everything. The man looked like the Indian version of a good ol' boy, but he is sharper than he seems."

"What's his name?"

"Ah . . . Wes, Wesley? Something like that. I have it in the notes I can send you. He acts as the office manager and personnel clearinghouse. He's a Navajo dude, probably in his early thirties. Give me your email, Manuelito, and I'll send you my full report."

"OK, but just summarize it for now."

"Wes said they blocked the virus we sent and asked me who I really was. I stuck with that lame cover story, acted insulted, and requested a chat with Mr. Begay Perez, the man we still assumed was behind KHF. Wes told me Begay Perez was unavailable. A big Asian guy with a diamond stud in his ear showed up, addressed me as Agent White, and said it was time to leave. I tried to play dumb, using my fake name and demanding to talk to Begay Perez. But Wes said the big man would escort me to my vehicle. There was nothing else I could do. That was it."

"So you never got into the computer."

"I never even saw it. But we know from our re-mote investigation what operating system they've got. It's not in the report, but I will send it to you, too. Boring, but it could be important. Anything else, Officer?"

"Other than the guard with the truck and the big dude, did the place have much security?"

White took a moment to answer. "I didn't get a good look, but my gut says they have what they need. The big guy didn't give me time to investi-gate on the way out."

"Did you notice a new black Mercedes there? A model that looks kind of like a sports car?"

"I didn't. Unless you have more questions, it's my turn. Tell me again why the Navajo Police are interested in this."

"First of all, they are operating on our land." She mentioned the fatal collision involving the car traced to KHF, the neighbors' complaints, the threats and the dead dogs, the increase in traffic and garbage along the road, and the company's al-leged practice of hiring children too young to le-gally work, all in violation of the agreement with the Navajo Nation. She told him how the Nation's attempts to resolve the issues with KHF had been ignored. She told him about Begay Perez's rela-tives' concerns.

"We think Begay Perez is out and a man named Kelly is running the show now."

"Good to know. Where is Begay Perez? What happened?"

"I don't know."

She mentioned the call to the substation about the missing man and her hunch that his name was Dr. Zhou. "The New Mexico State Police are investigating the fatality, but last time we checked, they hadn't been able to identify the victim. And the KHF car involved in the accident hasn't surfaced either."

"If you go to the farm, be careful. You've seen that they play for keeps. Things out there are more complicated and sophisticated than they seem on the surface. Want some advice?"

"Go ahead."

"Don't take these guys lightly. Behind that black plastic is more than just a farm. I think the place is a front for a well-run, highly organized operation. Some of what's out there is hemp, but we suspect that they are producing other botanicals for the recreational use, legal or otherwise. My money is on special varieties of high-grade marijuana with some designer engineering for the black market, but we haven't intercepted enough to nail them for it."

"Did you see any labs where they could do genetic modification to refine the product or run other research?"

"I spotted some modular buildings, but I didn't have a chance to check them out before the Big Guy arrived. The property stretches back quite a distance and . . . hold on."

Then he was back. "Sorry, I've got to go. Here's my cell number, in case you think of something else." He rattled it off. "Remember, those guys have a lot to lose if that operation gets busted. If you go in there, watch your back."

White sent his report and the computer information as promised. Bernie read it twice. If the operation was as dangerous as White made it seem, he was fortunate to be alive. But she'd known more than a few people in and out of law enforcement who exaggerated. The information would be helpful if Largo approved the assignment; she wished he'd written more.

She was almost finished with her own reports when Sandra buzzed her. "When you've got a minute, the captain wants to see you. He said to tell you to finish whatever you're doing first."

She sped to the end of her writing and knocked on Largo's open door. He looked up from his monitor and motioned her to come in and sit down.

"Did you talk to Agent White?"

"Yes, sir. He didn't spend much time out there." She mentioned the photo recognition program that had identified him, and his suspicion that Begay Perez was no longer running the operation. "He said it was dangerous, but we already knew that."

"Like I said, the Navajo Nation isn't the only one interested in that operation. After I made some interagency calls today, I decided you ought to be in on those conversations. I arranged a follow-up conference call for early tomorrow."

"So, I've got the assignment?"

He nodded once. "You said you wanted a challenge."

"Thank you."

They discussed strategy and agreed that she would show up at the farm and say that she'd heard they were hiring. She would ask for a job, explaining that she had experience in farmwork, which was the truth, and also with computers—which was accurate to some extent. If anyone wondered how she knew about the KHF operation, she'd give Arnold's name, of course not mentioning that she had arrested him.

"What will you say if they ask why you want to work there?"

"I need a job to help my family. When they see my car, they'll believe it. I'll stress that I'm ready to work, and I want to start as soon as I can. Right after the interview is done."

"What if you run into someone out there who knows that you're a cop?"

Bernie didn't have to think about it. "I'll say I got fired."

"And what if they ask why?"

"How about insubordination?"

The captain raised an eyebrow. "That works for me. You have to come up with a story to tell your mother and sister. I know you stay in close touch with them several times a day, but it might be impossible to call while you are doing this job. I don't want them blowing your cover."

Bernie hadn't considered that, but it made sense.

"When you figure out your story for them—a sick friend who can't be disturbed, or maybe you just lost your cell phone—tell me so I can reinforce it. The simpler and closer to the truth, the better."

"What if I tell them I have to study for the detective test and need to focus?"

"That's good. What about Chee?"

"I'll tell him the truth. He's a cop. He knows how things work."

She tried out the studying-for-the-investigator-job story on Darleen. "I'm going to be out of touch for a while, prepping for the detective test and the interview."

"What do you mean, out of touch?"

"I'm not going to answer texts, make phone calls, send emails. Incommunicado. I'm going dark so I can concentrate."

"How long?"

"I'm not sure. As long as it takes."

"The rest of today? Twenty-four hours? A week? A month?"

"Probably only a day or two."

"Incommunicado, huh? I don't understand why you're so concerned about this. You're smart. You graduated from college, and you aced a bunch of classes for your police work. Why is this such a big deal, Sister?"

"I'm concerned about making the transition from patrol to detective. Part of the job involves going to court, you know, speaking in public? That scares the stuffing out of me." The more she told the truth, the better.

Darleen laughed. "I know you. You'll do fine. You're one tough overachieving babe."

"Thanks, I guess."

"Can I ask you a question?"

"Sure."

"So, remember how I never focused when I was in school? Studying wasn't my thing, you know."

Bernie recalled it well. She waited to hear what Darleen wanted to ask.

"I checked out Navajo Technical University, and it seems cool, but, well, do you think I'm smart enough?"

"Oh, sure."

"Really?"

"Really. You have all the brain power you need to do whatever you want."

"Thanks." She heard the grin in Darleen's voice. "Are you going to tell Mama you'll be muted?"

"Yes, but I'm not sure she'll remember. Remind her if she asks why I'm not calling, OK? I don't want her to worry about me." Bernie called Mama every day after her morning prayers.

"I'm with her now. You wanna say hello?"

"How is she?"

"Kinda tired. Me too." Darleen laughed. "Mrs. Darkwater's dog barked all night. Kept us both awake."

"I'd like to talk to her."

"I'll get her for you."

Mama sounded alert when she came on the line. "My daughter, is everything OK?"

"Yes. I'm fine. But I want you to know I have to

study for a test and some interviews in Window Rock this week, so I won't be able to telephone for a few days."

Mama seemed to be absorbing the news. "Oh. Is it long distance?"

Bernie hadn't heard that term for a while. "Yes. The police headquarters is in Arizona."

"OK." And then Mama said something unexpected. "Don't worry about your sister. I'll take care of her. You focus on your studies so you can graduate. We will talk when we can."

Bernie smiled as she put the phone down, thankful that at least for now, Mama's memory troubles worked to her advantage. Her worry had been wasted. As usual.

She drove home and called Chee, excited to share the good news of her assignment.

He answered on the first ring. "Hey, beautiful. I've been thinking about you, too."

"How's the case coming?"

He told her. "I spoke to a person who had known the dead man for a long time, and he mentioned someone who had a grudge against the one who died. And it also looks like he may have had at least one secret girlfriend."

"Any progress on the cave?"

"Not really. What's happening with you?"

She told him about her undercover assignment, and the story she'd left with Darleen and Mama.

"The captain is on board with this?"

"Yes, of course." She didn't like the question. "He's the one who suggested the undercover part. Why wouldn't he be?"

"Because it's dangerous. Because you don't know what you'll be walking into."

Chee's comment and concern surprised her. "You worry too much. Largo is setting up a conference call first thing tomorrow with the other agencies that have information on the operation. I talked to a DEA agent who gave me some tips on the phone and sent me a couple reports. I've got some heavy reading ahead tonight."

"So is there a chance the assignment could fall through?"

"I guess. I hope it doesn't."

She could almost hear him thinking over the phone. Then he exhaled. "Will you let me know what happens after the meeting tomorrow? If you can't call, just text. Sweetheart, I know this was your idea, and that it's a big step forward, but I . . ." He stopped. "Do you know how long you'll be undercover?"

"The captain wants me to do what I can in a day. Then we'll regroup. Don't worry about me."

"I'll work on it."

"I worry about you, too." She paused for a moment. "This matters a lot to me. I have to understand why that man is dead." She thought about mentioning the nightmare where she saw the murder car approach an innocent person, and how it ended with her inability to stop the driver and save the victim. But as she was considering if and what and how to share that, Chee told her he loved her and said goodbye.

13

Sunfish repeated herself. "If you want to find out why Curtis is dead, focus closer to home."

Jim Chee looked at her. "What do you mean?"

"It's a long trip from Navajo Mountain to Crimson Beach. If someone wanted to hurt Curtis, they could have found a lot of easier places." When she shook her head, her curly hair bounced with the motion. "You're the professional crime solver, but if I can do anything to help, just ask. I understand this landscape really well. I'm in love with the rocks and the water."

He thought her suggestion made sense and told her so. What she said about knowing the area gave him an idea. "Have you heard of a big cave along the lake near a beach that a boat could pull up to?"

"How large a cave?"

"Huge enough for a dozen people to be inside." Chee remembered the Lieutenant talking about the kidnapping case that had brought him to the site.

"Yes." She smiled at him. "I've been to some caves that big and heard about others."

"I might need someone with a boat to take me to one."

"I'd be happy to do that. Just ask. But it'll cost you lunch."

Chee stopped to fill Omar's gas tank and went inside the convenience store for more coffee and a bottle of water, thinking about the challenges of the trip ahead. Then he sat in the truck and called the cell phone number Doug had given him for Wanda. He heard a generic message telling him the person who owned the number had not set up voice mail. Doug had mentioned that she worked for either the tribe or her local chapter. Navajo Mountain was a small community; she should be easy to find. He'd start with the chapter house.

Chee was ready to start the drive when his phone flashed with an incoming call. Recognizing the number, he tapped accept.

Desmond didn't waste his breath on small talk. "I asked my buddies in Shiprock about you, and they say you're all right. Come up here so we can talk face-to-face. Maybe I can help you figure out why that man died." Desmond paused a few beats. "I have been thinking about the other question you asked me."

Chee knew he meant the cave. "Thank you for considering it. Where shall we meet?"

"At my house." Desmond gave him directions.

Chee turned Omar toward Navajo Mountain

and reached for his travel mug. The insulated cup had been a gift from Bernie before they married. It was his favorite, classy and functional. It felt good in his hand, and every time he held it he thought of her.

He'd use the drive to think of the best way to tell Wanda about her friend Curtis's death. Despite the many times he had done it, he never felt comfortable giving bad news to strangers. He wondered if she would be surprised.

He followed Desmond's directions and found the house with less than the expected number of U-turns and backtrackings. A gray-haired man in a blue flannel shirt came to the door as Omar pulled toward the house. He stepped outside and watched Chee park. A dusty-looking brown mutt barked, received a reprimand, and trotted up to pee on the truck's back right tire. Chee grabbed the cookies and headed toward the building.

"You must be Chee. Took you long enough. Did that beast break down on you?"

"No, sir. But it's an aged truck. He complains if I try to drive the speed limit, so I didn't want to push it too far."

"I know about age. Come on in."

A black potbelly stove with the flames visible through a window in front dominated the room. The smell of burning juniper made Chee nostalgic for his uncle Nakai and the time they had spent together as Chee learned the Blessing Way prayers. Like Desmond, his uncle kept his living space exceptionally warm.

Even though more homes now had electricity,

many elders continued to heat with woodstoves. Their relatives helped provide the fuel, and it came with a bonus, a link to the community. During the time of isolation because of Dikos Nitsaa'igii-19, volunteers delivered firewood to many elderly residents, warming their lives with both fuel and human kindness.

"Sit where you want. I like it close to the stove."

Chee selected a chair across from the old man, farthest from the heat source. Before he settled in, he gave Desmond the box with the cookies. The elder sat the treats on the table next to him and inched it toward the visitor with the back of his hand. "There, help yourself."

Chee selected a shortbread shaped like a leaf. "It's nice to meet you, sir. Doug says of all the people here who knew him and his brother back in the day, you probably were the closest to them." He assumed that Desmond followed the custom of not saying the names of the dead. "I appreciate you speaking with me."

The older man took an oatmeal cookie from the box. "Some coffee would be good with this."

"Would you like some?"

"I would, but I didn't make any."

"I could do that."

The older man nodded. "I would enjoy that, but the can is empty."

Desmond took a bite of the cookie and chewed it thoughtfully. "I have been remembering that Walker family. Doug, the older son, and his mother got along, maybe because they were more alike. Those two always had to be moving, you know, doing things. The younger one, well, he was different. Quiet, sensitive, hard to read. He liked to come over here with me. I taught him to carve a little—he had the sensibility of an artist. And I helped him learn how to speak some Navajo."

Chee looked at Desmond's strong brown hands, sturdy nails trimmed short. He noticed that the right thumbnail had ridges and a purple bruise at the nail base. It looked like it must have hurt. They'd been speaking in English, but Desmond continued in Navajo.

"When the boy became a teenager, he made some friends who helped him get in trouble, but underneath all that, he was still a good boy. That was one of the reasons Doug decided to move away after that accident that killed their mother. You know about that?"

"No, sir."

"She died in a car wreck. Doug had graduated from high school a few years before . . . I think he was twenty then, and had a job at the lake. His brother was still in school. Anyway, they lived here together for a few more years. Then Doug started that tour business and found a place to live closer to Antelope Canyon. When they left here, and he put his brother to work that summer, it made a big difference."

Chee pictured Curtis as a motherless young teenager living in a different environment, and probably working hard in Doug's new business. "I'm supposing that Doug's decision to start fresh in a new place had something to do with wanting to move his brother away from those kids you mentioned."

Desmond broke his cookie into two pieces, looked at them, and put the smaller one in his mouth. He chewed slowly and then spoke. "Doug is a good man. His brother left those friends behind when they moved."

Chee thought about that. "Did Doug's brother have a girlfriend?"

"There was a girl he liked. She went into the service. The marines. That was that. She died not long ago."

"You mentioned a man named Chill earlier. Was he one of the wild boys Doug's brother ran with up here?"

"No." Desmond broke the remaining piece of cookie in half again. Chee waited while he chewed and swallowed.

"Sir, you mentioned that Chill and the man who died had their differences, and that they had made peace. How do you know that?"

Desmond smiled at the question. "I know because I brought them together. I heard Chill's anger, and then, after some time, they spoke to each other with the clarity of *k'é*. I saw them embrace."

"I'm still curious about the wild boys. I wonder if one of them had an old grudge that could have led to violence."

"No. Trust me on this. The dead man lived here as a young teenager, a long time ago. Some of those boys he ran with grew up, got their heads on straight. Some died. Some, like the girl, left here for the service or a job and never came back."

Desmond looked at his hands.

"I did what I could to help Doug's brother after they moved away. He would come up to see me once in a while; I would go to see him and Doug. Then Dr. Pete came into his life. Things shifted toward the light." The older man leaned back in his chair. "Do you know about Dr. Pete?"

"I have met him."

"Well, then you know that Dr. Pete has fire in his belly. He wants everyone who has ever heard of the lake to understand that it is more than just a playground for people in houseboats. He wants people to understand that this old, sacred land deserves our respect. I think that man must be part Diné. He spoke at schools, at churches, at the Fourth of July and the rodeo. He could talk!

"Anyway, a spark from Dr. Pete's fire lit inside the boy. Dr. Pete started some volunteer programs to help kids understand archaeology, and Doug's brother signed up. The boy couldn't get enough. He even made friends with Paul Hendrix, Dr. Pete's son." Desmond paused, studying the front of the woodstove. "Sergeant, you asked me to tell you what I could about the man, my young friend, who died. That's his story."

"Sir, I am wondering if the visits back here led in some way to the man's death. Why did he begin to come to Navajo Mountain again?"

Chee waited, watching Desmond break his remaining piece of cookie into several smaller bites. The old man smiled.

"You are sounding like a detective now. The one who died and I shared a secret." The old man picked up the largest piece of the broken cookie and studied it, then placed it in his mouth as carefully as if it were sacred corn pollen. "Now that he is gone, I hold that secret."

Chee's curiosity struggled with his sense of decorum. He knew Desmond would say what he wanted to say without prompting and when he was ready, but the investigator in him wanted to scream *Get on with it!*

Desmond chewed carefully and swallowed, then closed his eyes.

"Sir, I would like to talk to Chill about the one who died. Even though you saw them make peace, I have worked with enough angry people to realize that peace doesn't always last."

"I understand." Desmond opened his eyes. "You mentioned a cave. The cave you asked about, it has its secrets. Tell me again why you want to know about that."

Chee recounted the story he had told Desmond on the phone, the story of Joe Leaphorn discovering the trove of sand paintings as he worked a case as a young policeman. This time, he added as many details as he could remember about the place itself and what Leaphorn had seen.

"My colleague believed that he had stumbled upon a treasury of our ancestors' heritage. He described the collection as a library of the Diné world of spirit. He told our historical preservation leaders about it, and he heard that some medicine people came to look at the dry paintings in the cave. The years have gone by, and he wonders if what he saw survived the rising of the lake. He wonders if the paintings still exist, or if that legacy of stories about the Holy People has been preserved. I told him I would do everything I could to find the cave. That's all I have to say."

"You said you had some training as a *hataɫii*. Why did you abandon that?"

The question caught Chee off guard. An unexpected flood of emotion rose inside him. In the split second before habit built its wall of self-protection, he attempted an answer.

"My teacher was Hosteen Frank Sam Nakai, my uncle. He died before I could learn many of the healing rituals. I needed a new teacher, but I had fallen in love, and I realized that I could not be a husband, a policeman, and a singer, and do justice to any of those. I made a choice."

Desmond nodded, not so much in agreement, Chee thought, as in understanding. "Jim Chee, you have the opportunity to do many things with your life, or to decline to do them. To make many choices. Why did this choice bring you here today?"

Chee took time to think about the answer, appreciating the silence Desmond left.

"Grandfather, I came in part as a favor to my mentor and in part as a favor to myself. I came because my wife could have died a few weeks ago at the hands of an evil woman, and now she's ready for a change that would take her career in a new direction, perhaps away from me." As he spoke, he felt unsummoned tears rise in his eyes, and he let them. "I came because I have loved police work for a long time, but I wonder if I am ready for something new. I came to say a prayer at Tsé'naa Na'ní'áhí, to look for the cave, and think about what might be next for me, for my job and for my relationship with the woman I treasure."

Chee took a breath, thought he had more to say, but realized he had said it all.

Desmond raised a finger. "But instead of doing what you came to do, you are helping us understand why a good man is dead."

"Sir, what happened to Doug's brother and why it happened bothers me, like a sliver under my thumbnail."

"The death of this good man is like a stone in still water. The ripples stretch. Many people feel the loss in many ways. I am sitting in deep sadness." Desmond studied the stove, then spoke again. "There is more to the story of the man you found dead, and there is more to the story of the cave, and there is more to your story, too."

The room fell into comfortable silence. Chee was glad he had made the trip.

"Doug said his brother had been visiting you more often, and that he also saw a woman here. Wanda. He didn't know much about her and has never met her, but he suspected that his brother might have loved her. I would like to talk to her."

The old man nodded. "What Doug said is true. Wanda Nakai was becoming an important part of that man's life." Desmond leaned toward the table and picked up a pen and his pad of paper. He wrote something and handed it to Chee.

Desmond closed his eyes again. "After I rest, I will call Chill and tell him to come here so you can speak to him. In the meantime, talk to Wanda. Be gentle when you tell her of the dead man."

The slip of paper was a phone number. Chee called it and got a recorded message in Diné Bizaad telling him no one was available to answer his call to the Navajo Mountain chapter house. Instead of leaving a message for Wanda, he drove there.

On the way, his phone chimed with a text. After he parked, he read it. The message was short and important.

Autopsy results back on Curtis Walker. Proceed with murder investigation. Details to come.

He wanted the details, but the news confirmed what his intuition had told him. And in terms of the questions he planned to ask, really nothing had changed.

A young woman was energetically sweeping the chapter house porch. She looked up as he rolled down Omar's window.

"That must be an endless job."

"I don't mind. I like to stay busy. May I help you, sir?"

"I'm trying to find a person named Wanda Nakai."

"You're in luck. That's me."

Chee turned off the engine and climbed out of the truck. Wanda looked considerably younger than he'd expected, maybe in her late teens. She had onyx eyes and lovely clear skin, with a dim-ple in her chin. No wonder Curtis was attracted to her.

He'd thought about how to say what came next, but that didn't make it easier.

"I'm Sergeant Jim Chee. I have some bad news about a man you know, Curtis Walker."

"Bad news?"

"I regret to tell you that his body was found in Lake Powell. I'm working with the police on the investigation."

"Body? You mean he's dead?" He watched her joy drain away. She stood in stunned silence.

"I'd like to talk to you about him for a moment, as part of the case."

Her eyebrows rose.

"Is there a place we can sit for a moment?"

"Ah, yeah. Sure. OK." She opened the door, and Chee followed her into a large room, noticing the slump in her posture. She motioned him toward a well-worn couch against the north wall, the direction for death. Was it a coincidence, he wondered, or did this young one understand something of the old ways?

He sat a respectful distance away from her. Although he wanted to ask her directly about her relationship with Curtis, and whether she knew anyone who might try to harm him, he started with a safe question.

"Tell me the story of you and the one who died. How did you know each other?"

"Curtis came here looking for me, kind of like you. It was late in the spring. I'd just graduated from high school, and I felt so lucky to get this job, full-time and everything. He came in and asked for me. I'm glad I was here that day."

Chee noticed that unlike traditional Navajos, she had no hesitation in speaking the name of the dead man. Her story surprised him. "Why did he ask for you?"

"He said he had been a friend of my mom's. He told me he was sorry she had passed, and that he would have come sooner to pay his respects, but he had just learned the news. He told me he hated to bother me at work, but he didn't have my phone number."

"Did he tell you how he knew your mom?"

"He said they went to school together. When we got to know each other, he showed me the yearbook with their pictures, and he said that I reminded him a lot of her. Curtis told me some stories about her that, I don't know, made me happy."

"What was he like?"

"Nice. Quiet. Sincere." She stopped. "Kind. Generous. Funny, when I got to know him. I really enjoyed being with him."

"I'm sorry to give you such sad news."

She sighed. "Somebody had to. How did he fall into the lake?"

"We're not sure exactly what happened. That's why I came to ask questions."

When she shook her head, her long hair moved like a shiny dark curtain. "Curtis said that not knowing how to swim was one of his big regrets. He told me I should take swimming when I get to college next fall, and get credit for learning something that could save my life. It was one of the few times he gave me advice."

"How long have you two known each other?"

"About six months. It's funny, Curtis said he felt as though he had known me my whole life."

"When are you starting college?"

"I planned to start in January, because Curtis offered to help pay for it. I don't know now." She looked down a moment, then sat straighter. "He always told me how strong I am, how good I am at solving problems. He was like the cool dad I always wanted."

Chee thought of Desmond's image of the rock with the ripples. Whoever was responsible for Curtis's death had probably not considered the losses left behind and what happens to those in the tragedy's wake, people like Wanda, Doug and his boys, Ramona, Pete and Paul, and even Sunfish.

He shifted a little on the couch. "Besides you, did he know other people up here?"

"He only mentioned Mr. Desmond Grayhair, an elder who had been a friend of his family back in the day. He would visit with him when he came to see me."

"Wanda, did Curtis ever mention anything or anybody that frightened him?"

"Well, yeah. A guy I know flattened his tires, but they worked it out. The only thing he ever talked about that bothered him was drowning. And now that happened. Oh gosh. How awful."

He saw her tears. "Young lady, I didn't say he drowned. I said his body was found in the lake, and law enforcement is investigating."

She looked startled. "What, what do you mean?"

"I mean, we don't know for sure why he died. I gather that Curtis wasn't your boyfriend."

Her eyes widened. "Boyfriend? No. Chill, Brian Chinchili, is kinda like my boyfriend, when he's not working or riding his mountain bike." She shook her head. "No," she said again, more forcefully. "Curtis was a friend of my dead mom. Curtis was old. You're creeping me out."

The dead man was younger than he was, and Chee didn't consider himself old.

He held out his hands, palms toward the young woman. "I didn't mean to upset you. It's my job to ask questions. In addition to Chill, did Curtis ever mention anyone he didn't get along with or, you know, complain about people?"

She thought about it. "Yeah, a few times. One day he said that he thought an old friend was jealous of him. Sometimes Doug, that's his brother, got bossy. He'd tell me about that, but it was just family stuff."

She paused. "And the man he worked for at the marina gave him grief once in a while. He told me that guy wasn't very nice."

Chee took out a business card, using his pen to scratch off his Shiprock office number while he spoke. "I'm working with the National Park Service and the sheriff's office to find out what happened to your friend. You can call this, my cell number, if you need to. Or call the Shiprock office and they'll get a message to me."

She looked at his card. "Shiprock. Isn't that where Navajo Technical School is?"

"That's right."

"And Diné College?"

"We have a branch, but the main campus is in Tsaile."

She put the card in her pocket. "Thanks for telling me about Curtis. He was a really good guy. I know it's hard to give people bad news."

As he walked back to Omar, Chee considered the relationship between Wanda and Curtis. The young woman was attractive and focused, but just out of high school; Curtis was at least in his thirties. Wanda's denial of romantic interest rang with sincerity, but perhaps the lack of attraction hadn't been true for Curtis. He'd known men with a preference for women half their age. And with some, the thrill of the chase intensified if the object of their desire spurned their advances. The fact that this beautiful girl reminded him of his old high school friend may have enhanced her appeal.

And Chill's aggressive behavior raised more questions.

An interesting conversation, he concluded, that might have brought him closer to learning why Curtis was dead. Or might have been a waste of time.

14

Bernadette Manuelito got up in the dark. She had gone to bed exhausted and excited about the next day's challenge. She'd fallen asleep quickly and dreamed the same bad dream she had the previous night, except this time the victim she couldn't save from the speeding car resembled Jim Chee.

After making a cup of tea, she sat quietly, reexamining the events of the previous workday. Then she thought of Chee. She missed his company, and while she knew his concern for her safety came from a place of love, it still frustrated her that he was meddling in her work. The pessimist in her remembered the conversation with Mama; her mother had been too agreeable to her period of silence. But her inner optimist said, *Be thankful, go back to sleep, and trust Darleen to handle whatever comes up.* Finally, tired of arguing with herself, she had returned to bed and fallen asleep. This time she dreamed of her handsome husband, the beauty of Antelope Canyon, and photographs she had seen of graceful, holy Tsé'naa Na'ní'áhí, the stone bridge shaped like a hope-affirming rainbow.

She awoke again earlier than usual and ran in the dim predawn light. Bernie prayed with extra concentration, then dressed for her assignment in her snuggest jeans, an orange tank top, and a denim shirt she could leave unbuttoned. Instead of a ponytail, she wore her hair loose and put on some large hoop earrings. She left her makeup on the counter to remind herself that she needed to look like a down-and-out woman in search of a job, and not a cop.

Then she read through Agent White's reports and discovered something interesting. The man he'd referred to as Wes on the phone, he'd called Les in the reports. She wondered if this could be the same Lester Nez whose phone was used for the call about the missing brother. She appreciated the warning White had given her about the facial recognition software. She would pick up some face putty at the station.

Her house phone rang as she was leaving. She let it go to message and heard Mama asking if her eldest daughter had forgotten to call. She made a note to talk to Mama later and remind her again that she'd be out of touch for a day or two.

She arrived at the station long before the phone meeting. Sandra's truck was already in the parking lot. Her friend had been working extra shifts.

"Bernie, you're here early. What's going on?"

"Oh, the captain asked me to come for a phone meeting."

"And then you're off, or what?" Sandra grinned. "Nice outfit. No uniform."

"I've got to study for the detective exam." That was true, Bernie thought, even though it didn't mesh with her plans for the day.

"I heard about that. Good luck." Sandra had dark circles under her eyes, and Bernie noticed that she wasn't wearing the silver and turquoise bracelet she usually had on. Normally, this woman vibrated with energy. Today she seemed lackluster, moving at half speed, as she had been ever since she came back from a brief unscheduled vacation.

"You look like you could use some caffeine and I could, too. Is there coffee?"

"I'm making coffee now." Sandra's voice had a bite to it. "Come on back in a few minutes and . . ." She stopped and Bernie saw the start of tears. "And . . . thanks for not bugging me to tell you what's going on."

"Some secrets are too heavy for one person to carry. I have strong shoulders."

Sandra offered a subtle shake of her head.

Bernie jotted down questions to ask the other agency people about KHF during the phone call and started a column of details to discuss with the captain. She worked until a familiar, enticing aroma drew her away. Sandra stood at the coffee maker, adding sugar to her mug as she waited for the last of the drips to reach the pot.

She gave Bernie the hint of a smile. "How did you enjoy your time off?"

"We all had fun at Antelope Canyon. After I left, Chee hiked to Rainbow Bridge."

Bernie poured some coffee for Sandra on top of the bed of sugar and gave herself some coffee, too.

"I heard that Chee found a man who died out there." Sandra put a spoon in her cup and stirred. "The investigators are lucky to have him. And even though he's working, it's good to be someplace different."

"I miss my husband, but having him gone makes it easier to focus on studying for the detective test. The timing is good." Bernie wondered if Sandra went "someplace different" those days she was mysteriously absent from work. Wherever her friend had been, it wasn't on vacation. Sandra looked more troubled than ever.

Through the back windows, Bernie saw Captain Largo's SUV pull into the lot.

Sandra glanced that way, too. "If you get that promotion, will you still work from Shiprock?"

"I guess it depends on what cases I'm looking into."

"The Nation's a big place. Good thing you like to drive."

A few minutes later, Largo joined them, filled his mug with coffee, and turned to Bernie. "Come to my office. We need to talk before the phone meeting."

She followed him. Largo closed the door behind them.

"Did you know that Chee called me this morning?"

"No, sir." She felt a hot wave of anger and raised her voice. "If he asked you to pull me off the assignment, I hope you said no."

"Manuelito, get real. He just wanted to make sure backup would be available in case things go south. But so you know, this assignment isn't a go until after the conference call. I don't want you, or any of my people, at serious risk. We need all the facts from every angle."

Her lapse into emotion embarrassed her. "Did Chee say much about his Lake Powell case?

"A little." Largo filled her in. "It looks like he'll be tied up another day or two out there. By then, you should be back on regular duty."

Largo glanced at the time. "Any questions before we start the meeting?"

"Yeah. How did those scumbags get a foothold out here on our turf to grow cannabis?"

"That's an interesting story. The council, the executive branch, and the ag board all debated the pros and cons of hemp for months, and while they were talking, these guys found a hole in the fence and climbed through. Anything else?"

"Besides the FBI, Homeland Security, and the DEA, who else is interested in the cannabis operation?"

"A whole cast of characters." Largo tapped them off with his fingers. "The New Mexico attorney general's office. The San Juan County Sheriff's Office. ICE, because of the immigrants rumored to work there. And maybe even the Bureau of Indian Affairs."

"Wow." She hadn't expected such a long list.

"I'm anticipating conditions for workers at the farm to be grim. If you're out there, expect to see some bad stuff."

Bernie nodded, recalling the terror in the hitchhiker's eyes, the same look she had seen with victims who'd been kidnapped and sex trafficked.

Largo said, "Those entities are involved, but today, it's us, DEA, FBI, and someone from Homeland Security." He looked at the computer. "Are you ready for the session?"

"More than ready. Let's do it."

Largo initiated the video conference call. The DEA representative, a pale, thin man named Patricio Worthman, came on, followed by Sage Johnson from the FBI, and then Bob Jimenez, the mustached representative from Homeland Security. Bernie knew Agent Johnson and jotted down the other names.

Largo introduced her to the group, encouraging her to move closer to the computer's camera. "Officer Bernadette Manuelito has volunteered to go undercover to help investigate a suspected homicide. She has some questions for you."

Largo gave her a look that said "go ahead."

"Captain Largo filled me in on the K'é Hemp Farm operation from the Navajo Nation's perspective. I'd like you each to tell me what your agency knows that I should be aware of. And if there's something I can assist you with, tell me now."

"I'll go first. The DEA's connection is obvious." Worthman looked and sounded like a person who would rather be doing something else. "As you know, these big producers like isolated spots for their operations. The Navajo Nation was perfect, and the distances have made it harder for us to do our job. We believe that the marijuana grown out there ends up in Kansas, Wyoming, Idaho—states where it's still not legal—but we don't know for sure. We've heard that they also grow extra-high-octane weed for special markets, and we could use verification on that." He cleared his throat. "As you may have heard, our agent failed when he tried going undercover there."

Bernie absorbed the words *tried* and *failed*. She didn't want that ever said about her. "What happened?"

"Long story short, he raised too many questions."

"Tell me the long story."

She noticed that someone entered Worthman's office, placed something on a table behind the man, and left again. "Officer, are you Native American?"

"Yes. I'm Navajo."

"Our agent tried going undercover as a computer expert. The man who interviewed him got suspicious and said something to him in code about Yahtzee and tea. Our guy didn't know the correct response."

Bernie heard the captain stifle a laugh. "Could it have been *yá'át'ééh*?"

"Whatever. What does that mean?"

"It's 'hello' in Navajo."

At the bottom of the screen, she noticed a message in the chat box and clicked on it. From Agent Johnson: Do you think the agent really failed the test? Or did the screener decide the guy was just too rude to work there?

"We were in the process of finding someone else to go in there when Captain Largo told me that you'd volunteered. Whatever you can learn about how the products get from the farm to the distributors, we'll welcome. That's it from me." Worthman turned off his video, his picture replaced with the U.S. Department of Justice Drug Enforcement Administration logo.

Jimenez had an office with a window that cast light on him and the bookcase behind him. He looked at the screen instead of directly at the camera when he spoke, so his eyes seemed half shut. He explained that Homeland Security's involvement grew from evidence that KHF had ties to violent gangs in Los Angeles. Their investigation had turned up several names, but none that matched law enforcement records. "We know these guys are vicious and cagey, but we haven't yet linked the operation to any known players, at least not convincingly. We're hoping you can get some names. Photos would be great. It smells like they've violated immigration law as well as the labor standards you guys are aware of."

"Do the Chinese workers come willingly?" Bernie remembered the dead man and the terrified voice on the phone.

"Some do. Some probably not. They seem to be a mix of legal and illegal immigrants. Our contacts in Los Angeles report that recruiters provide their transportation to the Navajo Reservation and promise them housing and all the paid work they want. But when they get there, we hear that they're treated like pond scum, and they don't have a way to get home." He tented his hands beneath his chin. "That's all I have for now."

Agent Johnson jumped on the call. Her office looked so neat that Bernie wondered if she was using a canned backdrop. "The FBI got involved because of claims of kidnapping by the families of some of those Chinese workers, but we haven't been able to substantiate the charges because we haven't located the victims. We believe some of these missing persons are laborers at the Navajo farm, but we don't know for sure. The families told our agents that their loved ones had recently lost their jobs at another agricultural plant. Many of them spoke little or no English. The families believed that, if they weren't actually kidnapped, they had been lured into working at the marijuana farm with false promises."

Bernie noticed that Johnson called the enterprise a marijuana farm, not a hemp operation.

Agent Johnson leaned into the camera on her desk top for emphasis. "With the help of these families, our Southern California office eventually traced some calls to the Navajo Nation and then to KHF. But none of the families heard from the missing persons after they made that call." She frowned. "I understand that the man killed on the highway hasn't yet been identified, but we think the circumstances of the death, as Officer Manuelito described, point to his involvement with the marijuana enterprise."

Worthman turned on his video again and seemed to be talking.

"You're still muted." Largo motioned to the bottom of the screen. "Turn on the microphone."

Worthman complied. "Give me some background here, Officer Manuelito. Is marijuana legal out there on the . . . on Navajo land?"

"We call it the Navajo Nation." She was glad he hadn't said "reservation" like Jimenez. "And no, it's not. The operation has approval for hemp, and that's part of what's happening at the farm."

Largo spoke. "The request to launch the hemp farm came from a well-connected and respected tribal member, a man named Dino Begay Perez. He obtained permits for water use, but now the farm seems to be using considerably more water than its allowance. Water is scarce out here. We're looking into that as a way to shut them down, but it's complicated."

Bernie wondered if people who lived where rainfall exceeded the Navajo Nation's average of ten inches a year could appreciate how moisture was worth fighting for. The saying "Water is life" rang true for most of the Southwest.

Worthman said, "We also hear rumors that there are going to be some tribal labor complaints against the operation in addition to what ICE may be working on."

Largo nodded. "The Navajo workers—and there's probably some Utes and Pueblo people, and maybe some white guys—all of those are paid as day laborers. The operators have to hire Navajos because of the agreement with the Navajo Nation. Workers may get a choice of cash or weed—or some of each—and that management

encourages them to work for drugs. Tribal prose-
cutors will bring a case for labor law violations as
soon as they can get solid information. The farming takes place in an isolated area. The operators
have scared most of the neighbors out there from
complaining."

Bernie remembered the woman whose dogs
were killed.

Jimenez spoke. "We understand that the Navajo man who applied to run the farm—Mr. Begay Perez—is no longer actively involved in the
operation. Can you verify that?"

Bernie spoke. "Not yet, but my calls to him
have gone unanswered, and his relatives can't
reach him either. One of my goals is to talk to
him about this mess. When I spoke to DEA agent
Russ Bright White, he had some evidence that
Begay Perez was out, and that a man named Kelly
ran the show."

Jimenez said, "We'd appreciate substantiation
and names of the other big fish, as high up the
food chain as you can trace them. I'm sending an
encrypted file with what we learned about Kelly."

Johnson said, "Bobby, cut the encrypted crap.
Give us the short version. Let's get on with this."

Bernie saw his shoulders tighten on the video
screen. "OK. Kelly has links to a dangerous mul-
tinational operation with a base in Los Angeles.
Running a business on the Navajo Nation with
water and labor violations seems to be his first
major misstep. The parent company follows the
same pattern of cheap labor and broken business
promises with clandestine operations across the

globe. We are picking up rumors that KHF hopes to expand to a custom line of high-grade designer marijuana and other cannabis products." They saw him roll his shoulders. "We're grateful to the Navajo Nation for their professionalism. I know you have your own challenges without this mess in your backyard."

The backyard, Bernie thought, was sixteen million acres populated by more livestock and wildlife than people. And some cannabis, along with bootleg liquor, went with the territory. But nothing on this scale.

"If this is part of an international drug operation," Largo said, "I guess these guys didn't understand that the Nation is sovereign and makes its own laws. They underestimated us. We don't appreciate exploitation."

Worthman spoke. "Before we end this, we need to talk about the bust."

Largo's voice rose in surprise. "What bust?"

"Don't get your shorts in a knot, Captain." Worthman laughed. "It's still tentative, in the planning stages. You guys will be invited to be a big part of this."

Johnson took charge. "Captain, besides the increasing violence that the highway death speaks of, there's another reason to move on this. We hear a big shipment leaves this week. We need to make sure the drugs are there when we do the bust."

Jimenez's phone rang, and he muted the mike.

"So how long do I have to get in and out of there before something goes down?" Bernie asked.

"We don't have anything on the immediate horizon," Worthman said. "Don't worry. You'll have all the time you need."

Largo frowned. Bernie knew what he thought. "Don't worry" always preceded something grim on the horizon. It was code for *Pay attention and watch out*.

"I won't put Officer Manuelito at risk if a raid is in the works," Largo said. "Especially with the shipment about to leave. Everyone out there will be on edge."

"Captain, the details are still influx," Johnson said, "and some of what happens depends on what Officer Manuelito discovers. Everyone on this call will get all the information necessary when the time comes. And, Bernie, you don't need to worry. I'm sure—"

"That's right," Worthman cut in. "This is the end of harvest season. Everyone at the farm will be working hard, distracted by getting the job done. Manuelito can ask questions without stirring up too much suspicion. Her timing is perfect."

Later those words would come back to haunt Bernie.

"Officer Manuclito," Johnson said, "when will you start the assignment?"

"I hope as soon as we're done with this call."

"I'm done. Good luck, Bernie."

"Yeah. Be careful out there," Jimenez said. They both left the meeting.

Worthman added, "Thanks in advance for the information, and stay safe."

After that, Largo printed the file from the

DEA summarizing their involvement in the case. He gave Bernie the pages, knowing that she liked to read important documents that way, then reached into a lower desk drawer, pulled out a black iPhone, and handed that to her, too.

Bernie glanced at the report, then turned on the phone and looked at the screen. She scowled. "What's this for?"

Largo said, "You'll contact me only on that phone, on the number programmed for Howard. It has a good camera, an excellent microphone for recording conversations, and plenty of battery life. Program it to open with a finger scan, not a password."

She moved to settings and arranged it to respond to her right thumb.

They devised a plan for her to safely call or text, including a special word: *shimá*. If she mentioned her mother, the captain or whoever monitored her communication would realize that she was in danger. Bernie never knowingly walked into a perilous situation without her weapon, but this assignment was different. After what Agent White said, she expected to be searched, and her police-issued gun would mark her as a cop; any other gun, according to his narrative, would have to be locked in her vehicle or confiscated.

"Manuelito, keep your head down, your eyes and ears open, and your mouth closed as much as possible. Trust your instincts and remember your training. And get out of there as soon as you can."

"Yes, sir."

"One more thing." He reached into a desk drawer and handed her a small white case.

"What's this?"

"Your going-away present. Inside are special glasses that will distort your eyes and ought to help you skirt the facial recognition software. They'll make things a bit fuzzy, but wear them as much as you can, especially until you're sure you're hired. There's also some material to create fake scars and some spray-on color. You've got the facial putty already. Use everything. I want you back here safely."

Bernie left Largo's office with feuding emotions. The assignment and the chance to set things right for the dead man made her proud, although Mama had always warned her about that. And, she had to admit, she felt some apprehension about what came next. Good nerves, she told herself; they'd sharpen her reflexes and make her more careful.

She ran into Sandra on the way out.

"How was your meeting?"

"Fine. I'm glad it's over."

"Are you going home?"

"Yes." It was true. She had to get her disguise in place and leave her personal cell phone there. And she needed to call Mama before heading to KHF.

"Good luck with everything. You seem kind of nervous."

"I guess I am. What's coming up is a big deal."

She left with the going-away present, glad that Sandra had not noticed the white case and

she hadn't had to fib. Lying didn't come naturally
to her. She planned to follow Largo's advice and
keep her mouth shut.

She drove home and made the call to her mother
the first order of business. It took her *shimá* longer
than usual to answer.

"Hi, Mama. Hope your day is off to a good
start."

"Daughter? I thought you didn't want to talk to
me. That's what your sister said."

"I have to stay really focused for the next few
days. I needed to wish you a happy morning before I dove into that."

"Come here and stay with me. I'll cook for you
while you study. No problems."

"Thank you, but I can't do that."

"Well, I hope it all goes well for you, my daughter. But what about that man you take care of?
Who will take care of him?"

The comment caught her off guard. Jim Chee
took care of himself. "Are you talking about my
husband?"

"Husband?" She heard anger in her mother's
voice. "My daughter, how could you get married
and not even tell me?"

Bernie took a calming breath. "Mama, this is
Bernie. My sister is the one who was taking care
of that elderly man."

"Bernie? You said you couldn't talk to me because of your police work. Are you playing a joke
now?"

"No, Mama. I'm sorry I confused you. Is my
sister there?"

"No. She drove off somewhere. I think to be with that one she likes." Bernie knew Mama meant Slim. "Did you talk to her about that man?"

"No, I haven't."

"When will you do that?"

"I don't know."

"My daughter, you are a disappointment to me." The anger in Mama's voice came over the phone like an electric shock. And then Mama hung up.

Bernie collected her emotions and called Mama's neighbor, Mrs. Darkwater. The call went to voice mail.

"Hi, this is Bernie. I just spoke to Mama, and she seems upset and confused this morning. I'm going to be out of reach for a day or two. Darleen will be there, but I'd appreciate it if you'd keep an eye on Mama for me, too. Thank you."

Then, with Mama's confusion and Darleen's absence weighing on her mind, she made the preparations for the assignment. She slipped her own cell phone into a drawer and experimented with the special phone Largo had given her, snapping some photos and recording her voice. The captain was right. The camera had a good lens and a high-quality optics for both close-up and distance pictures. The record feature was easy to use. She practiced turning it on and off without looking, pleased that she quickly mastered the skill.

Then she put some food for the road, a book, and a change of clothes in her backpack, filled her water bottle, and headed into the bathroom to work on her disguise, including a long scar on her right cheek. Satisfied, she put the glasses and her new phone in the backpack and set off.

The drive gave her time to think; she did some of her best thinking when she drove. Unlike the Lakota, she didn't need a fancy reason to go to the farm. She'd present herself as a down-and-out gal on a desperate search for a job. Once she got behind the fence, she would find Lester Nez, look for the mystery man who made the call, track down the elusive Mr. Begay Perez, discover who drove the black Mercedes involved in the wreck—and get to the bottom of the neighbors' problems, including the dead dogs. The list of tasks challenged her; all she needed was time and a dash or two of good luck.

The questions Agent Johnson and the others had raised during the call might get her attention, too, but not at the cost of her own assignment. The captain had been clear on that. "Manuelito, you work for me, not them," he'd said. "If you can help them, too, go for it, but remember—your main job is to get out of there unscathed."

Bernie drove to the farm without hesitating, even though she'd never been there, because the operation had stirred so much controversy. She thought it was deceitful that Begay Perez had sold the project to the powers that be in tribal government based on the fact that hemp used less water than the crops it would replace, that the product would be refined to produce natural medicine, and that Navajo workers had priority in hiring. But he hadn't acknowledged that, because of the greenhouses, his growing season would be longer and the number of plants involved higher, so actually the water use would be the same or possibly greater.

She cruised down the paved highway for a while, then turned onto a gravel road. The route gradually became dirt that, she noticed, had been graded. The road climbed, and in the distance she could see grayish oblong domes she recognized as plastic-covered greenhouses. Beyond them she saw rows of oblong boxes. Modular buildings, she realized. Perhaps this was housing for the workers that the neighbors had talked about, or laboratory and office space for scientists working with cannabis genetics.

Her old Tercel left a fantail of dust in its wake as she bumped down the final few miles, past No Trespassing signs at regular intervals and a Dead End warning. She wondered how much swearing went on inside the truck cabs as the delivery van drivers negotiated this route in their rigs. As the road deteriorated, she decided that pickups must handle this part of the job, rendezvousing with the larger guys on the paved highway to unload their stash and send it to the big markets.

Up ahead, on the posts of the barbed wire fence, she noticed the small green-and-white signs with pictures of surveillance cameras that ran beside the road. She pulled onto the shoulder and checked her disguise in the mirror, putting on the glasses Largo had given her. She admired the colorful pink stripe in her hair and the fake heart tattoo on her arm and adjusted her removable eyebrow ring. In another few minutes, the barbed wire gave way to ten-foot-high chain-link fencing, shielded with black plastic on the inside.

A Ram 1500 blocked the road ahead, and she stopped. A young Navajo man climbed out of the truck and walked to her car. She spotted his gun on his hip. She turned on the phone to record.

"Help you, miss?"

"I'm looking for a job. I heard that the farm is hiring."

"Could be. A job doing what?"

She shrugged. "Whatever, man. I heard these guys pay in cash, and I need to work."

"What's your name?"

She gave him the name she and Largo agreed on. "Bernadine Blackman."

"Have you done farmwork before?"

"Yeah, for my . . ." She almost said *shimá*, her safe word. "For my *shichei*, you know, my grandpa. I worked with the corn and the irrigation. I'm strong, and I like to work."

"Where are you from?"

She shrugged again. "The rez, here and there. Are you the guy who hires people?"

"Me? Not at all."

"Can I talk to someone about getting a job here, dude? I drove all the way out from Shiprock. I need money for gas and rent and maybe . . ." She put her thumb and forefinger together, brought them to her lips, and inhaled.

"Hold on, sister." He laughed. "They want me to screen folks in case they're narcs or something. I gotta do this." He fiddled with his telephone, then walked to the back of her car. She was glad

Largo had told her to switch the license plates with an abandoned vehicle they had impounded. The search of that expired plate would lead to a dead person also named Blackman. While the guard was behind her car, she took some quick photos of her own and then returned the phone to her lap.

"OK. I'll call and let them know someone's coming." The guard stood closer and held the phone to his face, not only for the call but, she assumed, for a picture of her. She realized she'd forgotten to put on the distortion glasses, so she closed her eyes and kept them shut until he spoke to her.

"Drive ahead and then turn left. You'll see some vehicles. Park there and then walk to the shed with the red roof. That's the office. Talk to Lester."

"I'll do it. *Ahéhee'*."

"Good luck."

She followed instructions but slipped out the phone, took photos of the entrance area, and shipped them off to "Howard." She parked her Tercel between two pickups, where she couldn't see the surveillance camera. She said a quick prayer, then grabbed her backpack, opened the door, and climbed out to discover what she could learn that might give some meaning to a stranger's violent death.

15

Jim Chee left the Navajo Mountain chapter house, his conversation with Wanda still on his mind. He needed to contact Desmond and make sure Chill was there before he went back to the old man's place. But first, he sat in Omar and sent a quick text to Bernie.

> Sweetheart, thinking of you. I know you are being careful. Hope you are safe.

He closed it with a heart.

He waited a few moments for her response. When he didn't see it, he told himself she was busy, and called Desmond.

The old man got right to the point. "Chill is doing a job in Page today, but he said for you to call or text him." Desmond recited the number, speaking slowly. "I gave him your number, too. I figured that would make it easier for the two of you to get in touch."

"Thank you. Where does he work?"

"He's with a company called Community Construction. An electrician. A good one, too."

"I appreciate your help with this. I'm sorry that your friend's death was the reason we met. Take care of yourself." Chee thought about mentioning the cave, but he didn't.

"Jim Chee, you know that everyone dies. Usually, news of death concerns us old ones. When you solve the mystery of that body you found and rest in a calmer place with the woman you love, come back to visit and we will talk about the cave. And one more thing."

"Yes, sir?"

"When you come, bring coffee to go with the cookies."

The old man reminded him of his uncle Nakai and Chee smiled as he headed back to Page. He knew himself as a man who looked toward the future, but his time at the sacred bridge had reminded him how lessons from the past could guide the way. Even though he hadn't discovered much from the day's interviews, the investigation into what happened to Curtis Walker made him feel alive.

Learning that Chill had a job in Page moved the young man higher on the list of potential suspects. Page was closer to the lake, closer to the crime scene than Navajo Mountain. The incident of the tires, and Wanda's description of Chill as a sort of boyfriend, who could have been jealous of the attention Curtis paid to her, added more weight to Chill's possible involvement. Wanda said that Chill was a mountain biker. That spoke to a good fitness level and solid balance, both important if a person planned to hike over slick rock, bash someone in the skull, perhaps push the body into the lake, and return to the dock undetected.

He stopped to stretch his legs after an hour on the road and texted Chill, introducing himself as a police officer and saying that he had a few questions he'd like to ask in connection with a case. He kept it light and purposely vague, positioning the interview as a follow-up on his conversation with Wanda. He heard nothing in return. The silence made him wonder if he'd tipped off a murderer. More likely, Chill's phone was turned off, uncharged, or abandoned in his vehicle.

After half an hour, he called Chill's cell number and got a mechanical voice instructing him to leave a message. He hung up instead, and called Detective Malone. She was out of the office, he was told, and he got transferred to Sheriff Carter.

"Sheriff, I may have a possible suspect in the Curtis Walker death," Chee said. "It's Brian Chinchili of Navajo Mountain. He slashed Curtis's tires a few weeks ago and may still have a grudge against him involving a woman. Can you do a background check?" Chee estimated Chill's age, based on what Wanda had told him, and mentioned that he was an electrician.

"Spell that name." Carter paused to write it down. "I'll ask someone to get on it. What's the name of his company?"

"He works with Community Construction."

"Hold on, let me check something." The phone went quiet, then the sheriff was back. "The company is doing a remodel on the south side of town for a relative of one of my deputies. They say Chinchili is handling the electric for the place and ought to be working on-site." He gave Chee the address. "It's on your way back to Page."

The GPS led Chee to a single-family home in a neighborhood where basketball hoops occupied many of the driveways. He found the house easily because of the three white pickup trucks with red Community Construction signs on the doors. The place looked like it had needed remodeling for several decades. Chee parked Omar behind the nearest truck and skirted around wood scraps and drywall debris to the entrance. The door stood open. Inside, the rooms were bare of furniture, and thick protective plastic hid the wooden floors.

Following the whir of a power drill, Chee found two men installing cabinets in an otherwise empty kitchen. The air smelled of sweat and sawdust. When the sound stopped, he asked about Chill, and they directed him to the master bedroom, a room down the hall that collected northern light.

Chee knocked on the doorframe before walking in. "Chill?"

"Yeah?" The tall, lean, muscular Navajo stayed focused on the wires protruding from an outlet on the floor. "Did you bring me the cover for this floor box?"

"Nope. Can we talk a minute?"

Chill turned from his spot on the floor and took in Chee. "Who are you?"

"Sergeant Jim Chee, Navajo Police. Are you Brian Chinchili?"

"Yeah, that's me."

"I have a few questions for you."

"About what?"

"About who. Curtis Walker."

Chee had been in plenty of situations where an informal interview would have gone crossways from here, but luck stood with him.

"Huh. I don't know much about him, but sure, we can talk. I need a break anyway." Chill rose to standing with strength and graceful balance. "Can I see some ID?"

Chee obliged.

"You're from Shiprock. Nice up there. Not so hot. Was Mr. Walker from there, too?"

"No, he was born at Navajo Mountain. One of the Antelope Canyon guides. You've met him. He was a friend of your girlfriend, Wanda."

"Oh, right. That one. We called him Tahoma."

Tahoma. The name meant Water's Edge. An appropriate nickname for a non-swimmer.

"He's dead. I found his body in the lake."

Chill's expression moved from neutral to shocked. "Whoa. That guy. No kidding? He drowned in the lake? I haven't even had time to go to the lake in a month. Does Wanda know what happened?"

"Yeah."

"Does Desmond know about this?"

"Yes."

"How did they handle the bad news?"

Chee nodded. "They're OK." Chill's concern for others increased his opinion of the man.

"What did you want to talk to me about?" He

stopped. "Oh, I get it. The tires. Well, you're Navajo. You know about restorative justice. I made restitution. Tahoma accepted it. I shook his hand."

"But you were still angry that he was paying attention to your girlfriend."

"Not exactly angry. Irritated. Wanda said nothing sleazy was going on, but it seemed too weird. I won't lie, bro, I wanted that guy to leave my girl alone. But she liked him, and when it was the three of us, he was always respectful to her and, I gotta say, to me, too. I figured the easiest thing was to believe her when she said he was just a friend and let it be." Chill emphasized the word *just*.

"I hear you. Where were you last weekend?"

"Working here, all day Saturday and Sunday. The overtime money is sweet."

"When you and Wanda were with the man who died, did he ever talk about being afraid of anybody, or about any disagreements or arguments?"

Chill scratched his head. "Funny you ask about that. Last time he came up to see Wanda and I was hangin' with them, he said things weren't going well at work. Wanda mentioned something about how that must be tough when you worked with family. And he said, no, he and his brother got along great. I guess he works other jobs, too."

"Anything else?"

"He was complaining about paperwork." Chill took a step back from Chee. "Speaking of work, I gotta get back to it."

Chee thanked Chill for his time and headed to the truck. Before he got there, he felt his phone buzz. Bernie?

No, it was Paul Hendrix.

"Hey. Pop asked me to check in with you, and I thought that was a fine idea. Any news about what happened to Curtis?"

"Afraid not. How are you and your father doing today?"

"That why I'm calling. I'm OK, but my pop is taking Curtis's death hard. He's not eating, not doing much of anything except staring out the window and looking at pictures of Curtis or of the three of us from way back when."

"I'm sorry to hear that." The reaction seemed to lie well within the normal range for fresh, raw grief, Chee thought.

"He cheered up when you came by to talk to him about his work at the canyon. There's a map of his here that he'd like you to have. He asked me to call you for a mailing address, but I was hoping you could stop by. Pop can give you the map and tell you a story or two about Curtis. Work for you today?"

"It might. I need to write a report for Detective Malone. When I'm done, I can swing by, if it's not too late."

"Good. Can you call first?"

"I will. By the way, how are *you* doing with, um, with the loss?"

The phone was quiet, as though the question caught Paul by surprise. "Well, it was a shock, seeing him drowned like that. But having been there makes it easier for me to accept his death and the accident. Easier than it's been for Pop."

"I forgot to ask you. What do you know about those artifacts that were in the tent?"

"What do you mean?"

"The big broken pot, the old sandal, the grinding stones. You and Ted didn't seem especially concerned about that, but the idea that Curtis might have been looting up there bothers me."

Paul hesitated. "I can't answer that without raising more questions for you. It's complicated. Curtis and I were partners in a project to get a grant for some preservation work. Let's talk about it when you come to see Pop."

"Sure."

"Pop wants to keep discussing Curtis's accident. I hope you can distract him from that obsession. He asks me to tell him the details I remember. And then he weeps."

Chee drove Omar back to the sheriff's office, thinking about Paul's comments. Clearly, his father had had a strong bond with Curtis, and his unexpected demise had left its wounds. If Paul, who had lost a friend and business partner, could share his father's grief, that would make life easier for them both. But instead, Paul seemed closed down, pulling back from the emotion that usually came with the death of a friend.

In her office, Detective Malone arranged a spot for Chee to type his notes from the Navajo Mountain and Chinchili visits, but she wanted to talk to him about it first. Chee summarized what he'd learned from Desmond and Wanda and the futility of the other contacts.

"Was Chinchili at the work site?"

"Yes. The other good news, I guess, is that we can rule him out as a suspect. He confirmed that

he had slashed Curtis's tires in a jealous rage, and
then made peace with him and offered restitution."
The men had solved the problem the traditional
Navajo way, Chee thought, dealing directly with
each other to make things right, bypassing mainstream culture's notion of punishment.

Malone looked puzzled.

"I didn't ask for details," he added, "but that probably means he bought new tires and did what he
could to make up for the inconvenience he'd caused."

"That's interesting. Curtis never filed charges
over the incident."

"Chinchili said Curtis had told him and his girlfriend that he was having problems at work. I found
that interesting."

"At Laguna Blue?"

"Or Antelope Canyon Tours. And he also did
some work with Paul Hendrix."

Malone wrinkled her brow. "OK. I'd like you to
interview Robert and Ramona at Laguna Blue. See
if they had an issue with Curtis's work."

Chee hesitated, remembering the unpleasant-
ness of his initial encounter with Robert and Ramona's tears. "What if you talk to them and I talk
to Doug, Shawna, and Sunfish? Maybe there was
a problem with that business. Remember how you
thought I'd have some rapport with Navajos?" Sunfish wasn't native, but Chee knew she liked him.

"You're a pro, Chee. You can talk to anybody
and get them to answer. When you go to Laguna
Blue, start with Robert. I'll talk to Doug and then
Paul if we need to. You'll get further with Robert
than I will. Trust me."

"But Doug and I—"

Malone frowned and interrupted. "Three things. First, we both want to wrap this up quickly, so we share the load. Second, Ramona is Navajo, remember? And, finally, there's bad blood between Robert and me."

"Really? What happened?"

She grinned at him. "Short version: I'm married to his first wife."

"I can see how that might make things awkward."

Malone glanced at the time. "They ought to be there for another hour. Good luck."

Chee drove to the marina. As he pulled into the parking area, he saw an SUV with a magnetic Laguna Blue sign drive away, with Robert behind the wheel. He'd talk to Ramona first.

He parked and went inside. Speaking to Ramona might stir up her tears, but it would be easier without Robert there. She might be more likely to tell him the truth about Curtis.

Ramona was behind the counter, occupied with something on the computer. She looked up at the sound of his footsteps. "You're back."

"I'm still trying to figure out why the man you worked with died. Can we talk?"

"Sure. Just give me a minute to finish here. Let's sit outside on the bench and enjoy the view. If any last-minute customers come, I can see them from there."

He went out to wait, pleased that the area was virtually empty. He listened to the rhythmic clapping of the water against the boats and the dock.

The sun felt comfortably warm through his pants and shirt. It made the perfect setting for a nap. But Ramona arrived a few minutes later and sat a respectable distance away. She stretched her muscular, tanned legs straight out in front of her.

"Before you ask . . . no, I didn't kill Curtis, and I don't know who did."

He eased into the questions. "I spent most of the day at Navajo Mountain talking with people who knew him and everyone held him in high regard. Now that you've had time to think about it, do you recall him mentioning any arguments, disagreements, or irritations with people?"

She didn't answer immediately, then turned to face him. "I don't think any of this has to do with his death, but he and Robert were arguing about an idea Curtis came up with for some new tours. The disagreement upset Robert. He was very angry."

She looked away from him, toward the lake.

"Boat tours?"

"Yes. Educational excursions to teach visitors about the park's archaeological heritage. Boats and hiking."

"Would tours like that have conflicted with Doug's business?"

"I thought they seemed like a good overlap. We have the boats; they have the tour experience. When Curtis shared the idea with me, it sounded great, like a win-win for all of us. I imagined that we could eventually merge the two businesses. But Curtis didn't even want to talk about it, probably because of Robert's attitude."

"And what attitude is that?"

She sighed. "Robert rejects most ideas that he hasn't thought of himself. And he was jealous of Curtis because we worked together so well. Curtis showed up when he said he would, did his job without ever complaining, and gave more than the situation required. He saved us money by making sure we paid our taxes and bills on time. He has . . . *had* . . . a sharp mind, especially when it came to numbers."

Chee watched her twist the silver ring on her right hand.

"You know, Ramona, Curtis was wearing a ring like that one you're wearing when I found him. Ted Morris made sure that you were one of the first to know about the body. You went to some trouble to pack up his belongings and get them to Doug."

He stopped, and her hands grew still. When she looked up, he saw her tears. "We were more than coworkers. More than friends. That's one reason I encouraged him to start those archaeological tours. If he had more financial stability, he could focus more on his art and photography. I know that made him happy."

"Did Robert realize you were"—he recalled her words—"more than friends?"

"Yes, he sensed the chemistry between us, and I didn't lie about it. He wanted to fire Curtis, but I wouldn't let him until we found someone else who could do the job as well as Curtis could. I own half the business, so he had to listen to me. Robert was furious, but there was nothing he could do. Curtis had just told me that he wasn't going to work with Paul Hendrix anymore so he needed the salary and we needed his help at Laguna Blue."

"So Paul was firing him?"

"Not exactly. Curtis said the decision was mutual."

"Detective Malone indicated that Robert has a short temper. Is that true?"

"He can be intense. That's one thing that makes him good at business, and one of the things I've always loved about him, but it has a downside. When he loses his cool, watch out."

"Ted Morris told me he had to break up a fight between them. What did he and Curtis get into it about?"

"Robert accused him of stealing our idea for those tours. He went ballistic."

"Was he right?"

"Sort of. Curtis loved petroglyphs and pictographs. He liked to sketch the images, create photomontages with rock art and artifacts—you know, things like potsherds, arrowheads, those little corncobs you find at the old sites. Like I said, I thought it would be great if he and Doug worked with Robert and me to offer archaeology tours. I mentioned that idea to Robert, and next thing you know, he imagined *he'd* come up with it. He expanded it to include hiking to the ruins, picnics, a map of the sites, two-day overnight excursions."

"Was Robert with you the day Curtis died?"

"Yes." She answered without hesitation. "Mostly, anyway. We both worked late that evening because Curtis took the day off. Robert was still here when

I left for my aerobics class. I came home with a headache and went right to bed. I didn't hear him come in later, so I assume he was here all evening."

"Did you actually see him?"

"No. We sleep in separate rooms."

They looked out at the lake, shimmering navy-blue water in the distance against a panorama of tan and red desert cliffs, with the endless sky arching over it all. After a few moments Ramona turned to face him.

"If Robert wanted to kill Curtis, he would have found a more convenient place. And when and if the body ever showed up, everyone would have been convinced that the death was an accident—no investigation required. He's smart. Don't underestimate him."

"I noticed him driving away as I parked. Is he home now?"

"No. This is his poker night. You can probably reach him after ten, but the morning would be better. Their games involve beer."

A murder inquiry trumps a card game, but Chee let her comment stand, and asked for Robert's cell phone number. "Can you think of anyone else who might have wanted to harm Curtis?"

She shook her head. "Here's my theory about what happened. He went camping at the lake to get his head on straight because of the conflict with Doug and Robert about the tours and because of his decision not to work with Paul anymore. He was one of those guys who really needed space and time to figure things out. I can see him lost in thought, tripping, hitting his head before he could stop himself, and rolling into the lake." She shuddered. "I'm going to sit here awhile. Good luck with the investigation."

He left her on the bench, looking at the lake and waiting for the sunset. From his truck, he called Paul's number.

"I'm at the marina. I just wrapped up an interview about Curtis, but I need to do another. I might not make it over there tonight. How late does your father stay up?"

"He's a night owl. Did you learn anything?"

"Not especially. Another vote for the accidental drowning theory."

"I can't get that sight out of my mind. If you hadn't found the body, his family might never have known what happened to him." He heard Paul take a deep breath. "Here's an idea. Come over now and share a pizza with Pete and me. Nothing like pepperoni to erase the day's worries. You don't have to stay long, but I know it will be good therapy for Pop. And I want to explain something to you about those artifacts you saw at the tent."

The mention of pepperoni made Chee think of Bernie. That was the only pizza she ever ordered. And the puzzle of the artifacts gnawed at him. Why had Paul taken them back to Page instead of leaving them at the lake? Was what he had seen in the tent somehow connected to Curtis's death?

"Pizza sounds great. I'd like that. I'm going to make a quick call, and then I'll be there."

16

Bernadette Manuelito locked the car and put the keys in the front compartment of her backpack. Her phone, tucked away in a jacket pocket, was charged, muted, and ready to record. Her pack held lunch and water, an extra jacket, and another T-shirt. If she were working inside a greenhouse, she expected heat. Outdoors, it could be cool.

She walked toward the portable building with the red roof, noting the odd silence, the lack of birdsong or human noise except for the ongoing vibrating roar of a generator. The door to the office was open, and a brown-skinned man missing a lower tooth sat waiting for her. She pushed the record button.

"Yá'át'ééh." She introduced herself with her clans, the way polite Navajos greet Navajo strangers.

"Yá'át'ééh." He switched to English. "I don't speak much Navajo."

The irony dawned on her. **Agent White would**

have lasted longer on his assignment if he'd been schooled in basic Navajo manners. "Are you the guy to talk to about a job?"

"That's right, I'm Lester." He motioned her to the metal chair across the table from him. She removed her backpack, set it on the floor, and took a seat. "How did you find out about us?"

She'd expected the question. "I know a guy who worked here." She told him about Arnold. "He said there were jobs and that you didn't ask too many questions about, ah, about stuff that happened."

"I remember that guy. Tell me your name again."

"Bernadine Blackman."

"That's a mouthful. I'll call you Bebe."

"Fine with me."

"What can you do?"

"Lots of stuff. I helped my *shicheii* with his garden. I know about plants, thanks to my grandfather's teachings. And my auntie told me what herbs and roots were good for healing. I know how to work hard. I'm good with numbers and computers."

Mostly true. The number skill came as a side benefit of her mother's efforts to teach her the intricacies of weaving, with its mathematic patterns and requirement for perfection. As for computers? She had studied the supplemental information Agent White had sent, and figured she knew as much as she needed to find a personnel list and information on super cannabis cultivation.

"You're lucky, Bebe. It's Croptober. That's what

we call it. You know, time to harvest. We've been at it already, but there's more work out there."

"I can drive a combine." She pushed a strand of pink hair out of her eyes.

"Not here, sweetie pie. Everything's by hand. The flowers bruise easily. We have to keep the heads clean and the resin intact. We're cutting two-foot sections from the plants, mostly the top flowers. We leave the stems for oil, process them later."

He looked at her again. "You're a little short for that, Bebe. I think we're done hauling hoses and fertilizing with chemicals. You're lucky. That's all outside in the sun and tough work, especially for a girl."

Sweetie pie? Girl? Bernie forced herself to chuckle. "Whatever. You're the boss."

"Not me. I'm not the boss. You see those pictures?"

He used his chin to point, directing her eyes to the wall above the desk. She looked at colored photographs of men. One large, one lean. The lean one resembled the dead man.

"Those two are the top dogs. The one in the suit is Mr. Kelly, he's in charge now. The other guy's Dr. Zhou."

The name resonated with Bernie but she didn't let it show. "Wow. A doctor running a farm."

"Just Mr. Kelly runs it now. Dr. Zhou left a few days ago."

"Where did he go?"

Lester shrugged. "Mr. Kelly said he'd finished his work here."

She could tell that Lester knew more than he was saying, and she waited, but he opened a drawer of the desk and took out an old-fashioned clipboard with some papers.

"I thought a Navajo guy ran this. Dino Begay Perez. A Navajo like us."

"You're behind the times, honey. Kelly's the boss."

"What happened to Begay Perez?"

Lester shrugged. He put the clipboard on the table.

"I heard there's Chinese laborers here."

"Yeah, but don't worry. Most of them work outside, or loading trucks. You probably won't even see them. The boss likes them to all stay together. Says they work better that way. He keeps us Navajos working with whoever else shows up looking for a job."

"Somebody told me one of those Chinese guys got run over out by Shiprock."

Lester shrugged and looked away. "They don't want us to talk about things like that. You're a real Chatty Cathy."

She interpreted his attitude as confirmation that the dead man had a connection to the farm.

"So, Bebe, you looking for some hard work?"

"Yep. I hear you pay . . . good," she said, stopping herself just in time from saying "well."

"You work good, Bebe, we pay good. In cash or product." He swiveled his chair to face the open door. "You see those big puffy things out there?"

"The ones that look like big pillows?"

"Right. That's the greenhouses. With them and the fields, we have year-round farming."

"I bet the hemp grows best under the sun."

"That's where the CBD comes from. You know about that?"

"Sort of. Old people use it for arthritis. They say it helps their pain, but it won't get you high. Is that more hemp in the greenhouses?"

"No, special plants. The outdoor harvest is done, and the crew is trimming the buds of the inside crop. That's the job we're hiring for now. All the work is day to day. Cash when you leave. Or weed, or some of both."

Bernie appreciated getting that on her recording. "What's the pay?"

He told her. "And you can come back for more work the next day, if your supervisor gives the OK."

"What about loading the trucks? I could do that, too, work a double shift."

He smiled at her. "Trust me. Trimming is better. Start there, and if you want, we can talk about a double shift in a day or two."

"Sure." She paused. "You said the Chinese work with the special weed. Can I get some of that?"

"You sure have a lotta questions, Bebe."

Had she talked too much? "If I hadn't been curious, I wouldn't have found out about the jobs here, and I wouldn't have met you, and—"

The penetrating noise of tires crunching against the dirt road outside the office caught her attention. She turned toward the open door as a gold-colored sedan rolled past. "Wow. Those are some wheels."

"That's the boss."

"Nice car. Do you know him?"

"We've talked." Lester sat a bit straighter. "Yep. Mr. Kelly. He says this place was named for him: Kelly's Happy Farm. KHF."

She watched Les's face for a sign that he was joking. He wasn't.

"You don't see many fancy cars like that around here."

"He's from the big city—LA." He handed Bernie the clipboard, with two sheets of white paper on it, and a ballpoint pen. "Fill this out. Can you start work today?"

"I want to. I can use the money." She sat the clipboard on her lap. "You don't have a computer for stuff like this?"

"I got one." She saw him glance toward a closed door. "But I don't use it for work applications because some workers only stay a day. Too easy to hack. That's what Mr. Kelly says."

She took the opening. "We had trouble with that on my last job. I figured it out. Saved them a bunch of grief. I'm good with computers. If you ever get in a jam, I could help you, you know, off the record in exchange for some *naakai binát'oh*." She assumed he knew enough Navajo to understand the word for marijuana.

He winked at her. If he'd asked why she wasn't still at this imaginary job, she had the story of her imaginary firing cued up.

Bernie took off the vision-distorting glasses and turned toward the form, noticing that it didn't ask for a social security number, references, or previous jobs. She printed her fake name, age, and the number of the cell phone Largo had given her. She stopped at the check box to confirm that she knew the work was dangerous and waived her right to hold KHF responsible for any injury.

"On this part about injuries, what could happen?"

"Don't worry about it. We've got a first aid kit."

She signed the form and handed it to him.

"You forgot your address. Put that in, and then I'll take your picture and you can get started." He handed the clipboard back to her.

She put on the distortion glasses, grateful that Lester had mentioned the photo. "I don't exactly have an address. Since I lost my job, I've been living in my car, you know, or couch surfing with some relatives."

"You gotta put something there."

"Why?"

"Because." He winked at her again. "You're cute. Got a boyfriend?"

She winked back. "Nope. Not today anyway."

She used the address of the Shiprock Women's Shelter and handed back the form.

He glanced at it and put it on the desk. "I have to take your picture and your fingerprints. Come on."

"Fingerprints?"

"Yeah."

"What about my right to privacy?"

He laughed. "Are you kidding? It's routine. Part of the deal if you wanna work here, Bebe."

"Go ahead." She hadn't anticipated finger-prints, and knew that as soon as Lester received the results—and that could be within twenty-four hours—the gig would be over. The clock was ticking now.

He opened the door to the adjoining room. She saw a laptop computer on the desk, the only com-puter she'd spotted so far. Across from it, a camera sat on a tripod in front of a single metal chair.

"I'll do the photo first. Right there." He pointed to the chair.

She sat, and he snapped the shot. "Now without your glasses."

"I have to wear them. I can't see, and—"

"It's the rule."

He took a picture. "No. Keep your eyes open."

She squinted as he snapped another. "Better."

He took the fingerprints on a device she was familiar with through her law enforcement work. The machine transferred the prints right to the computer and sent them off for analysis. He pushed some keys on the laptop, put her applica-tion on the scanner, and then took it out and ran it through a shredder. "They'll call me if there's any problem."

She nodded. The statement added urgency to her assignment. "I'm ready to get to work."

"In a minute. I need to read you the rules." As he led the way out of the office, he pulled a card from his back pocket and cleared his throat. Again, she was glad the recorder was on. "You get fifteen minutes for a meal and fifteen for the john. You get paid at the end of the shift. No complaining. If you've got a gripe, quit. No talking about what you do here with anybody." He stopped. "That means relatives, the cops, your girlfriends, anybody. No socializing during working hours. You get paid to work. No smoking, drugs, or drinking on the job. No texts or phone calls."

There were rules about when shifts started and ended, what to bring to the job site, and what to do if she got injured. And how anyone, any time, could be fired without notice.

"By accepting a job, you agree to the possibility of being searched on entering and leaving."

She looked at Lester and raised her eyebrows. "Why?"

"That's to make sure nobody helps themselves to the product."

She thought of the dead man, wondering how he had managed to escape with the seeds and so much marijuana or hemp, or whatever was in those baggies.

Lester put the card back.

"Do I get a copy of that?"

"No."

"I just wanna make sure I don't mess up."

"You won't."

He pulled a pager from his belt.

She heard static and then a female voice. "Lester. Whatcha got?"

"Just one. She seems more with it than average. Just waiting for the background check."

"That's slow today. Go ahead and bring her out to number three. Them and shipping need the most help."

She thought about the fingerprints and remembered her cover story of getting fired from the police department. She hoped she didn't have to use it.

Lester turned to her. "I'll take you to the bud room. You'll like it better than shipping because you'll be . . ."

He stopped, distracted by something.

Bernie heard footsteps. She turned toward the open door as a small Chinese man in a blue T-shirt stepped inside.

"What are you doin' in here?"

"My brother? Where he is?" The man stood still, legs apart, grounded as though he expected a blow.

"I don't know a thing about him. You could have gotten me fired by using my phone like that. The cops called me. Get outta here now. What's your name?"

The man didn't speak. Bernie smelled his sweat.

"Oh yeah, now I remember. Limp Lick or something like that." Lester looked at her and smirked. "If your brother's not here, he probably ran off."

"No." The man shook his head once. "What happen to him?"

"People come and go all the time. Your brother is not my problem. Nobody cares."

"Tell me or . . ." He squeezed his hands into

tight fists. A vein at his temple pounded, his fury palpable.

"I'm calling security." Lester held up his phone.

The man glanced at Bernie, and she saw sadness as well as anger. He said nothing as he turned and jogged away.

Lester stood. "Let's go. You need to get to work."

"Can I pee first?"

"Be quick. Come on."

She picked up her backpack.

He frowned. "You can't take that in the greenhouse. You can leave it here or—"

"I'll put it in my car after the restroom."

She followed him outside, noticing the keypad lock on the door again.

They had walked a few yards when an idea came to her.

"Oh shoot, my water bottle fell out." She patted an empty pocket. "I really need it."

"OK." They returned, and she watched him punch in the code, memorizing it. He opened the door, and she made a show of looking beneath the chair where she had been sitting. "Shoot. I guess it must have fallen out in my car."

He closed the door and she heard it lock. He waved an arm toward a trail leading to the row of green portable toilets.

"I gotta take care of something at the main headquarters. Wait up there when you're done, and I'll meet you."

She selected a toilet at the end of the row,

locked the door, and took her phone from the inside front pocket of her jacket. The recording was audible. She added a few observations and sent the file to the captain as they had agreed, then slipped the phone back into her pocket. As she opened the door, she noticed the man who had come to the office coming out of a toilet, walking away from her quickly.

"Sir? Wait."

Luck rode with her. He stopped. When he turned, she realized that the blue T-shirt he wore matched the one she'd seen on the dead man.

"I want to show you something." She walked toward him as she spoke.

He stared at her.

She had moved two images onto her new phone: the image of the dead man from the scene of the hit-and-run, and the photo of the woman and child that had been in the Bible she found in the duffel.

She showed him the group picture first.

"Our family. My niece and my brother's wife. Where you get this?"

"A man put his bag in my car. This was inside it."

He shook his head. "Who are you?"

Bernie put a finger to her lips and showed him the picture of the body. She had chosen the least offensive shot.

"Is this your brother?"

He shuddered, and looked away. His voice was barely a whisper. "My brother."

"I was there when he died. He was hit by a car."

"Who are you?"

She shook her head. "What was your brother's name?"

He took a step away, distracted by the sound of a vehicle in the distance. He said something that sounded like "Zhou."

"Say that again. What was his name?" She spoke more slowly this time. A dusty pickup truck was heading in their direction, kicking up road dirt with its oversize tires.

The man bolted toward the giant white domes of the greenhouses that rose behind them.

Bernie stood watching the truck pass, absorbing as much as she could of the driver's appearance. She memorized the make and model and the license plate, and saw it head out the gate. Whatever was loaded into the back had been covered by a black tarp, but it filled the truck bed.

She scanned the area for Lester. When she didn't see him, she ducked back into the outhouse, pulled out her phone again, and spoke into it, recording the information on the truck, the name Zhou, and the fact that he and Kelly had been running the place and now it was just Kelly, with both Zhou and Begay Perez out of the picture. She sent it on to Largo and turned off the phone.

Still no Lester. She jogged toward the parking lot, passing the office. The door was closed. She tried the handle and found it locked. She knocked. "Lester? You in there?" and was relieved at the lack of response. She knew she'd have to work fast.

She typed the code she'd memorized onto the small black keypad and entered, quickly shutting the door behind her.

Lester had left the back room unlocked. The laptop sat on the desk, lid raised. She left the door open and listened intently for him or anyone. As she tapped the mouse on its pad, she expected the device to ask for a password. Instead, the display brightened with a background of healthy, green, narrow-leaved *Cannabis sativa* plants.

She looked at the icons on the screen and found the file with fingerprints. She opened it. Hers came up first as most recent. She deleted them, but couldn't tell if they'd gone to another computer that would tie them to Officer Bernadette Manuelito. She remembered something she'd read in the manual White sent her and used the information to corrupt the larger file where her prints could have been stored. It seemed to work.

She went to the search bar and quickly typed "Zhou." The machine brought two hundred results, the ones on the first page all in Mandarin. She added "Dr." in front of "Zhou" and came up with ninety. She added "cannabis," and the number went down. She added "research" and got eighteen hits. She scanned the first page of those responses and saw the words *children* and *epilepsy*, along with *Cannabis ruderalis*, a lesser-known species in the marijuana universe she recalled from her earlier research. She found the slot for the flash drive she'd brought with her, and inserted it to copy the files she had highlighted to drive D. She saw the light on the little device blink, indicating the copy function had begun.

She searched the Zhou files for a picture, and . . .

"Les?"

She froze. The woman's voice came from the front room.

"Lester? You there?"

When she heard it again, she realized the sound wasn't a flesh-and-blood human but from a speaker, some sort of intercom. The voice fell silent, and she returned to the computer, hoping to find an image to confirm or deny the identity of the man she'd seen run over. She clicked on a file.

The screen filled with photos of cannabis plants, words, and charts, one of which was a distribution schedule. She noticed the date—that month. She cued it for the next download to her USB. But as the data flow continued, she realized that it was too slow. She tried to close it, but the drive didn't respond. The information froze on the screen. Her heart began to beat faster.

Then, she heard a conversation outside the building: a pair of male voices, speaking English, coming closer. Neither sounded like Lester, a tiny bit of good news. But she couldn't leave the office while they were there.

She followed some of the advice she had read in Agent White's memo, and either by skill or luck, brought the frozen screen to life. She typed in her search terms again for Dr. Zhou's picture, and a menu of possibilities came up, about half of them in Mandarin. She clicked on one in English.

The men now sounded as if they were standing directly outside the office front door. Her stomach tightened. She could pick out bits of the conversation from one guy with a loud voice.

They were talking football. Cowboys or Broncos? What about those Cardinals? If the men decided to come in, it would take them a moment to type the code to open the door, and a few more to discover her in the back room, time at least to remove the drive.

Her heartbeat accelerated.

The file came on screen slowly, filled with charts and color photos of children and hospitals and groups of medical workers. She scanned the identification beneath the photos. At least one said "Zhou." She instructed the machine to copy the data and willed the conversationalists outside to walk on so she could leave as soon as the download finished.

The men's discussion continued, and a woman's voice joined them. Bernie picked up the word "Lester" and male laughter. Finally, the voices grew silent. She stood and rolled back the desk chair, ready to grab the portable drive and vanish. Then someone knocked on the locked door.

"Lester. Here's lunch."

Maybe the woman would leave whatever she'd brought outside. No, the electronic beeps of the code box came next, and Bernie heard the door open.

The woman's voice. "Les?" She was inside.

For a fraction of a second, Bernie considered calling out a hello and pretending Lester had asked her to fix something on the computer. She took the only other option, and dove under the desk as quietly as she could. She thanked her lucky stars that she'd rolled Lester's chair out of the way, that he used a pad for its potentially noisy wheels, and that she had only grown to five foot two. She squeezed into the tight space, grateful that the desk had three drawers that could block the woman's view. She hunched close to the wall, pulling the chair in as close as possible

Boots clicked against the floor. The steps stopped, and Bernie pictured the visitor looking around the empty front room. Then the steps started again as the woman moved toward the back office.

Bernie held her breath, hoping that she'd hidden well enough and that the open computer wouldn't draw the woman's attention. The scuffed black boots stopped close enough that she could have wiped away the dust.

After an eternity, the boots retreated, and she heard the main door open and close again.

Bernie crawled out from her hiding place. The light on the flash drive had stopped blinking. She shoved the device into her jeans pocket, clicked to end the program, grabbed her backpack, and left the back office as she found it. She hunkered down to look out the window, saw no one, opened the front door, and rushed away from the scene of her trespass.

She steadied her breathing as she walked to her car, put the flash drive in an inside zip pocket of the backpack, and grabbed an energy bar. As she shoved the pack under the seat, regretting that her hatchback didn't have a trunk, she heard the sound of an approaching vehicle. She squatted down to let the car shield her and again saw the long gold sedan, a sporty Mercedes with dark tinted windows. She sent a quick note to Largo about the flash drive data and where to find it, then sprinted back to the outhouses to meet Lester. If he asked why she was late, she'd say she couldn't find her car keys. She had just reached the edge of the outhouse trail when she saw him ambling in her direction. By the time he got there, she had caught her breath and turned on the recorder again.

He handed her some disposable gloves and a paper face mask. "You don't have to wear these, Bebe, but some people choose to. If you want a full day's pay, you'll have to skip lunch and stay until the next shift."

"Thanks." She slipped the gloves and mask into her pocket. "Let's do it."

As they walked down the road, she began to realize the huge scope of the operation. She could see ten large greenhouses, and beyond them fields where she assumed the hemp plants grew. Portable buildings sprawled on one side of the road past the greenhouses, and across from them she noticed a collection of old motor homes and camping trailers.

"What's all that? An RV park?"

"That's where the Chinese workers live."

"How come they get a bed, and us Navajos don't?"

"Sweetie, you don't want to live in one of those. Believe me. I've been inside. Give me a tent and the fresh air any day."

As they approached the first greenhouse, the noise of the generator grew louder. Bernie could see the shapes of workers and plants through the plastic walls and estimated perhaps thirty people inside. If each of the ten was similarly staffed, that would make the number of employees here close to three hundred.

"What are those guys doin', Lester?"

"Working. Trimming the buds for the shipment. We've got a big order to ship this weekend."

He stopped at the second greenhouse and pushed some buttons on the keypad, blocking Bernie's view with his body.

When the door opened, the steamy heat hit her like a slap to the head. Unwashed bodies, moist earth, and an overnote of cannabis filled the stale, damp air. Workers, mostly Navajo and almost all male, stood at a waist-high table. A few looked up when Lester entered and studied the newcomer with him. Most stayed focused on removing buds from stems with knives and clippers and separating the two piles with quick, efficient movements.

A heavyset Navajo woman came up to them. Lester nodded to her.

"This is Bebe. She knows the rules. She's ready to work."

"OK, thanks."

He turned to Bernie. "If you ever need a boyfriend, look me up after work."

She smiled. "I just might do that." Then she slipped on the mask he'd given her.

Lester left, and the Navajo woman focused on Bernie. "I'm Chastity. Watch and learn. It's not rocket science."

Something about her stirred a memory, but

Bernie couldn't quite retrieve it. She followed Chastity down the row to an empty spot at the table.

"Stand here. Pay attention."

"Yes, ma'am."

The woman grabbed a plant stem and some snippers, and in half a breath trimmed the buds so they fell in an empty plastic jug. She brushed the stem into a pile of naked stems next to her.

"When you're done with this batch, push the button." Bernie saw her extend her hand beneath the table. "The guys will bring more plants. When the jug is full, push this twice, and they'll pick it up and bring you an empty one. Understand?"

Bernie nodded.

"If you're too slow, you won't be back. I decide who stays and who goes." She stopped, offering Bernie a chance to say something or ask a question.

"Is this hemp?"

"This is a hemp farm, right?" Chastity handed her the clippers. "Get to work. I'm gonna watch you."

Bernie clipped her first buds and dropped them in the container.

"You have to move faster. Show me your trim again."

She snipped the next set of buds.

"Quicker. Don't worry about getting a little nick."

"What happened to your fingers?"

The woman extended her mangled right hand,

missing the first joint on the middle and ring fingers. "An accident. Don't worry about it. I didn't do it here." She lowered her arm. "I know lotsa people wonder, but most don't ask."

"I'm sorry about your hand."

"No biggie. It still works. Do another trim."

Bernie obliged.

"Better, but you're still way slow."

"Where does all this go?" Was she posing too many questions? But Chastity didn't seem to mind.

"From this line, the buds go to California for processing. You know, to make CBD oil, drops, lotions, and gummies. Stuff like that. The stems get treated and put to use, too. The whole plant is valuable."

Lester had installed the new girl in the legit part of the operation. He was smarter than she'd given him credit for. "These are the guys that grow outside, right?"

"Right, but they're all girls. We want the buds."

"Lester said I could get paid in product. I thought that meant some real bud, not the stuff my *shicheii* uses to help him sleep at night."

Chastity exhaled. "Honey, if you wanna get paid in weed, Lester will do that. But take the cash. You can't pay the bills with ganja."

Bernie picked up another stalk and the clippers. "How long will I have to do this kind of stuff before I can get a job like yours?"

The woman made a snorting sound and then lowered her voice. "Trust me. You don't want my

job." Chastity's phone buzzed. She pulled it from
her waistband, looked at the screen, and then took
a few steps away, her back to Bernie.

"Yeah?"

While Chastity dealt with the interruption,
Bernie wondered if she'd already blown her cover.
She focused on studying the other workers. Only
a few wore gloves; more wore masks, despite the
heat. Many looked much too young to be working
on anything except homework. Most were Navajo,
though a few could have been Ute or Pueblo people, and some were non-natives, including Asians.
No one made eye contact with her.

She wouldn't have recognized the Chinese man
if it weren't for his blue shirt. He pretended not to
know her as well.

She strained to eavesdrop on Chastity's conversation, but the woman spoke softly. The only
word she picked up was *problem*, until her new
boss raised her voice.

"I don't know nothin' about that. It's not my
issue, bro. I'm focused on making the quota for
the shipment. Hold on." Chastity took her conversation outside.

Bernie had just gone back to trimming when
she heard a loud grunt and then a crashing sound
on the other side of the table. The man in the blue
T-shirt had collapsed. Those near him stopped
and stared. Even before someone yelled, "A guy
needs help," Bernie's training took over, and she
moved toward the fallen man.

"Hey, let me in." She knelt next to him, noticing the shaking in his stiffened limbs. His open

eyes seemed to see nothing. "My uncle has seizures," she told him. "I know what to do." She made sure there was nothing close by that could hurt him, and gently moved his head to the side. She raised her voice to the onlookers. "Give him some privacy. It's nothing contagious."

The others went back to work, but Bernie stayed with the man, pulling out her phone to keep track of the time. If the shaking didn't stop in five minutes, she knew he would need medical help, maybe a trip to the hospital. As she watched the time, she surreptitiously snapped a few photos of the room and the working conditions. The seizure ended, and the man slowly returned to consciousness. She put the phone back in her pocket.

When he tried to sit up, Bernie spoke to him. "Stay down a minute. You had a seizure."

She saw him relax a little.

"Do you know what that is?"

"Yes. I take medicine to control it, but I can't get it anymore."

"Why not?"

"My brother, he get me what I need for me and my little girl, but—"

She felt a presence behind her. Chastity. "What happened here?"

Before Bernie could speak, the Chinese man stood and shakily dusted himself off. "I slip. So sorry. She hep me good, I'm OK."

"Get back to work."

She turned to Bernie. "Lester says you know something about computers."

Bernie nodded.

"You remember the place you went to check in?" Chastity didn't wait for an answer. "Go back there. He wants to see you."

"You mean now?"

"Whaddaya think?"

"OK."

Outside of the greenhouse with its suffocating heat and pungent smells of plants, soil, and her fellow workers, she took off the mask and enjoyed some deep breaths of fresh dry air. She grabbed her phone, stopped the audio recording, and took pictures of the exterior of the greenhouse and of the compound. She could get some great shots of the RV park and the temporary buildings on her way back to the office. Then all she needed was a photo of a black Mercedes used in the hit-and-run and a heart-to-heart conversation with Begay Perez. The timing was perfect. What could go wrong?

17

As Bernie walked toward the admissions shed, she checked her phone's battery, sent the photos and recording to the captain, and, after receiving a quick "Got it," turned off the phone and hid it away. She'd only been inside the compound half an hour, she realized, looking at the time.

She wondered what Lester wanted. She had been careful in her exploration of the office laptop, doing exactly what she'd learned from Agent White. If Lester had discovered the corrupted fingerprint file, there was no way he could know she was behind it. She hoped he had sought her out because of the impressions she'd worked hard to leave—that she could help him off the record with computer issues, and that she liked flirting with him. The timing of the invitation to come back to the office worked, too. The assignment had fallen into place more quickly than she'd hoped. If things continued to go well, she'd be done there soon.

But before she left the farm, she needed to spot the vehicle involved in the murder. Otherwise, she knew KHF could claim that the car had been stolen or sold. Assuming they were as clever as Agent White believed, they might even cobble together an authentic-looking bill of sale. If Dr. Zhou and Kelly had had a disagreement, and Zhou left with some of the product, that could be enough motive for murder. Who had driven the car that killed him? Was it the mysteriously unavailable Dino Begay Perez? Had he offed the doctor and then disappeared?

As she knocked on the door of Lester's office, she clicked her phone to record.

A thin white man in a muscle shirt opened the door and stared at her. She noticed his tattoo, a parrot that stretched from shoulder to elbow. Behind him, she saw Lester pacing. He called to her, "Come on in, Bebe."

Parrot Man stepped back just enough for her to get by. He smelled good, like geraniums. But he gave off negative vibes.

Lester spoke quickly. "We have a problem here. I remember that you told me you'd worked with computers, and I was hoping you might have an idea."

"What's the trouble?"

"A program I need isn't responding." Lester looked at Parrot Man. "He's the in-house marketing guy, so he knows something about computers, but this has us both stumped. You said you outsmarted some hackers, so I thought, you know . . ."

"Usually Lester and I can figure things out." Parrot Man's voice was higher than she would have expected, and had a defensive edge. "But this isn't working. Lester thinks you can help. Quietly, you know, because you weren't hired for this."

A challenge, an opportunity. She turned to Lester. "I'll try. If I can't fix it, you're no worse off than before, right? If I can fix it, you guys get the credit. But it will cost you."

"More ganja?"

She gave Lester the most beguiling smile she could muster. "I wanna hear what happened to that guy's brother. I've been thinking about that ever since he came in here."

Parrot Man looked at Lester. "What's she talking about?"

"Oh, Dr. Zhou's brother came in asking about him. Bebe was here and saw how I ran him off."

Parrot Man frowned. "Dr. Zhou. That's the medical stuff, right?"

"Yeah."

Parrot Man spoke more quickly. "You and Les can jibber-jab later. Fix the computer."

She nodded. "What kind of network are you on?"

He told her. "It's special to Mr. Kelly's businesses."

The computer came on, and she noticed that one of the Mandarin files she had inadvertently accessed earlier was still loading in the background. No wonder they were having trouble. Hoping to distract them, she kept talking as she quickly x-ed it closed, hoping to distract them.

"I don't get why that man's brother would

run off . . . I mean, without saying goodbye or even letting him know. Especially if he was a bigwig in the business."

Lester shifted from one foot to the other. "It happens that people run away. Maybe they get homesick. Like I told you, Mr. Kelly expects everyone to work their butts off, and he expects those Chinese guys to work harder. I don't know why Dr. Zhou left."

Parrot Man frowned. "What does Zhou's brother do? Is he a researcher, too?"

Bernie grabbed the word *researcher*. She fiddled at the keyboard, grateful for the opportunity to undo what she'd done earlier. She looked at the fingerprint file again and was pleased to see it was still corrupted.

"He's just a grunt," Lester said. "But I found him in here after hours yesterday. He had a broom and said he was cleaning, but I caught him sitting at the computer. When I called him out, he told me he had to send an email to his wife about their kid. What BS. I fired him and told him to get out, but he begged me for another chance, practically bawling about a sick baby." Lester snorted out a laugh. "I said OK, he could stay, but at half pay."

Parrott Man scowled. "He might be the reason this thing is screwed up. I wish you'd mentioned that sooner."

"I think I can solve this problem here, but you have to tell me more about the computer network. You said it serves the businesses? You mean this farm?"

"More than that. The whole enterprise, the

other offices, the shipping, the distribution, phar-maceutical research—"

"Hey," Lester interrupted him. "We're not sup-posed to talk about that."

"Bebe works here." Parrot Man gave her a half grin. "All this is just between the three of us, right?"

"I wouldn't have it any other way." Bernie gave them her deepest scowl as she highlighted the fin-gerprint file. "This looks bad to me. Maybe the man in the blue shirt . . ."

Parrot Man frowned. "That little bastard. Les, I think he—"

The intercom buzzed, and Lester ignored it. "No. I doubt that guy's smart enough to do any damage. He's a farmer, not a—"

The intercom buzzed again. "Are you in the office, Lester?"

He pushed a button. "Yeah. I'm here. What's up?"

"Kelly wants to talk to you. Right now." Bernie recognized the voice; it was the same person who had come around with news of lunch.

Lester pushed the button. "Tell him I'm on my way."

"Hurry. You know he's been impatient ever since that wreck."

"Stop nagging. I'm leaving."

"Don't get pissed with me."

"Sorry. I'm dealing with a computer issue. Nothin' personal."

Parrot Man said, "Get outta here. I'll handle this." He turned to Bernie. "Show me the bad file again."

She wiggled the cursor. "Here."

"Thanks. I'll take care of it."

Lester smiled at her. "I appreciate this, Bebe."

Bernie stood. She still wanted a picture of the black Mercedes with the damage from the accident and the license plate, but her instinct sensed danger. Lester's summons to the office left her uneasy.

Parrot Man sat at the screen. "If this doesn't work, we might—" He looked away from her toward the window, stopped talking, and stood a bit straighter.

A large man in a dark suit, a light green shirt, and a gold necktie stepped into the room. Two even larger men entered behind him and stood at attention. The man in the suit glared at Parrot Man and Lester. Then he focused on Bernie. "Officer Manuelito. I am Mr. Kelly. How endearing of you to come to visit." The way he smiled at her was pure evil.

18

The two big men with Kelly moved toward Bernie.

Kelly looked at Lester and Parrot Man again. "Fools. Get out of here."

Parrot Man headed to the door before Kelly had finished. Lester gave Bernie a wide-eyed look, then rushed to follow.

Kelly studied the room, motioned to the guard with a diamond in his ear, and said a few words in what she assumed was Mandarin. Diamond nodded and walked outside. Bernie noticed that the door stayed open. Kelly turned to the second guard, who had a mustache, and said something else she didn't understand. That man went into the office and emerged with the laptop under his arm.

The distractions gave Bernie time to plan her response, and she took the lead. "I assume you are the person in charge." He didn't correct her.

"I have to compliment you on this operation.

From what I have seen, you run things with tremendous efficiency. I've been wanting to talk to you. I have some questions."

"And I have some for you, too. And I anticipate that we can work together." Kelly motioned toward the couch. "Please."

Bernie sat. The guard with the neatly trimmed mustache stood so close to her, just over her right shoulder, that she could smell his aftershave. Kelly gracefully lowered himself onto the chair across from her. A strong man, she thought, and fit. With an element of surprise, she might have been able to evade him and escape, if it came to that. But not with the two bodyguards. She wondered why he needed them, especially at his own workplace. That idea in itself sparked some hope in a bad situation.

"When your photo and fingerprints entered our system, as well as realizing that you were not Bernadine Blackman but Navajo Police officer Bernadette Manuelito, I discovered that you have a background in botany. I find that highly appropriate for this conversation. But first, tell me why you are here, Officer. Or should I call you Bebe?"

His arrogance made her teeth hurt. "I could give you several reasons, all of which concern illegal activity. A man died in a collision with a car KHF owns. Another man intimately involved with this company is missing. My phone calls to learn what was behind these two serious incidents remained unanswered." She paused for effect. "Can you explain why I am speaking with you instead of Mr. Begay Perez, the registered owner of the company?"

"Mr. Begay Perez is no longer with us. I acquired the business from him a few days ago." Kelly leaned back slightly. "Again, why are you here, pretending to need a job?"

"When I called to talk to Mr. Begay Perez about the dead man, I also wanted to speak to him about KHF's lack of respect for the agreement he signed with the Navajo Nation. Another officer who came on official business got the runaround. To work undercover seemed the most direct way to get my questions answered and find justice for the man killed by the KHF car."

"Regretfully, KHF has had some communication problems with the Navajo Nation's government. Mr. Begay Perez no longer speaks for the company. I know nothing of an accident involving one of our vehicles. You must be mistaken."

"I'm not mistaken. Let's start over. As I'm sure you know, the Navajo Nation approved this operation because of Begay Perez's tribal connections and his reputation. The tribal council believed his promises regarding water use, labor laws, and respecting the rights of the neighbors. And, of course, only growing hemp for CBD. We have evidence that all of those agreements have been violated."

"Officer, that is preposterous. You have observed the hemp processing. I can show you how we monitor THC levels carefully to make sure that our cannabis products meet the guidelines. If you had approached me directly instead of resorting to this undercover ruse, I could have explained everything."

"I would have talked to you if I had known you were in charge, but no one here would respond to me. I get more determined when I'm ignored." She took a breath. "Let's move on. I know that you pay your workers in weed as well as cash, because Lester offered to pay me that way. That's illegal, and I'm sure you knew that."

"The payments are a small misunderstanding. I apologize for Lester's lack of clarity. After they receive clearance from a doctor, we offer our workers medical cannabis because the strenuous jobs many of them do lead to muscle aches and spasms. We make that option available through kindness, but if it upsets the Navajo Nation, we can consider discontinuing the practice."

He was one of the smoothest liars she had ever come across. "What about the illegal immigrants who work here, the abuse of water rights? The dead dogs?"

He held up a manicured hand. "Nothing but jealous rumors. The neighbors don't like change."

"Let's go back to Dino Begay Perez, the face of the business for the tribe, the man who signed the agreement. What happened to him?" She nodded to the wall where Kelly's photo hung. "Why isn't Begay Perez's picture there, with you and the other man, Dr. Zhou?"

She saw his face stiffen for an instant. "While Mr. Begay Perez strongly supports KHF, he is not able to continue his active role with the company. It's really not police business."

"Mr. Begay Perez's relatives have asked the police to follow up on his disappearance. That's another reason I'm here."

"Disappearance?" He gave her a cool smile. "How rude of him to neglect his extended family. KHF valued his contributions to the farm, and we were all saddened when he resigned. I can tell you truthfully that no one has seen him in the past week."

A pair of trucks rumbled by. Bernie turned to look, and Kelly changed the subject. "For your information, those are filled with our unique CBD products going to market to reduce arthritis pain, help cancer patients with nausea, and ease sleeplessness and anxiety. Those sales finance the medical research arm that my dear friend Dr. Zhou led so well. And each product's label mentions that it was produced on the Navajo Nation."

"What happened to Dr. Zhou?"

"He and I had a slight difference of opinion. He left one afternoon, and, as you know, was the victim of a pedestrian-vehicle collision." Bernie hid her surprise that Kelly would confirm that Zhou was, in fact, the victim. "Dr. Zhou was a fine plant scientist, and a founding partner, along with myself and Mr. Begay Perez, in KHF. Dr. Zhou had just developed a new medicine. Alas, as you know, he died in that tragic accident."

She remembered the vehicle's unhesitant assault on the man—intentional, unapologetic murder. "What illnesses did Dr. Zhou focus on?"

"Mainly epilepsy, especially childhood conditions. He had a relative with the disease, and that

motivated him. The medicine currently available costs more than the average person earns
in a year. And, besides the expense, the existing
cannabidiol medications help only those children
with a specific type of the disease. Dr. Zhou developed a new, broader-range treatment. We are
presenting it to the FDA for approval and hope to
get major drug companies to partner with us for
massive production and, of course, profits."

"Profits?"

"You sound offended, Officer. Making a profit
is the American way, is it not?"

"But not on the backs of sick people. Not by
exploiting desperate workers."

"You sound like Zhou. He wanted to practically give the medicine away. He kept quoting the
Christian Bible to me. Can you imagine?"

She could imagine clearly, having seen the Bible in Dr. Zhou's bag at the time of his death and
having known people with medical bills many
times larger than their incomes. "Is that what you
argued about?"

Kelly said something to Mustache, and a few
moments later the guard returned with a single
bottle of water that he gave to his boss. "He was
a good worker, a fine scientist, but stubborn. No
one is irreplaceable. My sister, Mai Kelly, is now
running the lab."

"If, as you say, everything here is on the level,
why all the secrecy and security? And why do this
research here, instead of at a hospital or university
with state-of-the-art equipment?"

"We have everything we need here, and access

to the plants is important to the researchers." He looked at Mustache. "I believe we have exhausted this conversation. My associate will walk with you to your vehicle."

"No. I can't leave without knowing who killed Dr. Zhou. Where were you at the time of the accident? I know you would not let just anyone drive that expensive new company car. Who else had access to it?"

Kelly moved his head slightly, his perfectly barbered black hair shining in the sunlight that flowed into the office through the front window. She looked into his eyes, something her mother had taught her not to do with a stranger—especially someone who might harm her. She shivered as she recognized the identical coldness she had found in the eyes of the Mercedes's driver. Kelly, she realized, was the same size and shape.

"So Dr. Zhou talked about taking his discovery someplace where making money wasn't as important as helping people feel better?"

Kelly nodded. "A fine scientist, but a poor businessman. Why does it matter so much to you, Officer?"

She exhaled and played her trump card. "Because I was there. I saw him die."

Kelly moved his chin, and she could tell by the scent of aftershave that Mustache now lurked behind her. She rose from the chair. The guard put a heavy hand on her shoulder and pushed her back to sitting.

"What are you—"

"Listen and learn. Now the situation becomes

more interesting. As you must realize, I have a large investment here, and planning comes as natural to me as breathing. I appreciate your vulnerability, Officer. And we can use your mistake in coming here to our mutual advantage."

Bernie shook her head. "My department, the FBI, the DEA—the whole alphabet soup of agencies—know about this assignment."

"Of course they do. That doesn't matter. I'm going to show you the laboratory where Dr. Zhou worked. And you are correct, of course; we also have scientists who work to develop more potent strains of cannabis for the recreational market as well as for medicinal uses. Why wouldn't we?"

"Because of something known as integrity? Because of living up to one's word with the sovereign Navajo Nation?"

"When you meet Mr. Begay Perez, remind him that he was the one who signed the agreement. But before you go, let's take a tour." He stood and made a subtle motion with his chin. Mustache moved, too. "First, Officer, I need your cell phone. Lester told you they were not allowed."

"My phone? Are you—" Before she could say *crazy*, Mustache towered over her and brushed his arm against her chest. Bernie pressed herself back in the chair to avoid the contact, but he increased the pressure against her chest and let his arm linger there before he moved his large hand into her upper interior jacket pocket, squeezed her left breast, and removed her cell phone.

She felt hot anger rise. She jumped from the chair, and just as quickly, he pushed her down again, hard enough this time to make her teeth chatter.

Mustache gave the phone to Kelly, who opened it, studied the screen, and then passed it back to Mustache with a few words of Mandarin.

"Officer, I suggest that you cooperate when the guard reaches for your hand. The screen responds just as well to broken fingers. Which one do you use for the scan?"

It made no sense to resist. When the time came to escape, she didn't want to unnecessarily hamper herself with avoidable pain. "My right thumb."

She extended her hand and felt Mustache press her thumb against the phone screen. He winked at her, and she spit in his face. He wiped the saliva off with the back of his hand and smiled.

The guard passed the phone to Kelly, the screen now bright. Largo had assured her it was complicated enough that only a serious techie could uncover its inner secrets. Kelly spent a moment studying the phone without comment, and then, instead of destroying it as she expected, slipped it into the breast pocket of his custom-fitted suit coat. He said something else to Mustache, and the guard grabbed her arm and pulled her to standing.

They left the office. The cool October air mixed with her anger, invigorating her. She waited for the stirring of another idea and watched for a chance to escape.

The men walked quickly, Mustache guiding her with his hand heavy on her upper arm. Diamond stayed next to Kelly, a few yards behind them. It was exactly the way she would have orchestrated the situation if she were in charge. No chance of an easy getaway.

They headed to a part of the compound she had noticed at a distance earlier, an area with portable buildings. They reminded her of those supposedly temporary classrooms often used in poor rural areas, including parts of the Navajo Nation, except that these looked new.

They kept walking, past the first building. Closed blinds covered the windows that faced the road, but she could see the glow of lights inside and an occasional human-size shadow. Two more loaded pickup trucks cruised past, stirring up dust.

The second portable seemed exactly like the first. Diamond punched in the entry code, and Bernie heard the door unlock. He opened it and stepped aside so that Kelly could enter ahead of him. Then Mustache pushed her forward. Judging from the cannabis, the scales, microscopes, test tubes, beakers and burners, computers, and other equipment, this was a botany lab. Perhaps new varieties of *Cannabis indica* and *Cannabis sativa* were born here. Perhaps they even worked with the special kind of cannabis that had helped prevent seizures.

The man in the white coat at the desk closest to the door rose, greeted Kelly, and said something Bernie didn't catch. He left, and in a few moments a fortysomething Asian woman, also in a white lab coat, came over to them. She glanced at Bernie and then smiled at Kelly. "Sir, is there something specific I may show you?"

"Dr. Mai, my guest has some questions for you."

"Of course." She turned to Bernie. "Please go ahead."

"Tell me what sort of research you are doing here for people with epilepsy."

The woman had obviously expected the question, and her answer sounded like something she had said many times before. "We are exploring pharmaceutical uses for cannabis in various neurological protocols. Some cannabis compounds seem especially effective with certain forms of epilepsy. We are researching those that may reduce the number and intensity of seizures."

"How do you do that?"

"Different varieties of cannabis have different chemical footprints. When we find those with most of the elements that alleviate the neurological symptoms, we work to genetically enhance them to contain more of the beneficial substances. For example, *Cannabis ruderalis*, first discovered in southern Russia, holds special promise for medical uses because it has very low levels of THC—tetrahydrocannabinol, the chemical that produces the plant's intoxicating effects—and is rich in CBD, cannabidiol. Do you know what cannabinoids are?"

"Tell me."

"They are interesting chemicals—more than one hundred of them in cannabis including CBD and THC. They interact with special receptors in the human brain and adjust the release of neurotransmitters in an effort to keep the body's functions in balance."

"Neurotransmitters?"

"They are the molecules used by the nervous system to send messages between neurons, or from neurons to muscles. There is considerable research underway to explore the benefits of cannabinoid substances for people with neurological diseases, including intractable epilepsy." *Cannabis ruderalis* is a more popular choice among those researchers and patients who are interested in the natural healing benefits of cannabis.

"Why do this here, in the middle of nowhere, in an improvised laboratory?"

She glanced at Kelly. He nodded.

"We wanted to conduct our research free of the threat of espionage, and we wanted to minimize distractions for our staff. Also, we wanted the lab to be as close as possible to the source of the plants."

Mai relaxed as she talked, Bernie noticed. "Dr. Zhou's niece is living with the disease, so finding a way to make things better for her and children who share her diagnosis motivates the work he and his staff do."

"Who are they?"

"Excuse me?"

"The staff you mentioned. What are their credentials?"

"Dr. Zhou and I, as his research partner, assembled an international staff at the beginning, when our focus was strongly on medical cannabis uses. But now, sadly, without his assistance, I—"

Kelly scowled. "Mai, enough."

The woman cringed as though she'd been slapped.

Bernie felt Mustache's hand on her shoulder again. This time they walked down a narrow hallway. Diamond opened the door into a small, sparsely furnished room. She paused at the doorway, looking for alternative exits and finding none, only a pair of couches and a coffee table. Beyond that, she saw a small kitchen on one side of the room and a long horizontal window on the other.

Mustache shoved her forward. Kelly and Diamond had entered before them, and Mai followed, enough people in a small space to make Bernie uneasy and slightly claustrophobic.

The window on the opposite wall looked into an area with a table that held two sets of headphones, microphones on their stands, and two padded roller chairs. Gray foam that reminded her of egg cartons covered the walls for sound dampening. It was a hybrid between an interview room at the police station and a radio recording studio. She had spoken on the San Juan College station in Farmington twice. Once she was one of three panelists talking about a multiagency program to combat drunken driving. And once she came with a public health person to encourage her Navajo people and everyone in the Four Corners to stay home during the pandemic.

"What's that little room for?"

Mai said, "We do a lot of video meetings and online consulting to involve the brightest minds outside the company in our cannabis research.

Because technology is still a challenge in much of this area, we put this studio together to ensure smoother interactions. When our dear Dr. Zhou—"

"Quiet," Kelly cut in. Mai turned away from him, her jaw clenched. He said something to Mustache, who took Bernie to a chair.

"Officer, you've seen the research lab and heard about our important pharmaceutical work. Now, it's time for you to focus closer to home."

Diamond dimmed the lights. A screen dropped from the ceiling.

"How fancy. Your operation must be doing very well to warrant all this expense."

Bernie saw Mai smile and nod. "Of course. We are—"

"Enough chatter." Kelly spoke loudly, and Bernie heard the anger. "Pay attention."

There on the screen she saw Mama sweeping the porch at her little house, her walker parked by the door.

"Why are you showing me this?"

"Watch." Kelly's voice had a disturbing smoothness to it. "Watch and learn."

A truck drove up into Mama's driveway, and she stopped working. A Navajo man, a person Bernie had never seen, climbed out and greeted the old lady. Bernie saw Mama frown. Then a second person, a woman, climbed out and started to talk. Bernie didn't recognize the woman either. As she watched Mama's reaction on the screen, she could see her body relax. Mama seemed to trust these strangers. She opened the door, and they all went inside.

Bernie watched as an old SUV pulled up to Mama's neighbor's house and parked where Mama wouldn't see it. She watched Mrs. Darkwater's dog bark, as it always did, and charge toward the vehicle. She saw the driver's door open and a man wearing a dark hoodie with a ski mask over his face come out. He kicked the dog, landing a hard blow to its ribs. The animal staggered away, and then came back. The video had no sound, but she could almost hear it growling. In the meantime, the man had opened the hatch and removed a shovel. He swung it at the dog and connected. She saw the dog fly and land heavily on its back. It didn't move as the camera stayed on it. Bernie wasn't fond of dogs, but she cringed to see the creature Mrs. Darkwater loved so cruelly abused.

The man took some red plastic gasoline containers out of the vehicle. Bernie watched him walking toward Mama's house. Then the screen went black. Someone turned on the light, and Kelly stood in front of her.

"What was that guy doing with those gas cans at my *shimá*'s house?" She used the safe word, hoping the phone in Kelly's pocket was still transmitting. "Who are those two people in the truck?"

"My employees. They told her they were her relatives and were in the area and stopped by for a visit. As you saw, and as we expected, she invited them in, so our other workers could prepare to burn the woodpile, the old corral, and her home."

The corral, where Mama had kept the sheep back in the day when she could still weave, was an important part of her heritage. Her home meant the world to her.

Bernie inhaled to calm herself. The video had left her profoundly shaken—and she realized that was their intention. "My *mother* has nothing to do with this. She's a harmless old woman."

Kelly must have set up the encounter in Toadlena as soon as they understood that she was not Bernadine Blackman. The idea that someone would harm Mama made her both furious and anxious. She realized that, like Agent White, she had severely underestimated the depth of evil here.

"The two will stay with your old mother until I tell them to kill her. Or until I tell them to let her go. That depends on you. How tragic for an old woman's body to be found in a blaze at her home. But old ladies catch things on fire all the time." Kelly laughed.

"And her police officer daughter simply disappears. A double tragedy. I'll spare you the painful details for now, but it won't be pleasant for you either."

"You'll never get away with it."

He flashed a smile, and she noticed his perfect teeth and the icy focus in his eyes. She had no doubt he meant exactly what he said.

"Let us talk about you and your work and how you can save your mother's life. When Dr. Zhou left the farm, our surveillance cameras captured him running away with a small duffel bag. After an extensive investigation, we are certain that Zhou stole some proprietary material, specifically samples of unique types of cannabis under development and seeds from those plants, which we intend to patent. We believe he had that material with him on the highway where he died, and that his bag is now in the custody of the Navajo Police. Am I correct in this assumption?"

"You are." She understood where Kelly was headed. She had to buy time for her backup to arrive—assuming they had received the safe word. Time for Mama to stay alive. "What does this have to do with me or my mother?"

"I will offer you a business deal. A trade."

"What is it?"

"After the accident, one of our associates went to the scene to search for the bag, but it was not there. We contacted the New Mexico State Police officer who investigated the accident. He informed us that a Navajo officer, Officer Bernadette Manuelito, was the first responder and may have found the bag. We believe what Dr. Zhou stole from us is in that bag. If you can retrieve it, your mother will live. Dr. Zhou's bag in exchange for your dear *shimá*'s life."

"That's impossible. The bag is locked in the evidence room of a police station."

"You work there, Officer, and you know how to solve problems. And you love your old mama."

"Let me think about it. I'm sure we can work something out."

"That's what I knew you would say."

Bernie understood two things clearly: The

cannabis that Kelly sought, the reason he wanted the bag, had been shipped to the law enforcement lab for analysis. And he would kill her as soon as she did what he asked, but until then both she and her mother would stay alive.

She had to buy time.

"OK. The best time to get the bag is in the evening, when there's less activity." She put her best actress skills to use. "I can probably do it for you, say, around ten p.m." She paused again. "I know the man in charge of the evidence room, and that will be near the end of his shift. I'll tell him he can leave, and I'll lock up when I'm done." She sighed deeply.

Kelly motioned to Diamond. She saw the Taser, but by then it was too late.

19

Jim Chee listened again to the politely worded
message on Bernie's cell phone that came down to
Leave me alone, I'm studying. He hoped she would
have finished her undercover assignment by now.
He called their old-fashioned landline but she
didn't answer.

She's fine, he told himself. She's a highly competent police officer. The job must have been more
complicated than she expected, and the captain
and his crew have her back. No need to worry.

He worried as he drove toward Pete's house.

Dinner with the two would be a good distraction. He enjoyed the old man's stories. It wasn't his
style to arrive empty-handed as a guest, so he
stopped at the Food King on his way to their
house. He remembered the older man's comments about watermelon and grabbed a small
one to take with him.

Paul met him at the door.

"The pizza just got here. Come on in. You want a beer to go with it?"

"Water is fine."

Paul took the watermelon. "Looks like you brought dessert. Thanks."

Chee followed Paul past what had once been a living room and now stored rocks, books and magazines, and treasures from their active days in archaeology. Chee paused to study a dusty black spearpoint on the large tabletop, next to some old leather straps.

"Paul, is this onyx?"

"That's right." He handed the artifact to Chee. "Take it in and let Pop tell you the story of how he found it."

"And what's this?" Chee motioned to the straps.

"It's an old sling the indigenous people used for hunting. They killed rabbits, maybe even larger creatures, with the rocks they could launch."

"Interesting. I've never seen one before."

Paul handed it to him, and Chee noticed a pouch where the ancient hunter would have placed the projectile. "Pop showed Curtis and me how to make these when we were teenagers. I got pretty good with it. One time I hit a vulture in flight."

"Wow."

Paul laughed. "Stunned the poor sucker. He staggered around awhile and then took off again."

The house looked messier than before, perhaps because Chee was seeing it now without the dramatic distraction of the view through the windows. Dr. Pete sat facing the closed blinds, and seemed more slumped than he had on the previous visit. Someone had arranged three small tables, one in front of Black Beauty and the other two at opposite ends of the couch. Chee noticed that the old man had not shaved.

"Hello, sir. Thank you for the dinner invitation."

"Chee, glad you could join us. Have a seat there, close to me."

Before he obliged, he handed the man the black spearpoint. "This caught my eye on the way in. Paul said there's a good story that comes with it."

"He's right about that." But instead of telling the story, Pete felt the weight of the worked stone in his palm and then set it aside. "What have you learned about Curtis? Any idea yet what happened out there?"

"No, sir. Nothing more definite than we talked last time. I think—"

"Have you talked to that scumbag guy he worked for?" Paul interrupted, bringing the pizza, plates, and napkins.

"Robert Azul?" Chee assumed Paul wouldn't speak of Doug that way.

"Yeah, and his slimy wife."

Paul set the pizza next to his father. "They took advantage of Curtis. He worked hard for them with nothing much to show for it. Curtis said Robert was beyond angry when he told him he was starting rock art tours with Doug."

"Talking with Robert and Ramona is my part of the investigation. That's all I can tell you."

"I'm glad you're looking into them. How long before the autopsy report comes back, so we'll know what killed him?"

"Autopsies don't work like that."

"Are you sure?"

"Yes. Despite what you see on TV. The coroner or medical examiner will come up with a cause of death, say a bullet to the heart. And explain the angle at which the bullet entered, the damage it did to other organs, things like that. And sometimes they come up with a manner of death."

"Cause? Manner? What's the difference?"

"Well, the cause of death is the specific injury or disease that leads to the person dying. For instance, if Curtis died from drowning, that would be the cause of death. In that example, the manner of death would be a determination that the drowning was an accident—he slipped and fell in—or a homicide if someone held his head under water."

"How long will your investigation stay open?"

"It depends. I have at least one more person to talk to."

"I still can't believe you found his body out there in the water," Pete said. "A cop on vacation. Our poor, poor Curtis was so afraid of water. I wonder . . ."

Paul had begun to distribute the plates. "Pop, let's talk about something else."

Pete leaned back, frowning. Paul served his father a piece and motioned to Chee. "Help yourself."

Chee took a slice. As he did, he looked at Pete and saw the tears on his cheeks.

"Sir, I never got to know the man who died. I wish I had. I'd like to hear some stories about him. How did you meet?"

Pete studied his untouched slice of pizza and took a sip of his beer. "Well, I was doing talks at schools out here, and Curtis was in the class. And then he came to my Saturday programs, and then he volunteered. I mentored him. He was like a son to me. A nice, smart boy who became a fine, talented man."

"He was a saint, right, Pop?" Chee heard the sarcasm in Paul's voice. "Little Curtis's biggest problem, at least according to my old man, was that he didn't get enough attention. My father ended up practically adopting him."

"I did what I could to help him. I didn't love you any less because of him." Pete's voice had more than a touch of anger. "Don't sound so jealous."

"I was sad, not jealous. I lost Mom to divorce. I lost you to Curtis. I know he meant a lot to you, and he was like a brother to me. But he's dead, Pop. We have to move on together." He stood. Chee saw the pain on his face. "You want another beer?"

"Sure."

Paul looked at Chee, who shook his head.

Pete drained the beer at his side and handed his son the empty bottle.

Paul was back in a moment and gave his father an open long-neck.

"I was happy when Curtis and Paul became friends," Pete said. "How long did that last?"

"Until he died," Paul said. "We got along. We just didn't want to work together anymore. Curtis

helped Doug as a tour guide and he worked for Laguna Blue at the marina. Even though he already
had two jobs, he was a great help on the grant at
first. But he really couldn't commit to it."

Paul resumed eating, and Chee enjoyed his own
pizza in the room's soft quiet.

Pete sat motionless, his food untouched. "That's
not true," he said. "Curtis liked being busy. You
and he used to work together well. You have the
drive and ambition and see the big picture. He
loved sharing his stories about this place, taking photographs, making sketches, talking to me
about the details. The tours would have been first-
rate."

"Details? Pop, Curtis was taking advantage of
you, of your experience and your passion to try to
make some money."

Pete put the plate with his uneaten pizza on the
table and stretched back in the recliner. "It broke
my heart when you two decided you couldn't get
along."

"We got along. That's the beer talking. But I
didn't like the way he was using you. I didn't like
that he didn't pay back the money you loaned him."

"You're wrong, as usual. Curtis loved the soul
of this place as much as I did. He wanted to share
it with people, to educate them on what had been
here before the dam and the lake. For you, it's all
academic. Get another grant. Do another mean-
ingless study."

Chee realized he sat as an observer to a long-
standing disagreement between father and son.
He kept quiet, waiting for the bickering to sub-

side. Paul squeezed his lips together, as though he were imprisoning the words that could further fuel the argument. The room had begun to darken as the after-sunset glow filtering through the shades faded. Silence hung over the three of them like the stealthy approach of night.

Then Paul stood and turned on the overhead lights. He walked to his father, patted his shoulder, and took the empty beer bottle. "Another?"

"Yeah, but you better watch it. Alcohol doesn't go well with your antidepressants."

Chee saw Paul tense and turn away.

"Pop, our guest might be interested in that project we were doing with Curtis, for the insight it provides into the man. Why don't you tell him about it?"

Pete looked at Chee. "You curious?"

"Sure."

"We, the three of us—Paul, Curtis, and me—were going to try to re-create some of the excitement that I experienced decades ago as one of the leaders of the Glen Canyon archaeology salvage work. You've heard of that." He said it as a statement, not a question.

"By way of background, that was the job that brought us out here so many years ago. My obsession with the project led Paul's mother to divorce me, but that's another story. We ran short on almost everything—time, funding, and personnel topped the list—but we did the best survey we could. We developed a comprehensive overview of the human history of Glen Canyon." Pete paused, lost in the memory. "It was beautiful here before the rising water destroyed what nature had built and ravaged thousands of years of irreplaceable artifacts and information and—"

Paul handed him another beer. "Pop, stop. Without the lake we wouldn't be living here. Doug wouldn't have his business. You wouldn't have met Curtis, or Sergeant Chee for that matter. Don't be so negative." Paul turned his attention to Chee. "You may not know this, but my father and his associates changed the course of American archaeology with their work at Glen Canyon. Before the Glen Canyon project, research moved very slowly and focused mostly on specific problems and the reconstruction of ancient societies. After Pop's work here—and the work of others, my old man doesn't get all the credit—archaeologists began to focus more on the big picture. Pop's passion is what brought me into the field, and Curtis, too, to some extent. I've rarely regretted a day of it."

He stood. "You guys talk awhile. I'm going upstairs to work on the grant. Chee, let me know when you need to leave so I can help Pop."

"Sure thing."

Pete put the round mouth of the bottle to his lips and swallowed. "I'm fine, son. I don't really need—" But before he finished the sentence, his son had begun to climb the stairs.

Chee offered a second slice of pizza to Pete, even though the first remained untouched. The old man declined.

He took a piece for himself. It was good, with sausage in addition to the pepperoni. Bernie, a pepperoni-only gal, would never have approved. He missed her.

"It seems like the man who died had been your friend for a long time."

Pete nodded. "It sounds corny, but I really loved that guy. Curtis had such a bright, inquisitive mind. I liked him from the first day I met him.

"We used to talk about some of the other places that disappeared in addition to the Indian sites. Historic gold mines, and sites like the Crossing of the Fathers, where the Spanish explorers Escalante and Domínguez forded the river in 1776. And the spot on the Hole-in-the-Rock Trail where those Mormon families struggled." He took another swallow of his beer. "The glen that John Wesley Powell enjoyed and that gave the canyon its name sits beneath hundreds of feet of water."

"Did you take him and Paul on field trips to show them where you'd worked?"

"I sure did. The boys loved it, especially Curtis, even though being in a boat made him nervous. He always wore his life preserver. Paul acted like a big brother and said if anything happened, he'd save Curtis and then I could save both of them." A smile lit his face for the first time since Chee had arrived. "Most people know this area because of the lake—a boater's playground. But the deeper story, what I talked to the kids about, is beginning to reemerge as the water level lowers. It gives us another chance to set things right and focus on the bigger story of the people who lived here." Pete paused for a bite of pizza.

Chee was relieved to see him eating. "I'm glad

to hear you say that. This is sacred land, and we all have an obligation to protect it."

"That's the reason the three of us started the education project. Paul found the initial money, and he's looking for more. I provided a list, based on my research, of some of the places with the best rock art. Curtis loved being outside, so he was doing the legwork, figuring out what's left of some of the sites, taking pictures, making sketches. Sometimes he'd bring a few props to use in the photos or his drawings." Pete ate another bite of pizza. Chee sipped his water, remembered the camera he'd seen in Curtis's backpack, and silently wondered if what he'd characterized as looted artifacts were really props for pictures.

"Curtis wanted to open the most accessible sites for guided tours, in some cases while the fieldwork continued. He liked the idea of giving visitors a chance to see archaeology graduate students in action, even from a distance. And we'd include women in the project this time."

"What do you mean?"

Pete shook his head. "The teams I led were all men. The profession frowned on women archaeologists out here, sweating in the sun. I'm glad times have changed."

"Me too."

"Anyway, Curtis discovered that some of those places where I'd worked years before were visible, just barely, above the lake's surface. I'm too unsteady to be climbing around out there but Curtis enjoyed taking photos or sketching the places where I worked, the sites I told the boys stories about. He thought the archaeology tours would be hugely popular."

Chee watched as Pete adjusted the oxygen tube in his nose and shifted in his recliner, craning to see the table in the other room. "There's a brown sketchbook in there. Bring it here. I want to show you something."

Unlike the other things on the table, the sketchbook looked new and practically dust-free. Chee brought it, and the sling Paul had mentioned, and gave them to the old gentleman.

Pete sat the book on his lap and picked up the sling. "This was a rare find, an ancient tool. Take a look."

The old man extended it to him, and Chee examined the item more closely, then handed it back to Pete. "Paul pointed it out to me. It's an ancient slingshot, isn't it?"

"That's right. I found it way back when. I imagine the hunters may have killed squirrels with it. Maybe the skilled ones got a small deer."

Chee knew that such an artifact should either be returned to the site of origin, repatriated to the ancestors of the person who made it, or perhaps displayed for educational purposes in a museum somewhere.

"You have some interesting artifacts. Back when you were excavating out here, I guess the rules on collecting cultural material were different, right?"

Pete smiled. "I know what you're getting at. It's not exactly legal for me to have this stuff, but not exactly illegal either. If I hadn't saved it, the sling and much of the rest of what I have would have been lost to the water. In the end, my collection goes to the University of Utah and NAU, and they can deal with the repatriation issues."

Chee nodded. "What's in the sketchbook?"

Pete opened it to the first page. "Look at this."

He glanced over Pete's shoulder. The meticulous drawings captured ancient stick figures, spirals, and four-legged creatures. The page across from it was a color photograph that showed a rock art panel filled with ancient handprints and the scenery around it.

"Wow. Did Curtis do that?"

"This was part of his exploration for where the tour might go and for use in the grant proposal."

"He had talent. I'm sorry I never got to know him."

Pete turned a page and then another. "This is some of what we want to save, Curtis and Paul and I. I'm worried that now Curtis is gone, this won't happen."

"You still have Paul."

"Paul likes the research idea, but not the public education part of it. That was crucial to Curtis and me. Paul doesn't understand the role of the tours in enlightening the public, in building a bigger cadre of people who would work to protect these sites. He can't get past the fact that the tour operator would be making money and that visitors might damage the sites. But it's a double-edged sword. People who want to harvest these antiquities already know about them. Curtis and I strongly believed that if we can educate the average guy, show him this resource, and enlist his help, we've got a better chance of protecting what's out there."

Chee considered that. He believed most archaeologists would side with Paul in the discussion.

Pete closed the sketchbook. His chest expanded with a deep breath and then sank. "Have you figured out how he died?"

"The autopsy says it wasn't drowning. All my interviews so far have been blind alleys. I'm wrapping things up today, probably heading home in the morning. If you could tell me anything else about the cave I mentioned, I'd really appreciate it."

Pete reached for his beer, studied the brown bottle. He took a sip and slowly set it down again. "I'd like to take you to the rock art Curtis drew. Are you up for another trip onto the lake?"

"I would love that. I hoped you'd suggest it. Do I need to rent a boat?"

"No. We can take mine." Pete studied his freckled hands. "I want to see the place where you found Curtis in exchange for my petroglyph stories. Can you show me that inlet?"

Chee nodded. He'd ask Sunfish for help to make sure he could find it again.

"How about tomorrow morning, when you've finished your work with the sheriff?"

"It's a deal. Are you sure you feel up for it?"

"Never better." Pete smiled. "I won't hike up to the panels at Crimson Beach, but I'll tell you which way to go. While we're out tomorrow, we can talk about the cave. Around ten sound OK?"

"Fine."

"Call me when you're on your way here."

"I'll do that. Good night. I'll head upstairs to say goodbye to Paul."

At the base of the staircase, Chee checked his phone and saw that there had been no response from Robert Azul. He texted the number with a message that he was on loan to the Coconino County Sheriff's Office, and if Robert couldn't talk to him tonight, Detective Malone would conduct the interview. Chee slipped the phone back in his pocket and had climbed the six steps to Paul's office when he felt a vibration. Robert texted back, suggesting that they meet at a restaurant bar just off North Lake Powell Boulevard. Chee confirmed: On my way soon.

Paul was working on the computer. He minimized the screen and turned to Chee. "You leaving?"

"Yeah. Thanks for the pizza. Pete and I had a nice talk. He seems a little less upset about the death. He wants to show me some rock art tomorrow."

"Did you set something up?"

"I'm stopping by at ten." Chee paused. "Is Pete OK with a boat?"

"Not really. I'll come along. Curtis took him out a couple weeks ago, and Pop forgot his portable oxygen. It took him a full day to recover. Where does he want to go?"

"He plans to show me some rock art panels and talk about the artifacts at Crimson Beach. And he wants to see where we found the body."

"Maybe that will give him some, what do they call it? Closure."

"He seems concerned that without Doug's brother, the tours won't happen."

Paul nodded. "They won't if I can help it. Pop got on board too early. We have to do the science first, see what survived all those decades underwater. Curtis couldn't wrap his brain around that. He only pictured the money."

Chee said good night and drove to the restaurant. As soon as his eyes adjusted to the dim light, he spotted Robert Azul at a seat at the end of the bar. He slid onto the stool next to him. They didn't speak until the bartender had taken the order for club soda for him and a Jack and Coke for Robert. The room, quiet except for some generic background music, held few other customers. Chee appreciated the decor—a thirty-foot etched-glass wall with an image of the Glen Canyon Dam.

Robert opened the conversation. "Ramona said you talked to her about Curtis, wondering if he had any enemies. I guess I made the list."

"This is a routine investigation that follows an unattended death. I heard that you were at a poker game. Thanks for doing this."

"I was having a terrible night anyway, running bad. What can I tell you about the dead man?"

"Ramona said you were unhappy with Curtis and wanted to fire him. Why was that?"

"Unhappy? That's a nice word for it. He ripped me off in a business deal. I wanted to kill the bastard." He stopped. "I guess that's the wrong thing to say to a cop investigating a possible murder."

Chee sipped his drink, letting silence do its work.

"And even though I just said I wanted to kill him, I respected him. He worked hard, never complained, did more than we asked him. Even though he stole my idea and my wife had her eyes on him, I'm sorry he's dead. Makes my life more complicated."

"I hear you." No criminal Chee had spoken to had ever admitted on their first conversation that the idea for murder had crossed his mind. And conflicts over a woman drove more murders than the theft of an idea. "Tell me about Curtis and Ramona."

Robert studied the ice cubes in his drink. "OK. Curtis worked for us about a year. He was smart and reliable, but I noticed that he and Ramona were becoming real, ah, cozy. I thought about firing the guy when I realized what was going on. But she'd strayed before. And I love her." Robert picked up the glass and adjusted it so it sat directly in the middle of the coaster. "So I assumed she'd have some fun with him and get it out of her system. It didn't work that way."

"That's tough."

Robert took a long swallow of his whiskey. "Curtis and I had an odd, strained relationship, you know, because of Ramona. And that was before he double-crossed me in business."

"You mentioned that Curtis stole an idea from you. Is that what you mean by being double-crossed?"

"They call it an anger management issue now.

You know, when you want to bash someone's head in? So, Chee, have you seen the bathtub ring around the lake?"

"Are you changing the subject?"

"No."

Chee waited as Robert put the glass down exactly as it had been, with the establishment's logo of Glen Canyon exactly in the center.

"I'm gonna tell you a story about Curtis. Pay attention.

"Bathtub ring is what we call the thick white band of mineral deposits you see on the rocks around the lake. It's formed because the water level has been steadily dropping due to drought, evaporation, increased demand downstream, and the sandstone soaking up the water.

"One of our regular boat rental customers asked if the lower water level meant that some of the old Indian sites and the drawings they left on the rocks might be visible now, not underwater anymore. He and his girlfriend wanted to hike in and see what they could find.

"I knew Curtis was into that rock art stuff, so I mentioned to him that maybe Laguna Blue could promote some self-guided tours. You know, encourage people to rent boats for day trips with a map of places to visit. He got excited and did some research to see if some of the archaeological sites Dr. Pete and the other crews had researched were visible now. He said he'd talk to the old man about my idea, that maybe Pete's memories of the area before the lake filled could be part of a guided tour—part nostalgia, part science, part adventure hiking. That sounded great, and I gave him paid time off to investigate out there and see what he could learn about the Indians who used to live here." Robert stopped. "Or should I say Native Americans? I don't want to offend a cop."

"If you know that they were Navajos or Pueblo ancestors, you should say that. Indians is OK with me. I'm not offended."

Robert continued. "Curtis and I brainstormed my idea. He said that he wanted to get Dr. Pete more involved, you know? He said nobody knew what impact being under the water for decades would have on ruins, stone tools, rock art, that kind of thing. We talked about a promo video and using it to help sell the tours. We called it Lake Powell: Home of Untold Mysteries. Catchy, huh?"

Chee nodded. "Have you seen any of the sites that are exposed, now that the water is lower?"

"Yeah. I love to hike. The ones Curtis liked best aren't easy to get to, a bit out of reach for a balding guy on a houseboat in his flip-flops."

"So, these tours wouldn't be for the average Joe?"

"That's right. This would have been adventure tourism for people who love the idea of doing something extraordinary. Lake Powell: Home of Untold Mysteries." He smiled as he said it. "The name makes it easier to monetize. I called Dr. Pete to talk about it, and Paul Hendrix answers. He's a downer. He says he's sure his old man will not want to be part of anything like that for a few more years, until all the archaeological reexamination is done. And he told me Doug Walker might be doing something similar.

"So I got in touch with Doug, and yeah, he and Curtis are planning something: Art and Adventure with the Ancient Ones. He says Curtis told him Dr. Pete would introduce the trip, and Curtis would lead the groups." Robert's voice had grown louder, and Chee could feel his anger. "I wouldn't have even heard about it except that Dr. Pete's son clued me in. The bastard stole my idea and gave it to his brother."

He took a long swallow of his drink. They sat in silence again until Chee spoke.

"Did you kill Curtis Walker?"

"No."

Chee waited. Often the guilty elaborated on their professed innocence or grew defensive; Robert didn't.

"Where were you the day Curtis died?"

"Hold on." Robert pulled out his phone and checked the calendar. "It looks like a typical day. Work, an hour at the gym around noon, home. The gym has a sign in/sign out sheet, if you wanna check. That was the night for the city's Visitor Promotion Advisory Board meeting. I'm involved with that group and our sessions run a couple of hours, seven to nine or so in the evening. They get taped for our archives if you want to check my alibi."

"You knew Curtis well. Why do you think someone wanted him dead? And who would that be?"

"I can't think of anyone with a better reason than I had, and I didn't do it."

"Other than Ramona, who were his friends?"

"He hung out a lot with his brother and his sister-in-law and his nephews and Sunfish. You know her, right?"

"Yeah."

"She's a flirt. She acted as though she really liked Curtis. I think she was jealous of my wife. You might look into the woman-scorned aspect. And she's athletic. If someone pushed him into the lake, she could have done it." The ease with which he floated the idea suggested that this wasn't the first time it had come to him.

Chee listened as Robert elaborated on the case against Sunfish. He didn't buy it, but it wouldn't hurt to suggest that Malone talk to her.

Robert switched tracks. "You might talk to Dr. Pete about Curtis's friends and foes, get his ideas. Curtis respected that man. He probably told Pete things he didn't discuss with me or even Ramona. He kept his secrets to himself."

Chee finished his soda and left Robert ordering a second drink. He'd have plenty of time to chat with Pete when they were on the lake.

He called home and then Bernie's cell— surely she was done with her assignment by now. He hung up when the messages clicked on. He texted: Call me. Then he returned to the motel, got ready for bed, watched a bit of news, and read for a while. He turned off the light and waited for sleep. Because she hadn't called or texted, he assumed Bernie must still be undercover. He knew she was smart and careful; he hoped she was safe.

20

Jim Chee wouldn't have described himself as a worrier, but he worried now.

No word from Bernie last night. Nothing this morning.

As soon as he awoke, long before it could be considered civilized behavior to make a phone call, he called Captain Largo's home number and then his cell. Both calls went straight to voice mail.

When he called at the station, Officer Bigman told him he hadn't heard from Bernie, and reminded him that his lovely wife was studying hard for a test and the interview to become a detective. Chee knew that was her cover story, and he let it sit.

"Sergeant, want some advice from another happily married guy?" He didn't, but Bigman continued anyway. "Chill. You might be able to survive without hearing her voice for a day or two. She'll sound even better when you talk to her after this. OK?"

"I guess."

"Calm down, bro. When will you be back?"

"Probably tomorrow evening. I'm done here except for a couple loose ends."

"Did you find out what happened?"

"No, but I've done as much as I can. Maybe the other detectives have figured it out."

He hung up, unsatisfied, but impressed that Bernie's cover story had held up so well. Maybe Bigman was right to tell him to relax about it. His competent wife knew her way around an investigation. One of the many reasons he loved her was because she kept a cool head.

He showered, thinking of what lay ahead for his own day. He needed to call Malone, tell her what he had learned from the interviews, and suggest that she follow up with Sunfish. He wanted to contact Desmond to see if he had any more thoughts on the Lieutenant's sacred cave. After the trip on the lake with Paul and Pete, he would either return to Navajo Mountain or roll on home.

He told himself, again, not to worry about Bernie, but his nagging anxiety about her wouldn't go away.

He dressed for the boat trip, packed up his things, and took them to the truck. He'd settled into a breakfast of hotcakes with syrup and a tempting side of crisp bacon when his phone vibrated. The caller ID read "County Sheriff." He answered.

"Chee, it's Detective Malone. You learn much yesterday?"

"Not really. I was going to call you after breakfast."

He filled her in about his interviews. "I learned that Curtis was camping there because he was helping Pete Hendrix with a project. Pete asked him to check some of the major sites where the salvage archaeology crews had worked. Now that the lake is lower, Pete wanted Curtis to see if the receding water had uncovered pictographs or anything else from the project's excavations."

"That would explain why Curtis was out there in the middle of nowhere by himself."

She had news for him, she said. "I read through the coroner's full report. Like I told you yesterday, the autopsy shows that Curtis was dead before he hit the lake."

"A heart attack?"

"No sign of that or a stroke. He had a fractured skull. You want the other highlights?"

Chee remembered the bloody rock. He hoped death had come quickly. "Go ahead."

"The coroner estimated that the body had been in the lake less than twenty-four hours, although the cold water made it hard to confirm time of death. And there's another curious thing. You and Ted mentioned that gash on the head, and you took a picture of the blood on the sandstone and some of the boulders. The autopsy mentions that wound, but it wasn't what caused his skull fracture. The autopsy showed a fracture on the back of the skull, caused by something that made contact with great force.

"If you guys had found a baseball bat or a hammer or the like up there, I'd suspect someone had snuck up on our victim. Someone with really good aim and a strong arm could have thrown a brick and hit him in the head hard enough to do that damage. An old-fashioned way to kill somebody." She stopped. "Speaking of that, Ted Morris went back to Crimson Cove for the tent and found two more of those round stones that resembled the one you saw."

"Is that right?" Chee waited for the punch line. Finding rocks that looked like other rocks wasn't exactly big news.

"Hold on. The stones aren't from around here. Ted knows something about geology, and he says he did not expect to see them along the shore at Crimson Beach or anywhere near Rainbow Bridge. They came from the north end of the lake."

"So Ted thinks the killer brought those special death rocks with him, and had a strong arm and good aim on the third try?" He said it as a joke, but Malone took him seriously.

"I'm not going that far, but I'm wondering at the coincidence. You want to see a picture of the rocks Ted found?"

"Of course I do. Send them to my phone, OK?"

"They look like ordinary rocks to me, but Ted took the full face and profile. See here? Like mug shots."

Chee studied the images she sent. "I'm going to

Crimson Beach with Pete Hendrix later. I'll keep an eye out for rocks like that. Can you send that to my phone?"

"Sure. And speaking of mug shots, your tip about Robert Azul paid off. He's a convicted felon. Drug charges, embezzlement, assault. He served time in California but has been a good boy, as far as we can tell, since he and Ramona moved here. And FYI, she hasn't ever been arrested."

"Tell me about the assault."

"Some man was flirting with Ramona, so Robert broke his jaw with a tire iron. Nearly killed him. Ramona told the jury it was self-defense."

Chee thought a moment. "Robert told me he's a seasoned hiker. The fact that whoever killed Curtis didn't use a gun, and Robert isn't supposed to own one, is an interesting side note. Let me know how it shakes out. It's been a pleasure working with you. Good luck, Detective."

"Thanks. We'll get it done. And Chee, someone called for you. A Mr. Grayhair from Navajo Mountain. I asked if it was about Curtis Walker, and he said no, it was something personal. Wants you to call him. And before you head home, remember to stop by and pick up a check."

He'd forgotten. "Will do."

Chee finished his pancakes and then called Doug. Sunfish answered. She sounded more upbeat.

"So, you ready to go cave hunting with me?"

"Not today. Pete Hendrix is giving me a rock art tour. Evidently, he's heard of the cave and wants to talk to me about it."

"Where are you going to see the petroglyphs?"

"Some place Dr. Pete researched back in the day. It's near Crimson Beach. He also wants to see where I found the body."

"Be careful out there. High winds are forecast for this afternoon. Tell Dr. Pete hello for me. I'm fond of that guy. Will you stop by the office when you get done?"

"I don't think so. I'm heading home to Shiprock after that, perhaps with a detour to Navajo Mountain."

"OK." He heard the disappointment in her voice. "Don't be a stranger. I'm serious about wanting to take you out on the lake. Next time?"

"Sure." As he said it, he hoped there would be a next time, and that Bernie could come with him. Despite the murder, this austerely beautiful place had eased his spirits. After the boat trip he looked forward to a closing visit with Desmond and then a quiet drive home to think again about what might be next.

His phone vibrated again. "P. Hendrix." Probably Pete calling to find out when he planned to arrive.

"Hello?"

"Hey, Chee, it's Paul. Pop's not feeling well this morning, and he asked me to show you that rock art above Crimson Beach. I'll pick you up."

"I'm sorry your dad is under the weather." The stinging disappointment made him realize how much he'd wanted to hear Dr. Pete talk about a place he clearly loved.

"No. I'm on the way to your motel. We can

chat about Robert and whatever else I can help you with when we're on the lake."

Chee considered it, letting the phone go silent.

"You still there?"

"Yes. I'm thinking."

"Come on. You can't weasel out of this. Pop made me promise to be his substitute, and I'm looking forward to it. He wants me to take some photos of those magnificent panels for him, as well as the spot where we found Curtis. I can tell you more than you probably want to know about the area. Rock art is one of my specialties."

When would he have another chance for a guided tour of petroglyphs and pictographs at Lake Powell with an archaeologist? "Well, sure, then. Thank you. I hope your father feels better. I was looking forward to hearing his stories about the work he did out here."

Paul laughed. "I can tell you a few of those tales, too. I've listened to him relate that history more times than I can count. I'll be at your motel by ten."

Chee waited outside the lobby and recognized Paul's truck when it arrived on time, with the boat trailer in tow but without the boat. Paul lowered the window and called to him, "Ready?"

"Yeah, but aren't you missing something?"

Paul chuckled. "It's already in the water. I took care of that earlier. The boat is waiting for us. I even packed a lunch."

"How's your father?"

"Still feeling puny. I think he must have eaten too much pizza."

Odd, Chee thought. He remembered Pete refusing the second slice of pizza and barely touching the first. He climbed into the cab of the big truck, and they drove off to the dock.

Paul parked, and they walked to the boat, which was tied to one side of the dock, away from the foot and water traffic. Paul started the old outboard motor and guided it away from the marina.

The day was beautiful, as, Chee realized, were most autumn days near this massive human-made lake. Sunny, pleasantly warm. They saw a few other boaters, but the morning's quiet dominated the vast open space.

"Is it usually so peaceful this time of year?"

"Oh, it depends. Columbus Day, oh wait, Indigenous Peoples' Day, or weekends can get busy, but October tends to be slower. Most of the children are back in class then, and that limits family lake time."

"It sounded like Pete really enjoyed the work he did with schools."

"Yeah. He loved other people's kids. Are you a dad?"

"No. Not yet, anyway. How about you?"

"No. The one woman I fell hard for is married to someone else. She still has a roving eye and wouldn't have minded a little extracurricular with me, but that's not my style. Of course, kids and marriage don't always go together, but they do in my book. So it's just been me and Pop for a while now."

"You two and Curtis?"

"Yeah. Curtis. The brother I never wanted."
Paul laughed. "How about you?"

"I have more clan brothers and sisters than I
can count." As he said it, Chee realized that the
term he recalled Paul using to describe Curtis
most often was business partner. Not brother, or
even friend. "Were you and the dead man close?"

"Why do you ask?"

"Because of your tone of voice when I mention
his name. And because your father is mourning
deeply, and you seem more detached. Last night,
Pete told me that he'd always hoped you two
would get along."

"Pop sincerely loved Curtis. I knew he'd take
the death hard."

"What happened to drive a wedge between you
two?"

"Long story." Paul pushed the boat to acceler-
ate through the smooth lake, leaving the question
unanswered. "You said you might have some additional things to talk to me about. Go ahead."

"OK. I'm puzzled over those items you removed
from Curtis's tent. What's your take on that?"

"What do you mean?" Paul eased up on the
speed and maneuvered the boat to gently cruise
over the wake of a houseboat.

"I saw the pot, the sherds and old tools, and
the sandal. Why were they there? Why did you
remove them?"

"My guess is that he was doing some illegal digging or he had borrowed that stuff from Pop's collection to use for his photos at the site. I figured

I'd rescue the items and let Pop figure it out. You know about Curtis's photographs?"

"Yes. Nice pictures. Your father showed me his sketchbook, too. He was a good artist."

"He was."

"Detective Malone is wrapping up the case now." Chee put his hand in the water. The surface felt warm, but he knew it was icy a few inches beneath. Even though the years of drought, evaporation, and use by agriculture and communities had lowered the water level here, the lake was still deep and filled with buried secrets. Just like most people he encountered, even those who seemed transparent. "What do you know about the dead man's finances?"

"Finances? That's a joke. Curtis spent money as fast as he made it. Faster sometimes." Paul paused. "Oh, you mean in case he owed someone money and they argued over it? Something like that could get a man killed."

"Right. There are three basic motives for murder: jealousy, profit, and revenge. Beyond that, you have the rarer occurrences such as people who kill for the thrill of it, or to conceal another crime. Some experts say that at the bottom of any murder, you'll find at least one of the three *L*'s— love, loathing, and loot."

"Catchy."

"Did Curtis's money issues cause any trouble for his work with you?"

Paul laughed. "No. Pop thought he was volunteering, but I hired him because I knew he needed cash. And if I hadn't, Pop would have given him a loan and then not ever have collected. My father often helped his precious almost son that way. I figured I should give the guy an opportunity to work for his keep."

The motion of the boat and the warmth of the sun reminded Chee that he had gone to bed late and that worry about Bernie had awakened him too early. His eyes grew heavy, and he stretched out his legs. He let the droning sound of the motor lull him into deep relaxation as he replayed Paul's comments about Curtis and the job. Something didn't sit right. He felt his brain activate and his lethargy vanish.

"I've got some questions for you about Curtis and Robert."

"Go ahead."

"You mentioned earlier that Robert took advantage of Curtis. What did you mean by that?"

"He asked Curtis to work weird hours. On several of the days when he and Pop and I had planned to focus on our archaeology project, Curtis would call and say he had to put in an extra shift at Laguna Blue. Also, Robert didn't pay him what he was worth. Stuff like that."

They were closer to the beach now. Chee noticed the color of the water changing to lighter blue, then green as it grew shallower.

"Did my pop mention that Curtis wanted him to be part of the archaeology tours?"

"He did, and he said you opposed that idea."

"You bet. Bringing in tourists didn't sit right with me in terms of protecting the sites here, especially before anyone has had the opportunity to seriously look at what's left after the flooding. But Curtis, Robert Azul, and Doug Walker all loved the idea, each for his own reasons, of course. Robert assumed the tours would be with Laguna Blue but Curtis wanted to help Doug grow his business. When he told Robert, Curtis said, the man went ballistic and threatened him." Paul sighed. "Did you know that Curtis and Ramona were lovers, and that Robert knew about the affair?"

"Robert told me about that himself, although not in so many words."

"If Curtis was murdered, here's how I see it. Robert asks Ramona where Curtis goes on his days off. She tells him he's scouting sites for the tours. Robert loves money even more than he loves Ramona. Robert's a strong hiker, and he knows the area as well as Curtis and I do. Ramona could have told him where Curtis liked to camp. She's been calling me for comfort since Curtis died, and I hear guilt in her voice. There you have it. My theory."

"Interesting." Chee paused a moment. "Were you in love with her, too?"

Paul laughed. "I still am." He cut back the throttle, and the boat slowed as it headed toward shore.

"This looks familiar."

"That's right. Pop asked for a picture of the place where we found the body. And I want to show you some more of the archaeology here at Crimson Beach. I know a good spot to pull ashore. It's a long walk to the sites, but I need to leave the boat here for safety in case the wind comes up."

Chee admired the stark, rocky beauty of the

place, the contrast between the blues of the water and ever-present sky juxtaposed against the sandstone's desert colors. He watched Paul's skillful navigation as he asked the next question. "Here's something that puzzles me. Ramona said Curtis left his job with you because he thought you were going to fire him. Why was that?"

Paul flinched. "Ramona told you that, huh?" He took a breath. "Curtis quit because the work of setting up the new tours, combined with the Laguna Blue job, didn't give him any extra time. The real friction was between Curtis and Robert, but I might have fired Curtis if he hadn't quit. I couldn't stand to think of him and Ramona together, especially because that jerk had another girl—someone named Wanda—and he was giving her money. Ramona has her faults, but she didn't deserve that kind of treatment."

Chee had no doubt that Curtis's relationship with Wanda and her boyfriend was platonic. Paul had misread the situation, and hadn't bothered to ask Curtis for clarification.

He watched Paul bring the boat closer to the coastline and let it drift toward the beach.

"We'll see the rock art up there beneath the overhang. The climb is worth the effort because the carvings are spectacular. You'll find the habitation compound amazing, too. The ruins are well preserved." Paul paused. "I should say, *were* well preserved. I haven't been here since Curtis started his photos and sketches. I think he took things from the ruins for his pictures. I'll show you what's left of the structures by the lake, and then we'll hike. Pop loves this site, but despite the bull Curtis sold him, it deserves more study before anyone opens it to tours."

"After that, I'd like to go back to Curtis's campsite," Chee said. "I need to take a look at something."

"What?"

"I'll talk about it when I find it." The bloody rock Chee had seen earlier weighed on his mind. He wanted to hand it to Detective Malone as part of the trail that pointed to Robert Azul. With the autopsy results implying murder and the other two rocks raising Ted's suspicion, he knew a similar stone stained with the victim's blood should be part of the evidence. He hoped he could find it.

"I could use your help here." Paul motioned to a boulder. "I'll toss you the rope if you don't mind jumping onto the beach and tying us up."

"Sure."

"You can leave your gun here. You won't need it on shores and it's safe in case you slip into the lake or something."

"I never leave my weapon unattended."

"Me neither." Paul laughed. "I guess some guys feel naked without their guns."

Chee leaped to the shore with the rope Paul gave him and securely tied the boat to a rock.

Paul moved onto the beach with agility. "The petroglyph trail starts up there by those trees, but we'll explore down here first. Pop wants a photo or two of what's left of the old irrigation works. You might see some interesting pictographs, too, images of handprints. That is, if they survived the flooding. Pop named this area the Open Hands complex and brought his school groups here to enjoy it. Curtis and I tagged along for years. I got tired of coming, but Pop and Curtis kept visiting until walking along the shore got to be too hard for my old man."

"When was that?"

"Oh, a few years ago. In addition to the irrigation works and the rock art here, there's a habitation complex, granary storage, and a kiva up high." Paul looked toward the cliffside. "We'll go there next to look at the art and assess the damage Curtis has done."

If he hadn't been with Paul, Chee would never have found the irrigation site. Time and the lake had destroyed much of the old system, but the rock walls remained. Paul pointed out the pictographs—zigzag designs that could have been lightning or a snake, a few faint red handprints, and some four-legged creatures with bodies shaped into half ovals with stick antlers.

"These are beautiful." Chee studied the animals. "Being submerged didn't seem to hurt them."

"The amount of degradation depends partly on how much boat traffic cruised by when the water was higher, and the wave action that created. This part of the lake isn't very popular, and that saved these. I'm sure the images on the cliff face fared even better. See how the overhang provides some shelter? According to what Pop and the other archaeologists learned, very few of the people here built permanent habitations. Ruins like the ones you'll see are rare."

"How old are they?"

"A thousand years or maybe a bit more. The area may have had heavier rainfall then, and the extra moisture would have made the place more habitable. You know, water is the story of the settlement of the West."

Chee nodded. Then as now.

They walked quietly for a while.

"Curtis told me he came up for some preliminary scouting, photography, and to do some sketches of the rock art. But the ruins drew him back here. I think the jerk was looting, digging illegally. He exploited my father's memories to make a few bucks on the black market, and in the process violated every principle Pop stands for."

"Looting?" The charge struck Chee as wrong. Most Navajos shied away from places where the ancestors could have died. "That's serious. Do you have proof?"

"That's another reason I brought you here. We're going to hike up there and assess the damage. You'll be my witness. Pop thinks I'm too critical of his favorite son, but he'll trust your opinion."

Chee thought about that. "You know, even if we see proof that the ruins have been exploited, that doesn't implicate Curtis."

"Of course it does." Chee heard Paul's impatience. "Very few people know about this site, and of those who know, only Curtis is blackhearted enough to steal from the past."

"Blackhearted? From what you and your father said, I thought you liked Curtis."

"I used to love the man. Things change." Chee noticed Paul's shoulders sag as he said it. "He got involved with his old buddies on Navajo Mountain again, but wouldn't talk to me about what was going on with that. His trips there and his other jobs took priority over the research project he had agreed to help me with. He'd come over to make nice with Pop, but when I brought up the work, the job I was paying him for, he only wanted to talk about bringing in the tours. I realized he wasn't interested in the research, in learning more about who lived here and why. He only wanted the money. I think that had to do with his new girlfriend, that Wanda."

Paul stopped talking for a moment and focused on the route, which grew slippery as the sandstone and water met.

"I'll get some photos here for Pop, and then we'll hike on up. I'll take a picture of the place on the lake where you found the body before we head back."

While Paul took the pictures, Chee considered the situation.

"So, you were here when Curtis pitched camp?"

"Not exactly. I dropped him off close to this spot, where the hiking is easier, and then came to get him the next morning. I hiked up to the tent. He wasn't there, but I saw what he had inside. Disgusting." Paul shook his head. "Let's head to the overhang. I want you to verify the damage he's done to the ruins."

Chee followed on a whisper of a trail. They climbed up the slope, sometimes over the sandstone, sometimes through places where dirt had accumulated. It was tough going, but after a few minutes Chee let himself relax, following Paul's well-placed steps. The man's stamina surprised him.

"You're in good shape for someone who spends a lot of time inside."

"Yeah, I get to the gym whenever I can and focus on strength, both upper and lower body. I figure if I ever have to lift Pop, I'll need that."

Up ahead, the slope grew steadily steeper before it reached the cliff face. Chee noticed a cornice-like overhang and a long natural stone wall with a wide ledge at its base. He assumed that was their destination. Although he couldn't yet discern the images, he had looked at enough rock art panels to recognize a natural easel when he saw one.

"So, is the old pueblo near that rock face?"

"Yeah. We'll stop at that art exhibit first. Pop wants some pictures. Then we'll look at what Curtis did to the ruins. After that, we'll take the boat to the spot where you found his body, and then I'll show you a couple of places Pop thinks the cave you are interested in might be."

The trail vanished in the slick rock as they moved uphill, but they didn't need it. No matter which way they climbed, they'd reach the destination that rose before them. As the incline increased, the view of the lake below them grew incrementally more beautiful.

Paul paused to enjoy the view. "The ruins up here are, or were, spectacularly well preserved.

That makes the desecration Curtis caused even worse."

Chee felt his unease increasing. The places where the ancient ones had lived and perhaps died both attracted and repelled him. As a modern man, he found this look into the past fascinating and moving. As a person with deep roots in the Navajo way, he cringed at an association with the long-dead.

And he realized he was probably sharing the trail with a murderer.

"The ruins are hard to spot. The stone from what's left of the buildings is the same color as the cliff. The overhang sheltered the little settlement. It's just around the corner from where you'll see the art. Look up to the right of that big streak of desert varnish, and you'll spot the edge of the compound. Pop brought Curtis and me here when we were teenagers. It hasn't changed much."

Chee spoke. "This hasn't changed much, but the three of you have. Did those changes drive you to murder?"

When Paul turned to face him, Chee saw the gun pointing at his chest. "So, let's see. Curtis stole my father's love. He was sleeping with the woman I wanted to marry. For good measure, he screwed me in business, and by looting ancient, irreplaceable material from these sites, he violated a basic code of ethics."

"Put the gun down. You don't want to hurt me." Chee took a breath to calm himself. "I understand about those grievances. But why kill him?"

Paul didn't seem surprised at the question. "Curtis's arrogance. He asked me to drop him off here so he could make sketches of the site, or so he said. On the ride over, I talked to him, begged him actually, not to involve Pop in that archaeology tour scheme, although I didn't use that word. He said Pop was enjoying working with him, and I should back off. He told me I worried too much and accused me of being jealous of him."

Chee said, "I get it. And if I hadn't hiked up here for the view, Curtis would have slipped beneath the waters of Lake Powell."

"There's no question about it."

Chee looked at the weapon again. "Put that down. You're a smart man. I'm on your side."

"Remember when you told me you don't like unsolved riddles?"

"I do."

"Well, I admire that, so when you said you were working the case, I assumed you'd figure out what happened. That's the other reason we're here."

Chee looked at Paul's steady hand holding the gun and realized the man had nothing to lose. Chee said, "Like I told you earlier, I try to understand what makes people act as they do. Did you confront Curtis about the looting?"

"Of course. That's why I offered to give him a ride here. I thought we could talk. He always denied doing anything wrong, but I figured it was worth one last chance before I told Pop. Curtis was a hardheaded son of a dog. He said I should mind my own business, that I was wrong and that

I was jealous because my father loved him more than he loved me."

"So you killed him?"

"I didn't plan it. After I dropped him off, I circled back, waited, then I followed him up here to get proof of his looting, but he intercepted me, denied it, argued with me, and told me I was a jerk. He said I neglected Pop for my work, and that without him my father would die of loneliness."

"But wasn't he a brother to you?"

Paul laughed. "Yeah. That's right. Have you ever read the Bible? He was a brother like Cain to Abel. Humanity has a long tradition of fratricide, right? It wasn't a bad death, you know."

"You were clever to use the sling."

"I'd been practicing on pigeons in the backyard. The rock knocked him down, and the fall knocked him out, as far as I could tell. He rolled into the water without lifting a hand to stop himself."

Chee assumed he could overpower Paul, but he didn't want to take a chance on getting shot at close range. "You don't have to kill me. I can help you. Curtis's death could have been self-defense, you know? It was just the two of you. I've spent a lot of time in court listening to lawyers talk, and I've seen cases dropped with more conclusive evidence than this one. I can work with you to construct a story so you won't have to worry."

"I'm not worried. And I'm not planning to kill you. I'll just start the process and let nature do its work. As it will, because no one knows we're here."

"What about Pete?"

"I told him you called when he was in the shower; that you had to head home and you'd catch him next time. Enough talk. Get going. You first."

Chee set off at a trot up the steep slope toward nearby boulders that offered cover. He slipped on the loose stones and felt his right ankle twist. Ignoring the pain, he shielded himself behind the first boulder he reached and pulled out his gun. Paul yelled an obscenity.

From his hiding place, Chee watched as Paul lost interest in pursuing him and proceeded to the cliffside.

Chee limped his way up the slope, quietly advancing to the edge of the rock overhang, looking for easy access to the mesa top, where he would have a clearer view of Paul. He didn't want to kill the man, but he would if his own life were endangered. He took a deep breath and noticed the shadow of a hawk against the rock. His gaze followed it toward the sky, and near the cliff summit, he saw a small but definite indentation in the rock face. Then his eyes found another and another— an ancient ladder to the mesa. He stood half a foot taller and was many pounds heavier than the ancestors who had used the hand- and footholds, but urgency fueled him. He maneuvered himself up, holding his breath with each shift from hand to hand and leg to leg and ignoring his throbbing ankle. The higher view would give him a better option for self-defense.

After a dozen excruciating steps, he rolled onto the clifftop and lay on his back, panting from the exertion and adrenaline, waiting for his heart to calm and the agony in his ankle to subside. Then he scanned the ruins below. It looked as though no one had visited here since the builders left it to the mercy of the elements; he saw no evidence that Curtis or anyone had been looting. He pressed himself facedown at the edge of the overhang, watching and listening for Paul, working to separate the sounds perhaps caused by the approach of the troubled man from the whistle of the restless, strengthening wind and the thunder of the blood in his veins.

The October afternoon sun glowed warm in a cloudless sky, the same intense blue as the lake's deep water. The raucous caws of ravens filled the dry air, which carried the faint scent of the dust Chee had stirred up. As he waited for Paul, he became aware of the growing stiffness in his back and the intense throbbing of his right ankle.

Then, echoing off the cliffsides, he heard footsteps. Paul emerged at the end of the rock art panel. Chee had barely glanced at the drawings, but Paul stopped and studied them as if that was his only goal. Then he approached the ruins. Chee watched as he slowly moved from one untouched room to another, and then surveyed the hard unbroken earth beyond the walls. The man repeated the route slowly, several times, intent on his inspection, squatting to examine something, then straightening up to repeat the procedure.

Paul certainly must have noticed the same lack of disruption, the same undisturbed, unlooted ancient dwellings, the same unviolated site that Chee had seen. Without the looting, the justifications Paul had given himself for killing his friend and brother fell away. Chee watched as the man slowly moved away from the abandoned habitation toward the edge of the cliff. There he stood, studying the expanse of blue water. Chee saw sunlight reflect off the gun. Paul looked at the weapon for a few moments, then pressed it to his chest.

Chee stood and yelled, "Paul! Wait! No!" And before he could rush to prevent the tragedy or turn away, he saw the man collapse and then, propelled by the energy of the blast that caused the fall, the steepness of the slope, and the pull of gravity, tumble toward the lake. Simultaneously he heard the retort of the shot as it echoed off the ancient stone walls.

21

By the time Jim Chee had maneuvered himself down the stone ladder, blindly feeling for each small indentation and wincing with pain each time he put weight on his right ankle, Paul Hendrix's *chindi* was roaming free to cause trouble. Chee limped to the edge of the cliff, but couldn't see where the body had come to rest. He called to Paul, waited, heard no response, and called again. He could tell by the amount of blood on the golden sandstone that he had no reason to make the dangerous climb down to verify Paul's death.

Chee knew he had to return to the boat, report the death, and let Detective Malone know that Curtis's killer wouldn't be a threat to anyone else. Before that, he spent a few moments looking at the amazing pictures the ancients had left and calming his spirit. Even though Paul threatened to shoot him and leave him to die, the suicide profoundly saddened him. He recalled what Pete had mentioned about his son taking antidepressants, and Paul's own references to depression. He had killed his adopted brother on an assumption that proved to be wrong, motivated by fierce, protective love for his father and his profession.

And now, Chee thought, another good man was dead.

He began to limp toward the lake. Because of his ankle, the angle of the slope, and the slickness of the rock, progress came slowly. He paused when the pain spiked beyond the high bearable category. After an hour or so, he looked down at the injured ankle, noticing the swelling, now tight against the fabric of his pant leg.

Chee sat for a moment and reconsidered the options.

The section of hiking that came next involved negotiating a steeper slope covered with loose rocks. That didn't appeal to him. October's shortening days would soon bring sunset, and less light to help him find his way down without the risk of inflicting serious self-damage. And if and when he made it to the boat, he would then have to find his way back to the marina in the dark.

The safest plan would be to wait until morning. He looked at the beautiful shining blue water of the lake and sat with his thoughts. His memory flashed on the handprints, large and small, he had seen on the cliff face. *K'é*, he thought. Kinship and connection. He thought of Paul and Pete and Curtis with sadness. Then he thought of Bernie, and a wave of unease came over him. He remembered his unanswered phone calls, his texts that garnered no response. Even on an undercover assignment, disappearing totally didn't match her nature.

The unease transformed into cold fear.

He stood, wincing as his injured ankle spoke to him, and moved as quickly as he could down the rocky slope to the lakeshore, the boat, and his Bernie.

22

Bernadette Manuelito had been tased before in training exercises. She knew what to expect, but that didn't make it hurt any less. She assumed, correctly, that she had been stunned to make it easier to tie her up. And that she would be left that way until it was time to go to the station to steal Dr. Zhou's bag. After which, she would be killed, and her mother would die, too.

She feigned unconsciousness until Kelly, Mai, and the two big guards left, locking her alone in the room. After much effort, all the while wondering if her backup had arrived and, if not, why not, she slipped her hands free. She gave thanks for the fact that the warmth of the tight, enclosed space made her sweaty. Now she faced new problems: leaving the building, reaching her car, calling for help, and getting to Mama's house. All, of course, while staying alive.

Once she untied herself, she searched the room for something to use as a weapon, finally finding a sturdy knife in the small kitchen. She looked in vain for an item of clothing to use as a disguise against the surveillance system. She assumed that Kelly would have someone check on her periodically, so she needed to leave the room, the building, and KHF itself as quickly as possible.

She used the knife blade to unlock the door and carefully opened it a tiny crack. The passageway that led to the studio seemed clear. She raced through the hall and had almost reached the research lab when she heard deep male voices speaking in Mandarin. She edged to the first place that offered a view of them. They had their backs to the hallway, so she quietly slipped into the laboratory space and crouched behind a counter, appreciating the fact that the researchers were so focused they didn't notice her. She snuck into the restroom and removed her facial putty. A white lab coat hung near the door, and she put it on. It was too big but at least offered some kind of disguise. She moved back to the lab and headed for the door.

It was locked, with a key pad to open it. She pushed down disappointed panic and tried the code she remembered from Lester's office. The door remained locked, but at least no warning alarm sounded. She stood, waiting tense moments, until finally someone approached from the road and pushed the right buttons. She rushed out before the man who opened the door could come in.

Outside, she started to run, heading for her car. She had just reached the outhouse area when at a distance she saw the truck that had blocked the entry road approaching her. She hid behind the closest green stall, watching as the truck pulled into the parking lot and stopped in front of her Tercel. She saw the guard get out, test the car's locked doors, and then climb back in his own vehicle. He was waiting for her.

She took a breath, inhaling the stench of the toilets, and wondered again why her backup wasn't there. Behind her, she heard the rattle of a pickup heading for the exit. As she watched it lumber toward her, she planned and, when the time was right, sprinted toward the truck. She jumped onto the bumper, nearly losing her balance, and then squeezed herself beneath the black tarp that covered the pickup bed, hoping that whatever she landed on wasn't too gross. She lay as still as death, praying that neither the guard watching her car nor the driver of this truck had noticed anything suspicious.

As the vehicle picked up speed, the vibration increased and she became aware of the pain in her legs and arms, agony amplified when the truck hit a bump or a pothole and jarred her to full consciousness. Her head ached, and she was nauseous.

Her hips hurt from where they held her weight against the metal truck bed. Never mind that. She had a chance to save her mother. She wrestled the gnawing pain into submission.

She couldn't see much beneath the black tarp, but the road noise was intense, and it was cool enough that she wondered if she was still wearing her jacket.

Her mental fog from the tasing had begun to

lift. She remembered being in the room with the recording equipment. She remembered watching the video of Mama welcoming strangers into her home, the vicious attack on the dog, and the man with the gasoline cans.

The entirety of the terrible scene came into her consciousness more quickly now. She recalled Mai pressing the reasons she should return Dr. Zhou's bag with its mystery drugs, appealing to Bernie's brain and heart.

"No matter what else is under way here, exploring new medical uses for the compounds found in cannabis that affect the brain is the core of our research. Our drugs will bring such relief to people with diseases like seizure disorders, Alzheimer's and other dementias, Parkinson's disease, ALS, MS, the whole alphabet of neurological disaster."

"That's great. I'm all for it, but I can't help you unless I know what happened to Dr. Zhou and to Mr. Begay Perez."

Mai nodded. "Neither gentleman is with KHF anymore. That's all the information you need. Don't waste your energy thinking of those men."

"I saw Dr. Zhou die. I want to bring his killer to justice."

"Justice?" Mai spit out the word. "Is it just that some families have a child, a harmless baby, with a life plagued by seizures? Is that just?"

"It isn't."

"The new drug Dr. Zhou and I created will offer hope for many, and an opportunity for wealth for Mr. Kelly and his associates."

The truck hit a rut, and when the agony that

followed settled, Bernie went back to reviewing her conversation with Mai, trying to recall if anything she heard might save Mama's life.

"I need to know why Dr. Zhou is dead."

"My dear, the man was in the middle of the highway with oncoming traffic at seventy-five miles an hour. A terrible accident."

"State police told us the vehicle was registered to KHF."

"That must be a mistake. Or perhaps it was stolen." Mai paused. "If you don't agree to help us, your mother will die."

Bernie moved her head against something that felt like plastic, and the motion took her headache past excruciating. She surveyed the rest of her body for damage and added ribs and shoulders. Nothing seemed broken. She wiggled her toes and then ordered her legs to stretch out. They complied until they pushed against something with some flexibility. More plastic. She kept pushing and pushed harder, even though the movement added to her nausea. But the plastic, or whatever it was, remained in place.

Her nausea increased. If she were going to throw up, she didn't want to choke. She rolled as gently as she could from her back onto her side. As she waited to heave, or for the nausea to subside, she considered her situation. Kelly or one of his employees would come into the room to retrieve her around nine that evening. When they saw she was gone, they would begin searching for her. They might also start the fire at Mama's house.

Suddenly she realized why she was nauseated.

The air around her held a disgusting stench. She'd smelled it before, the fetid odor of death. She needed to see what dead thing shared her space, but the tarp blocked the light.

The ride had become relatively smooth, and she appreciated that they were traveling on pavement. After a solid stretch of time, the pickup slowed and made a turn to the right. Bernie slid with the motion, slammed against something, and momentum pressed her harder against the object. The noise increased; the road had grown rough again. She visualized the tires rolling over hard-packed earth. The stench and her nausea had grown, and she realized that the putrefying dead thing now lay next to her.

She scooted toward the place where the tarp and the sides of the truck didn't quite meet, closer to fresh air. She reasoned that the driver planned to leave the rotting thing out here somewhere off the unpaved road. She needed an idea.

Now that her eyes had adjusted to the dim light beneath the tarp, she found the cab of the truck and saw rows of boxes, all the same size. This had to be cannabis, on its way to a rendezvous with a larger truck. She stared at the garbage bag again and noticed something shiny protruding from a rip in the plastic. Although the low light made it hard to tell for sure, it looked like the silver-covered toe of a black cowboy boot. She wondered about it for a split second, then realized with gut-wrenching clarity that the rotting thing inside the bag had once been known as Dino Begay Perez.

She pushed herself to kneeling in the airspace

between the tarp and the tailgate, and vomited over the side of the truck. She kept her head in the wind as the truck slowed, pulled off the dirt road, and bounced into open territory, making its own rough trail. Flushed with the glow of sunset, the sky shared its soft light with a landscape devoid of humanity but rich in piñon and juniper trees. A good place to dump a body. She slid back under the tarp and waited.

Bernie knew that after the truck stopped, the driver would get out to do the job. The boxes blocked the back window, which meant he wouldn't see her moving. Her best bet would be to jump out and conceal herself. Before he realized she was free, she would use the value of surprise to overpower him. She assumed he would be armed. If she could get the advantage quickly and disarm him, she'd survive.

She based her plan on the presumption that the driver had come alone. She doubted that Kelly would have given Diamond and Mustache the job, but if that was the case, she'd need a different plan. They wouldn't hesitate to kill her, so her best option was to flee and live to tell the truth about the KHF operation.

She tugged as hard as she could on the side of the tarp, attempting to loosen it enough so she could squeeze through. The cover was taut but, luckily for her, a bit shorter than the truck bed. She had room to leap from the space at the back, near the tailgate. But the angle would put her in view of the driver if he glanced that way. It was a risk she couldn't avoid.

The truck slowed, weaving its way between large rocks until it approached the edge of an arroyo. The driver pulled around so the tailgate faced the gully, and the bed was slanted. Gravity would be on the driver's side as he unloaded the bag. Right before the truck stopped, she maneuvered herself to the edge of the closed tailgate. At the last minute, she remembered the rearview mirror on the passenger side; the driver might be using that as he backed up. She waited until the truck came to a full stop, then jumped and stayed there, crouched behind the truck, listening for anything that might indicate a second person in the cab. She heard nothing.

The driver's door opened, and a slim person stepped out, then walked a few feet from the truck. Bernie watched as the figure lowered pants and assumed a squat. When she heard the sound of urine hitting the dirt, she rushed toward the driver, reaching her as she was pulling up her jeans. The driver yelled "Yee naaldlooshii!"—"Skinwalker!" in Navajo—as Bernie tackled her, grabbing her sweatshirt as she struggled to get away. The driver was taller and heavier, but Bernie had strength and surprise on her side, and used her legs, leverage, and training to pin the woman to the ground.

The driver looked to be in her late twenties. She stopped struggling. Stunned and terrified, she said in Navajo in the softest of voices, "Please don't kill me."

Bernie eased up, but kept her pinned.

"Are you a skinwalker?" the driver asked.

"No. I'm a cop."

"How—"

"Do you have a weapon?"

"Yes. A gun. It's in the truck. Don't shoot me." The woman was panting now. Her breath smelled like cigarettes.

"I'm going to move off you. Stay flat on the ground and pull up your pants. I won't hurt you. I need your help."

Bernie stood carefully. The woman followed instructions.

"OK. Sit up slow."

The woman did.

"Do you know what's in that big garbage bag?"

"Dead animals."

"Why?"

"Mr. Kelly's security guys shot a couple dogs that had been causing trouble. They didn't want the neighbors to find them, so they said to dump them out here. That's all. They said to just roll the bag out of the truck and then go on with the delivery. I thought it was mean to shoot them and not tell the people their dogs were dead, but I'm just the driver. I need this job."

"What's your name?"

"Lauren."

"I'm Bernie. Officer Manuelito. We need to get to Toadlena as soon as possible."

"But I've got to—"

"No. You'll do exactly as I say."

The woman sucked in a breath. "What's in the bag, if it isn't dogs? It's heavy. It stinks."

"You don't want to know."

"Oh my God . . ." The young woman's voice cracked. She glanced toward the bed of the truck and then quickly looked away.

"Lauren, stand up. We need to leave."

The woman rose. Bernie noticed scratches on the driver's arms from where she'd pinned her to the ground and a bruise on her shoulder. No, not a bruise. A tattoo. It reminded her of something, or someone.

"What's your tat?"

"A feather. A blue eagle feather."

"Are you Lauren Lapahie?"

Even in the fading sunset light, she saw the woman's eyes widen. "Are you a witch?"

"No. I'm a cop. I met your uncle George in Kayenta at a restaurant. He asked me if I knew you. He's very worried about you."

Lauren was speechless.

"He was helping with a flea market for one of your relatives with seizures. A cute little girl."

"Morgan, my baby sister. Was she there?"

"She was."

"How did she look? She's been so sick, and—"

Bernie put a finger to her lips. "Let's go. We'll talk in the truck. Do you have a phone?"

Lauren began walking. "Yes. It's in there. Service is spotty out here."

Bernie couldn't make a call until they reached the crest of a hill. The phone at Mama's house rang more than a dozen times, but Mama didn't answer. Frantic, Bernie called the Shiprock substation.

She could tell Sandra wanted to chat, but Bernie got to the point. "Tell the captain I have to talk to him right now. This is an emergency."

Captain Largo listened as she told him about the threat against Mama.

"Hold on while I get someone on the way over there. Don't hang up." He paused. "I don't recognize the number you're calling from. What happened to your phone?"

"Kelly, the new boss at KHF, took it. Call me at this number. And tell the responders to be careful. These guys are smart and vicious."

The captain put her on hold for a few minutes as he dispatched the officers. Bernie gave him a tight summary of KHF's operation and her attempted murder.

"What happened to my backup?"

"We never heard the emergency word. We lost touch with you completely. We didn't want to blow your cover. We thought that would really jeopardize things."

"I could have died either way, but we'll talk later. I have to help Mama."

She hung up before he could protest.

Bernie noticed Lauren's tight grip on the steering wheel. "You put up a terrific fight back there," she said. "I can tell you're a strong woman. This will be OK."

"I heard what you said about Mr. Kelly and Mai. And the trouble they are causing for your family. I'm scared to be with you."

"We'll be just fine." Bernie felt her own confidence rise as she said it. She hoped it was true.

Largo called back. "Someone will be at your mother's place in about half an hour. No one was patrolling nearby, but she's a priority. Now tell me everything."

She started with the body in the truck bed.

"Are you sure the dead man is Begay Perez?"

"It's him, unless somebody stole his boots. I didn't open the garbage bag, but I will when we stop. The body has started to putrefy. I hope I can recognize him."

"Get your driver to take the body to the Shiprock hospital. I'll make arrangements for refrigerated storage. An officer will meet you. Where are you now?"

Bernie turned to Lauren and got an estimated location, then gave the captain Lauren's name and a description of the truck. "I'll give them five minutes to unload, and then the guy in the bag is coming with us. I've got to get to Mama's house."

"We've got that covered. Chill."

But Bernie had seen too many things go wrong to be able to relax. And, unlike Largo, she'd seen what happened to two of Kelly's business partners.

"Manuelito, are you listening?"

"Yes, sir."

"An officer will meet you at the hospital and take you to your mother's place. How did she get involved in this anyway?"

"Because of me. They tried to use her to leverage me into doing what they wanted." She filled in the details, ending with Kelly's words: "'Old ladies catch things on fire all the time.'"

"I've requested a fire truck and an ambulance." She heard him take a sip of something. "Manuelito, you know, we're both lucky you aren't dead."

She didn't want to think about that.

Largo told her again not to worry about Mama and ended the call. But Mama's endangerment hung over her like a nightmare. She looked out the window. Lauren was driving too fast, but Bernie didn't complain.

"How come you became a cop?"

"I wanted to do something to make the world better, and I figured the best place to start was in my own backyard." There was more to the story, but she didn't feel like sharing it. "Here's a question for you. What happened that caused you to lose touch with your family?"

"I'll give you the highlights, or I guess I should call them lowlights." Lauren pressed her lips together. "I started drinking too much and met a man who wasn't good for me. My relatives tried to warn me off, told me I was throwing my life away on booze and a bad husband, but I didn't listen. We got arrested a few times. We split up, and when I left him, I stopped drinking. I went to work for KHF because I needed a job where they didn't ask too many questions. A job where I could be by myself to figure out what comes next."

"That makes sense. But why abandon your relatives?"

"I broke too many hearts. I am ashamed."

Bernie let it sit, grateful for the woman's honesty.

"Are you really a cop?"

"Yes. Why?"

"Well, you didn't show me any ID. No uniform. No cop car. No gun. No phone. The pink hair. The tattoo." Lauren paused. "You're not a guy, like most cops, and you're kind of short."

Bernie laughed. "Lots of women work in law enforcement these days, although the men still outnumber us. I've always been short. I was on an undercover assignment at the farm, so that's why no uniform and all the rest of it."

Lauren chuckled. "I guess that assignment didn't go so well."

Bernie changed topics. "What's it like to work with KHF? Have they been good employers?"

"I loved Dr. Zhou. Mr. Kelly doesn't have much to do with us."

"Tell me about Dr. Zhou."

"He specialized in childhood epilepsy. When he found out our little Morgan had seizures, he told me his niece had seizures, too. That was why he went into his research. He said his brother had to work at KHF because her medicine was so expensive. He and his brother made a deal with Mai and Mr. Kelly so the medicine Dr. Zhou created could help the little Chinese girl."

"A deal? Couldn't they just buy it for her?"

"No, that's the problem. The new treatment is a big secret until they figure out how to market it for top dollar. Dr. Zhou told me he wanted as many people as possible to have it, but that wouldn't happen with KHF. But he gave me some for Morgan."

"It sounds like you two were friends."

A vehicle approached in the opposite lane, high beams on. Lauren flashed the truck's lights, and the other driver adjusted.

"Sorry. What?"

"It sounds like you knew Dr. Zhou well."

"Sort of. Well enough to know he wasn't happy. And then he just disappeared. Kelly announced that he'd left the company." Lauren cringed. "Was he in the bag?"

"No. I think that was Dino Begay Perez. I saw the silver toe guard on one of his boots."

Lauren shook her head. "I liked him. He spoke up for us Navajos and he objected to the way the Chinese workers were treated, and next thing he was missing, and now . . ." She didn't have to say it. "I heard you mention two murders. Is Dr. Zhou dead, too?"

"Yes."

"What happened to him?"

Bernie told her the story.

"What kind of car hit him?"

"A new black Mercedes sedan. Sporty-looking." Bernie looked out into the dark night as she remembered that afternoon.

"Mr. Kelly told me he hit a colt on 491. He said the accident did some damage, so I drove the car to Flagstaff to the body shop the dealership recommended. I believed him because there's a problem with feral horses out there."

"When was this?"

The date Lauren gave was the day after Dr. Zhou died. "Did they fix it?"

"Yeah, and they took before-and-after pictures so I could show Mr. Kelly and Mai, knowing they would appreciate it. The body shop even got the color right."

"What do you mean?"

"The colt—" She stopped. "The collision left some blood. The car was black but he wanted it repainted gold. The shop did a great job, and quick, too."

"Gold?"

"I heard him saying that color brought *affluence*. As if he needed more money."

"Do you have those before-and-after pictures?"

"Yes. They're on my phone."

"Let me see them."

Bernie looked at the photos and sent herself copies. "Where is your gun?"

"In the console."

Bernie opened the compartment and removed it carefully. "Loaded?"

"Yes. I mean, why bother to have a gun with me otherwise? You're lucky I didn't have it on me when I got out to pee. If I had seen you roaming around out there, I would have tried to kill you—or at least scare you away. I thought you were a skinwalker."

Skinwalkers, shape-shifting evil ones, *yee naaldlooshii*, took the form of animals, often wolves, and used an animal skin as a covering when they were on the hunt in their human body. Some called them Navajo witches. Most people didn't speak of them at all.

Lauren slowed for a curve and then accelerated

again. "I see those evil things out here sometimes. They run along the highway, trying to distract me. I ignore them, but they are scary."

"I've seen them, too, when I'm driving at night." Bernie remembered several incidents, and turned her thoughts away from them.

"Now that I know what's in that bag back there, I'm nervous. I don't like driving with a dead man. My grandmother also told us about *chindis*."

"I don't like it either." Bernie's voice was almost a whisper.

They said nothing more. Such talk was dangerous and taboo.

Lauren signaled to pull the truck off the dark road.

"What are you doing?" Bernie said.

"This is the mile marker where I deliver my boxes."

"Not tonight."

"If I don't stop, I'll lose my job. I really need the money."

Lights approached, and a passenger car zipped by.

"No stopping. Don't worry about getting fired. KHF will be out of business anyway after Kelly and Mai are arrested."

Another set of headlights appeared through the truck's windshield.

"That's the van that is expecting the order. When he doesn't get it, he'll call KHF. I don't want them to hurt me. Or you."

Lauren's phone chimed with a message for Bernie.

"You don't need to worry. I just got a text that

the farm has been raided and the illegal drugs seized. Mr. Kelly, Mai, and the rest of the management are in police custody."

They drove in silence for a while, and then Lauren spoke. "How much farther to the hospital?"

Bernie thought about it. "Maybe half an hour."

"After I connect with the van, I head back to the farm, turn in the truck, and go to sleep. What should I do tonight?"

"After you drop me off at the hospital, you'll need to wait until the bag is unloaded. And some officers will be there to remove the boxes, as evidence against KHF."

"Then what? Can I take the truck to my family's house?"

Bernie thought about it. "I guess so, unless one of the officers there tells you otherwise."

"I'd like to see Uncle George and little Morgan, and apologize for making them worry. And I have the medicine Dr. Zhou gave me for her." Lauren shifted in the driver's seat. "I don't want to get busted for stealing it."

"I'll explain. Don't worry."

"Thanks." Lauren focused on driving for a moment. "I'm really hoping your mother doesn't die."

"Me too."

Bernie realized she was bone tired. Drained. Exhausted. "I'm closing my eyes a minute. Tell me when you see the lights of Shiprock."

She awoke when Lauren pulled into the hospital parking lot. A Navajo Nation patrol car and a police department pickup truck were there, lights flashing.

Lauren looked confused. "Where shall I park?"

"Drive to the emergency entrance. I'm sure someone will meet us."

A security guard appeared and motioned the truck into the well-lit bay. Two people in scrubs rolled a gurney toward them.

Bernie climbed out.

"The body is in a bag in the back of the truck. The driver is Lauren. I've got to go."

One of the hospital staff members, a tall, hefty man, nodded to her. They'd known each other for a while. "What happened to your hair?"

Bernie shrugged. She'd forgotten about her disguise.

Officer Bigman, her clan brother and friend, waved to her from the window of his unit.

"The captain briefed me. He told me your mother could be in trouble." Bigman spoke faster than usual. "A couple officers are on the way already." He stopped. "If we need to ID the body, I can do it. You've had a long day already and I know Dino . . ."

"No," she practically yelled at him. "Go." She climbed in and he accelerated as she fastened her seat belt. "I'm glad you're here. I just hope—"

An announcement from fire dispatch on the unit's radio interrupted her. The address the dispassionate voice gave for the fire was Mama's house.

23

Bigman turned on the light bar and siren, and they sped away. "We may get there before the other units."

"Good. I hope so." Bernie didn't know what else to say.

"Your mom is tough and smart. Is Darleen with her?"

"I don't know. I assumed so, but I didn't see her on the video they made to threaten me."

Bigman, her clan brother, knew the way to Mama's house without directions. His driving gave her time to think, a better plan than worrying. She looked out the window, where the darkness suited her mood.

Whatever evil had gone down at Mama's place was on her. She'd allowed the death of Dr. Zhou to cloud her judgment. If she'd stayed at Lake Powell another day with Chee, as he had so fervently wanted, she wouldn't have been witness to the murder. She wouldn't have gone to KHF. She

wouldn't have been captured in the failed undercover op, or encountered the corpse of Dino Begay Perez. And, finally, Mama's house wouldn't be
on fire.

In every way, with the exception of discovering
that Begay Perez was dead and that the car that
killed Dr. Zhou had been repaired and repainted,
she considered her assignment to have been an
epic failure.

"It's about half an hour to your mom's place.
You wanna talk about what happened out there?"

She appreciated Bigman's gentle tone. "What
did the captain tell you?"

"He told me you were coming to Shiprock in
a truck with a dead body, and that you'd gathered
enough information to begin to shut down KHF.
He said you did well."

"You're kidding."

"Wanna hear something else?"

"Sure."

"The captain said that you'd asked someone
to translate the Mandarin writing that was on
those T-shirts the dead guy had in his bag. It was
a verse from the Christian Bible. Hold on. He
gave me the translation."

Bigman took his right hand off the wheel to
fish into his pocket, and handed her a slip of paper. She couldn't read it in the dark, so she folded
it and slipped it in her own pocket for safekeeping.

"What does it say?"

"Something about sickness. I can't remember
exactly."

The news that the captain approved of her work

didn't counterbalance the disaster she anticipated up ahead.

"Bernie, why so quiet?"

"I think Mama is probably dead." She took a deep breath to choke back the tears. No point wasting energy on that, when she knew they would have to gather evidence at the crime scene, and she was already running on fumes.

He sighed. "Tell me what to expect up there."

"OK." She filled him in. "Kelly said they would stay there until I did what he wanted—steal the evidence against them we had at the station. If I didn't cooperate, he told me they would kill Mama and disguise the murder with a fire."

"Were the two people you saw on the video Navajo?"

"Yes. Even though she hadn't met them, she let them in because she believes in *k'é*." She remembered the third person and the gasoline and felt her panic rise. "I escaped from KHF hours ago. I assume they've killed her. And if my sister was there, she's dead now, too. Kelly said after they killed Mama, they would set the fire. We heard the call for the fire truck. This is all on me."

"Hey, don't give yourself so much credit. We both know there's serious evil in the world. That's why you and I wear this uniform and do what we do."

"And sometimes it isn't enough."

"But we try our best and move on. I know your mother. She's tough and wily. Don't give up on her."

As she watched for the glow of the flames from

Mama's burning house to appear in the distance, Bernie stretched her legs. Her foot bumped against something. "I kicked something on the floor here. I hope it's OK."

"I forgot about those. That box has some great flyers your sister made for a missing woman out by Kayenta, and she added good general info for anyone dealing with a missing relative. That girl has a lot of talent."

"I agree. She's not sure."

"We sent some of the flyers to Lieutenant Leaphorn. He was so impressed that he wants Darleen to help with that task force he's on for missing indigenous women. You know about that?"

Bernie nodded, then realized he couldn't see her in the dark with his eyes on the road. "I've heard of it. What would she do?"

"They want some graphics for their new website, for letterheads, business cards. All that."

"That's good." An idea came to her. "Is that poster about a woman named Lauren Lapahie?"

"I think so. Open the box and take a look. Use my phone for a light."

"I will, but first, may I make a call?"

"Go ahead."

She called Mama and, as she expected, got no answer. She dialed Darleen's cell, and the call went right to voice mail. They she called Chee, not knowing exactly what she'd say.

She didn't have time to fret about that, because he answered immediately.

"Bigman! What's happening with Bernie? I've been trying—"

"It's me. I'm OK."

"Thank goodness. Darleen's on the other line. We're dealing with an emergency. I'll call you soon." And he hung up.

"That was the shortest phone call ever," Bigman said.

"He mentioned Darleen and an emergency. I don't like it. I'm about to jump out of my skin."

"Chee's a good man. Calm down. Take a look at those posters."

She used the phone's light and recognized the photo Darleen had used as the one they'd seen at the sale to benefit little Morgan.

"Lauren is going home to her family." She explained how she recognized the truck driver. "You know, Darleen could have wandered into a crime scene at Mama's house. She's probably in danger."

"She couldn't have called Chee for help if she was being held at gunpoint, right? Think positive."

The unknowing left her profoundly uneasy. She needed to find out what situation she and Bigman were headed into. They were only a few minutes away from Mama's house now. She searched the horizon for the glow of a fire but saw only a few security lights.

Bigman's phone buzzed. It was Chee.

"Bernie. Are you at your mother's place yet?"

"We'll be there in about ten minutes."

"Bigman's with you?"

"Yeah. You mentioned Darleen. What's going on?"

"I'm driving toward . . ." Chee's voice cut out. Then, "Your sister asked me . . ." He said something else, but she couldn't understand.

"I didn't get that."

"The fire . . ." Then the call died. She dialed back, and it went to voice mail. When she put the phone down, she noticed a faint orange glow ahead of them. "Can't you go faster?"

Bigman seemed to speed up. The illumination ahead grew brighter.

Bernie had expected to see the lights of one or more police cars, maybe an ambulance. But the only vehicle outside was Darleen's old sedan.

Bigman slowed down. "Bernie, do you have a weapon with you?"

"No."

"I have a second gun. Take it." He told her where it was, and she picked it up. Knowing she could use it if she had to eased her anxiety.

Bigman parked where she would have, safely away from the fire, and left the flashers on. The truck and SUV Bernie had seen on the video were gone, and there were no other vehicles.

Behind them, they noticed red lights approaching in the distance. Help on the way.

Flames rose from the stacked firewood and had begun to engulf the old corral. The fire had spread to the weeds and grass and marched brazenly toward Mama's house. They saw no one in the smoky darkness.

"Hey, you cops. Over here. I need help bad."

Bernie's eyes followed the male voice to a figure standing with a shovel near the house. Remembering the man who had attacked the dog, she yelled, "Police! Put the shovel down. Now."

Bigman pulled his gun, and she raised her own in the man's direction.

The shovel clamored to the ground. "I'm trying to put out the fire before it gets to the house." The man sounded familiar.

"Slim?"

"Officer Bernie? Thank God you're here."

"Where's Darleen?"

"Helping the lady who got hurt."

"Mama?"

"I think your mom's OK. She's in the house."

"What happened to the bad guys?" Bigman said.

"They left after they started the fire. She's alone."

"Who's hurt?" Bernie said.

"The lady next door."

Bigman turned to Bernie. "I'll check on her and Darleen. You deal with your mother."

But Bernie was already racing to the front door.

Mama's house sat in darkness, illuminated only by the reflection of the flames in the kitchen window. When Bernie stepped inside, she noticed the eerie quiet. She flicked on the light switch, but nothing happened. She realized that the electricity was off—no buzzing of appliances or electronics. She passed Darleen's empty bedroom, heading toward the odd beam of light seeping from beneath Mama's door.

"Mama? Mama? It's Bernie. Everything's all right now." She hoped that was true.

"Who?" Her mother spoke softly.

"Bernie. You're safe now. I'm coming in."

She assumed her terrified mother would have tried to barricade the door, but it swung open when she turned the knob. Mama was in bed, a magazine facedown across her chest and a flashlight pointing to the floor. Clearly, she had fallen asleep reading.

Mama looked like she always did if Bernie awakened her: surprised and slightly disheveled. She in no way resembled a person held hostage a few hours earlier. Or a woman aware that a fire was destroying her empty sheep pen and moving toward her house.

Bernie's relief surged so strongly that it came with tears. "Mama, you're OK, aren't you?"

Mama wrinkled her forehead at the question. "It's late, my daughter. Why are you here?"

"I heard you had some trouble."

"It was nothing much."

"What happened?"

"Oh, some people came by. They were lost, I think, and confused and nervous. I tried to help them. Then your sister got home, and that man she likes came with her." Mama stopped talking to plump her pillow.

"And then what happened?"

"Oh, we heard a noise, and those people went away. They were scared of something." Mama frowned. "What happened to your hair? And what's that poking in your eyebrow?"

Bernie remembered her pinkness and the eyebrow ring. "Oh, I had to dress up like this for work. It's nothing permanent."

Mama patted the bed beside her. "You look tired, my daughter. Share this bed with me."

"I have some things to do. If you're ready to sleep, may I use the flashlight?"

"Flashlight?"

"That thing there beside you."

"Oh." Mama handed it to her.

Bernie went outside, feeling as though the weight of the world had lifted from her shoulders. The fire seemed no larger and a second police car—the unit the captain promised—had arrived. An officer was helping Bigman and Slim keep the fire away from the back wall of Mama's house. If Mama had outside spigots, they could have used a water and a hose, but they made do with what they had.

Like Mama's place, Mrs. Darkwater's house was pitch-black. Bernie ran to the front door using the flashlight, instinctively nervous about the dog who always guarded the porch, until she remembered how the man in the video had bashed it. She yelled for her sister and Bigman as she stepped inside.

Bigman answered. "In the kitchen."

"Thank God." This time her sister's voice roared through the house. "We're back here."

She followed the voices through Mrs. Darkwater's unlit living room. "I can't find you."

Bigman shone his flashlight toward her, and Darleen said, "Sister. Here."

She saw them on the kitchen floor. Mrs. Dark-water lay sprawled, blood on her face and her blouse. Darleen sat next to her. A beam of light caught the fear in the neighbor's open dark eyes before it captured the blood seeping through Darleen's fingers pressed to the woman's head.

"I'm checking on the ambulance and the fire truck," Bigman said. "They should have been here by now. Darleen has things under control."

"I'll stay with her. Find us some towels before you go."

Bigman returned in a moment with a pair of dish towels that Bernie had noticed hanging on the oven door and handed them to her sister. Bernie sat next to Mrs. Darkwater. "Hi there." She spoke softly, keeping her voice steady and calm. "It's Bernie. An ambulance will be here any minute. You're going to be fine."

The woman closed her eyes.

"What happened?"

Darleen grabbed a towel to use as a compress against the wound before she spoke. "Mrs. Dark-water said she saw the fire and was running to help us and fell."

The neighbor spoke in a whisper. "The dog saved me."

"Really?" Bernie had seen the dog lying motionless after the shovel attack.

"That's right." Darleen swallowed. "Even though it could barely walk, the poor thing figured out how to tell me Mrs. Darkwater needed help." She paused, then mouthed the word, "Mama?"

Bernie gave her two thumbs up.

Darleen took a shuddering breath. "She could have died. We all could have . . . This is so awful."

Bernie put her arm around Darleen and squeezed her into the best hug they could manage.

"Tell me everything. It'll help."

She felt Darleen's ribs expand with her breath. "OK. When Slim and I came home, we saw a strange truck in the yard. Mama had invited these people into the house, a woman who smelled like cigarettes and a muscular man. He didn't seem like her husband or boyfriend or even a brother. Too weird.

"I asked who they were, and they came up with a lame story about being related to us but they didn't even know their clans. Slim introduced himself, the traditional way. They just looked at each other. I could tell Mama was not happy with the situation. She told them she needed a nap and they had to leave, but they said they couldn't go until they called Mr. Kelly, whoever that was. I didn't want to be rude, but I told them Mama was in charge of her own house, and they shouldn't be disrespectful. Then it got weirder."

Darleen turned back to Mrs. Darkwater and stroked her arm.

Bernie waited for Darleen to compose herself.

"The man showed us a gun. He said they were staying and that Slim and I were the ones who should never have come in, but now it was too late for us to leave and he'd have to talk to Mr. Kelly about us. We sat there for a while, thinking. I coughed. Slim nudged me real quick and winked. Then he pretended to cough. He'd cough and I'd cough, and even Mama started to cough. We kept doing that, and the woman told us to get a cough drop or something. I told them we had just discovered that we had a new virus, like Dikos Nitsaa'igii-19, and that the man next door had died from it. The lady asked what that virus was because she didn't speak Navajo. I said it was like COVID, the Big Cough, but worse. Slim did a good job of acting even more sick. The couple started fidgeting, getting nervous.

"Then there was a terrible noise outside, like a moaning or something. Mama said, 'Oh, it's the *chindi*—the bad ghost of our neighbor man who died from this new sickness. He knows us but doesn't like strangers.'"

"Mama said that. Really?"

"Really. We kept hearing the noise Mama called a *chindi*, and she convinced them. She kept talking about how terrible that ghost was and we all kept coughing. Those two got in that truck and drove away."

Bernie smiled at their cleverness. "What happened to the third man?"

Darleen shrugged. "I never saw him."

Bernie told her sister about the person in the SUV and how he'd hurt the dog and then walked toward Mama's house with the gasoline containers.

Darleen twisted a lock of hair. "He left before I got here. But that explains how those two crazies started the fire so quickly when they left."

"Tell me about that."

"The woman was a smoker. She had about six cigarettes while they were here. I think she must have dropped one of those, or a match or something, to start the fire. The grass is really dry. And the fire or those two killed Mama's electricity. Mrs. Darkwater says it's off here too because we're on the same circuit."

Mrs. Darkwater whispered, "The dog."

"Oh, right. The noise Mama called a *chindi* kept going after the people left, so Slim and I went out to check. It was the dog."

"He saved your mother." Mrs. Darkwater's soft voice rang with conviction.

"That's right. Something had happened to him. He could barely walk, and he was crying at Mrs. Darkwater's back door. If it hadn't been for him, we wouldn't have seen the flames. Slim went to put out the fire, and I said I would help with that as soon as I took care of the dog. He wouldn't leave so I thought maybe he needed water. I knocked on the door to let Mrs. D. know, and when she didn't answer, I came in to get him something to drink. That's when I found her here."

Darleen smoothed the woman's hair. "Your dog saved your life, and he saved Mama."

"Like you saved me." Mrs. Darkwater squeezed Darleen's hand. Then she looked at Bernie. "Your hair. Your eyebrow."

"It's nothing permanent."

"Shine the light on your face, Sister." Darleen stared. "OMG. What a look! Did it hurt to get that piercing?"

"No, it's—" Bernie saw pulsing red lights in the window. "The ambulance is here. I'll go out to tell them about Mrs. Darkwater's fall."

She took the flashlight and walked into the starlit night just as the vehicle stopped. She explained the situation.

The crew chief listened. "No burn victims?"

"No, only one woman who had a fall. I saw a scalp wound. She's lost some blood, but she seems lucid."

"Thanks. Anything else?"

"The lady, Mrs. Darkwater, had a dog that saved her life. It was hurt by the people who started the fire and I don't see it around anywhere."

"We'll keep a lookout for it. Thanks for letting me know." He went inside.

Bernie noticed that the air was less smoky as she looked toward Mama's house. She saw Slim, Bigman, and then another familiar shape among the firefighters. She called out to him as she ran closer, and he looked up at the sound of her voice. Then Jim Chee dropped the shovel and stepped back from the flames to wrap his arms around her. They held each other close for a long, long time.

24

Finally, they sat in Mama's kitchen, Chee and Bernie and Darleen and Slim, all four of them exhausted. Bigman had gone back to Shiprock with a report on the damage to Mama's corral and woodpile, as well as portraits Darleen had sketched of the intruders. Bernie appreciated how close the pictures came to the way she remembered the couple from the video.

Slim made coffee, and the aroma alone began to revive Bernie. Darleen located cookies Mama had squirreled away, which reminded Bernie that she hadn't had anything to eat for a very long time. Chee was beside her at the table, his warm, strong hand on her leg. She noticed the way Darleen sat straighter and smiled when Slim spoke to her.

"Sister, I saw that poster you made for Lauren's family. You did a good job."

"Thanks. I like your tat, but it's fake, right?"

"Yeah. They were part of my new identity."

"I thought you were studying."

Bernie explained a little about her assignment at KHF. "The woman on the poster, Lauren, had a job as a truck driver there. I got a ride with her and . . ." She paused. No reason to share the horror, but she would talk to Chee about a healing ceremony. "Lauren had some of the medicine Dr. Zhou developed for epilepsy. It might help Morgan."

"Zhou? That's the man who got killed, right?" Chee asked the question, and she appreciated the generic way he phrased it, sparing her sister and her boyfriend the bloody details. "Did you figure out the motive for his death?"

"Money. Dr. Zhou wanted to make the medicine he developed widely available at low cost. Kelly saw it as a way to make a fortune."

Talking about it brought up the memory. Then she remembered something else. Bernie reached into her pocket for the slip of paper Bigman had given her that evening.

Chee watched as she began to unfold it. "What's that?"

"Dr. Zhou and his brother had T-shirts with a slogan in Mandarin. Captain Largo found someone to translate it, and gave this to Bigman for me." She put the note on the table and read it out aloud. "'I will take away sickness from among you. Exodus 23:25.' The captain wrote that the shirts were sold by a church in Los Angeles at a fundraiser to find a cure for childhood epilepsy."

"That's a slogan for a doctor," Slim said. "There's more to that in the beginning: 'Worship the Lord your God, and his blessing will be on your food and water. I will take away sickness from among you.' I guess that would be too much for a T-shirt."

Chee got up to bring the coffeepot over for refills. Bernie noticed that he was limping.

"Did you do that fighting the fire?"

"No." He thought a moment about how much of his long day to share and how to share it. "I twisted it at Lake Powell. An archaeologist took me up to see some amazing rock art. I had a little misadventure when we went to look at some ruins." He would tell her the rest of the story, but not tonight.

"Did you ever find out what happened with Curtis?"

"Yes. It was an interesting case. Sad, too. He was murdered by a man he considered his brother."

"Why?"

"A combination of jealousy and misplaced suspicion. The murderer thought Curtis was exploiting a friendship with his father."

"Did you arrest him?"

Chee shook his head. He remembered the pop of the fatal gunshot as it echoed off the stone, the sight of the definitely dead Paul Hendrix at the bottom of the cliff trail, and the long, lonely boat ride back to the marina, guided by the moonlight, instinct, and perhaps the Diyin Diné, the Holy People.

He switched to something more positive. "There was another guy who I thought might have done it. It's an interesting story."

"What, you almost made a mistake?" Bernie smiled at him. "Go ahead."

He started at the beginning, recounting how the case had taken him to Navajo Mountain to research Curtis's past acquaintances. "The victim had been driving up there to see a beautiful young woman named Wanda. His brother assumed they were dating. Another guy, Chill, called himself Wanda's boyfriend and slashed Curtis's tires. Chill looked suspicious at first, but I learned he and Curtis had made peace."

"They decided to share the same girlfriend?" Darleen said.

"No." Chee remembered when they had talked on the phone earlier that day and simplified it for Darleen. "Wanda was Curtis's daughter. Wanda's mother never mentioned the pregnancy to him because they had broken up, and she had moved away. And she never told Wanda who her dad was. Curtis had learned about his daughter only recently from a mutual friend, a medicine man actually, after Wanda's mother passed on." He studied his coffee. "Curtis died without telling Wanda he was her father, but at least she got to know him."

Slim stood and turned to Chee. "I need to start for home. Dee drove me, but she's beat. If you're going that way, maybe you could pick me up later. It's hard to hitch a ride this time of night."

"Don't be silly," Darleen said. "That's too far to walk. I can take you. I'm not that tired."

Bernie gave her a look.

"Sister, I'm fine. Really. I'll just have a little more coffee."

"Bro, we're all tired," Chee said. "Stay here and

sleep on the couch. Let Darleen drive you home in the morning."

Slim looked at Bernie, the acting matriarch.

"That's a great plan," Bernie said. "You two behave yourselves."

Darleen laughed. "If she gives us a hard time, I'll tell her the sleepover idea came from Cheeseburger. Do you think she'll ever like Slim?"

Chee sighed. "Maybe. Someday. It took her a long time with me. You know, in the old days, mothers-in-law weren't even supposed to see their daughters' husbands. Don't let her get in the way of whatever might be good between you two."

Bernie nudged her sister. "Remember that question you wanted to ask my husband?"

Darleen smiled. "About how to tell if a guy likes you? I think today helped me figure it out."

Chee's fine face sagged with fatigue. Time to go. Then Bernie flashed on an old hesitation that always arose when she left Mama's house. "What about the dog? Is it still alive?"

Darleen nodded. "The ambulance guy said he thinks he has a fractured rib, but he was breathing OK. He said Mrs. Darkwater might want to take him to the vet, but the main thing is just rest. The guy told us we could give him an aspirin, so I did." She rubbed her hands over her cheeks, and Bernie noticed the lavender nail polish. "I'll take care of him until Mrs. Darkwater gets home from the hospital. I know you don't like dogs, but don't worry. He won't hurt you."

They walked to Chee's truck, and Bernie saw

the dog on the mat in front of Mrs. Darkwater's door, the place from where it usually leaped to bark at her. This time it stayed silent. She went to it, took a deep breath, and put her hand gently on its head. The dog looked at her, and she whispered, "*Ahéhee'*. Thank you for saving my *shimá* and my sister and the man who loves her."

Chee opened the passenger door, and leaned down to kiss her. "I've been wanting to do that all night. I missed you so much. I was worried sick when I didn't hear from you."

"I missed you more. My heart sang when I saw you here."

He closed her door, and slid in behind the steering wheel.

They drove in silence for a while, appreciating the gift of each other's company even in their exhaustion. Bernie reached for his hand. "What happened with your search for the cave?"

"It's a long story. I'll give you details tomorrow. But I found several people who know that area and seem to have heard of it. They have different ideas of where it might be."

She watched the night pass by outside the truck window, realizing that for the first time in days, she felt relaxed and safe.

Sleepiness had begun to seduce her when Chee spoke again.

"I met an elder there, a *hatałii* named Desmond Grayhair, who confirmed that what the Lieutenant saw in the sand on the cave's floors did once exist, but he doesn't know if the lake washed away this sacred treasury. We spoke on the phone tonight as I was heading here. I want you and the Lieutenant to come with me when I go back to Navajo Mountain. I think talking to Grayhair will stir his memory of what he saw."

"Well, you might have to wait a while for Leaphorn. Captain Largo got a postcard from him. He and Louisa really did go to Hawaii."

"That's a long boat ride."

She laughed. "Believe it or not, they flew. The Lieutenant himself set up the flights. There's a rumor that a honeymoon might be involved."

"You're teasing."

"We'll have to ask them when they get back. Or see if they have rings."

"Speaking of that, what's that new look for your eyebrow?"

"I knew you'd like it. You need one, too."

He squeezed her hand. "I mentioned to the *hataɫii* that I was driving home, and he told me I didn't need to worry about you tonight, even though I never mentioned your assignment. He told me you were a brave woman." He chuckled. "Of course, I knew that already."

"Did you mention to him that you might be interested in resuming your own *hataɫii* training?"

"Yes. He said that before he could decide whether he wanted to teach me, he needed to meet you."

The statement surprised her. "Did he say why?"

"No." But they both knew that studying to be an *hataɫii* would bring huge changes for Chee and, correspondingly, for her.

"Did he say anything else?"

"He told me I wasn't quite ready to stop my work as a policeman. He told me that the job I do now makes a difference in the world and not to discount that, but to give myself more credit. And he . . . he told me I was a good man."

"He was right about all of that." She put her hand to his cheek and brushed away the tear. "You are a good man."

They drove home in blessed silence.

When Chee brought the truck to a stop in front of their home along the river, he turned off the engine and sat a moment, enjoying the quiet after the drive. His Bernie had fallen asleep. He touched her shoulder, and she opened her eyes.

He kissed her gently. "I worried that I might never be able to do that again. What a terrible ordeal for you."

"It was, but Kelly is in jail and Dr. Zhou will have justice. I still want to be a detective."

"Undercover work might be a strong suit for you. You look great with that pink hair." He smiled at her and fell silent for a moment. Then he kissed her again.

"Thinking of you doing that scares me because I love you so much. But if that's what your heart says, you should do it."

She moved closer and put the palm of her hand against his cheek. "The thing is, what if I want to have kids?"

Acknowledgments

This final chapter of a new book always challenges me. Writing it is saying goodbye to a dear friend. While my relationship with every new book ranges from difficult to joyous, in the end it is a love affair filled with deep rewards.

The Sacred Bridge was shaped by the COVID pandemic that hit New Mexico (where I live) and the Navajo Nation with tremendous force beginning in the early spring of 2020. The sorrow, fear, and anxiety the disease brought also resulted in a change in my writing process reflected in this book. In each of my previous novels I was able to visit the main sites on the Navajo Nation I used as my setting. For *The Sacred Bridge*, however, I had to rely on my memories of previous visits to Lake Powell and the surrounding landscape because of the extraordinarily restrictive and successful measures the Navajo Nation took to keep its people safe. Those memories, plus photographs, videos, and conversations, fueled my imagination as I wrote.

This book also arose from my personal journey of transition, my experience as a widow after more than forty years of happy marriage to photographer Don Strel. He was my enthusiastic fan, sounding board, and safe haven. Don's journey to what my father called "the next great adventure" in part inspired me to think of what the future might hold for Jim Chee.

As always, none of my books, including this one, and none of Tony Hillerman's Navajo mysteries would have been possible without the real-life commitment of the men and women who work so diligently in law enforcement on the Navajo Nation. My deep respect and admiration go out to you. Gratitude to the reporters at the *Navajo Times* and the *Albuquerque Journal* for their stories on a real-life problem on the Navajo Nation, which provided some inspiration for *The Sacred Bridge*. And a tip of the hat to Duke Rodriguez for information on marijuana legalization in New Mexico.

Like all good books, this novel was a team effort. My squad of what I call beta readers helped me refine and improve the manuscript. My gratitude to Benita Budd, Rebecca Carrier, Charmaine Coimbra, Cheryl Fallstead, the irreplaceable Gail Greenberg and David Greenberg, Lucy Moore, and Dave Tedlock. A thank-you to Arin McKenna, who took on the daunting job of handling my social media presence and reminding me how important it is. A shout-out to my friends Charles

Mullins and Jann Wolcott, whose enormous support and encouragement helped me move forward from grief onto writing.

Thank you to all the bookstore owners and staff who go out of their way to make my stories available to their patrons. Special shout-outs to Dorothy Massey at Santa Fe's Collected Works, Noemi de Bodisco and Betty Palmer of op.cit. bookstores, Treasure House's John Hoffsis, Craig Chrissinger and the rest of the helpful folks at Page 1, and Wyatt Wegrzyn and Danielle Foster of Albuquerque's Bookworks. More big thank-yous to the owners and staff at Maria's Bookshop in Durango, Colorado; Mystery Galaxy in San Diego; Barbara's Bookstore in Chicago; and Murder by the Book in Houston for hosting my talks and helping new readers learn about Bernie and her colleagues. And to Barnes & Noble nationwide for their enthusiastic support of all things Hillerman.

I also appreciate the great networking and encouragement offered by my professional colleagues in Croak & Dagger—the New Mexico chapter of Sisters in Crime—Western Writers of America, New Mexico Press Women, and my special *commadres* in our Literary Ladies Lunch group.

I would never have published seven novels without the support and advice I receive from my agent, Elizabeth Trupin-Pulli of JET Literary Associates, Inc. Thank you, Liz! Sincere thanks, too, for my team at HarperCollins—senior editor Sarah Stein and her assistant Hayley Salmon; director of publicity Rachel Elinsky; vice president and marketing guru Tom Hopke; Marie Vitale, assistant production editor; as well as the talented copyeditor Miranda Ottewell and designer Bonni Leon-Berman.

In the end, there would be no new books about Bernadette Manuelito and her associates without the ongoing support of readers. I value the opportunity to speak with you directly at book clubs, public libraries, college extension classes, and in bookstores. I'm also happy when we can connect remotely on Zoom and its cousins or by email and with social media. I appreciate everyone who has helped arrange those visits, both face-to-face and through technology.

Onward!

Glossary

A Few Navajo Words

aak'ei: Autumn

ahéhee': Thank you

bilagáana: A white person

chindi: The spirit of a dead person

Dikos Nitsaa'igii-19: Big Cough, aka COVID-19

Diné: The Navajo people's word for themselves

Diné Bizaad: The Navajo language

Diyin Diné: The Holy People of Navajo legend

hatałii: A person who knows the sacred healing ceremonies; a medicine man

Hosteen: A term of respectful address in Navajo meaning man, grown man, elder, or husband; often *Hosteen* may be used before a last name, functioning in a way that is similar to the English honorific "Mr."

hózhó: A philosophy of harmony, beauty, and mental and spiritual wellness; more broadly, *hózhó* refers to a way of walking this earth that is inherently good

Jo'hanaa'éí: The Sun, personified as the Hero Twins' sun father and Changing Woman's husband

k'é: Kinship, a unifying relationship among the Navajo people

Késhmish: Christmas

naakai binát'oh: Marijuana

Naatsis'áán: Navajo Mountain, a Diné community in Arizona near Lake Powell

shicheii: Maternal grandfather

shimá: Mother

Tsé Bighanilini: Antelope Canyon

Tsé Bit'a'í: Ship Rock

Tsé'naa Na'ní'áhí: Rainbow Bridge

yee naaldlooshii: Skinwalker, an evil shapeshifter

yá'át'ééh: Hello; it is good